CURSED BY COLD

JAMIE DALTON

Home Away From Home

Scarlet

I stick to the shadows out of habit, glancing over my shoulder periodically to ensure no one follows me. Finding the nondescript wooden door tucked into a particularly gloomy corner, I rap out the secret rhythm that gains me entrance.

The door swings open, spilling warmth, light, laughter over me in welcome. I stride inside, the tang of woodsmoke and ale mingling with perfume immediately enveloping my senses. This feels like home. The Gilded Grafter Guild, or GGG as we like to call it. Fairy Godmother's thieves guild where only the "good" are allowed to join. One of the best kept secrets in the kingdom partially because Fairy Godmother spelled the name itself. It's already a tongue twister, but you only learn the name of the guild after you join and if you try to say it out loud or write it down it jumbles up and never comes out correct.

My eyes sweep over the crowded room, taking in the scarred oak tables surrounded by a ragtag mix of chairs accumulated over the years as our ranks have grown. Intricate tapestries in jewel tones cover the stone walls, muffling sound and lending a cozy feel despite the cavernous size of the hall.

A massive hearth holding a fire big enough to roast a boar keeps the room balmy as we head into winter. I make my way toward the usual table, nodding greetings to the familiar faces I pass. Some are old friends, some rivals, some I only know as aliases around this table. But we're all family of a sort.

"Scarlet, fashionably late as always I see," Lucius greets me with his signature roguish grin as I take my customary seat. Before I can respond, he's flagging down a barmaid and pressing a fresh tankard of ale into my hands.

"The usual for you then, Scarlet?"

Lucius jumps in. "Come now, Polly my dear. Tonight's a celebration! Bring a round of your finest ale for the whole table, on me!"

Polly arches an eyebrow. "That's quite generous of you. Trying to impress someone?" Her eyes flick to me teasingly.

"Only the best for our Scarlet," he proclaims with an exaggerated courtly bow that makes me snort.

Gen laughs, giving him a playful shove that nearly up-ends his own drink. "You're just angling to get her drunk in hopes she might finally take pity on you."

Lucius places a hand over his heart. "A man can dream! Maybe tonight's the night, eh Scar?" He gives me a wink.

I fix him with a wry look I've perfected over the years of fending off his ridiculous advances. "Keep dreaming, Lucius." But the familiarity of his harmless flirtation makes the hint of a smile tug at my lips all the same.

He grasps at his chest as though deeply wounded. "You cut me to the quick! But I'll win you over someday, just you wait." He winks, dropping the act. "Truth be told, we rogues like a lady who can stand her ground. Keeps that window of possibility open, eh boys?"

Raucous laughter greets this. I roll my eyes good-naturedly at his antics. Lucius may be a shameless flirt, but his nonsense has always entertained me.

As Polly heads off to fetch the drinks, Gen leans in with a grin. "You know, Scar, you could stand to buy a round yourself every now and then. Always hoarding that coin of yours."

I wave her off. "And miss the chance to keep these scoundrels paying my tab? What would be the fun in that?" But inwardly, I cringe. They assume I'm just being miserly, when in truth every copper I scrimp and save goes to keeping my family's estate from falling into total ruin. Ever since Father died, Stepmother and her daughters bleed our accounts dry with their frivolous spending, willfully ignorant of the crumbling legacy around them. I'm the only one trying to preserve what's left for when I can inherit. When I can finally take back control. Unfortunately, as long as my stepmother is around that won't happen, per my fathers will.

So I ply my trade, doing whatever jobs I must to slowly rebuild the estate they're so content to fritter away. Let my guild mates tease me for a stingy purse. The laugh is on them in truth.

Just then, Polly returns balancing a round of foaming tankards. As she places one before me, the firelight glints off the pale golden waves of my loose hair. I toss it back from where it has fallen across my face, meeting Polly's smile with my own vivid green eyes.

"Many thanks for your generosity, Lucius," I proclaim grandly, hoisting my drink in mocking salute. Laughter ripples around the table. As I look out at their mirthful faces, so different yet bonded by our shared fates, warmth fills me that has nothing to do with the ale. However strange a family this guild has made for me, I cannot imagine a home beyond it.

We're soon joined by the rest of our motley crew, the table growing louder and more crowded. Eli and Tabitha are deep in an animated tale, finishing each other's rambling sentences like the lifelong partners in crime they are.

Jonas slides in beside them, not even trying to hide his smug grin. The ostentatious ruby ring now adorning his hand makes it clear his recent jewel heist was a success. Evie plops down with soot still smudged on her cheek, fresh from a narrow chimney escape but eyes bright with victory.

In between swigs of ale, stories are swapped of our various escapades and close calls. Elaborate re-tellings designed to impress newcomers and one up each other's daring deeds. Razzing those who fumbled their latest job. But it's all in good fun—around here we know how easily the tables could turn. When it matters, we have each other's backs.

As the night stretches on, I feel the comfortable buzz of ale dulling my ever present sharp edges. I allow myself to relax into the feeling of camaraderie, letting down my guard among fellows who have proved themselves time and again.

My eyes drift across the room and land on Rose holding court among her gaggle of admirers. With her daring silk gowns and perfectly painted face, she takes the more sensual jobs I tend to avoid. We may differ in our methods, but I respect her skills all the same. She catches me looking and lifts a glass in cheeky salute. I find myself returning it with a genuine smile.

"Let's liven things up with a round of Never Have I Ever!" Gen suggests with a wicked grin.

A chorus of approval rises up around the table as tankards are refilled and pushed to the center. I lean back in my chair, swirling my drink absently. This could get interesting.

Gen starts us off. "Alright...never have I ever been caught in the act on a job."

A few groans sound as several people take sips of their ale. Jonas grimaces as he drinks. "That damned lord still has no idea how I got his entire silver collection out right under his nose. As far as he knew I was a servant of his mistress, fetching her before his wife arrived."

"My turn!" Lucius chimes in eagerly. "Never have I ever...seduced someone as part of a disguise."

More drinks are taken, along with some bawdy laughter. "Come now Lucius, we all know that's your specialty," Rose calls out from across the room, lifting her glass with a wink.

When it's my turn, I consider for a moment before stating, "Never have I ever accidentally betrayed the guild." A bold statement, but I know it will hold true for everyone here. My loyalty is unshakeable when it comes to my found family.

"Getting cocky there, Scarlett!" Elias jokes. "Alright, never have I ever botched a job so badly I had to lay low for weeks."

I begrudgingly take a sip at that, along with several others. The room fills with teasing and colorful stories of close calls and bungled jobs. Though rivals, we can all sympathize with the unpredictability of our line of work.

The game continues, secrets and entertaining tales flowing along with the ale. Lucius regales us with a story involving a noblewoman's missing jewels that has us all roaring. Gen reveals she was once stuck in a chimney for an entire night waiting for the household to sleep.

When it's my turn again, I consider for a moment before stating, "Never have I ever had to hide from guards inside a noble's privy."

Everyone laughs as a few people sheepishly take drinks.

"No way, I have to hear this story!" Tabitha crows, pointing at Jonas who is glumly sipping his ale.

"Let's just say the lord's digestion issues provided an opportune distraction," he mutters, to even more howling from the group.

"No!" Gen gasps. "You mean he was in there with you hiding?"

Jonas only finishes his drink and pours another, shaking his head no.

Elias calls out next, "Never have I ever accidentally robbed the wrong house on a job."

Again drinks are taken amidst colorful stories of bungled plans and mistaken addresses. I don't partake, but get my fair share of good-natured ribbing all the same.

"Of course pristine Scarlet would never make such a mistake!" Gen teases.

I spread my arms magnanimously. "Some of us are simply more adept at our work than others."

Their heckling continues fondly as the drinks flow. Surrounded by my odd little family of scoundrels and thieves, I feel light and warm, all sharp edges smoothed away by companionship. Here, I belong.

I'm still flushed with laughter and camaraderie when a hand grasps my shoulder. I turn to see Lucius gazing at me intently.

"When did you get up and leave?" I laugh as I stare at my mug trying to remember exactly how many I've had by now.

"Fairy Godmother wants you," he states.

Puzzled, I follow him through a side door into the private chambers used for sensitive guild business. There I find Fairy Godmother seated at an ornate desk. She gestures for me to sit, as Lucius leaves the room.

As I sink into the plush chair, curiosity warring with unease in the pit of my stomach, she passes me a parchment. I scan the document and inhale sharply—the payout listed is astronomical, enough to sustain the estate for a full year. But a job promising such riches means unprecedented risk.

I meet Fairy Godmother's steady eyes, feeling an anxious twist in my gut. She regards me solemnly from across the desk.

"I know it is a bold task, child. But you are my best. I would trust no one else with this."

Her unwavering faith steadies me. I nod slowly, resolve hardening as I accept the parchment. My fingers worry at a lock of golden hair as I process the enormity of what I've agreed to. The candlelight flickers over the contract, making the inked letters seem to dance with possibility and danger, in equal measure.

This will be the most daring - and potentially deadly - job of my career. But for Fairy Godmother, I can do anything. For the future of my family legacy, I must succeed.

I meet her gaze again with firm determination, my mentor's pride washing away any last traces of doubt. She believes I am up to this task. I refuse to fail her now.

Complaints at Court

Remme

I slouch on my golden throne, chin resting on one golden-gloved hand as I half-listen to the drone of voices below. My assembled council of advisors chatter and squabble amongst themselves like gulls fighting over scraps. I've heard enough of their ceaseless petitions and minor quibbles to last a lifetime.

At the foot of the dais, Vladok meets my gaze, his hawkish features set in an expression mirroring my boredom. As my First Minister, he suffers through these tedious meetings at my side. I catch his subtle eye roll at Lord Demir's latest long-winded complaint regarding grain shipments. My lip curls in a hint of a smirk.

Lord Greystone looks to be napping in his seat, a curtain of dark hair concealing his face. I honestly don't even know why he comes to these, other than to make sure I don't forget that he exists. Our resident mage, Lord Caius, toys absently with a dancing flame in his palm, ignoring the withering look Minister Darius shoots him. Only Sofia remains attentive at her post, scanning the murmuring nobles for any hint of threat. Ever the vigilant guard.

I shift on my throne. How much longer must I endure this monotonous pageantry posing as counsel? I contemplate adjourning the session early, propriety be damned. Before I can act on the impulse, the smaller side door creaks open to admit a new arrival.

Vladok straightens, giving me a meaningful look. The interruption must be important then. I lean forward as the man I recognize as one of our senior intelligence agents strides up to murmur in my First Minister's ear.

As Vladok's expression hardens, I feel a curl of anticipation. Finally, something of significance. I cut off Lord Demir's rambling with an impatient slash of my hand.

"Enough! Unless the kingdom faces imminent threat, I've no interest in such trifles." All eyes turn to Vladok as he steps forward. "It seems you come with more pressing news."

His features are grim as he gives a short bow of apology. "Indeed, your majesty. There has been another robbery..."

I scowl. "Again? That's the second in as many weeks."

"Indeed. They somehow stripped an entire gallery of priceless artwork without stirring Hendrik's household."

"And no doubt Duke Geralsh expects compensation for his stolen treasures," I fume. That greedy old weasel will be pitching a fit at court, blustering about his close friendship with the crown. As if I need another noble begging at my heels. It's not my job to fund the results of his poor security.

I begin to pull off my gloves in irritation before thinking better of it. Revealing bare skin around others is unwise, no matter the circumstances. With an effort, I restrain my temper.

"What of this thieves' guild you claim is behind these brazen crimes? Have you made progress tracking them down?"

Vladok's frown deepens. "Unfortunately, they cover their trail well. We have turned up no solid leads yet. However, I have taken the liberty of doubling the guard patrols near estates containing significant valuables..."

I hold up a hand, cutting him off. "A stopgap measure. We must go on the offensive." I rise to pace before the hearth, the firelight glinting menacingly off my golden armor.

"Sire, perhaps a bounty on information would loosen tongues..." Vladok ventures hesitantly.

A spark of interest kindles in my chest. "Intriguing notion. And once we have a name, we can stamp out this pestilence for good."

I turn and stride toward Vladok. "See that it's done. Once we have a target, eliminating them shall be swift."

"At once, my king." Vladok bows and takes his leave.

Alone now except for Sofia, my personal guard, I stride to the fireplace and drum my fingers on the mantel, lost in thought. Out of habit, I reach to pull off my restrictive gloves, the day's grievances almost making me forget caution. But I stop myself just in time. Revealing my deadly curse, even for a moment, is unwise.

Sofia approaches silently to stand at my shoulder, face carefully averted. It saddens me that my closest friend and protector cannot even meet my bare skin. But after accidentally turning her favorite childhood doll to solid gold with an affectionate touch, we learned to take precautions.

No one else alive knows of the curse that transforms anything I touch into gold. None but Sofia, who has kept my secret these long years without falter or fear. A living fortress, shielding me from a kingdom that would recoil in terror of their deadly king.

Her quiet presence soothes my simmering temper. "Crippling these criminals subtly may prove difficult, if their skills live up to rumor," she says. "I could assemble a covert team suited for such a task."

I nod slowly, ever grateful for her counsel. "See that it is done. Use whatever methods necessary to excise this growing threat."

We stand in pensive silence as the fire slowly gutters. With each brazen theft, these mysterious interlopers endanger my kingdom's stability and my own rule. I cannot allow such defiance to spread unchecked.

Soon enough the serpentine guild will find itself in my grasp, its leader chained and kneeling at my feet to face fatal justice. Sofia will help me keep my curse secret even as I crush these rogues publicly. None can be allowed to defy their king and live.

My gloved hands clench with anticipation. Once we have them in our sights, their days are numbered. I will finally satisfy this craving for retribution simmering in my cursed veins. None escape my wrath unscathed.

THAT'S NOT SO WEE

SCARLET

I crouch in the shadows, thankful for the cover of darkness tonight. With the moon tucked behind the clouds, even the guards' watchful eyes would struggle to see me sneaking past.

My knees ache from holding still so long, but I don't dare move. Patience is key for any good thief, as Fairy Godmother always says.

The shadows welcome me like a friend as I sneak past the clueless guards.

Staying low, my steps are light and measured as I walk across the open courtyard. Grateful that this job requires pants instead of a skirt as I stalk over areas that would have snagged my hem. I occasionally pause to check my surroundings, listening for any signs of movement. But so far, the castle seems asleep.

At last, I reach the castle wall. I study it carefully, looking for any signs of a breach. But the wall seems solid and intact, without any prominent weak spots. I sigh in frustration. Getting inside the castle is going to be more difficult than I had anticipated.

What are my options? The wall has no doors or windows, and I can see no way of scaling it. It's far too smooth with no cracks or vines. The only way in is through one of the guards' posts. But getting past the guards will be tricky.

There is no other choice, though. I have come too far to turn back now. The client has given a two month's timeline to get the Bodian crown and is offering a hefty bonus if it is stolen within the first few weeks. I need this money. Taking a deep breath, I begin making my way toward the nearest guard post.

As I move closer, the low murmur of voices comes from inside. The guards are talking, seemingly unaware of my presence. I creep closer, my heart in my throat. I am almost there when one of the guards suddenly steps outside.

I freeze, but he doesn't seem to notice me. He steps away, and I quickly take advantage of the opportunity. I slip through the gate behind him, light and quick as a breath.

My dagger poised, I catch the lone guard inside unaware, and end him with regretful necessity before he can raise the alarm. As his body slumps down, I offer a whisper of prayer for his soul.

The room is silent now, but I know the other guard will soon be back, and if they find me here, it will be straight to the dungeons. Taking a deep breath to calm my nerves, I make my way through the narrow space toward the castle's inner chambers.

I am in.

I take a moment to compose myself before continuing. While I'm not new to this, I hate breaking into larger places. The bigger it is, the harder it is to get back out. The king's castle? It's massive. So many more people to avoid. Not to mention, King Remme is not known to be kind. Many who come in never make it back out. It's never a public execution. There's never an announcement of any sort. They just disappear as if they never were there.

The castle's inner courtyard is even darker than the outer one, and I can barely make out the shapes of the buildings. I wish the clouds would part for only a moment to let me catch a peek before covering the full moon again, but luck is never something I can rely on. In fact, I am often called a very lucky, unlucky person in the guild. Rather confusing, but that's how it goes for me. If it can go wrong, it probably will. And on the rare occasion that it doesn't, it's as if fate has been saving up all of my good luck to happen at once. At this point I just expect it and have become very good at pivoting and finding new opportunities to complete the missions I take on.

I begin walking, keeping close to the walls for cover. I peer inside the windows as I pass, trying to get a sense of where I am. After a few minutes, I come to a large, imposing building. I recognize it immediately—the towering spires and grand arched entryway mark it as the royal palace. My target stands in front of me.

A shiver runs down my spine, but I push my fear aside and move closer. I will make it out of here. I send up a quick silent prayer to Halisar, god of thieves, that I won't run into King Remme tonight.

Guards are patrolling the palace grounds, but I manage to stay out of sight. Finally, I reach the entrance of the palace. A large metal door bars my way, but I know how to open it. Going into my pocket, I pull out two thin metal tools. I insert them into the door's lock and begin to pick it.

It only takes me a few seconds. The door clicks, and I push it open just enough to slip inside. I have made it into the palace. Now all I have to do is find the Bodian crown and make my way out without being caught. Hugging the shadows, I creep down the deserted halls, my eyes slowly adjusting to the new level of darkness. I move swiftly but silently, glancing around warily with each step. Fairy God-mother's map guides me up concealed stairwells and along back passages. I don't belong here, and discovery means certain death.

Up and up through the castle I climb, avoiding any signs of life.

I stop in front of the door made of solid gold that slides inside the wall, it matches what Fairy Godmother told me to look for. It seems an odd choice for a door. The wall must have been carved out through solid stone to make this possible. Why would they put that much effort into something when a swinging door would work just as well? Gold is so heavy and soft. A poor choice of metal to keep things out if you ask me.

On the first try, the door doesn't budge. Pulling my tools out, I slide one through the tiny crack and slowly work around the seam, cautious to not mark the soft metal, until I feel resistance. With a wiggle and a quick flick, I hear a slight clink. I reach my hand out, careful to avoid making any noise, and slowly slide the door open.

The room is too dark to really see. The only light coming from large open windows with a golden frame. The cold floor feels like a frozen golden lake beneath me. The dust that lingers in the air is fine and powdery, like a mist made of the same warm metal that makes all other furniture in the room. What kind of egotistical, wealthy, and extravagant person would live in a room like this?

I creep inside, looking around for something that could be the Bodian crown. I search through bookshelves and chests but can't find anything. Around a corner I find only a giant golden bed which I can only see the very end of clearly. I am about to give up when I notice a faint glimmer from a box on the desk. Squinting in the dark, I realize it is the perfect size to fit what I'm looking for in it.

Heart pounding, I pull out my lock picking tools again and go to work on the tiny lock. After several tense moments, it finally clicks open, and I open the lid with trembling hands. Inside is an exquisite crown made of emeralds—the Bodian crown! Quickly grabbing it, I start to turn away when suddenly a deep voice speaks from behind me.

"Stop!"

My heart skips a beat as I whirl around to see who has spoken. A tall figure stands in the darkness—a man completely naked save for golden tattoos covering his muscular body from head to toe. He is beautiful in a strange way—his dark brown eyes are piercing, short blonde hair a mess, and his features sharp. Yet despite his intimidating presence, there is something strangely hypnotic about him that holds me in place.

His gaze shifts from me to the crown I hold in my hands. "So you've come here for this," he says softly, admiring its beauty. "You must have courage beyond your years if you think you can take this from my palace."

He pauses thoughtfully before turning back to me with a smile playing across his lips. "But courage alone won't be enough if you want this crown."

I grasp the glimmering Bodian crown tightly in my hand and prepare to run, but before I can take so much as a single step, my foot catches on the leg of a chair. I crash to the floor with a heavy thud and watch in horror as the crown flies from my grasp and skids just out of reach across the cold hard ground.

Frustrated, I scramble on my knees to grab it, but just as my fingers are about to wrap around it, a large foot suddenly stomps down between me and the crown. I look up at the man in alarm—he has moved with lightning speed. I meet his piercing dark brown gaze, but my eyes quickly travel down his bare body, taking in the chiseled muscles of his chest and shoulders. The way the golden tattoos flow all of the way down his abs and down to...

My eyes dart back to the floor as my face grows hot. Well, that isn't so wee, now is it?

He towers above me, his golden tattoos glowing. "You should have known better than to steal from me," he says quietly. His voice is like ice water down my spine—cold and calculating yet strangely hypnotic at the same time.

"I'm sorry," I stammer, looking into his eyes. "This was a mistake."

He only stares at me impassively, as if he hasn't heard my apology.

Taking one long last look at it lying there on the floor, I grab his foot and pull as hard as I can, knocking the large man to the ground. My heart sinks as I realize that I have failed—I won't be able to get the Bodian crown tonight. Hopefully, the client will be understanding and give me another chance.

Fear races through my body like an electric shock as I scrabble towards the open door and sprint away from the bed chamber, my heart pounding with each frantic step. The opulent halls blur past in a dizzying kaleidoscope of marble and gold as I flee blindly, desperate to put as much distance as possible between myself and that cursed king.

The telltale clanks of armored boots echo from a crossing corridor ahead, signaling the approach of palace guards. Panic claws at my throat as I veer sharply down a shadowed alcove, pressing my back against the cold stone as they march heedlessly past my hiding spot. I hold my breath, every muscle taut with dread until the sounds finally fade into silence once more.

Only then do I allow myself to suck in a ragged gasp, my trembling fingers finding purchase against the rough edges of the wall. That was too close - I cannot afford another near miss like that if I hope to make it out of this unholy fortress unscathed. With renewed determination, I force my wildly thrumming heart to settle, and begin meticulously mapping an escape route through the maze of hallways and ante-chambers.

The journey seems to stretch into an eternity of breathless suspense, skirting the edges of a now awakened palace as I slink from shadowed nook to shadowed nook. More than once, I have to flatten myself against an alcove as a squad of guards or group of nobles pass within mere paces of my hidden form. But finally I find myself crouched beneath a deserted portico that opens onto the palace courtyard and the tantalizing promise of escape beyond its walls.

With a last glance over my shoulder, I dart across the moonlit expanse like a wraith and throw myself at the servants' entrance gate tucked into the rear corner. The latch opens with a metallic groan of protest, but I'm already squeezing through the narrow gap and spilling out onto the dark, winding backstreets of the outer city ring, before any alarm can be raised. Only then do I finally allow the full brunt of my harrowing flight to wash over me in shuddering waves as I gulp in greedy lungfuls of the cool night air.

A lingering sense of dread follows me through my journey back to report my failure to Fairy Godmother. She is going to kill me.

She's Not Gold!

Remme

What the hell just happened? She didn't turn into gold. She didn't turn into gold! She did just try to steal the only item I actually care about in my entire castle, but still, she didn't turn into gold! What did this mean?

I rise unsteadily from the cold golden floor, memories of my fateful coronation flooding back. Privately, I had been granted two wishes, the first being endless wealth so I'd never worry about money again. A childish desire that became my curse.

The moment the magic took hold, my clothing stiffened and transformed to gold, as did my throne and everything else I touched. I cannot even eat or drink, only watch helplessly as my world turns to unfeeling metal around me.

For my second wish, I begged for a way to survive the golden plague I had brought upon myself. But when I pled to undo the spell entirely, I was refused. Instead, I was given gifts - my body, sustained without food or water, and the Bodian crown. I was told if I gave the crown to one who truly loved me, their touch would break the curse.

But who could ever love a king who turns all to cold, lifeless gold with a mere brush of his hand? I have lived mostly in isolation for years, turning away any who drew close, for fear of harming them too. Consumed by grief, I became the very monster I wished so desperately to escape. Not the king I wanted to be.

I storm into the hall, ignoring that I always sleep in the nude. My personal guards already know this about me even if they don't know why. It's not like anything truly becomes comfortable once it's turned to gold. Definitely not comfortable enough to sleep in for clothing. So layers of thin gold blankets over me are the most I can hope for at the moment to keep me warm at night.

"Guards!"

Moments later, a guard scrambles over, face drained of color. "Y-your Highness, we did not see—"

"Silence!" I snap, cutting him off. "Your incompetence has allowed a thief into my private chambers. A woman with blonde hair, dressed in leathers. She was after the Bodian crown!"

The guard pales further. "I will raise the alarm immediately, Your Highness! We will search every corner of the castle and beyond to find her."

I point angrily back into my room. "First, return the crown to its box, fool. Then mobilize all your forces. I want her found!"

Nodding nervously, the guard rushes to retrieve the crown with shaking hands. I tap my foot impatiently as he gingerly lifts it and places it back in the box.

"Now go!" I bark. "Turn the entire kingdom over if you must, but bring the thief to me unharmed. I want answers from her."

The guard bows and scrambles away, shouting for the castle guards. I seethe quietly, fists clenched. Incompetent fools! I should turn the lot of them to gold, for this failure. But I restrain my temper. For the first time in a decade, I can touch something without it turning to gold. Has more than just her changed?

I make my way over to the window, watching the moonlight filter through the trees in the courtyard below. Soldiers scurry below as the castle wakes.

I've spent so long living in isolation, surrounded by my golden possessions, afraid of losing another person who has worked their way into my heart, that I've forgotten what it feels like to be loved. I've chased away anyone who's ever become close to me, consumed by my own greed, grief, and power. But something about the thief...someth ing about how she looked at me, with those piercing green eyes...makes me believe that maybe, just maybe, this curse may be over soon.

I shake my head, trying to clear my mind of such thoughts. How can I expect someone to love me when I've become a monster? Perhaps they were wearing gloves and I missed it.

Lost in my thoughts, I hear a soft knock at the door as I pace the room. I hesitate for a moment before calling out, "Come in."

The guard from before steps hesitantly into the room, his expression unsure. "Your Highness, they've escaped. The grounds are clear."

My heart sinks. I had hoped that perhaps they would find her and I could have answers tonight. It appears that won't be the case. "Leave."

The guard nods, bowing before quickly exiting the room.

I stay in my room for hours, listening to the silence and contemplating what this means. Ultimately I need to find out if this incident is because the spell is weakening or changing, or because of this woman specifically. I look around my rooms for something I haven't already turned to gold.

Eventually, I hear a faint buzzing sound coming from somewhere in the corner of the room. I approach cautiously, not wanting to startle whatever it is that's causing the noise. As I near, however, I realize what it is: a small beetle flies past me, its wings shimmering in the moonlight.

Without hesitation, I reach out and grab it with two fingers. Instantly, it turns into pure gold and falls lifelessly onto the floor at my feet. I cry out in frustration. The curse is still within me - it has simply been this woman who has been able to resist my touch.

I sigh deeply. If anyone else knows about this woman's ability to resist me - if anyone else learns about her - then surely they will come for her too? Maybe even use her against me.

I need to find her, and I need to do it now.

FAIRY GODMOTHER

SCARLET

Looking around me to ensure that no one is watching, I enter a small back alley in a residential area and make my way to a small garden of a middle-class stone home. A barking dog sounds in the distance, but I can't hear any footsteps or sounds of anyone nearby, so I make my way to the back door.

Three quick knocks followed by two slow ones, and I wait for what feels like forever but must have only been a few moments before a tall skinny man opens it. I offer a slight nod, which he returns as he opens the door wider to let me in. I've come to report my failure. I can taste the bile in my throat as I enter.

Fairy Godmother turns to face me in the kitchen, her pale face like porcelain in the fading light. She has round cheeks with tiny dimples, like two pockmarks filled with powdered sugar, and heavy doe-like eyes that flicker with irises like black mercury on the sea. Her silver hair piled high on her head, a few strands escaping the perfected style revealing that today has not gone smoothly for others besides just me. An unassuming woman who if you really know her history, would both terrify and enthrall you. Even the name of her thieves guild is enchanted so you can't say it to anyone outside of the order. Not that you could say it easily anyways.

"Scarlet," she says, her voice as soft as dandelion fluff. "You've returned."

I nod, unable to speak. I want to tell her what has happened, but the words catch in my throat. I failed. I'm a failure. I don't fail missions. That's why she gave me the job to begin with.

Fairy Godmother steps closer and places a gentle hand on my arm. "What is it?" she asks. Her gaze is kind, yet probing.

I shake my head, feeling tears prick at my eyes. "I didn't get it," I whisper.

Fairy Godmother looks at me expectantly. "What happened?"

"I had it. It was in my fingers, but then he showed up."

"Who?"

"He was large," I say. "Covered from head to toe in gold tattoos." I shake my head. "I panicked and ran."

Fairy Godmother nods, her expression unreadable. "Was it a guard?"

"No. It was..." I pause, my voice catching. The entire way back, I have played the scene in my head over and over again. He had told me who he was, hadn't he? He said the place was his. The crown...his. "It was King Remme."

Fairy Godmother's expression turns hard. "Ah. I see. Did he see you?"

Fidgeting with my fingers I nod yes.

She pauses for a moment, her gaze distant. After a few moments, she looks back at me. "You need to lay low for now," she says. "We will watch for a better opportunity to sneak in and get the crown."

I nod, feeling a wave of relief wash over me. "Thank you," I say quietly.

Fairy Godmother smiles and pats my arm. "We've got time. If it's too difficult, I can always ask another to take the job."

"No!" the word escapes me before I remember who I'm talking to. Clearing my throat I begin again. "I mean, you don't need to do that. I can do it. It was only a small mistake. Please. You know I need the money."

Fairy Godmother nods her smile still in place. "I know, dear. I believe in you. But you don't know what you are dealing with. King Remme is a dangerous man."

I swallow hard, feeling the weight of her words. "I understand."

"Good. Now go rest. You've had a long day." Fairy Godmother walks me to her door and opens it, her silver hair glimmering in the light. I can see the tiredness in her eyes. With a small smile I wave goodbye and leave.

As I walk home alone, I can't stop thinking about King Remme. When he emerged from the shadows, so imposing and yet...beautiful, with those shimmering gold tattoos adorning his body, it stirred something in me. But no, I mustn't think that way. He is the enemy, a dangerous man drunk on power. I cannot forget why I was there.

And yet...the way he looked at me, with such intensity in his eyes. As if he could see into my soul, uncovering secrets that even I don't fully understand yet. What is it about him that lingers in my mind?

Shaking my head, I quicken my pace through the dark streets. This is no time for distraction or weakness. I need to figure out a plan to get that crown before my chance is gone.

Upon arriving home, I collapse wearily onto my bed, seeking rest. But as I close my eyes, visions of golden tattoos dance through my mind.

***

I jolt awake as the first rays of dawn creep into my cramped attic bedroom. Shivering, I pull the threadbare blanket tighter around my shoulders. The chill morning air seeps through cracks in the walls, cutting straight to my bones. This place was never meant to be lived in.

Rubbing the sleep from my eyes, I peer around at the sloping walls and exposed beams, so different from the well-appointed rooms below. My gaze falls on a few faded floral scraps I had pasted up, the only decoration I could manage. It will have to do for my makeshift refuge.

Swinging my legs over the side, I wince as my feet hit the icy floorboards. Last night's activities took their toll, leaving my limbs heavy and sore. Thoughts of the failed heist still haunt me. But dwelling on it now won't help.

I force myself to stand, stiffly making my way to the rickety wardrobe. My fingers tremble as I tie on an apron over my dress. The trembling has nothing to do with the morning chill. I know what awaits downstairs - the disdainful glances, the mocking laughter. My courage threatens to falter, but I straighten my back. I must be strong.

Taking a deep breath, I turn the brass knob of my door. I want to cling to the safety of this room, but it's time. I descend the narrow stairs on silent feet, mentally bracing myself. Let them deride me all they want. Their words cannot touch my spirit.

My stepmother has been badgering me for months to marry off and "contribute" to this decaying family. As if I owe her anything. She and my vain stepsisters have bled our estate dry ever since my father died, leaving me scrambling to pay the bills before the house crumbles around our ears.

Not that they care if we lose the roof over our heads. As long as they have silks and ribbons to flounce about in, the future means nothing to them. Nevermind my father wanted me to inherit. As long as that hag lives, this remains her domain to destroy.

That's why I work for the Guild, driven by desperation. Every coin I manage to secure postpones the collapse a little longer. But it's never enough with their ceaseless frivolous spending.

And now she wants me married off, like breeding stock to be bartered away. She knows full well no decent man would take a penniless bride, one that cannot offer a decent dowry. This is just her latest scheme to be rid of me, content if I'm swept away in ruin.

Over my dead body. I'll see them on the streets first. This house is my legacy, and I won't surrender it to their poisonous hands. So let my stepmother harass and mock as she pleases. When the time comes, justice will be served.

I leave my room and step into the hallway, dreading the sounds that will come from the kitchen. But instead, all is silent. I allow myself a moment's relief before I descend the stairs.

Entering the kitchen, I make a mental note of everything I need to do. The embers in the fireplace emit a feeble glow, barely denting the cold. Shivering, I load up the grate with fresh logs and kneel to coax a flame. It eventually catches, and warmth slowly returns to my numb fingers.

Rising, I fill the dented kettle from the pump and hang it on the rod above the growing fire. While waiting for it to boil, I take out a loaf of bread. My mouth waters as I slice off three pieces and butter them generously. I pry open a jar of raspberry jam, the summer sweetness transporting me back to brighter days. I lavish the toast with purple syrup before placing the slices on a tray into the brick oven.

The kettle starts whistling just as I retrieve the tea tin. Scooping leaves into the pot, I pour over the bubbling water. As the tea steeps, I inhale the aroma of freshly baked bread perfuming the kitchen. But I don't indulge. Those are for my stepmother and sisters. I merely prepare their breakfast, as I have since my father passed. They are family in name only, discarding me until there are chores to be done. But I cling to my morning rituals - they give me purpose, even if those I serve do not.

My heart pounds in my chest as I finish preparing the tea. Just as I am about to bring the pot to the table, I hear the footsteps of my stepmother and stepsisters coming down the stairs. I take a deep breath, steeling myself for the encounter. I place the pot on the table, then hurry back to the stove to fetch the bread.

My stepmother's icy voice strikes my ears before she sweeps into view, her severe raven bun pulled tight enough to smooth the wrinkles from her pinched face. "Good morning, Scarlet."

I paste on a smile as false as her cordial tone, avoiding the steely glint in her narrow eyes. Behind her, my stepsisters saunter in, a study in contrasts. Petunia with her head held high. Her luxurious auburn curls are pinned up in an elaborate style, not a strand out of place. An air of haughtiness surrounds her as she glides across the room in an extravagant emerald gown. The neckline plunges low, adorned with intricate gold embroidery that matches the heavy jewels dangling from her ears. Her gaze sweeps over me disdainfully, as if I'm an annoying insect to be flicked away.

Starla trails behind, rail thin, her sharp elbows poking through lace sleeves. She wears her long raven hair pulled back severely, amplifying the sharp angles of her hollow cheeks and pointed chin. Her pale skin is nearly translucent, giving her an almost ghostly countenance. It amazes me what the rich, and those attempting to be rich, find to be desirable and beautiful.

They titter softly between themselves, beady gazes fixed on me, alight with cruel mirth at my discomfort.

"It's about time you started contributing to this family," my stepmother remarks, her claw-like nails examining the chipped varnish.

I clench my jaw, smothering the bitter retort on my tongue. The same passive-aggressive jab punctuates our mornings. It's best if I stay silent and let her finish whatever suggestion she has this time for how I could better contribute to the family.

She yawns delicately, puffing out sunken cheeks, before gliding to the table on slippered feet, my sisters trailing in her wake. I release the breath caught in my throat and slip back to the stove, my legs trembling beneath my skirts. At least she remains oblivious to my unease.

When I return balancing the plate, the three have already claimed their cups, sipping daintily while watching me over the rims with judgment in their small, dull eyes. Their haughty expressions make my skin crawl, but I force my lips into a facsimile of a congenial smile.

An agonizing silence drags on, broken only by the clink of porcelain and the crackle of the hearth fire. At last, my stepmother sets down her cup with a soft clatter and levels her gaze at me once more.

"I heard that Lord Gouten was looking for a new bride," she says, standing up. "He makes 50,000 a year so I imagine his bride price would be quite the sum."

So that's it. We're back to my least favorite game of what is the worst possible husband we can tie Scarlet to.

"Oh yes," Petunia's giggle holds a wicked tone, "You would be a perfect match for him. I've always thought of you as having an 'old soul'."

Of course, my stepmother would think a man with only one eye and a severe case of gout who was near his deathbed was a good fit. She has blown through all of my family's money after my father's death, so she only sees her own profit from such a marriage.

"How about Lord Greystone. He's quite charming, don't you think?" Starla adds, giggling so hard that her tea spills when she snorts. "He will inherit, and I'm sure could offer a large bride price for someone... even someone as humble in appearance as you."

Lord Greystone is at least much younger. He is also known to spend the majority of his days in the brothels gambling his family's money away. Soon they will be in a worse situation than my own family. When I inherit this home, if he's my husband it would probably be sold to pay of his debts immediately. Much better to stay single than marry a useless man like that.

It's not like they would ever consider these men as their own marriage options. Only I am lowly enough to be considered a good fit.

"Scarlet, you are quite the bore," my stepmother says.. "Leave my sight and clean the carriage. We will head to the market for lunch. I'm in the mood for some new ribbons."

I nod mutely, my stomach twisting itself into knots. Without another word, I take my leave as their shrill laughter pursues me down the hall.

Blinking back tears, I steel my resolve and continue putting one foot in front of the other. Their cruelty cannot break me, for I have a higher purpose.

Stepping outside into the bracing morning air, I try to calm myself down - no matter how difficult they try to make my days, I will persevere. I must, if I hold any hope of saving this house and legacy. With that truth ringing in my mind, I get to work cleaning the carriage, focused on the task at hand. My future depends on it.

THE MARKET

SCARLET

The scent of spices and baked goods fills the market, making my mouth water. I had been so busy that I forgot to grab any food for myself before we left.

I trail behind my stepmother and stepsisters as they flit from stall to stall, cooing over frivolous hats and garments. My arms ache from the pile of boxes and packages they continue to add to my load. We will need a second carriage at this rate. I bite my tongue to refrain from complaining.

A flash of royal blue catches my eye. A man in an embroidered tunic heads purposefully to the central bulletin board, parchment in hand. My pulse quickens - could it be a warrant with my face? No, I was wearing a mask. The king didn't see my face. Holding my breath, I edge closer, packages teetering.

The man tacks up the parchment and walks away. Letting out a relieved sigh, I step fully into view and read the elegant script: An announcement of a royal masquerade at the palace. My heart flutters as I imagine the glamour and mystery. I chose to ignore the voice of warning in my head that asks why the king who normally stays shut away is suddenly holding an event?

My stepmother and stepsisters have wandered over and are giving the announcement their own examination. Starla looks particularly intrigued, her eyes sparkling with excitement.

"Oh, a masquerade!" she exclaims. "Can we go?"

"It's a great opportunity for the two of you," my stepmother says, nodding at my stepsisters. "Perhaps you can even catch the eye of the king."

Her eyes sparkle with enthusiasm as she looks around the room, expecting agreement from everyone. Petunia and Starla giggle together as they immediately start looking for the most sumptuous fabric and ribbons to make new dresses for the event.

I sigh, feeling my shoulders grow heavy at the prospect of another event that requires purchasing a new outfit and learning a new set of dance steps. Of course, I wouldn't be going. Not only would stepmother never allow it, but I also need to stay as far away as possible until we figure out how to get the crown. A night where there would be extra guards is not it.

But I can't deny the thrill of anticipation that surges through me as I imagine what the masquerade would be like. As I turn away from the bulletin board, I catch sight of a masked man watching me from across the market. He is tall and lean, with piercing blue eyes that seem to look right through me. Dressed all in black, his clothes tailored perfectly to his form. Lucius.

Is he here for me? Probably not. The guild is large and they have many missions going on constantly. This is probably just a fluke.

Just as I am about to turn away, he steps forward, approaching me with purpose.

"Excuse me, miss," he says, his voice deep and smooth. "I think you may have dropped this."

A small note slips into my hand, and I blink, surprised that Fairy Godmother has contacted me in the open like this. "Yes, thank you," I reply.

With a wink and a smirk Lucius walks away leaving me alone. I shift the packages I carry and read the note.

Come see me at Herlads. We need to talk.

F.G.

The sketch of an ornate capital G transformed into a flower sits on the bottom corner of the page. The sign of the GGG, or really one of many. The G is the important part. It is always transformed into something unassuming by whoever it is that uses it to make it clear who the sender is, their matching mark inked onto their skin. My own is hidden on my upper thigh. An area that would be easy to show, but difficult to accidentally sneak a peek of.

I glance back at my stepsisters and see they are thoroughly engrossed in their search for the perfect dress. I quickly tuck the note away, thankful for this opportunity to slip away unnoticed.

No one makes Fairy Godmother wait.

Taking a deep breath, I hurriedly weave through alleyways and narrow streets until I arrive at Herlads, a small tea shop tucked away in the corner of the market. It is almost empty this time of day, so it isn't hard to spot her. She is sitting in a booth near the back, wearing an elegant blue dress and sipping a cup of tea.

She waves me over with a kind smile. "Hello dear! It's good to see you again. I trust your family is doing well?"

I nod politely playing my part as I slide into the chair opposite her, placing my packages on the floor beside me. "Yes, ma'am, we're all doing fine," I say hastily before getting down to business. "You wanted to meet with me about something?"

Fairy Godmother's voice drops to a hushed murmur, though her words seem to reverberate strangely in my mind. Perhaps she is using magic to ensure privacy, even here in the open. It is unlike her to take such a risk.

"The masquerade is the perfect chance to infiltrate the castle and reclaim the Bodian Crown unnoticed," she says, eyes intent on mine. "With all the guests coming and going, you can blend into the crowds."

My pulse quickens at the thought. Ever since my failed attempt to steal the crown, just setting foot near the castle makes my hands tremble. A royal ball surrounded by guards seems like a death wish.

Sensing my hesitation, Fairy Godmother gives my hand a gentle, reassuring squeeze. "You're more than capable, my dear. Just get inside and reclaim the crown, then disappear into the night."

I force a shaky smile, wishing I shared her confidence. As a thief, I prefer the shadows. Deception and charm are not my strengths. But I cannot fail at this job again. That crown is my one chance to earn enough gold to save my inheritance from my stepfamily's clutches.

Taking a deep breath, I meet Fairy Godmother's expectant gaze. "I'll do it. No matter the risk, I will get inside the castle and take back that crown."

Pride lights up her eyes. She raises a hand to flag down the server, her words once again muted. "Excellent. Now about your gown, I think red would be quite striking..."

A smile tugged at my lips as her enthusiasm proved infectious. "Red sounds perfect," I said, a twinge of excitement welling up inside me. "Thank you for all of your help."

Fairy Godmother waved away my thanks with a dismissive gesture. "It's my pleasure, dear. Now, let's talk strategy. We'll need to get you an invitation, and a mask, of course. And we'll need to figure out how to get inside without attracting too much attention..."

As she spoke, her voice began to fade into the background, my mind racing with the possibilities of the masquerade. I couldn't believe I was actually going to do this - slip into the palace, surrounded by people, and try to steal the Bodian crown again. But the thought of the rush, the adrenaline of the perfect heist, made my heart race with anticipation.

This was going to be one for the history books, I thought with a grin.

With her words of encouragement ringing in my ears, I left the tea shop and made my way back to the market, my mind racing with plans and schemes. I knew that this would be a risky venture and that there was a possibility that I might not make it back out.

Masquerade Preparations

Scarlet

I step into the parlor, sunlight streaming through the tall mullioned windows, illuminating clouds of dust kicked up by my stepsisters' frenzied activity. Petunia and Starla are a whirlwind of chatter and fluttering silks before the towering gilt mirror.

"Oh Petunia, you must try this one - the color pairs divinely with your complexion," Starla gushes, holding up an emerald gown against her sister's ruddy cheek.

Petunia gasps, pressing a hand to her ample bosom. "You're so right, dear sister! Let me slip it on."

I shift the cumbersome box of family jewels in my weary arms and glance toward Stepmother ensconced in the corner like a queen holding court. Pillows nearly overwhelmed her thin frame in the delicate rosewood chair as she observes the proceedings, thin lips pursed in perpetual displeasure. The tea and pastries I rushed to prepare at dawn sit untouched beside her.

"Girls, you must select gowns that properly flatter your best features," she pronounces in clipped tones. "We can't have you looking like tavern wenches."

Petunia preens before the mirror in the emerald dress, which highlights her ginger curls beautifully but strains at the seams.

Stepmother tsks under her breath. "Perhaps something with a more...forgiving cut."

Petunia's face falls momentarily before brightening again. "You're so right, Stepmother. This shade washes me out dreadfully. Now this!" She flourishes a garish fuchsia gown against her frame.

I ache as I shift the jewel box again, simmering resentment. Just one piece sold could finance such urgent repairs, yet here I stand, enabling such wanton indulgence while our family legacy crumbles.

"Oh yes, much better!" Starla claps. "The king himself will beg for your hand when he beholds you in fuchsia."

At the mention of the king, anxiety coils in my gut. I recall his piercing eyes when I stumbled into him at court after the failed jewel heist. My pulse quickens, imagining his reaction if I'm recognized at the ball, even masked.

The hours drag on as I mute my protests and watch bounties of silk unfurled and critiqued. Stepmother finds fault with each gown in turn - too bright, too formal, too revealing, too matronly. The grating discontent in her voice frays my nerves while Petunia and Starla become increasingly desperate to please.

"Oh please mother, I must have this one!" Petunia grasps the fuschia gown to her chest defiantly despite Stepmother's lukewarm reaction. "I'll be the belle of the ball!"

Starla scoffs delicately. "Don't be gauche, sister. Simplicity and taste are what His Majesty will want in a bride." She dons a sleek black gown and gazes at her reflection approvingly.

As they argue over styles and fabrics, my thoughts drift to the imposing king who almost ensnared me. I picture Petunia dripping in gems, hardly able to move under their weight. The king would be dazzled initially, but unlikely to endure her preening.

Starla glides by in a slinky dark gown with a plunging neckline. Much too provocative, I think. The king struck me as rather conservative. Well besides his obsession with gold. The man's entire room was gold, but that was it. No frills, no jewels...just gold.

The afternoon wears on as dress after dress is modeled and critiqued. My hands ache from clutching jewel after

jewel. Just one would keep the manor solvent for month
s... No, stop. Stay focused.

Petunia sweeps by in a massive ballgown, grinning excitedly. "This is the one! I'll be the belle of the ball!" The king
would find it overwhelming, I suspect.

Finally, after what feels like an eternity, they have both
decided on their dresses — though I am sure that neither
of them is truly happy with their choice. I walk out of the
room, my heart heavy with sadness for the wasted money,
but hoping that at least one of them will feel some sense
of joy and satisfaction as they glide in their chosen gowns
through the masquerade.

***

I stand in the darkness, watching the carriage slowly pull
away from the estate. The white horses glow in the moonlight, their manes and tails flowing behind them like a gentle river. In the carriage, my stepmother and stepsisters are
leaving for the masquerade, and I will soon be following
them. Not that they know it.

The thoughts of the upcoming night fill me with nerves.
I am excited to go to the masquerade, to dress up and
become someone else for a night, to escape from the restrictions of my family. But at the same time, I am afraid

of what will happen if I am discovered. I know the consequences of such an action would be dire. I'm not just going to dance the night away. I have a job to complete.

My gaze follows the carriage until it is nothing more than a tiny dot in the darkness. I sigh and turn away from my home and set off in the opposite direction, towards the home of Fairy Godmother. I wrap my cloak tighter, hands buried in its folds against the chill. My breath mists before me as I hurry along the deserted road.

Arriving at the unassuming home, I rap sharply on the weathered door, shifting from foot to foot. Mercifully, the door swings open, spilling warm golden light over me.

Fairy Godmother welcomes me inside with a warm smile, shutting out the chill night air. "Come in, come in! We've got work to do."

I eagerly step over the threshold and breathe a sigh of relief to be out of the cold darkness. Her cozy cottage envelops me in warmth - a crackling fire, the rich aroma of beef stew bubbling. It already feels more like home than the drafty manor I left behind.

Fairy Godmother puts a kettle on to boil. "Let's get you warmed up with some tea while we prepare."

I extend my numb fingers toward the fire. "Bless you, it's miserable out there tonight."

She pats my shoulder affectionately as she passes, kettle whistling. Soon I'm cradling a steaming mug, breathing in the floral scented steam.

"Drink up! Can't have you catching a chill before the ball." Fairy Godmother winks, sipping her own tea.

I laugh softly. "No indeed. Thank you for everything, truly. You've always taken such good care of me."

Her eyes crinkle with a smile both maternal and wistful. "Of course, dear one. Anything for James' little girl."

At the mention of my father's name, a lump forms in my throat. Fairy Godmother had been one of his dearest friends since their youth, closer than kin. She was the one who took me in when I was left bereft and alone after he passed.

Her wrinkled hand reaches out to pat my own where it rests on the worn tabletop. "You have his spirit, you know. That stubborn spark that pushed him to achieve the impossible, no matter the odds."

I glance down, touched and sad all at once. It's been years since his booming laugh echoed through our home, yet the grief still ambushes me at odd moments.

"He would be so proud of the resourceful young woman you've become," she continues gently. "Proud, and utterly unsurprised at your boldness!"

A watery chuckle escapes me at that. She isn't wrong - Father always encouraged my adventurous streak, much to my ladylike governess' chagrin. The memory kindles a faint, bittersweet warmth in my chest.

Fairy Godmother squeezes my hand, her eyes faraway for a moment. "He did everything for you, Scarlet. Just as I will. Whatever it takes."

I clasp her hand tightly in return, vision blurring with grateful tears. With her guidance, I will find a way back to the home and life that was stolen from me.

She smiles, a glint of familiar stubbornness in her gaze. "Now then! We have a ball to prepare for. Try it on," she says as she hands me a delicate mask.

I turn to face a mirror hanging on the wall and hold the mask up to my face. It is cold and smooth to the touch, decorated with drops of mist that drip onto my face and run like trails of rain down my neck. This must be part of Fairy Godmother's magic.

"People become uncomfortable around people who cry. You will be a sad beauty that turns the crowd's heads away, giving you an anonymity that should work in your favor to sneak out and steal the crown. Now hurry, get dressed in my room, so you aren't late."

Fairy Godmother leads me into her bedchamber where the beautiful ballgown awaits on a mannequin. I reverently run my fingers over the intricate beading and rich, vibrant fabric.

The ballgown shimmers with a red so vibrant it is almost translucent. The gown is strapless and tight-fitting, with just enough room for my breasts to move up and down as I breathe. The skirt is full like a red and gold cloud, mimicking the stormy sky outside. It flares out at the hips like a bell that continues down to my feet and dances with my every step. The red fabric is embroidered with gold thread and glittering beads that drape across my body like a river of blood and diamonds.

"It's stunning," I breathe.

"Only the best for you, my dear. Now go behind the screen and put it on."

I carefully remove the gown from the mannequin and step behind the screen. The cool silk slips luxuriously over my skin as I wriggle into it.

"Are you decent? Let me lace you up," Fairy Godmother calls.

I emerge and turn my back to her. Deft fingers work quickly up the gown's back, tightening and securing the laces. Her weathered hands are gentle and warm on my bare skin.

When she finishes, I turn and clasp her hands gratefully. "Thank you. For everything you've done for me."

She cups my cheek tenderly. "You deserve the world, child. Now come, take a look."

We stand before the full length mirror, her hands resting proudly on my shoulders. I hardly recognize the elegant lady staring back at me. No trace of the scorned servant girl remains. Tonight I can be someone new.

Fairy Godmother smiles at my reflection. "You're perfect. Now they'll never suspect who's under that mask. My masterpiece." She pulls my hair into a delicate bun and secures it with ruby clips. My face is painted delicately to bring out the green of my eyes, a bright red painted on my lips. I am finally ready.

I clasp my hands around Fairy Godmother and hug her tight. "Thank you so much," I say, tears forming in the corner of my eyes.

"You're welcome." She smiles softly and runs a hand over my head. "Be brave. Come back in one piece."

She helps me into a thick velvet cloak to shield against the night's chill. I pull the hood up to conceal my identity.

Fairy Godmother embraces me one last time. "Now hurry, your carriage awaits."

I step outside into the darkness, my cloak swirling around me. A carriage waits to whisk me off to the palace. As we pull away, I glimpse Fairy Godmother watching from the doorway, the warm light from inside framing her kind face until we round a bend.

I gather the cloak tightly against the cold night air as I peer ahead. In the distance, the glittering lights of the palace beckon. Soon, the real game will begin.

***

The carriage rocks to a halt, and I spin around, questioning the driver.

"What's going on?" I demand, voice shaking with confusion.

The driver tips his hat low over his eyes. "Fairy Godmother gave me strict orders. Said I had to wait here." He gestures out the window at the night sky.

I swallow hard, nerves buzzing in anticipation. "Wait? Wait for what?"

The driver shrugs and taps his fingers against the reins. "Don't know. Don't ask me."

The door opens, and Lucius climbs in with me carrying a box. He sits across from me with an amused look on his face.

"Good to see you, Scar," he says.

"Right back at you, Lucius," I reply.

The carriage clatters along, bringing us ever closer to the looming palace. I try not to think about how many guards will stand between me and my goal tonight.

Lucius gives me a roguish grin, no hint of nerves in his relaxed posture. "Well Scar, shall we review the plan one more time?"

I make a face at him. "Please, I could recite it in my sleep by now. You've gone over it often enough."

He holds up his hands in mock surrender. "Forgive me for double checking before our most daring heist yet! I know how you hate to be unprepared."

I have to smile at that, some of the tension easing from my shoulders. Beneath his swagger, Lucius is one of the most meticulous thieves I know. We make a good team.

"All right, surprise me then," I say, leaning back and crossing my arms. "What's in that suspicious box you've been guarding this whole ride?"

"Ah, straight to business! I thought you'd never ask." With a flourish, Lucius opens the box to reveal the most exquisite pair of glass slippers. They glimmer in the faint carriage light, carved into the shape of delicate goblets.

I gasp in genuine delight as I lift one shoe, turning it to admire the craftsmanship. "These are a work of art. Fairy Godmother outdid herself."

"She wanted you to have something suitable for a royal ball," Lucius says. "Can't wear your usual muddy boots tonight. I added some padding inside, given they're made of glass and all."

I carefully slip off my practical boots and slide my feet into the slippers. The smooth glass molds comfortably to my feet. "A perfect fit! Fairy Godmother thinks of everything."

"We're almost there." Lucius nods out the window at the looming palace silhouetted against the night sky. I feel my earlier anxiety returning. But one look at Lucius' rakish smile steadies me.

"Just promise you won't actually make me dance tonight," I quip.

He presses a hand to his chest. "You wound me! You've got to blend in but I promise I will keep it minimal. After-all, there are plenty of other damsels to keep me occupied."

It is strange to see the palace ahead when I am actually invited. Well, sort of invited. I am using Fairy Godmothers invitation since I wouldn't be arriving with the one sent to my own family.

Standing tall and looming over Fallwatch, the castle is made of dark stone encircled by thick walls. Lanterns light up the road that gets busier as carriages start to move toward the gate. We stay among them, waiting to leave and heading toward the main entrance.

As the carriage pulls up to the entrance of the palace, I run our plan through my head for the millionth time. We have a small window of opportunity and have to act fast.

"We'll have to be careful," Lucius says as he adjusts his mask. "The guards are always watching."

I nod in agreement, my heart racing at the thought of being caught. I am about to break into the most heavily guarded castle in all of Fallwatch again. If we are caught, we will be jailed without hesitation. Worse for me, considering it wouldn't be my first offense.

"Once we're inside," Lucius continues, "we need to stay together until it's time for you to grab the crown. Several other guild members will create a distraction, and I will be on guard for you. Make sure you get it as quickly as possible."

I swallow hard, my hands shaking in my lap as I try to remain composed. "You got it," I say with more confidence than I feel.

"Good luck," Lucius says with a wink before disembarking from the carriage and heading toward the entrance.

I follow him shortly after with my head held high and a smile on my face, trying not to look too nervous or out of place among the many other guests that have been invited to tonight's masquerade.

Inside, music fills the air, laughter echoes off of walls covered in fine tapestries, and golden decorations are everywhere as if they are doilies. Someone really has a thing for gold apparently. The atmosphere is electric, and people are mingling and dancing with one another like no one has a care in the world. I slide my mask on, take a deep breath, and wait at the top of the stairs to be announced and join those in the ballroom below.

THE MASQUERADE
REMME

The music swells as the first masked guests begin their descent down the grand staircase. I fix my gaze upon them, eyes narrowed, searching for any hint.

My heart pounds a steady beat in my chest that thrums through my veins. I arranged this lavish masquerade for one purpose only - to lure the wretch who stole into my very stronghold back into my clutches. She won't escape me again.

These simpering aristocrats mean nothing to me as they preen and glide across the polished ballroom floor below. I care not for their whispered gossip or displays of wealth and status. They are oblivious pawns in the trap I have laid tonight, one far more dangerous than their petty politicking.

Only one holds my interest now - the elusive thief who managed the impossible and breached my palace defenses once before. But I learn from my mistakes. She will find no such easy fortune this time.

My eyes sweep the colorful whirl of guests critically, searching for any sign of suspicious movement, any hint of concealed intent. For now, the crowd seems composed only of the usual vain, shallow nobility trying to curry favor. None stand out. But the night is still young.

I try to calm my racing thoughts, stilling my tapping foot and loosening my white-knuckled grip on the throne. Patience is key now. I must remain vigilant and wait for the perfect opportunity to present itself. And when she slips up, I will be there to catch her in the act and deliver ruthless justice.

The guests descend the stairs, their steps light and sure. Some of them are laughing, others whispering secret words amongst each other. They all move with a grace I envy, and I admire the sophistication and confidence each one commands. I remember when that was me, long ago in my youth. Before I could no longer touch another person.

Most are people I immediately recognize. Their masks and costumes match their personalities perfectly. Rarely do I throw any events like this. While my court whispers about my greed and harsh behavior, I keep my mouth shut. It isn't anything like that. Honestly, I am afraid of accidentally turning someone into gold again, of my curse affecting another.

I see everything that happens in this room. The secret touches. The leaning whispers. The one woman in the red dress who seems to stand out from the rest and interacts with no one.

She struts down the stairs, her cheeks flushed as she draws nearer to the ballroom floor. I watch her closely, my eyes never leaving her. She is familiar, yet a stranger to me. No name comes to mind to match her with.

Is this her?

The woman walks up to the food table and begins to fill her plate. My mouth waters as a pang of jealousy hits me. I would give almost anything to taste food again. She glances around the room, her eyes darting from one guest to another before finally landing on me. Our eyes meet and lock. I can feel a jolt of electricity run through me.

For a moment, the entire room stands still. When a man in a peacock mask bumps into her, the spell is broken.

I watch her closely as she moves gracefully amongst the other guests. She is clearly a master of disguise, and despite my best efforts, I still cannot identify her. She is definitely the most suspicious person here, at least to me. The rest of the crowd seems perfectly content to ignore her completely.

As the night wears on, I my curiosity only grows. Who is this woman in the red dress? Why does she stand out so much? And why does she captivate me so completely?

I watch her from afar, studying her every move. She seems to glide effortlessly across the dance floor, her body swaying in time with the music. The same tall man in black dances with her every few songs, and she dances with no other. How I wish I could take a turn just once and talk to her. Her mask obscures most of her face, but I can see a hint of a smile playing at the corner of her lips.

She slips through the crowd and stands along the edge of the ballroom, almost as if hiding between dances. Always with some sort of food and a glass that she never drinks from in her hand. Who is she?

A yell from near one of the food tables draws my eye for a moment. I cannot see what is happening, but when my gaze returns to where she last stood, she is gone. I search the crowd for her but she is nowhere to be found.

Is she making her move now?

I leave the ballroom and head toward my rooms, both hoping and dreading that I will see her.

My heart races as I walk down the hallway, my feet pounding against the floors. Is she here? Had I been right about her identity? It is too late to turn back now.

My footsteps echo down the empty corridor as I approach my chamber doors. Pressing an ear to the polished gold, I'm met with silence - no hint of an intruder within. Still, caution slows my hand as I reach for the handle. The doors glide open soundlessly to reveal an undisturbed room, precisely as I left it. Relaxing slightly, I step inside and let the doors swing closed behind me.

A cursory scan shows nothing amiss, the moonlight cascading over familiar furnishings. But instincts honed from years on the throne keep me alert. I prowl the perimeter, peering into shadows, watchful for any sign of trespass.

There - a faint creak from the direction of the balcony makes me freeze. In three swift strides I cross the room and fling back the heavy curtains. Moonlight spills over a familiar figure, freezing her in the act of climbing through the open balcony doors.

For a split second shock roots me in place. It's her - the mystery woman in red, an unmistakable silhouette against the night sky. Victory surges hotly through my veins. I knew it!

"What are you doing?!" My voice booms through the room, echoing off the walls. Startled by my sudden appearance, she drops whatever she is carrying into an open bag at her feet and scrambles to cover it up with her skirt before turning to look at me with wide eyes.

"Nothing..." Her voice quivers with fear as she speaks, clearly trying to hide something from me but unable to find enough courage to fully meet my gaze.

My jaw clenches as I study her face. Is this the same woman that had tried to steal the Bodian crown?

"What did you take?"

She hesitates before finally speaking up again, "Nothing. I took nothing." Her voice shakes with nerves as she speaks, but there seems to be an underlying defiance there, too.

"Show me," I growl out.

"There's nothing to show."

I lean in close enough to scent the rose perfume she wears, "You should know better than to lie to your king. What are you doing in my room?"

I want to touch her. To see if she is the same woman that stole from me before, but what if I am wrong? I don't want to kill her if I can use her to find the woman.

She places her hand on my gold breastplate, and a coy smile emerges on her face. I freeze. No one has touched me—even my armor—in ten years. But this woman, standing in front of me, has the nerve to do so.

I fight to maintain my control as she looks up at me with those big green eyes, clearly trying to determine how she should proceed. I want to ask her questions, but I know it will be better if I can draw some information out of her by playing along with whatever she is up to.

"One night," She whispers, her breath warm against my skin.

My stomach flips as the implication of her words sinks in. What does she mean? I was cursed so young that I lack experience in romantic areas. Sure I have watched others court each other but I have never done it myself. Is she offering herself? Or is she planning something else entirely?

I feel an unexpected spark inside me as I consider the possibilities—if only I could find out why exactly she is after the Bodian crown...

Without warning, her hand touches my arm and then it is confirmed; this must be the same woman who had tried to steal from me before. But more than that, there is something different about her now—something almost seductive that makes my heart race with anticipation. A part of me wants to confront her and demand answers, but another part of me finds myself drawn in by the unknown possibilities that weren't possible only moments before.

I take a deep breath and step closer to her until our faces are mere inches apart. Her cheeks flush with color as she meets my gaze without flinching.

"What is it you want?" My voice rumbles through the room, sounding deeper than usual due to my sudden change in mood.

She hesitates before finally speaking up again, "I want you."

I can't believe what I am hearing. This woman not only tried to steal from me, but now she is making suggestive remarks like this? It is clear that she is up to no good, but something about her draws me in nonetheless.

I lean in closer to her, my lips dangerously close to hers. "You're playing a dangerous game," I warn her, my voice low and commanding.

Her eyes widen, and she presses her body against mine. I can't deny the desire that is quickly building within me, but I know I have to keep my guard up. This woman is trouble. She is clearly playing a game.

"What do you want me to do?" I whisper seductively into her ear.

THE KISS

SCARLET

His words hang between us. What do I do? I have a feeling that neither of us expected the conversation to take this route, but I can sense King Remme's curiosity stirring. I need to use this and think on my feet to figure a way out of there with the crown.

"What do you want to do?" I ask.

I hold my breath as I wait for his response, both of us frozen in time until his lips finally move.

"I don't normally speak of such things in a lady's presence," he says, his voice low and full of intrigue.

I smile, heart pounding in my chest. I can feel his gaze searching my face, no doubt trying to figure out what is happening. Why is my body reacting to him like this? I've never done anything like this. There's been a few quick dalliances when I was younger, but nothing that was more than a moment of convenience and inexperienced lust. I have to play the part and do it well, or I may not be able to get out of here alive.

"You said we were playing a game. What does the winner get?" I reply, my voice filling with more confidence than I feel.

He seems to consider my words for a moment before finally speaking.

"How about a kiss," he says simply, his eyes never leaving mine. I can feel the challenge in those words.

I feel a wave of heat wash over me. My body wants to do more than just kiss, and I'm afraid he can tell. But I have to remain in control of the situation, so I coyly raise an eyebrow and speak.

"I suppose that could be arranged," I say, my voice dripping with confidence that I truly don't really feel.

King Remme smiles, a sly smirk appearing on his lips. He leans down until the noses of our masks touch. I feel every inch of his presence. His eyes burn into mine as if he can see right through me as if he knows I am hiding something. I bite my lip, and can feel his gaze lingering there before he finally leans in and kisses me tenderly.

I am lost in the moment, completely forgetting the crown tucked away under my skirt. We stay like that for what feels like an eternity before he finally pulls away. His eyes still burn into mine, and his lips curve into a small, satisfied smile.

"So, who won?" he asks, his voice a low whisper.

I slowly shake my head, completely lost for words. He chuckles before pulling away.

A sudden sense of urgency grips me as my head clears, and I realize I need to get out of there with the crown now. Before I let my guard down enough to get thrown in the dungeons below. I shake my head, trying to clear my thoughts, my mind racing with ideas. Perhaps I can distract King Remme long enough to grab the crown and make a run for it.

"You won," I say with a smile, hoping to put him off balance.

King Remme raises an eyebrow, his eyes still locked onto mine. "Are you sure about that?" he asks, a hint of amusement in his voice.

I nod, trying to maintain my composure. "Absolutely sure. A mere kiss from me, though, isn't much of a prize," I add with a sly grin. "I have a surprise for you."

King Remme looks intrigued, and I can see the curiosity burning in his eyes. "What kind of surprise?" he asks.

I reach down to the hem of my skirt and pull out a small bag. "This," I say, swinging it between us.

"The Bodian crown," he says. "I'm afraid you won't be leaving with that. How about a trade? Anything else in the room, but you give me that."

I look between him and the bag. What exactly is this that he is willing to trade for it at such a hefty price? Anything? Only a fool would make that kind of offer.

I hesitate, weighing my options. The crown is valuable, but so is my life, and I can't risk staying here any longer. I toss the bag in his direction, watching as he jumps out of the way, refusing to catch it. That's odd; why isn't he interested in looking at what's inside?

Scooping up an identical bag from the floor, I'm already on my way out the door, running as quickly as possible.

The bag I tossed was a decoy; I always have a backup plan.

As I sprint down the hallway toward freedom, my ankle rolls, and I fall. Cursing under my breath, I scramble to my feet, feeling one glass slipper slip off in the process. Without pausing to think about it, I opt to leave it behind, choosing my life over a shoe-- for now at least.

I run through the castle, desperately trying to get as far away as I can. The guards and other masquerade guests are rushing around, making it difficult for me to stay out of sight. I duck into rooms and hallways, waiting until everyone has passed before continuing on my way.

Finally reaching the entrance of the castle, I pause for a moment to take off my other glass slipper before continuing on my way. Holding both the bag and slipper in one arm, I run through the courtyard and out into the streets beyond. As I emerge from the wealthy part of Fallwatch, I'm relieved to see that there is no one following me.

When I stop to catch my breath I open the bag to take a closer look at this crown everyone seems to want. A wave of dread washes over me as I realize what has happened. It's the wrong bag. How could I have been so stupid?

I curse under my breath as I realize that all my effort has been for nothing; now King Remme will undoubtedly hunt me down for stealing from him and probably kill me for disobedience.

I stared down at what little remained in my hands - a glass slipper and a bag filled with a dirty rag and an old horseshoe- realizing I only had two weeks left to get this crown and that there may never be a chance this good again. Sighing heavily, I tucked them away in a pocket before heading back to Fairy Godmothers home to report my failure. She was going to kill me.

A Shoe and a Plan

Remme

The bag lays on the ground taunting me. I can't open it myself, but I need to know if the crown is inside. I know there is no point in trying to chase after the woman. She has proven her skill the last time she escaped my castle, and tonight will be even easier with the crowd.

A tight coil of tension remains in my gut, despite the thief's escape. While we were clearly playing one another, my traitorous body reacted as if it were real. I let out a dark chuckle. To think my first kiss was with an unknown thief trying to rob me. How pathetic.

I blame this weakness on years without human contact, thanks to my wretched curse. Deprived of even the simplest touch, it seems I've become starved for intimacy. Still, longing for a connection with that thief is foolish, no matter my isolation.

I should feel only fury at her continued defiance and audacity. The woman has made me a fool twice over, evading my grasp. Next time, I won't be so lenient. When I catch her, there will be a heavy price to pay for her games. She will learn what happens to those who steal from me.

My hands curl into fists.

Slowly breaking that fiery spirit promises to be satisfyi ng...

I force my rage into cool calculation once more. First, I must find her. Then, her true penance will begin.

My personal bodyguard and confidante, Sofia, rushes up to me, panting. She holds a delicate glass shoe in her hand.

"I saw her!" she exclaims. "The woman with the red dress running from your room. I chased after her, but she got away! At least she left this behind." She presents me with the shoe.

Inspecting it, I ask tentatively, "A shoe? She left behind a shoe? What do you think it means?"

Sofia shakes her head. "I don't know," she replies. "It probably fell off while she was trying to escape. But if we can find who it belongs to..." Her voice trails off as our minds race with possibilities.

"Sophia, please check the bag and make sure the crown is in there."

She picks up the bag and opens it. "It's here."

Relief floods me.

"This thief is no ordinary criminal. She managed to evade some of our best guards twice now."

I nod, hesitating. Sofia is more than my bodyguard, she is my closest confidante. If anyone will understand, it is her.

"When she broke into my chambers tonight, we...had an encounter," I admit slowly.

Sofia's head jerks up, eyes wide with surprise. "An encounter? You don't mean she..."

"We had a moment. Yet she remains flesh and blood." I flex my gloved fingers at the memory.

"She touched you..." Sofia gasps, grasping the significance at once. In over a decade, no living being has made contact with my skin and survived.

"And when I kissed her, she did not turn to gold," I confess.

Sofia is stunned silent for a long moment. Then a smile tugs at her lips. "So that's why you're so eager to find this thief. She's immune to your curse!"

I shake my head ruefully but do not deny it. Sofia knows me too well. "I must learn how such a thing is possible. But she cannot be allowed to roam free."

"We will find her, and discover the truth together." Her eyes glint with renewed determination.

"Sofia," I say, "we need to be discreet. We don't want anyone else to know what we're doing. I don't know why she is after this crown or who is really behind it. If she was just a thief and it was random, she wouldn't have attempted to get the same crown twice."

She nods in agreement. "I have a few contacts in the city who can help us. They owe me a few favors."

"Good," I say. "Let's start with that. And we have to be quick. Who knows when she'll strike again." I pause as an idea forms, "What do you think about inviting her back onto our territory? Creating a trap of sorts."

"Remme, I like how you think. What do you have in mind?"

THE SUITOR

SCARLET

Sharp stones dig into my feet with every step, each one a fresh sting against my bare soles. My red ballgown flutters wildly in the wind, its hem catching on the cobblestones. My hair, a tangled mess, whips around my face, trailing behind me like a banner of defeat. I curl my toes, desperate for some grip on the unforgiving ground, but the cobblestones remain unyielding. Every hobbling step sends a jolt of pain up my twisted ankle, a relentless throb. I hug myself tightly, my arms a poor shield against the biting cold, shivers racking my body in waves. The night air feels like icy fingers pressing against my skin, every gust of wind a cruel reminder of my vulnerability.

Why did I not keep my cloak near me or grab something as I was escaping?

As I walk, the city seems to close in on me, the darkness swallowing me whole in its tight embrace. Every slight sound sets me on edge, as if the guards would emerge from the shadows and drag me back to the castle.

My chest tightens, each heartbeat a drum's echo in the silence of the night. Memories of the night's events swirl relentlessly—my hands clutching the crown, the cold rush of terror as the door swung open, the King's lips brushing against mine, the desperate scramble to flee. The vision of my abandoned shoe lodged in my mind, a symbol of my hasty retreat, brings a hot flush to my neck. My teeth clamp down on my lip, a futile effort to banish the thought, as my eyes lock onto the inviting glow of fairy godmother's house ahead.

As I stagger closer, my breath comes in short, ragged gasps, each step toward the humble entrance feeling like a small victory. The soft glow of fairy godmother's house is a beacon of hope. I pause, struggling to steady my breathing and calm my racing heart before swallowing hard and approaching the door.

The door creaks open, and there she stands—fairy godmother, her ethereal figure bathed in the warm light from within. Her eyes sweep over my dirtied gown and bare feet, taking in every detail before finally settling on my face. The concern in her gaze is palpable.

"My dear," she murmurs, her voice as soothing as a lullaby, "What has happened?"

Shame floods through me, my cheeks burning as I avert my gaze to the ground, searching for the right words. "I had the crown in my hands," I manage to say, my voice barely above a whisper. "But I got distracted and, ah, grabbed the wrong bag when I escaped." I force myself to lift my gaze and meet her eyes, feeling like a scolded child confessing a misdeed.

Fairy godmother's brow raises, a curious twinkle in her eye despite the seriousness of the situation. "Come," she says softly, her tone a blend of command and comfort, guiding me inside.

The warmth of the house wraps around me like a comforting embrace, melting away the tension that had coiled within me. Fairy godmother steers me to a chair, and I sink into it gratefully, my muscles finally beginning to relax. She busies herself around the kitchen, gathering first aid materials with practiced efficiency.

Her movements are swift and sure, yet there is a tenderness in the way she handles everything, a reflection of the maternal role she has played in my life. Once she finishes gathering what she needs, she stands in front of me and gestures toward my gown. "Let's get you out of that dress while you tell me about what happened," she says kindly, helping me out of the red ballgown and into my everyday blue and grey one.

As she tends to my twisted ankle, her gentle hands soothing the pain, I recount the night's events in halting breaths. "The ball was lovely, and everything seemed to be going smoothly. I slipped out and made my way to the King's chambers with no trouble. I admit that I probably spent too long looking at the crown, even though it was only a few moments, but I dropped the bag to carry it back in, and before I could pick it up, the King was in the room coming towards me."

Her eyes flicker with concern as she listens, her touch never faltering. "Is that how you were injured? Did he do this to you?" she asks, her voice a mix of worry and anger.

I shake my head, trying to wave off her concerns. "No, I twisted it as I was trying to escape. I should have worn my boots. It's near impossible to run in heels," I reply, my voice tinged with frustration at my own oversight.

When she finishes bandaging my ankle, she steps back and frowns slightly. "Where is the other shoe?" she asks, her eyes scanning the room as if it might magically appear.

Embarrassment wells up again, and I take a deep breath, forcing myself to admit, "After I kissed the King," I say quietly, unable to meet her gaze, "I twisted my ankle and had to leave the shoe behind to escape."

Fairy godmother's eyes widen in surprise, and she reaches out to take my hand. "You kissed him?" she asks, her voice a mix of astonishment and concern.

My face grows hotter. "It wasn't planned. I'm not entirely sure what happened, but at the time it seemed like my best bet to escape," I say, my voice small and unsure.

She looks at me, her brows furrowed in concern. "Scarlet, you know you're not one of our operatives that we send on those kinds of missions. Are you alright?" she asks, her voice gentle but firm.

I nod, taking a deep breath. "I'm fine," I say, trying to sound more confident than I feel. "It was a momentary lapse of judgment, and it won't happen again."

Her expression softens a bit, but the worry doesn't leave her eyes. "It's not that I don't believe you, Scarlet," she says, her voice filled with maternal concern, "it's just that this type of mission is usually reserved for our more... experienced thieves."

Panic rises in my chest. "Please don't do this," I beg, looking up into her eyes pleadingly. "I can do this—I've gone too far for it all to be for nothing. I NEED this."

Fairy godmother seems to understand the desperation in my voice and nods slowly. "Very well," she says finally. "But you must promise me that if anything goes wrong or if you feel overwhelmed at any point, then you will come back here immediately. Don't act rashly. We will keep our eyes open for another opportunity."

A sigh of relief escapes me, and I nod fervently. "I promise," I say with conviction, wiping away a stray tear.

Fairy godmother squeezes my hands, a soft, encouraging smile playing on her lips. "It's late, and I'm not as young as I once was. Do you need help getting home?"

I shake my head, still trying to steady my emotions.

"If you insist. Good luck, Scarlet. Be safe. We will be in touch soon."

With that, she leaves the room, her presence lingering like a warm hug. Left alone with my thoughts, a mix of nervous energy and determination courses through me. I lace up my boot carefully, double-checking that everything is in place before stepping back into the night. Fairy godmother must have used a bit of magic as she healed me. It's tender but doesn't hurt nearly as much as it did on the way here.

The cool breeze brushes my face as I hobble back home, feeling more and more like a hunted animal with each step. Every instinct screams to run, but the small amount of pain left in my ankle slows my pace. As I navigate the darkened streets, shadows seem to move in the corners of my vision, keeping me on high alert.

***

The sun is shining high in the garden, casting long shadows across the leafy green tops of the carrots. I carefully spread a bed of leaves over them to save them for a later harvest, taking care to sit down whenever the weight on my ankle becomes too much. My mouth waters, thinking of the fresh sweet crunch they will develop after another frost. My ankle, still a bit tender from the past few days, is on the mend, but I can't risk hurting it again.

Adjusting my position on the soft earth, I ensure my movements are steady and deliberate. I might be stubborn, but I'm not foolish enough to push my ankle beyond its limits. Each time it starts to throb, I pause, massaging it gently before resuming my task. The smell of the fresh soil and the thought of a future harvest keep me motivated, even as I balance caution with my work.

This garden, a sanctuary of sorts, offers me a momentary escape from the chaos of the household. The carrots are thriving, and the thought of their sweet crunch after another frost makes the effort worthwhile. I let out a small sigh, both content and cautious, knowing that every action here impacts not just the garden, but my own recovery as well.

Just as I am finishing up, I hear Petunia calling my name. I lift my head and see her standing at the garden's edge, her silk skirts gathered in her hands, her face twisted in derision. "You need to come inside," she says in a clipped voice. "We have a visitor in the parlor."

I sigh, knowing that I won't be able to continue with my gardening. If Petunia has been sent to find me, Stepmother is behind it. There is no other reason she would risk sunning her pale and delicate skin.

Taking a deep breath, I push myself forward, determined not to let my tender ankle slow me down. I rise carefully, doing my best to mask any sign of a limp, though a wince escapes as the soreness flares up. Petunia, of course, stands there useless, her eyes narrowing in disdain at the dirt smudging my clothes. Typical.

By the time I reach the house, I manage to maintain a steady pace, though my ankle protests with every step. Once inside, I head straight for my bedroom, moving as quickly as I can. I hastily change out of my gardening clothes, scrubbing away the dirt with practiced efficiency. Despite my efforts, I know it will never be enough to meet Stepmother's impossible standards.

When I finally make my way to the parlor, I am greeted by an unexpected sight. Duke Geralsh stands tall at the center of the room, flanked by Stepmother and Petunia. His white hair frames a shiny bald patch, and his cane trembles in his hand. The sight of Starla's cruel grin sends a chill down my spine. This won't be pleasant.

My heart sinks as the reality of their plans dawns on me. The teasing my stepsisters have tossed around about marrying me off to Duke Geralsh wasn't just idle chatter. How much does my stepmother hate me that she would resort to this?

I swallow hard, my stomach tying in knots. Every instinct screams at me to run, but I know better. Instead, I straighten my shoulders, lift my chin, and prepare to face whatever comes next.

"What is the meaning of this?" Stepmother says, her voice like ice, as she gestures to my hands.

I glance down and notice how the dirt from outside still lingers beneath my nails.

"Please forgive her appearance. She really can clean up quite well when encouraged."

She has a way of making me feel so small with just one look. I mumble an apology before stepping forward to greet our guest. I bow my head respectfully and speak, my voice shaking despite myself. "It's an honor to meet you, Your Grace."

He nods curtly in response before turning his attention back to Stepmother.

"It's been years since the old estate was passed down to me, and I'm still without an heir," he sighs heavily, running a hand through his already thinning hair. He pauses momentarily before continuing, "All these years of searching for the right partner, yet none were suitable."

My stepsisters watch eagerly, barely containing their excitement at the thought of what such a marriage could mean for them. Stepmother nods with each of his words, her face displaying only feigned interest as she listens intently to what he says next.

"Society these days cares more for flights of fancy than facts," Stepmother adds.

My stomach churns as the conversation veers into unsettling territory. The thought of being engaged to a rickety old man like Duke Geralsh ties my insides into knots. Each word from Stepmother and the Duke feels like a nail in the coffin of my freedom. I desperately search for an escape, my mind cataloging every possible excuse, every potential ally, every fleeting opportunity to slip away unnoticed. Anything to avoid this fate.

"Yes, I wholeheartedly agree. Money is what runs the world. It should not be this difficult to find a prime young lady who can bear me an heir... no, several heirs, to continue on my family name." Duke Geralsh grasps at his waistcoat with shaking hands, his gaze too direct for my taste.

Did he just say prime? I almost gag.

Stepmother gestures for me to serve them tea. I move clumsily across the room trying not to spill any on the expensive rugs beneath my feet.

Once everyone is served, they continue discussing business while I sit silently in the corner, my breath shallow and my eyes wide. They talk of business, money, and politics, but mostly of marriage. My heart pounds as I watch them discuss my fate with such ease and detachment, like I'm nothing more than a pawn in their grand scheme.

I want to speak up, to protest against being sold off like a piece of property, but I know better than to do so. Stepmother isn't one for arguing with her decisions, and my name has yet to be specifically brought up. Her sharp eyes have caught every mistake I've made thus far, and I am sure she will find more if I try to challenge her.

I glance around the room, my eyes flicking from Stepmother's calculating gaze to Duke Geralsh's trembling hands. The thought of being tied to this man for the rest of my life makes my skin crawl. Yet, I know that voicing my objections now would only make things worse. Stepmother would see to that. So I bite my tongue, forcing myself to remain silent, even as my mind races with plans and possibilities.

Even though I know better than to speak up against her wishes, hope begins to swell within me at the thought that there may be another option besides marrying Duke Geralsh. Perhaps there is someone else who could take me away from all this wretchedness and give me a chance for something more...

My mind wanders to a pair of soft forbidden lips. Ones that, if ever encountered again, would be more likely to announce my death than offer the tenderness I desire. I don't notice as my elbow slips off the chair's arm. My head drops suddenly, and I snort as my attention returns to the group.

"It appears I have overstayed my welcome," Duke Geralsh declares as he rises. A look of disgust is evident on his face.

"No, not at all!" Stepmother replies. She shoots me a glare as she continues, "I must thank you for visiting us today."

"I am most grateful for your hospitality and the wonderful meal," the Duke responds, bowing slightly and offering a quick smile.

Stepmother nods in acknowledgment, then gestures towards Petunia and says, "Allow me to escort you out."

The two walk together to the parlor door with Petunia trailing behind them, carrying the Duke's cape over her arm like a badge of honor.

Stepmother glances in my direction, her eyes still glinting with underhandedness. She bows gracefully as he makes his way to the door before turning towards me and mouthing "behave."

The room is full of palpable tension once he leaves. Starla is snickering in delight, undoubtedly at the thought of the punishments coming my way for my careless mistake.

I look around the room, and it feels as if time has frozen at that moment. All my hopes and dreams seem so far away now, lost in the shadows of what I know is expected of me. Tears well in my eyes, but I refuse to let them fall, determined not to break down in front of these people who see me as nothing more than a slave or a commodity for sale.

The silence in the room is deafening as Stepmother returns to face me. Her expression is stern, her eyes like daggers piercing through my very soul. I try not to cower away, but keeping myself from shaking with fear is hard.

"What were you thinking?" she demands. "This was a perfect opportunity for us, and you blew it!"

I don't know what to say, so I stand there in shock as she continues her tirade. She shakes her head before turning towards Petunia and gesturing towards the door.

"We will discuss your punishment later. For now, you are to leave this house and return when I am ready for you. Do not leave the property. Do you understand?"

Unable to speak without triggering the tears of frustration welling up in my eyes I only offer a small nod.

My stepsisters snicker as they watch me scurry out of the parlor and into the courtyard beyond. Tears stream down my face as I run, desperate to escape the judgmental glares of those I am forced to call family.

I hobble through the flower garden, my feet pounding against the cobblestones beneath me. The chill of the early evening air bites at my skin, but it does nothing to cool the frustration burning inside me. Tears stream down my face, mingled with the anger and helplessness of being treated like a pawn in Stepmother's schemes. She wants to sell me off to the highest bidder, and I need to find some peace, some refuge from this madness.

As I move through the garden, I force myself to remember the happy moments I shared with my father in this very spot. But instead of warmth, the memories bring a bittersweet ache. The way his eyes would twinkle when he told me stories, his gentle voice as he taught me about plants and wildlife—those moments seem so distant now, overshadowed by the reality of my current situation.

Though it has been years since he passed, thoughts of him linger like a comforting embrace. The way his eyes would twinkle when he told me stories, his gentle voice as he taught me about plants and wildlife. Most of all, I remember how he jokingly named me Scarlet because when I was born, I was bright red like a beet. My mother thought it was a beautiful name and agreed before passing away that night from an infection

As much as I want to stay in this place filled with happy memories, my worry for the future weighs heavy on my mind. With a sigh, I continue walking towards the back of our property, towards an area that holds some of my fondest childhood moments—watching clouds and finding shapes in them as Father pointed out different animals or places in the sky. Picnics of strawberry jam and butter sandwiches and cheese. Before everything changed when he didn't return from a business trip.

The trees around me sway gently in the evening breeze, their leaves rustling comfortingly. Fireflies light up the darkness around me like stars, and crickets chirp in harmony with one another—all these things making me forget my troubles, even if just for a moment.

But despite their calming presence, reality soon creeps back into view like a ghostly mist, and all too soon, I find myself standing at a small back gate of our property.

I stand there for a few moments, lost in thought, when I hear a rustle of movement from behind me. I whirl around in surprise, only to see Lucius perched atop the stone wall that runs along the edge of our property.

He smirks as he catches my eye, then leaps lightly down from his perch and saunters towards me. "What are you doing here?" he asks, amusement lacing his voice.

"I could ask you the same thing. After all, it is my home."

He chuckles before leaning in close and speaks quietly enough so no one else can hear us. "Actually, I've been looking for you since you left the party. There was quite the commotion after you left."

Careful not to give anything away in case someone is secretly listening, I reply, "Oh? Anything of interest?"

He reaches into his pocket and pulls out a piece of folded paper, which he quickly slips into my hand before stepping away again with a mischievous grin.

"No one knows what exactly happened," he says with a shrug, "but I heard the King was looking for someone. Someone who made quite the impression." He gives me one last wink before disappearing back over the stone wall.

Bewildered but intrigued, I unfold the paper in my hands and read its contents carefully: An announcement for an upcoming trial to determine who will win ownership of the rare Bodian crown—considered one of the most valuable jewels in all of Ovehan Kingdom!

This crown has eluded me twice already, and the thought of a third attempt sends a shiver down my spine. But as I tuck the letter safely away into my pocket, questions swirl in my mind. Who would dare put out a job to steal the crown if it's that important? And why would he be offering it as the prize for the tournament? It doesn't add up. Someone powerful and desperate must be behind this, and I need to know who and why.

I make my way deeper into the garden, seeking solace among the flowers and trees. Each failed attempt to steal the crown has been a reminder of how close I've come, yet how far I still am. This trial might be my last shot, but it feels like walking into a trap set by unseen hands.

I find a secluded bench under a large oak tree and sit down, letting the tranquility of the garden envelop me. Whoever orchestrated this must have a reason, and I intend to find out. Is it a ploy to lure out thieves and miscreants? Or perhaps someone wants to test the cunning and skill of the participants, hoping to recruit the best for some larger scheme? The possibilities are endless, and each one more dangerous than the last.

As I sit there, the weight of my previous failures hangs heavy in the air. This tournament could be my path to redemption, or just another twisted game in the web of power and deceit that surrounds the crown. But one thing is certain: I have no other choice but to enter and fight with everything I have. The stakes are too high, and failure is not an option.

***

I slowly shuffle through the massive crowd of eager faces with dreams of entering the King's Tournament. People of all shapes, sizes, and ages stand in clusters, hoping to be individually chosen as contestants. I take a deep breath and instantly regret it. My nose fills with overwhelming clouds of perfumes, sweat, and something so bitter, but I can't put my finger on it.

Approaching the entrance, a sense of dread washes over me, anticipating the inevitable rejection. I cautiously step into the building, eyes immediately drawn to a woman in armor seated at the table. The two wooden doors behind me slam shut, amplifying the sound of my footsteps as they echo off the bare walls. The chatter from the crowd outside fades away, leaving an eerie silence. With each step, I feel my insignificance in the grand scheme of things, a small figure in a vast, indifferent world.

There's no way I'll be selected. I'm surrounded by beautiful women, strong and able men, and people of all classes who appear much better than I am.

The woman raises her eyes from the sheet of paper she's writing on and looks directly into mine. She smiles, her expression at once both kind and austere. "Name and purpose for entering the tournament?" she asks, her voice carrying just the right amount of authority.

"My name is Scarlet Marheart," I begin, my voice shaking slightly as I speak. "I just want a chance to compete."

The woman nods, setting down her quill and leaning forward. "Very well. What is your shoe size, your weight, your height?"

I'm surprised by the list of questions she asks and the amount of detail she's looking for. I hesitate, unsure why she needs to know all that about me.

"What do my shoe size and weight have to do with entering the tournament?" I ask cautiously, curious as to why those details are so important.

The woman smiles and puts down her quill. "It helps us choose the best candidates who are suited for the tournament. It will also make it much easier when providing uniforms for the ones chosen," she says in a gentle yet firm voice. "Now, if you please, let us continue."

I nod, understanding that this woman isn't going to answer any more questions until I respond to hers. Taking a deep breath, I start listing my details. "Shoe size, eight. Weight, one hundred and twenty. Height, five five." I watch as she writes down my answers in neat, precise lettering, her quill moving swiftly across the parchment.

"Are you sure you need all of this information? It seems a rather odd way to select people."

"The questions came from King Remme himself. Only he knows his reasons," she replies smoothly, her tone leaving no room for further debate.

I pause for a moment, taking in the woman's words. King Remme's involvement adds an unexpected layer of intrigue and authority. Nodding slowly, I understand that these questions are not mere formalities but part of a larger, more calculated plan.

Taking a deep breath, I begin explaining why I should be chosen to compete in the tournament. "I've been training with a dagger since I was a small child and know a bit about healing," I say, trying to keep my voice steady and confident. "I am confident in my abilities and believe they would be an asset to any team."

"What if there are no teams?"

I shrug, "That sounds like their problem then."

The woman seems to consider my response before nodding her head. "Very well, this tournament will have a public element. There will be particular tasks that the civilians will be allowed to watch. Do you have anything else you would like to add?" she asks, her voice still carrying an air of mystery.

"No ma'am."

Hand outstretched, she smiles, "Scarlet Marheart, I would like to invite you to round two of the entrance process. If you wish to proceed, exit out of the door behind me. If you wish to reconsider, now is your chance. You may leave the way you came."

The woman's words hang in the air as I walk through back door and into a small courtyard. In front of me are several stations with different tasks to complete—swordsmanship, throwing daggers, lifting weights, identifying items and plants, and more. I had expected to sign my name and await an answer; this was much more involved than I anticipated.

Approaching the dagger station, I spot a man with short red hair and a scar running down the left side of his face. His stern, no-nonsense demeanor makes it clear this won't be a walk in the park.

"Let's see what you can do," he says gruffly, motioning to the table laden with daggers. Picking one up, I feel its weight in my hand and immediately notice the balance is off. I try to mask my frustration, but he catches the slight furrow of my brow.

"The tournament will be a challenge," he says, handing me another dagger, his eyes sharp and knowing. "You'll have to adjust your technique and work with what you've got. You won't always be allowed to bring your own weapons for the rounds."

Taking the second dagger, I give it a few practice swings, testing its balance and weight. It feels better, but I stay on guard.

Without warning, he lunges at me, a swift and calculated move aimed straight for my chest. I sidestep quickly, my instincts kicking in. I counter with an overhead strike, aiming to catch him off guard. He parries my blow, the clang of metal resonating through the air.

We circle each other, eyes locked. He feints to the left, then attacks from the right. I deflect his strike and counter with a low sweep, but he jumps back just in time. The intensity of our sparring escalates, each move and counter-move more precise and aggressive. His attacks are relentless, but I manage to hold my ground, my training with daggers serving me well.

After several minutes of this back-and-forth, he steps back, breathing heavily but with a look of approval in his eyes. "Impressive," he says finally, his voice carrying a hint of respect. "You have potential."

He motions for me to put down the daggers and then gestures toward the other stations. "Go on," he says, handing me a card with a signature on it. "You've passed. You need to collect three to make it into the final consideration of contestants."

Relieved yet invigorated, I pocket the card and thank him before moving on to the next station, ready to prove myself once again. The challenge excites me, and I can't wait to see what's next.

Next, I approach a table with a variety of plants on it. After years of growing the food we eat and scavenging medicinal plants because of my stepmother's spending habits, I am reasonably confident I can pass any test they give me.

At the table is a grey-haired woman wearing a simple brown dress and carrying a basket full of different plant specimens. She smiles warmly at me and gestures for me to come closer as she begins to explain her task.

"This is not as easy as it looks," she says, pointing to a few of the plants in front of her. "Some of these are poisonous if eaten raw, but safe when cooked in specific ways; others have medicinal properties when combined with certain other herbs." She looks up at me, her eyes searching mine for understanding.

I nod, excited, as I look at all the herbs and plants on the table. This is something I know I can do. "I understand," I say confidently. "I have experience with growing and identifying plants."

The woman smiles at me, her eyes brightening. "Excellent," she says. "Then this should be easy for you." She hands me a small vial filled with liquid and points to a plant on the table. "This is the herb you need to identify. Pour a drop of this liquid on it and tell me what it is used for."

I take the vial and walk over to the plant, examining it closely. It looks like chamomile, but I want to be sure. I carefully pour a drop of the liquid on a small section of the plant's stem. Immediately, a sweet, earthy smell fills the air. "This is chamomile," I say confidently. "It is commonly used to treat anxiety and promote relaxation."

The woman looks impressed as she makes a few notes on her clipboard. "You have a good eye for botanicals," she says, handing me another vial of liquid. "Now, try this one."

The next plant she points to is less familiar. Its leaves are broad and dark, and the stem has a slight purple hue. I rack my brain, trying to recall my training. I pour a drop of the liquid on the stem and wait. A sharp, almost metallic scent wafts up. "This is belladonna," I say slowly. "It's highly poisonous if ingested raw. However, in very small, controlled doses, it can be used to treat muscle spasms and pain, but it must be handled with extreme caution."

The woman nods approvingly, jotting down more notes. "Very good. Now, for the last one," she says, pointing to a plant with tiny white flowers and jagged leaves.

I recognize it immediately but pour the liquid on it to be sure. A pungent, almost peppery smell fills the air. "This is yarrow," I explain. "It's used in traditional medicine to stop bleeding and promote healing of wounds. It can also be made into a tea to help with digestive issues and reduce fever. It's very versatile but must be properly prepared to be effective."

The woman looks thoroughly impressed as she finishes her notes. "Very impressive," she says with a smile, handing me another card with her signature. "You have passed this round. You may proceed to the next station."

Feeling more confident than ever, I move on to the next challenge, eager to prove myself once again. Each step brings me closer to my goal, and I intend to make the most of this opportunity

The "Accident"

Remme

From my vantage point, I observe the woman with blonde hair as she navigates the courtyard, her movements deliberate and focused as she engages with the trials. Her determination is evident, each step calculated and precise.

So far, she's impressed me. Her use of daggers lines up well with the aftermath we found in the castle the first night she entered. The guard had been killed without defending themselves first with a short blade. Her second choice of challenges, the botany, had been unexpected. But I can see how that could serve a woman well in everyday life and be used by a thief.

I watch how her body moves as she decides what to do for her third test. She seems to have a similar build and the correct hair color for the woman I seek. Of course, so have several other applicants today.

"What do you think?" Sofia asks as she enters the room I conceal myself within.

Without moving my gaze, I reply, "Maybe. This is what, the fourth possibility so far today?"

"I think so."

"Good, keep the doors open and sign up until the sun sets if she comes late. Remember to select several others so as not to tip her off. Men and women both."

"Of course, your highness."

Sofia pauses, her eyes narrowing slightly as she watches Scarlet below. "Your Highness, there's something else to consider. What if she's working for the thieves guild we've been searching for? It's possible that the woman you're looking for is also involved, if they aren't the same person."

I turn to face Sofia, intrigued by the suggestion. "Go on," I say, my interest piqued.

"If she has connections to the thieves guild, she could lead us to them. Even if she can't break your curse, her knowledge and skills might still be useful to us," Sofia continues, her voice measured and thoughtful.

I nod slowly, considering her words. "You're right. We need to be cautious, but also strategic. If she's part of the guild, she could provide valuable information. And if she's not, her abilities could still serve us well."

Sofia's eyes glint with determination. "I'll look into her background further, see if there are any connections to the guild. In the meantime, we should keep her close and observe her actions carefully."

"Agreed," I say, my mind already racing with possibilities. "We need to find out everything we can about her, and the others who match the thief's description. Use your contacts in the city, but be discreet. We can't afford to alert anyone to our plans."

Sofia hesitates for a moment, then adds, "Considering your interest in her, it's worth exploring every angle."

I meet her gaze, understanding the unspoken concern. "Sofia, I assure you, my interest is not of a romantic nature. I need to understand how she defies my curse, and if she's connected to the guild, all the better. I'm not seeking love."

Sofia relaxes slightly, her expression softening. "I understand, Your Highness. I'll take care of it. We will find the truth, one way or another."

I turn back to watch Scarlet below, a sense of anticipation building within me. Whether she's connected to the thieves guild or not, there is something about her that I can't ignore. And I intend to find out exactly what it is.

The next test is about to begin. One not set up in an obvious way.

A servant walks into the courtyard, a goblet filled with wine and a small mound of fruit sits on the tray. I watch in anticipation as a servant approaches the woman. The servant stumbles, the tray tipping from her grasp.

Instinctively, the woman reacts, flinging out an arm to keep the servant from tumbling while reaching out with her other hand to steady the wobbling silver tray, her body coiling like a tightly wound spring as she braces herself. She grasps the silver tray just in time, allowing it to tilt and slow the fall of fruit spilling onto the dirt floor. Yet, it's too late for the expensive goblet—it smashes against the ground with a sharp crack.

Interesting. She could have moved to save the goblet but chose to save the fruit instead. It could have just been an accident, but how her body moves tells me the chances of that are slim.

I look up at Sofia, who nods at me in agreement. This is definitely someone we need to keep an eye on.

"What do you know of her?" I ask.

"Her name is Scarlet. Lord Marheart's biological daughter. It appears as if the family has fallen on hard times after he passed."

"I remember Lord Marheart. That would explain her use of blades. I want you to dig further. Find out what you can and see if there are any holes in her story, as well as the others who fit the thief's description."

Sofia nods and leaves the room, closing the door softly behind her. I continue to watch Scarlet below as she helps the servant gather the spilled fruit. There is something about her that intrigues me, something that makes me want to know more.

Observing Scarlet, admiration grows for her actions. She saved the servant from falling and handled the situation with grace and poise. Her skills and strength are evident, showing no doubt about her capability and composure.

I stand up from my chair and make my way toward the balcony. Scarlet is still below, now conversing with the servant she saved. Her face is kind, and her voice is gentle. Her voice carries up on the wind to my ears, but I can't quite pick out what they say in their hushed tones.

Sofia emerges in the courtyard below, carrying a slip of paper. She hands it to Scarlet, and the young woman bows slightly in acknowledgment before turning and leaving the courtyard.

A clocktower rings, signifying that it is half past three. I need to return to the castle. Meetings fill the rest of my afternoon. I make my way out of the building, my cloak carefully covering me without touching to prevent it from converting to gold. I don't want to draw too much attention, so I keep my head low as I walk through the crowd.

My guards are close by but not directly beside me. If they are too close it would draw too much attention.

I see Scarlet not too far ahead in the crowd, stopped by a group of noblemen. I watch as Scarlet is cornered against the building wall. A man steps closer, his face twisted in a menacing smirk. Scarlet appears uncomfortable and scared, her hands shaking slightly as she tries to retreat from him.

Why isn't she removing herself from the situation? With the skills she just showed us she clearly can. This doesn't make sense.

I want to intervene, but I have to be cautious. Drawing too much attention could ruin my plan and reveal my identity, so I sneak closer to hear what they say.

The man scoffs, "You must know that you'll soon be mine," he says to Scarlet.

Scarlet's lips tremble as she nervously stammers a reply, "No... No, I'm sure that won't happen."

He raises an eyebrow and continues patronizingly, "It is your stepmother's decision. It has already been made."

Scarlet's face pales, and her hands clench into fists at her side. I feel my blood boil with anger and rage as I watch this man. Does she have no clear way of escape, being surrounded by a group of five men? Does she feel that it's too much? Without thinking of the consequences, I step forward and clear my throat loudly, drawing both their attention towards me but careful to not reveal my face.

The man immediately steps away from Scarlet, eyeing me warily before quickly turning on his heel and disappearing into the crowd without another word. Scarlet looks at me with an expression of confusion and gratitude on her face before bowing her head slightly, mumbling thanks, and making her way out of the courtyard as well.

Who is her stepmother that would force such an unwanted marriage on her? I know the nobles often marry for alliances and not for love, but as far as I can remember, that is not how Lord Marheart worked. These questions rattle around in my mind as I return to the castle, eager to find answers that may or may not exist

ACCEPTED

SCARLET

I have been gone longer than expected, and upon my return home, I know something is off as soon as I step foot in the doorway. Stepmother stands with her back to me, holding a letter in her hand. She whirls around to face me, her expression dark and unreadable.

"You've been accepted," she says in a flat voice, handing me a piece of parchment.

Miss Scarlet Marheart,

You've been accepted as one of the participants in the King's tournament. Room and board will be provided, as will the uniform required for participants to wear during their trials. You will be expected to report in two days' time. If you fail to arrive, your spot will be forfeited.

Excitement and apprehension courses through me. But my stepmother's expression tells me she is far from happy about this news.

"Yes," I say hesitantly. "It appears that I've been accepted."

"And who will take care of the household while you're away, gallivanting around the palace with all those other lords and ladies?" Her voice is heavy with accusation.

I gulp, taken aback by her reaction. "I... I hadn't thought of that."

Why hadn't I thought this through? Had a plan in place already about how to handle stepmother while I was away?

"You never do," she spits.

"I'm sorry," I say quietly. "I didn't mean to upset you."

My stepmother sighs, her eyes narrowing with disdain. "It's not about you upsetting me, Scarlet. It's about your irresponsibility. Who will take care of the household while you're off gallivanting at the palace? Do you think your duties here will magically disappear?" she snaps, her voice dripping with accusation. "You never think of anyone but yourself. You're a grown woman, not a child. When will you learn to put others before your own selfish desires?" she continues, shaking her head in disbelief.

Her gaze turns even colder. "And what if you embarrass us? Do you think prancing around with lords and ladies will improve our situation? You've always been a burden, and now you're abandoning your responsibilities for some foolish dream," she spits, her words cutting deep.

Her anger is palpable, and I can see there's no point in arguing with her. She's only thinking of herself, as always.

"I will try to do better," I say. "I will ensure I come home in time to care for the household."

My stepmother smiles. "I know you will. You have my blessing as long as you fulfill your promise."

I smile back, relieved that she isn't refusing my opportunity entirely. "Thank you," I say.

With the letter from the palace in my hand, I leave my stepmother to head toward the kitchen to begin dinner. My mind races with everything that needs to be done before I can leave and figuring out how to work out my duties here and in the tournament. If I can win, everything will be different.

A knock at the window catches my attention as I enter the kitchen. A familiar dark-haired face appears in the window, his eyes twinkling with mischief. I scurry to the kitchen door and let him in.

"Congratulations!" Lucius says, a broad smile on his face. "I heard you were accepted into the tournament!"

"Thank you! How did you know?" I ask eagerly.

He shrugs as if it's no big deal. "You know me. I have connections everywhere, even at court. Word travels quickly when something like this happens. Anyway, I'm here on Fairy Godmother's behalf. She wanted me to deliver this message to you directly."

I wait for him to hand me a letter or really anything, but he doesn't. Arms crossed, I huff, "Where is it?"

He laughs and shakes his head, "You're too easy." He leans forward and whispers in my ear, "You're not the only GGG member competing for the crown. She sent in another girl too."

"What?!" I yell before remembering I don't want to draw my family's attention to the kitchen. "What do you mean, another girl?" I mutter angrily.

"To be fair, you've missed your opportunity twice. Perhaps you can work together and accomplish the job."

"I can't do that! You know I need the full payment for this job. Who is she sending?"

With a twinkle in his eye, he shakes his head no, "You know I don't have those details. Even if I did, do you really think I would tell you?"

I kick the toe of my shoe into the stone floor, frustrated. "That does sound like something you would do."

"One more thing," he adds as he reaches into his pocket. "Fairy Godmother asked me to give you these." He goes into another pocket and pulls out a small pouch containing two items—a silver needle to test for poisons and a small throwing dart.

A smile spreads across my face. If she is sending these to me, she expects this to turn deadly.

"Anything else?" I ask.

"She is offering help."

"What kind of help?"

"Someone to fill in your role here while you are busy elsewhere."

I don't know quite how to react to that. On the one hand, it would make things much easier. I could focus entirely on the trial. On the other, would stepmother allow it?

"In exchange for what?"

"I don't know. She didn't say."

"Fine, I accept."

"Don't act so pleased."

I roll my eyes. "You have no idea what that will mean for whoever she hires."

"Who said anything about hiring? I heard it's an inside job."

Eyes wide, I stare at him, not entirely sure what he means. "An inside job? You mean someone already in the guild?"

Lucius nods. "That's what I heard. But don't ask me for details. I don't know who it is."

I can't help but feel a little uneasy about this. Who could Fairy Godmother have possibly found to fill in for me? And what did they want in exchange for their help? But with the tournament looming, I don't have time to dwell on it. I have to focus on winning, no matter what it takes.

"Thank you for passing on the message," I say, trying to keep my voice calm. "And for the gifts. I'll be sure to use them well"

Lucius grins. "I have no doubt you will. Good luck, Scarlet."

With that, he slips out the kitchen door and disappears into the night. I turn back to the kitchen, my head buzzing with everything that has just transpired.

Deep breaths, Scarlet. Dinner first. Plotting can be saved for later. I need to focus on the immediate tasks at hand despite feeling uneasy about Fairy Godmother finding someone to fill in for me

***

I fold my simple dresses, leathers, and a few odds and ends that I feel may help me in the tournament and place them in my worn traveling chest. My stomach flutters with nerves as I think about what lies ahead. Will I be able to pass the tournament tests and win the crown? And who is this other girl Fairy Godmother sent? Is she a competitor, or could she actually be of help?

My grim thoughts are interrupted by the bell for the main door ringing. I hurry down the stairs, trying to get to the door before Stepmother arrives. My slippers skid slightly as I stop and pull open one of the heavy wooden doors.

Fairy Godmother stands on the steps. Her eyes hold a knowing glint.

"You needed some assistance. I'm here to help," she says softly.

Grabbing her arm, I pull her in and whisper, "You can't be serious."

"Am I known for my delightful humor?" she replies with a raised eyebrow.

I turn away. "I'll be fine. You've already given me items to assist while I'm there."

She gives me a sad smile. "Let me help while you're away."

"You don't need to lower yourself," I say stiffly. "The last thing I want is you serving my cruel family."

Fairy Godmother chuckles. "I'm not lowering myself, child. I have things to do here."

I turn to face her. "Things to ensure I succeed, no doubt. But what could be so important that you'd serve that witch!"

She reaches out, cupping my cheek. "All will become clear in time."

I sigh. "Fine, do as you wish. But I won't allow them to mistreat you."

She grins. "Oh Scarlet, don't worry about me. Have you ever known anyone to get past me?"

Before I can respond, my stepmother strides in. Her eyes narrow as she sees Fairy Godmother.

"Who are you?" Her tone holds thinly veiled disgust.

Fairy Godmother gives a slight bow. "I'm a friend of Scarlet's. I've come to help while she's at the tournament."

I look up in surprise, unable to hide my astonishment.

My stepmother frowns. "I wasn't aware Scarlet had any friends." She studies Fairy Godmother skeptically.

Fairy Godmother meets her gaze calmly. "There are many things you don't know about Scarlet."

Anger flashes in my stepmother's eyes at the slight challenge in Fairy Godmother's tone.

I hold my breath, hoping Fairy Godmother's words haven't caused irreparable offense.

My stepmother sighs. "Very well. An extra set of hands will be useful." Her dismissive tone makes it clear she sees Fairy Godmother as little more than a servant.

Fairy Godmother's eyes lock with mine, a shared understanding passing between us. I force myself to give a slight nod to show my acceptance.

My stepmother turns to leave but pauses at the doorway. "See that you do not displease me," she warns curtly before sweeping from the room.

Once she is gone, I let out the breath I've been holding. "Fairy Godmother, you shouldn't have—"

She holds up a hand, cutting me off. "I know what I'm doing, child. Now finish packing."

I stare at her, wondering if I'll ever truly understand this woman who feels more like a parent to me than my own stepmother. I return to my room with Fairy Godmother following. Silently, I finish packing my meager belongings.

Fairy Godmother places a reassuring hand on my shoulder. "You have a rare gift, Scarlet. Don't doubt yourself. This is your last chance before the deadline is up. The shadow patron is becoming impatient."

I look up at her, feeling tears prick my eyes. "Thank you," I murmur. "For everything."

She smiles softly. "Go now. Make me proud."

I hug her tightly, feeling like a small child seeking comfort from a parent.

Lifting my small, worn trunk, I make my way downstairs. My stepmother and stepsisters stand by the door, watching me with equal parts disdain and curiosity.

I hold my head high as I look at them, refusing to show any weakness or doubt. Then I turn and walk out the door without a second glance, my boots crunching confidently against the gravel path.

As I glance back at the imposing manor one last time, I see Fairy Godmother standing in an upstairs window, her face alight with pride and encouragement. A smile spreads across my face and I face forward once more, walking determinedly toward my future and whatever challenges it may hold.

With Fairy Godmother watching over my home and my stepfamily in my absence, I am now free to focus solely on the tournament ahead—and on finding a way to finally free myself from the bindings of the past once and for all.

ROSE

SCARLET

I step out of the carriage and hand my invitation to the guard at the palace gate.

"Name?" he asks curtly.

"Scarlet Marheart," I reply, trying to keep my voice steady.

The guard glances at the invitation, then at me. His eyes narrow. "Your business here?"

I tense, fearing he might recognize me from my previous attempts to infiltrate the palace. But I keep my expression neutral.

"I've been selected as a participant in the king's tournament," I say calmly.

The guard grunts, waving me through. "Go on then."

I breathe a sigh of relief as I enter the palace grounds. My trunk is unloaded, and a servant shows me to the living quarters for the competitors.

The last two times I have been in the palace, I've had guards chasing me out. I can't help the nervous flutter in my stomach as I walk the palace corridors. What if someone recognizes me?

I push those thoughts aside as I enter the room that will be mine for the duration of the tournament. My roommate stands up from her cot as I enter. My heart sinks as I recognize her—Rose, from the guild.

We make eye contact, acknowledging each other as guild members, yet remaining competitors.

Rose speaks first. "Fairy Godmother sent both of us. We should work together."

I eye her suspiciously. "To what end?"

Rose throws up her hands in a placating gesture. "No need to be hostile. I'm just saying two heads are better than one."

But I don't trust her. Rose would stop at nothing to ensure her success, even at my expense. I have no intention of allying with her until I have no other choice.

I study Rose carefully. I can see why Fairy Godmother has chosen her as a backup. We share similar hair color, eye color, and build.

But Rose is usually sent on seductive missions. An image of me kissing the king flashes in my mind. Alright, I admit that Rose might indeed be better suited for this job.

Yet I refuse to give up. I need this chance at freedom too desperately. I need to bring in enough money to fend off the marriage proposals my family insists on giving me. I have to prove myself useful without a grotesque man attached to me.

I speak calmly. "Let's work out sleeping arrangements first, then we'll discuss an alliance."

Rose eyes the cots warily. "I'll take this one." She claims the cot farther from the door.

We change into our tournament uniforms—simple leather pants and tunics. I see Rose's GGG mark on the back of her neck—chains and roses intertwined to create an elegant G. I instinctively touch my own mark on my upper thigh as I change—a G disguised as a woman sitting on the crescent moon.

Rose chuckles. "Different styles, same goal."

I sigh. "You're right. It might be smart to work together."

Rose studies me curiously. "What's holding you back?"

I hesitate, then admit, "I need this win more than you think."

Rose hums thoughtfully. "And yet here we both are." She extends her hand. "So, what do you say? Team up for now?"

I shake her hand, but my grip is firm. "For now." Our truce is uneasy, but it's necessary.

Rose grins. "Alright. What's your plan, partner?"

I look her in the eye. "We compete openly, keep an eye on each other for threats. As we get closer to the prize, we reassess."

Rose nods. "Fair enough. No double-crossing, then?"

"For now." I can't fully trust her, but we need to cooperate.

Rose smiles slyly. "Alright, we understand each other." She holds out her hand again. "Truce?"

I shake it. "Truce." Our agreement is tentative, but for the moment we have a common goal. I can only hope our fragile alliance will last long enough to get me what I need

TOURNAMENT BEGINS

REMME

The contestants file into the dining hall below. There are knights, thieves, nobles, and more—an interesting mix of competitors. My eyes scan the room with calculated precision. Several women could potentially be the one who kissed me, including Scarlet, who stands out with her quiet confidence. Another moves with stealth and grace, a skillful thief perhaps. I continue observing, analyzing skills and threats.

As I observe, several inexperienced pages enter, chatting excitedly. A dignitary sits by one of the women, smiling and introducing himself. She politely nods but does not smile back. Interesting, but not revealing enough.

As the contestants eat, none of them give any indication of being the woman I seek. Irritation gnaws at me. I will have to observe their interactions and reactions more closely. With a heavy sigh, I make my way down to the hall and ascend the dais. The chatter dies down as the contestants notice me.

"Greetings," I begin in a loud, clear voice, "I'm pleased to see such capable competitors. You were all handpicked from many who sought to enter."

There are scattered murmurs and nods in response.

"Though many trials lay ahead, the contest began the moment you entered these walls." I observe as the contestants exchange uneasy glances, their postures stiffening. A woman fiddles with her napkin, another bites her lip. I suppress a smile, relishing their discomfort. Good, let them feel the weight of what lies ahead.

"I must warn you—there are no safety nets. Accidents happen during tournaments. If that poses a problem, now is the time to leave." I pause while the room falls silent. No one dares to move. Excellent.

"As you compete in the trials to come, you will be awarded points for your placements and achievements. The one with the most points at the end will be deemed the winner."

I nod to one of my guards subtly. He withdraws, carrying out the next phase.

"For your first task, a foreign dignitary has been planted among you in disguise. Determine who they are and the country they represent. You have ten minutes. Write down who you believe the foreign dignitary to be and your reasoning, and bring your answers to me."

Excited chatter breaks out as the contestants begin examining clues.

I observe their reactions closely. Many seem overwhelmed, while others simply frown in concentration.

My attention turns to two women—Scarlet and someone who appears to be her acquaintance. They speak in hushed tones, poring over clues together.

I note one contestant touching various tapestries and paintings on the walls, while another returns to the food table, sampling different dishes. A few begin speaking to nearby contestants, listening intently for dialects in their speech. Can they not focus on the task at hand? This is not a leisurely gathering.

A tall woman with long red hair rises to bring me her answer. I take the paper solemnly but do not read it, simply tucking it into my pocket. One after another, they approach, each more oblivious than the last. Do they think this is a game? I repeat the process with each contestant as they bring me their deductions.

When Scarlet approaches, I study her face for any sign of recognition, any tell that she is the woman I seek. But her expression reveals nothing, and she hands me her paper confidently before returning to her seat. Frustrating. She remains a mystery, just like the rest of them.

With a sigh, I wait for the rest of the participants to hand me their papers and exit the hall to determine how well—or poorly—the contestants have done on their first challenge. None have revealed themselves as the woman I am searching for, but I must remain vigilant. The game has only begun, and my patience wears thin. I need results, not idle chatter and incompetence.

POISONED

SCARLET

Rose and I compare our answers for the foreign dignitary clue in hushed tones.

I shake my head. "I guessed Andalucia, but it must be wrong."

Rose frowns. "I said Meria, though now I'm not sure. Neither of us got it right."

"True, but we figured out it was the woman in green."

Rose nods. "At least we got that part. And we were observing everyone else."

I glance around apprehensively. "Who do you think will be the biggest threats?"

Rose considers. "The woman with throwing knives. And the man meditating in the corner."

"The knife thrower is skilled, but the meditating man..." I pause. "He seems too calm. I wonder what he's really thinking."

Rose hums in agreement. "Same. The quiet ones are often the most dangerous."

"Well that eliminates you then."

I choke on my laugh after seeing the look she sends my way.

Before we can continue, a stocky man with cropped brown hair steps forward confidently. He cries out and collapses to the floor, foaming at the mouth.

Poison.

I exchange an uneasy look with Rose. This is serious—we are truly fighting for our lives. Our alliance is needed to survive, but can I trust her? Only one of us can win.

Rose speaks first. "We'll watch each other's backs. Work together as far as we can, then split the winnings."

Her words ease my tension, but I can't fully trust her yet. "Agreed. But cross me, and you'll regret it."

"Likewise," Rose says coolly. "I have no interest in dying here. Do we understand each other?"

"We do," I say firmly. We shake on our renewed, if tentative, alliance. Together we have a better chance of survival, but only one of us can walk away the victor.

As the man continues to writhe in agony on the floor, I hesitate only for a moment before rushing to his side.

"I can help," I tell the shocked onlookers. "Please move."

Rose grabs my arm. "Scarlet, what are you doing? Helping him won't gain you any points."

I shake my head. "I'm not worried about points. I can't just let him die. Not when I might be able to save him."

Rose releases my arm with a frown. "Suit yourself." She sits back down, watching me closely.

I turn my attention to the poisoned man. His face is contorted in pain, his breathing labored. This isn't good. I take his arm to check his pulse. It's rapid and thinning. Panic rises in my chest, but I force it down. I need to stay focused.

"We need to purge the poison from his system," I say firmly. "I need boiled water and find me ginger root if you have any. I need it to be pure. Hurry!"

Several servants rush to get the items I request and return in mere moments. My hands tremble as I pour the hot ginger water into a bowl. Desperate to help the man, I hold his head up and force the liquid down. His body convulses violently as he gulps it down, while the other contestants watch with intense eyes.

What if this doesn't work? What if I make it worse?

Suddenly, his body relaxes and his breathing returns to normal—with relief. I exhale the breath I didn't realize I was holding.

I watch as a castle healer strides into the room, a long red cloak billowing behind him. He kneels on the floor beside the man and runs his fingers lightly over his arm.

After a few moments of observation, he looks up at me with surprise in his eyes.

"You did this?" he asks, his tone neutral.

My heart skips a beat. Is he accusing me of poisoning him? I nod slowly, feeling a bit embarrassed by the attention. "It's... I-I had to help him."

The healer's face softens into a smile. "You did a good job. If you hadn't acted quickly, he wouldn't have survived."

Relief washes over me. He's not accusing me; he's thanking me. My hands finally stop trembling.

He pats my shoulder in gratitude before turning his attention back to the man on the ground. I watch in silence as they continue their work, grateful that he is going to be alright.

Sitting back on my heels, I let out a sigh of relief. Rose approaches me, her expression calculating. "That was foolish," she hisses. "You gained no points and drew attention to yourself."

I watch Rose warily, my stomach sinking. Her cold indifference shocks me more than I expected. I thought she might be angry, but this level of callousness? It's an unsettling reminder that many other members of the guild are much more ruthless than me.

I stand up slowly, meeting her gaze. "Maybe," I mumble, my voice barely above a whisper. "But I couldn't just let him die when I had the knowledge to save him."

Rose shakes her head, her eyes narrowing. "Well, don't expect me to risk myself for the sake of others. Each person is on their own here." With that, she returns to her seat, eyeing the other contestants warily.

The healer finishes his work, and the castle staff takes the man away. The crowd soon disperses, leaving the room eerily silent. I remain standing in the middle of the room, my mind a whirlwind of emotions. Pride in helping someone in need battles with the shame I feel from Rose's heartlessness. I can't let myself become like her. I refuse to fall into that way of thinking.

Needing a moment, I sink into a nearby chair, my hands still trembling from the adrenaline. The weight of what just happened presses down on me. We're truly fighting for our lives, and not everyone will play fair. The room feels colder, emptier without the others, but I need this solitude to gather my thoughts.

I look around, my eyes settling on the remnants of the meal we never got to finish. My stomach churns, the food now unappetizing. The enormity of the situation hits me again—this isn't just a game. It's survival, and people like Rose will do whatever it takes to win.

Leaning back, I close my eyes for a moment, trying to steady my racing thoughts. The reality of the tournament and its dangers looms larger than ever. Rose's words echo in my mind, a stark reminder of the ruthlessness I'll face.

But I can't let that change me. I won't let fear or the cruelty of others dictate my actions. I take a deep breath, drawing strength from within. I have to stay true to myself, no matter what

Unexpectedly, I feel a presence behind me and jump slightly before turning around to see who it is. A tall figure with dark skin and bright green eyes regards me curiously, a faint smile playing on his lips. He is dressed in the competitor leathers, with a heavy woolen cloak draped over one shoulder.

"I apologize if I startled you," he says politely, bowing his head slightly. "My name is Darius."

I smile back at him in surprise. "No need to apologize, Darius. I just thought I was alone."

Darius nods in understanding, his gaze flickering around the room before landing back on me. "It seems like we both had the same thought—helping out a fellow contestant in need."

His words hang in the air, and I can feel my face flush as he studies me. He seems to sense my discomfort and smiles reassuringly.

"I don't mean to embarrass you, merely to express my admiration for what you did," Darius says kindly. "It's not often that I see selflessness in a situation like this. There were plenty of people here with the knowledge to save him. But they didn't. Most figured it was one less person to have to defeat later. You saw the value of another life."

"Thank you," I mumble, feeling a little more at ease now that the conversation has shifted away from me.

Darius chuckles softly. "You know, you were alone in the middle of the room after everyone else had left. I was worried you may have gone into shock."

He pauses, then adds with a mischievous grin, "Plus, I wanted to meet the person who had the courage to challenge Rose."

"You know Rose?" I ask, curiosity piqued.

Darius nods. "We've crossed paths before. She has a... reputation." His expression darkens briefly before brightening again. "But enough about Rose. Tell me, what's your name?"

I hesitate, unsure how much to reveal. But this man has approached me out of genuine curiosity and gratitude, not malice.

"I'm Scarlet," I say finally.

Darius smiles warmly. "A beautiful name for a brave woman." His tone is genuine, and it makes me blush slightly

"Thank you," I mumble shyly, tucking a strand of my golden hair behind my ear.

Darius laughs delightedly. His gaze is kind and open. "You are truly unique. May I sit with you?"

I laugh. "You've known me all of two seconds and already I'm so special? I think not. We can sit though. I have nowhere else to be. Tell me about yourself since you already seem to know so much about me."

He sits across from me, a smirk on his face. "I see what you did there. Very nice deflection. About me? I've traveled far and wide, from the icy tundra of Nordfjor to the deserts of Aswad."

"What was Nordfjor like?" I ask, curious to learn more.

He grins. "Beautiful and deadly. The landscape seems crafted by giants, with mountains towering over vast glacial valleys."

"It sounds breathtaking."

"It was. But the cold could kill a man in minutes if he wasn't careful. It has it's beauty though. I'll never forget staring up at the God's Lights dancing across the sky, every color imaginable."

I sigh wistfully. "I've never seen the Lights. Were they as spectacular as the stories say?"

"More so!" Darius exclaims. "Pinks and greens and blues swirling together in waves of light, shifting before your very eyes."

"Incredible." I pause. "You mentioned deserts as well?"

Darius' face lights up. "The deserts of Aswad! Sand as far as the eye could see, spreading out beneath a sea of stars. I spent nights camping beneath the dunes, listening to the wind create its own songs as it blew through the canyons."

"It sounds beautiful in its own raw way"

"It is. And the cities! Markets filled with spices from every corner of the world. Women in veils of gold thread, men debating philosophy over tiny cups of strong black coffee."

I chuckle. "You paint a vivid picture."

Darius smiles warmly. "Traveling opens your eyes to the rich variety of human experience. No matter where we're from, we all seek love, comfort, and meaning."

"Wise words." I hesitate before speaking again. "You must have many interesting stories to tell."

Darius nods. "More than I could ever share in a single night! But I'd be happy to tell you more if you're willing to listen."

"I am," I say gently. "I have a feeling sleep will evade me tonight anyways."

He laughs, delight dancing in his eyes. "In that case, my friend, prepare yourself. For I have stories enough to last through the night... and the dawn to come afterwards."

With a smile, I settle in to listen as Darius begins to speak once more, painting pictures with his words of places I have never seen and may never visit—but which now, thanks to him, I can imagine vividly in my mind's eye. His gift of storytelling breathes life and hope into this dark tournament, reminding me of the infinite variety and beauty that exists beyond these castle walls.

As we talk, I realize something—sitting here with Darius, I feel acceptance and kindness. Something I rarely feel from another person. There's always an agenda. A spark of hope that there are still good people in the world, even in places like this forms.

Darius listens attentively as I speak, his easy smile and warm gaze putting me at ease. But he presses me to share more about myself.

"What of your past? Your family?" he asks gently.

I pause, unsure of how much to reveal. "There's not much to tell," I say evasively. "I grew up on a country estate."

Darius seems unconvinced. "Come now, there must be more interesting tales. Your childhood, your dreams."

I struggle to come up with plausible stories that hide my true past.

"I learned to treat wounds and mix remedies from an old friend," I say, letting a bit of wistfulness creep into my voice. Truly it was a skill that everyone in Fairy Godmother's guild had to learn. "As a girl, I dreamed of seeing the world."

Darius nods encouragingly. "A noble ambition. What else?"

I cast about for something more to share that avoids revealing too much.

"I spent hours working in my family's gardens," I say, a genuine smile spreading across my face as I recall pleasant memories. "The scent of the flowers and earth comfort me."

Darius returns my smile warmly. "That sounds lovely."

We fall silent for a moment until Darius speaks again. "You seem hesitant to share much about your life." His voice holds no judgment, merely curiosity.

I sigh and look him in the eyes. "I've had to keep many secrets to survive this long," I say honestly. "Trust does not come easily to me."

Darius nods in understanding. "Some wounds leave deep scars," he says quietly. "But know this—you will always find true refuge in a heart open to mercy and grace. Whatever your past holds, that is all that matters now."

His kind words move me deeply. I take a long breath and feel some of the tightness in my chest loosen.

"Thank you, Darius," I say softly. "Your words give me hope"

The tension finally breaks as Darius laughs delightedly. "And that, my friend, is all I ever wish for!"

Darius rises to his feet, extending a hand to help me up. "I bid you good day, Scarlet," he says with a bow. He raises my hand to his lips and presses a gentle kiss there. "May the gods bless you in these trials.."

"The same for you, Darius. And thank you... for everything."

He inclines his head, a twinkle in his eye. "The pleasure was all mine." With that, he strides from the hall, his cloak billowing behind him

My Spy

Remme

I sift through the contestants' answers to our first challenge in my office. The papers crinkling between the fingers of my golden gloves. Some are clever while most are obvious guesses. Several I set aside as people to watch for possible connections to the thieves guild even though they can't be the woman I am looking for. There's been several more large scale thefts and no clues as to who has done it. Irritating would be an understatement for this. The longer this goes on, the weaker I appear to my court. Already I have to be careful not to reveal too much to them. The last thing I need is an attempt to overthrow me.

Footsteps in the hall slow as someone nears the door. I glance up from my papers and call out, "Come in!" The door opens, and a man steps inside the room, pausing to take in its contents.

Recognizing my visitor, I gesture for him to sit down in the chair across from me. "You encountered one of the contestants?" I ask, my tone stern.

Darius bows slightly before taking his seat. "Yes, my king. A woman going by the name Scarlet."

I narrow my eyes, scrutinizing his expression. "And what did you observe?"

"She hides details of her past but shares skills in healing and gardening," Darius begins, his voice steady. "She helped another contestant who was poisoned. I'm not sure she will last long in the tournament. I found her lost in thought, alone in the dining hall after the event."

I lean back, processing the information. This does not sound like the ruthless thief I seek. Yet, her observational skills and the peculiar circumstances around her actions keep her in my sights. I had seen her skills with daggers and agility myself, after all. I need more details. "What exactly did she do when the contestant was poisoned?" I inquire, my voice cold and precise.

Darius nods, understanding the gravity of my question. "She acted quickly, instructing the servants to bring boiled water and ginger root. Her hands trembled, but she managed to administer the remedy effectively. The poisoned man's condition improved almost immediately."

I mull over Darius's words. A healer, not a killer. Yet, the fact that she possesses such keen observational skills and remains calm under pressure makes her a person of interest. "And what of her demeanor afterward? Did she seem... concerned or calculating?" I probe further.

"Concerned, my king. She appeared genuinely worried for the man's life. But there was also a moment where she seemed to be lost in thought, perhaps contemplating her next move," Darius explains.

I tap my fingers on the desk, deep in thought. "Something doesn't add up. Still, she remains a suspect. Her skills could be a façade. We cannot afford to overlook any possibility."

Darius nods in agreement. "Indeed, my king. I will continue to observe her closely and report any significant findings."

"Good," I say, my voice firm. "Learn what you can, but do not reveal your intentions. We must tread carefully."

Darius bows his head. "It shall be done, my king." He leaves silently, the door closing with a soft click behind him.

As soon as Darius departs, I pull out another submission—Scarlet's, and read through it carefully. The writing is neat and precise. She has deduced that the foreign dignitary is Lady Emilia, the ambassador from Andorra. Scarlet explains her reasoning:

Lady Emilia was wearing jewelry in the Andorran style, though dressed in the competition leathers like the rest of us. Her hair was done up in the intricate braids typical of Andorran women. When she spoke, her accent had the distinctive Andorran lilt.

It is a well-reasoned answer, demonstrating keen observational skills. Yet Scarlet's nature does not match that of a ruthless thief. Of course, a good thief wouldn't give themselves away with thief-like answers, would they? Perhaps I'm overthinking this.

I pull out the other submission that correctly identifies both dignitary and country—Rose. Her answer is also logical but lacks Scarlet's precision. Still, her observation skills make her a suspect.

I sigh and rub my temples. The whole point of doing this set of trials is to set up tests that would help me potentially identify the thief that tried to steal the Bodian Crown. Everything in them has been set up to give the thief an opportunity to give themself away with the skills and behaviors that I saw them have. It seems I have two possible culprits—Scarlet and Rose. Neither fit the profile of a skilled thief, yet neither can be discounted. Both fit the physical description of the woman I seek. Darius's perception of Scarlet could be colored by his desire to deceive her. I will have to watch them both closely and make my own judgments.

For now, I proceed with caution. Give neither woman undue attention that might tip them off. But I keep a close eye on their behavior and progress through the tournament.

The true thief still remains hidden among these other skilled competitors. But I am determined to root them out, one way or another.

With a sigh, I set about compiling the points from this first challenge. The game has finally begun, and so too has my hunt for the woman who kissed me.

The Second Challenge

Scarlet

I rub my fingers over the rankings posted on the board, counting the names above mine. Fifth place. Not good enough.

A trumpet echoes from the dining hall. Ignoring the scores, I push through the crowd of contestants, curious about the noise. The contestants assemble in the dining hall, but I focus on the dais where King Remme stands, surveying the crowd.

Every inch of his being speaks authority and confidence. His face remains still, not giving away any of his inner thoughts. A commanding presence seems to radiate from him; it's something I can only aspire to emulate. It's astounding how he can always remain so sure of himself

King Remme begins speaking, his voice carrying easily over the gathered crowd. "For your next challenge, you will enter the forest and make your way to the caves hidden within. There, you will search for artifacts. These artifacts will match you to your team for the next trial. Forming effective teams is essential for success."

Excited murmurs ripple through the crowd. Those who have formed alliances exchange knowing glances.

King Remme raises a hand, instantly quieting the room. "You will have one hour to prepare before entering the forest. Gather any supplies you feel you may need."

A barely perceptible smile touches his lips, but there's a sharp edge to his words. "The challenges will become increasingly more difficult from here on out. Those who prevail will prove themselves worthy competitors. But be warned—not all who enter the forest will return. Only the most skilled, and perhaps the luckiest, will claim victory."

His eyes scan the crowd, meeting my gaze for a long moment. A chill runs down my spine.

King Remme's voice takes on a more solemn tone. "If there is anyone who wishes to withdraw from the competition, now is the time to do so with no shame or punishment."

The room falls silent, thick with tension. No one moves.

King Remme nods, satisfied. "Very well. You have one hour to prepare. From here on out, everything is at stake." His final words seem directed at me, and I meet his stare unflinchingly.

With that, King Remme descends from the dais and exits the hall, leaving the competitors to contemplate the challenge that lies before them—and the unknown threats that await in the forest

Rose approaches me. "We should team up," she says reluctantly.

I eye her warily. "For now."

Pondering what I should bring with me, I return to my room. I grab the silver needle and throwing dart from my belongings and tuck them carefully into my competition leathers. I won't fail this time. I refuse to walk away empty-handed like before. This challenge will be different. I have to win.

"Planning on poisoning other competitors?" Rose's derisive voice breaks the silence.

I turn to face her. "These are for defending myself," I say firmly.

She chuckles. "From what? The forest animals?"

Anger flares inside me, but I tamp it down. "From whatever threats arise," I say calmly.

Rose shakes her head in disdain. "Suit yourself. Don't come crying to me when your conscience eats at you."

I meet her gaze steadily. "Then it seems we understand each other."

Rose makes a show of examining her nails. "For now." Skepticism laces her tone.

My fists clench at my sides, but I refuse to lose my temper. "We have a challenge to prepare for." I meet her eyes. "Are you ready?"

Rose smirks. "I've been ready since the beginning." Without another word, she sweeps from the room.

I sigh and stare at my reflection. Doubts creep into my mind. Can I do what is necessary to win? Or will my conscience hold me back? I cannot afford failure now. Too much is at stake.

Squaring my shoulders, I leave my room to meet the others for the forest challenge. Whatever threats arise, I will face them head-on. Rose's disapproval means nothing. I have come too far to turn back now.

This challenge will be different. I refuse to walk away empty-handed again. I will find what is hidden in those caves and move up the rankings. Failure is not an option

***

I sift through my bag, ensuring each item is in place. The flask of water, the coil of rope, a small dagger, and a bag of nuts and dried meat nestle securely inside. I grab a sturdy stick, testing its weight and balance. It will serve as my makeshift staff to probe for traps.

Satisfied, I make my way to where Rose and the other competitors have gathered at the forest's edge. The woman who interviewed me stands before us, her presence commanding attention.

"You have all proven yourselves capable survivors," she begins, her voice carrying over the assembled group. "For your next trial, you will enter the catacombs deep below the castle."

Excited murmurs ripple through the crowd at this announcement. As I stand there, the weight of the challenge settles in. The catacombs—ancient tunnels that have swallowed many who dared to enter. My thoughts drift to the tales I've heard about the labyrinthine passages, filled with traps and guarded secrets. I imagine the darkness closing in, the air thick with the scent of decay and history.

Each shadow could hide a threat, each turn a potential trap. The unknown dangers lurking within those stone walls, the possibility of encountering something—or someone—left behind, sends a shiver down my spine. But alongside the fear, excitement bubbles up. This is what I have trained for, the kind of challenge that sets my heart racing. The adrenaline begins to surge, a mixture of fear and thrill. This is my chance to prove myself, to showcase my skills and bravery.

The challenge ahead is not just a test of survival, but of wit and courage. I glance at Rose, who appears equally resolute and excited.

The woman continues, "You will navigate the catacombs to find an artifact. Those artifacts will decide who you are teamed up with on the next challenge. Remember that this challenge has no rules."

A grim smile touches her lips. "The catacombs are dangerous and unforgiving. It's not that simple though. You will have to find the entrances in the forest first. Not all who enter will escape unscathed. The trials have truly begun."

My gaze sweeps the crowd, sizing up the competitors. I see Darius watching me. He offers a small smile and nod of the head which I return. A young noblewoman stands off to the side, nervously twisting her hands. She looks pale and delicate, likely unprepared for the danger ahead.

Two muscular knights glare at the other competitors, cracking their knuckles menacingly. They seem eager for a chance to show their strength and ruthlessness.

An older man wearing a healer's cloak looks around warily. His wisdom and experience could prove invaluable to any team.

As I watch the others, the woman's words echo in my mind. A mage standing beside the woman mutters a few words and sparks appear above us in the air signaling the trial has officially begun.

Rose joins me, and we head out into the forest together, choosing to move away from the rest of the competitors.

The forest quickly envelops us in its embrace. Tall trees stretch their limbs overhead, their dense canopy allowing only slivers of sunlight to pierce through. Shadows dance and shift on the forest floor, creating an ever-changing mosaic of light and dark. The usual chorus of birds and rustling leaves is conspicuously absent, replaced by an eerie silence that hangs heavy in the air, sending a shiver down my spine.

We walk in silence, our footsteps muffled by the thick layer of leaves and moss underfoot. The forest feels un-naturally still, as if holding its breath in anticipation. My eyes scan the undergrowth for any sign of the cave entrance while I use my staff to probe the ground before each step. The vibrant greens of the foliage seem muted, the usual whispers of the forest replaced by an oppressive quiet. The air is cool and damp, carrying the faint scent of earth and decaying leaves.

I listen intently for any disturbance that could signal a trap but hear nothing except for Rose's footsteps and my own. The occasional rustle of leaves or snap of a twig underfoot feels jarring against the otherwise silent backdrop. Every now and then, a gust of wind stirs the branches, creating ghostly whispers that seem to echo our movements. The forest, though not inherently frightening, exudes an unsettling calm, as if it is aware of the trials that lie ahead and is watching silently.

The path ahead winds and twists, each turn revealing more of the forest's secrets. The ground is uneven, with roots snaking across the path like hidden tripwires. The deeper we venture, the more the forest seems to close in around us, the trees standing like silent sentinels guarding ancient secrets. My heart races not just from the exertion but from the palpable tension that the forest exudes. The stillness makes every small sound—every snap of a twig, every rustle of leaves—feel amplified, a constant reminder of the challenges that await.

I stop to get my bearings, closing my eyes and taking a deep breath. The scent of damp earth and decaying leaves fills my nostrils. Underneath, I detect something metallic and acrid that makes my stomach turn. I open my eyes and glance at Rose. She seems oblivious but on edge, surveying our surroundings carefully.

As we continue onward, a distant shout pierces the silence. Without thinking, I quicken my pace, Rose following suit. I can hear the sounds of battle now—metal clashing against metal and cries of pain. Whatever fight is underway, we want no part of it.

We push through thick bushes and low-hanging branches, the undergrowth seeming to fight our progress. Finally, I spot a dark cave opening ahead. Just as we reach it, a blast of frigid air rushes out to meet us. I shiver and exchange a grim look with Rose. Whatever lies ahead, it won't be easy.

I turn to Rose, "We should check in there."

She eyes the dark opening warily. "Something doesn't feel right."

I roll my eyes. "We won't find any artifacts by standing here. I don't imagine that catacombs are the most welcoming of environments anyway"

"Wouldn't you think the entrance would be more grand?"

"I don't imagine the entrance in the forest would be the one they regularly use. Instead, it's probably something that seems completely natural."

"Like a cave. You're right," Rose groans.

I step into the cave, the faint light from the forest quickly fading away behind me. Total darkness descends as I fumble for my torch, the staff tapping out warnings with each step. I hear Rose sigh in frustration beside me but say nothing, focusing my attention on putting one foot in front of the other without falling. Our senses on high alert, we make our way ever deeper into the freezing darkness, listening for any sign that we are not alone.

Rose reluctantly follows behind. As soon as we are both inside, thick fog begins rolling in, quickly filling the cave. Visibility drops to mere feet in front of us.

"Ugh. Should have known it wouldn't be that easy," Rose grumbles.

"Not a fan of the dark and unseen?" I tease.

"You and I both know this isn't the type of locale that my jobs take me."

I'm tempted to tease her more, but after tripping over a rock in the fog I admit to myself that she may have it right. This really is a more difficult location than even my jobs usually take me.

We slowly make our way deeper into the cave system, stumbling over loose rocks and jagged stalagmites obscured by the fog. We move cautiously through the cave, our vision limited to the small circle of light cast by my torch. My staff sweeps back and forth, testing the ground before each step.

Rounding a corner, I fail to notice a thin tripwire strung at ankle height. The moment my foot hits it, I hear a faint click followed by a swift release of tension. An array of darts shoots through the air directly at Rose.

"Look out!" I shout, lunging towards Rose and tackling her to the ground. The darts whistle past, slicing through the air with deadly precision. The sound is sharp, almost like the hiss of an angry snake, before they lodge into the cave wall behind us with a series of loud thunks.

Rose gasps, staring wide-eyed at the cluster of darts now protruding from the stone just inches above where our heads had been. The realization of how close we came to being skewered sinks in. The cave, which moments ago felt oppressive and silent, now echoes with the aftermath of the trap we've narrowly escaped.

"Thanks, Scarlet," Rose whispers, her voice tinged with a mix of relief and lingering fear.

My breathing is ragged as the adrenaline starts to wear off, leaving a cold sweat on my skin. "That was too close," I mutter, forcing myself to look at the darts embedded in the wall. Each one is razor-sharp, their tips glistening with what could only be poison.

Rose, ever the pragmatist, lets out a shaky laugh. "You know, Scarlet, dodging darts is usually something we do when we're making our grand escape, not just walking around."

I chuckle in response. "Yeah, it's almost like the traps have decided to come to us for a change. Makes you nostalgic for the good old days, doesn't it?"

Rose grins, her fear momentarily forgotten. "Did you retire? My last encounter was only last week. Nothing like a bit of adrenaline to start the day. Although, I do prefer to see the darts coming rather than have them surprise me."

I nod in agreement, still eyeing the darts warily. "At least when we're escaping, we expect this kind of thing. Keeps you on your toes."

Rose smirks. "We probably shouldn't let our guard down even for a second. There's a reason most who go in without a guide don't come out."

I sigh, the tension easing just a bit. "True enough. Let's try to avoid setting off any more traps, shall we? I'd prefer not to add 'human pincushion' to my resume."

Rose laughs, a genuine sound that cuts through the oppressive atmosphere. "Deal. But if we do, at least we know you're getting pretty good at the whole saving-my-life thing."

"Just another skill to add to my repertoire. If the triple G doesn't work out I may apply for guard or kingdom hero." I reply with a grin. "Now, let's find that artifact and get out of here before the cave decides to throw any more surprises our way."

Rose nods solemnly. "Good thing you have quick re-flexes." The grudging gratitude in her voice takes me by surprise.

"I saw it just in time." Standing up, I hold out a hand to help Rose to her feet. For once, she accepts it without hesitation.

We examine the rope tripwire closely. It is nearly invisible in the darkness and attached to a mechanism that releases the darts at just the right height to hit a person in the chest. Had I been alone, I likely would not have noticed it in time.

As we walk on, I can't help replaying those frantic few seconds in my mind—shouting out the warning, lunging at Rose to yank her down, hearing the darts whistle past our heads. It had all happened so fast.

Rose glances at me, an uncharacteristically grateful smile tugging at her lips. "Maybe we make a decent team after all," she says reluctantly.

I hold her gaze for a moment before facing forward once more. "For now," I agree, then pry one of the darts free.

We continue deeper into the cave system, driven only by the light of my torch. Each corridor twists and turns, presenting new dangers at every corner—traps, mysterious artifacts, and shadowy creatures that call these caves their home.

Rounding another corner, we are faced with an enormous stone door set into the cave wall. The door is etched with strange swirling symbols and what appears to be a convoluted maze.

I study the puzzle intently. I point to four worn symbols. "These must open the door in a certain sequence"

Rose traces one of the mazes. "Each maze starts at a different symbol."

I crouch down to examine the door closer. "Let's press the symbols in order of the maze paths, from shortest to longest."

Rose agrees, and we begin pressing the symbols. Nothing happens. Disappointed, we step back to examine the puzzle again.

After several minutes, I snap my fingers triumphantly. "The maze paths that lead to the center are in order from longest to shortest, not the other way around!"

Rose shrugs. "Worth a try."

We press the symbols in the revised order: top left, bottom right, top right, and bottom left. This time, with a grinding of stone, the enormous door slides slowly open, revealing the chamber beyond.

"Well done!" Rose says appreciatively.

I can't help but smile back at her, our brief celebration putting aside competition.

Rose claps me on the shoulder. "Don't celebrate too much," she warns. "There will be more difficult puzzles ahead."

I sober at her words, knowing they are true. We have overcome this obstacle through teamwork and observation, but further challenges await.

We step cautiously into the chamber beyond the puzzle door. Torches flicker to life as we enter, illuminating a vast underground space hewn from rock. The air is cold and still, hinting at the age of this place.

Carved into the cave walls are burial niches filled with ancient remains. Bones, urns, and deteriorating cloth litter the floor amongst stone tools and weapons. We have stumbled upon a tomb.

Rose kneels to examine something on the floor. "Look at this," she says, beckoning me over. A mosaic depicts a many-headed serpent entwined around a horned staff. "The symbol of Cheribus," Rose notes. "God of the Underworld."

A sense of foreboding creeps over me as I take in our surroundings anew.

As we step further into the chamber, spikes shoot up from the floor while blades swing down from the ceiling, barely missing us.

Rose eyes the obstacle course of traps warily. "We'll have to move carefully."

I nod. "Agreed. You head right, I'll go left. Watch your step."

We quickly dash between two swinging axes, hearts racing. Rose eyes the obstacle course of traps warily. "Let's make this interesting," she says, a challenging glint in her eyes. "First one to the artifact wins."

I meet her gaze evenly. "You're on." This is our chance to truly test each other's skills. Something we haven't done in years. Once we were friends, in our training days. That was long ago though. Our respective missions keep us busy, and rarely do we have this sort of opportunity to see who is best.

We move through the gauntlet of traps. A flaming arrow launcher springs to life, firing a volley that we jump and roll beneath. "One point for me," I sing, grinning at Rose's scowl.

Sheathing my dagger, I swing on a rope across a chasm to the next section while Rose navigates a series of spinning blades. We both make it through unscathed. "Tied score," Rose says through gritted teeth.

A pressure plate activates below my foot, dropping a net from the ceiling that narrowly misses Rose. I cut myself free quickly. "Two points," I crow.

Rose smirks. "Not for long." She defuses a trap that would have set off a spiked boulder, saving us both. "There, we're even."

We continue through the chamber, adrenaline coursing through our veins as we test each other's speed, agility, and tactical thinking.

Finally, we reach the altar and golden scarab artifact. But as I reach for it, the floor starts sinking into a spike-lined chute.

Rose and I grab on, momentarily united in our will to survive. "Don't worry," I say confidently. "For members of the GGG, this is basically child's play."

Rose laughs. "Literally."

Together, we hold on, wondering if we'll make it out alive. This trap isn't meant for the clever or brave—only the lucky survive. And luck, it seems, is all we have.

As the stone floor sinks further into the spike-lined chute, Rose and I hold on for dear life.

Rose spots two heavy stones nearby and grabs one. "Help me swing these into the gears over there!" she shouts.

I grab the other stone, and we take turns swinging them at the gears powering the trapdoor. After several hits, the gears jam, and the floor stops sinking.

Rose laughs in relief. "We did it!"

We shout in celebration as I grab the golden scarab artifact.

Rose frowns. "That one's mine."

I shake my head. "I got it first."

Rose crosses her arms. "I was the one to figure out how to save our butts or neither of us would have made it out of her. I deserve it."

Annoyance flares, but I tamp it down. Fighting now would be foolish.

I sigh. "Fine. We work together to find me one as well though."

Rose smiles slightly. "Deal." She takes the scarab. "Come on. There will be more artifacts deeper in."

I nod. "Let's keep moving"

Staff of Halisar

Scarlet

Rose and I inch deeper into the cave system, every step taken with deliberate caution. The flickering torchlight casts eerie shadows on the towering stone pillars around us, each one intricately carved into the likeness of coiled serpents. The walls are rugged, their uneven slabs illuminated in the dim light. In the distance, shadows dance and twist, creating an unsettling, almost hypnotic effect. The air is thick with the stench of rot and stagnation, the musty odors of an ancient tomb pervading every breath.

As we navigate through the pillars, the stone floor beneath us groans ominously. Suddenly, without warning, the pillars begin to spin rapidly, crashing into each other with a deafening roar. The once-still serpents now become a deadly gauntlet, their immense stone spikes whirling and smashing together, threatening to crush us between them.

"Run for the door!" I shout, pointing to our only chance of escape.

We leap away from the giant crushers, the cold rush of air from each rotation whipping our clothes into flapping ripples. Dodging and darting between the spinning pillars, we race against time. The noise is deafening, stone grinding against stone, each near miss a reminder of how close we are to being pulverized.

Miraculously, we make it to the far wall, collapsing against its solid safety just moments before the crushers would have reached us. Rose meets my gaze, her eyes wide with adrenaline. "Another close call," she says, her tone grim, though a spark of excitement dances in her eyes.

After catching our breath, we proceed with even more caution. We edge along the side of a stone pool, its glowing green water roiling ominously below. Thick columns of vapor rise from the surface, the smell of sulfur and decay assaulting our senses.

"Lovely place," Rose mutters, her voice tinged with sarcasm as she eyes the bubbling pool warily.

I smirk, trying to lighten the mood. "Could use a little redecorating, don't you think? Maybe some fresh flowers?"

Rose chuckles softly, her grip on her torch tightening. "Yeah, and a bucket of scented oil."

We continue along the edge, each step calculated, each breath shallow. Rose's eyes dart around, her wariness infectious. "Something's not right here," she whispers.

I nod, every sense on high alert. Rose is right. Something is off. The silence is almost deafening, broken only by the occasional drip of water echoing through the cavern.

Without warning, thick tentacles burst from the depths, wrapping around Rose's legs. Her scream pierces the silence, raw and primal. The tentacles are slick and strong, pulling her towards the pool with a force that makes my heart skip a beat.

"Rose!" I shout, lunging forward. My hand clamps around her arm while my other hand draws my dagger in one swift motion. The tentacles writhe and tighten, desperate to drag her into the murky abyss.

I slash at the tentacles. The blade slices through the first one, then the next, spraying foul-smelling liquid all over us. The remaining tentacles recoil, releasing Rose from their grip. She stumbles back, gasping, as the severed limbs thrash wildly before sinking back into the pool.

Just when we think we're safe, more tentacles surge out, faster and more aggressive. One wraps around my ankle, yanking me off balance. I hit the ground hard, the torch slipping from my grasp and rolling away, casting wild shadows on the cave walls.

"Not today!" I growl, twisting to slash at the tentacle constricting my leg. The blade bites into the slick flesh, and the tentacle recoils with a hiss, spraying more of that foul liquid.

Rose, having regained her footing, swings her torch at the writhing mass, the flames licking at the tentacles and forcing them back. "Scarlet, behind you!" she yells.

I spin just in time to see another tentacle lunging for me. I roll to the side, narrowly avoiding its grasp, and come up swinging. The dagger cleaves through the air, severing the appendage mid-strike. The tentacle flails wildly before dropping to the ground, twitching.

We scramble to our feet, panting but determined, as more tentacles lash out. Working in unison, Rose and I fend off the onslaught, our movements synchronized from years of training together. The cave is a frenzy of slick limbs, flashing steel, and flickering torchlight.

Finally, with one last desperate push, we drive the remaining tentacles back into the pool. The water roils violently before settling into an eerie calm once more. We stand there, breathing heavily, the adrenaline still coursing through our veins.

"That was too close," Rose mutters, her voice shaky. She wipes the foul liquid off her clothes, her eyes wide with lingering fear.

I nod, still gripping my dagger tightly. "Yeah, I don't think that was the welcoming committee."

She laughs, a sound that cuts through the tension. "Let's get out of here before something else decides to say hello."

"Come on," I say, holding out a hand. "We've got to find another artifact and get out of here before this place kills us."

Time moves oddly when there's no sky to help track it. Eventually we stumble through a passageway that opens into a vast chamber filled with tombs lining the walls as far as we can see. The room is large; even from where I stand, I can see the walls disappearing into darkness. The silence is overwhelming. Not even our footfalls make noise as they scrape across the floor. We move in the pit of a tomb, lost to time and surrounded by the nobles and heroes of the past.

Rose and I walk slowly through the room, on high alert for any traps or dangers. After several minutes with no sign of artifacts, I sigh in frustration. "What are we looking for?"

She shakes her head. "No clue. Something will reveal itself, I'm sure. Mine was fairly obvious in its room."

We fall into silence once more, scanning the chamber for any hint of what secret lies within.

Suddenly, a hooded figure comes crashing toward us, desperate footsteps echoing off the stone walls. Behind them, a horde of animated skeletons gives chase, claws scraping against the floor.

Rose moves to hide behind a sarcophagus while I grab a staff from a tomb, having long lost mine while trying to save myself from the many other things wanting to kill us in here. I lunge forward to strike at the skeletons as the hooded figure races past us. Smashing their hollow skulls and shattered ribcages fills me with an energy I didn't expect as I send bones clattering to the floor

Always unable to stay out of a good fight, Rose comes out of hiding to join the fray, flinging daggers with deadly accuracy into skeleton eye sockets and between vertebrae. Finally, the last skeleton falls and the hooded figure turns to face us, hood falling back to reveal Darius' face. He breathes a sigh of relief. "Thank you, my friends."

Rose speaks first. "What were those things?"

Darius shrugs helplessly. "Guardians, I suppose. Dead but not dead." He eyes the staff in my hand. "Where did you find that?"

I glance down at the intricately carved staff. "I didn't. It was here." As I speak, runes appear along the staff, glowing with a warm light.

Darius gasps. "That staff belonged to the high priest of Halisar!"

I glance down at the staff glowing in my hand, recognizing the symbol of the God of Thieves carved in the wood. Of course now is when the God of Thieves would decide to claim me. Right when I need to keep those skills a secret.

"Seems sort of ridiculous that a high priest of the God of Thieves would have a staff. Why not a dagger or bow? What thief carries around a staff? It would just get in the way." Rose scoffs.

Darius speaks urgently. "The artifacts choose their owners. The staff has deemed you worthy."

Reluctantly, I tighten my grip on the staff. The wood feels warm, accepting my touch. How am I going to explain this?

Rose's eyes flicker towards me, a silent warning conveyed in her gaze. I know exactly what she is thinking because I am thinking the same thing myself.

"Have you found your artifact?" I ask.

Darius pulls a lute from his back. "It called to me, as a bard's instrument would."

Rose and I exchange a glance, curiosity and suspicion mingling.

Darius seems not to notice. "It's time we find the exit," he says confidently, taking the lead.

Rose falls into step beside me. "Can we trust him?" she whispers.

I watch Darius wander ahead, strumming his lute. "For now," I reply quietly. "But we both know better than to trust anyone."

Rose nods. "Very true."

Our partnership remains fragile, built on mutual gain and necessity rather than full truth or trust. But for now, it will have to suffice.

Two Suspects

Remme

I observe as Scarlet, Rose, and Darius enter the throne room. The entire space turned gold from one of my early mishaps. It feels too opulent. I hear the rumors of me showing off and wasting the kingdoms wealth. If only they knew what really caused the entire space to become gold.

Scarlet and Rose appear worn and weary from their trials. Though successful, they bear signs of their challenges—torn clothes, scrapes, and bruises marring their skin. Yet beneath the dirt and exhaustion, something glimmers in their eyes—a spark of triumph kindled by survival. Scarlet clutches an ancient wooden staff carved with runes.

Rose grasps a glittering golden scarab in one hand while blood drips from her knuckles. Straw-colored strands escape her tidy bun, falling around haunted yet triumphant emerald eyes. Darius holds an intricately carved lute against his chest. Though outwardly composed, an uneasy energy radiates from him as he casts furtive glances between Scarlet, Rose, and myself.

. As she recounts their trials, I find myself drawn to her earnest yet reserved nature. Her honor contrasts with my initial suspicion. Yet something hints at secrets. I steeple my fingers. "You claim compassion yet wield a thief's tools."

Scarlet meets my gaze calmly. "I use the skills I have to survive."

"Your dagger skills during the application impressed me." Scarlet's eyes widen, betraying her surprise. Then she smiles wryly. "You saw?"

Scarlet's honesty and admission refresh me. "Why did you compete? It seems at odds with your gentle nature."

She laughs. "I wouldn't consider myself gentle. I seek to change my circumstances. Escape a life I did not choose."

Scarlet's words mirror my own imprisonment. Two souls yearning for freedom. I speak softly. "You wish not just for victory, but purpose. For a place in the world where you can live the life you want. To be seen for who you are and not what you are."

Scarlet's eyes widen at my insight. "Perhaps," she says quietly.

I smile. "Your wisdom does you credit." I hold out my hand. "Thank you for speaking with me, Scarlet."

Scarlet nods respectfully. "Thank you for listening, Your Majesty."

Rose steps forward after Scarlet leaves, her matter-of-fact tone hiding any emotions. "Tell me of the trials you faced down there," I demand.

Rose recounts their challenges succinctly but precisely. I sense worlds of meaning between her words. Her keen wit and composure fascinate me even as I search for dishonesty. Yet my every question is met with a clever rebuttal that leaves me wondering. She holds something back, her glimmering emerald eyes hinting at secrets yet unspoken. I cannot determine if her silences stem from cunning or caution.

I search Rose's gaze. "Why do you compete, if not for mere victory?"

Rose pauses, considering. "Survival demands many skills. I apply them where needed." Her words mirror my own desire for freedom yet fall short of revealing deeper truths.

She stands, seemingly unmoved by our talk yet meeting my gaze. As she departs, my curiosity only grows. Beneath this woman's poised exterior glimmers ambition that intrigues me as much as it gives me pause.

After I dismiss Scarlet and Rose, my mind is in turmoil. I am no closer to knowing which one is the thief who tried to steal the Bodian crown twice. Both are very possible suspects. Though their artifacts point to dark potential, their actions hint at honor within.

The room now empty of those who are not my own I motion for Darius to step forward. "What have you learned?"

He shakes his head. "I don't have anything to share that you didn't just get out of them, Your Majesty."

Frustration rises within me. "One of them must be the thief who tried to steal from me. I need to know which."

Darius speaks gently. "When we label others, we risk missing their full truth. Give the women a chance. I'm sure they will reveal themselves in due time."

I sigh heavily. "You're right."

Darius nods. "Sometimes the truth lies in compassion, not suspicion."

STARGAZING

SCARLET

I've been tossing and turning in my bed for what feels like forever, unable to fall asleep. My mind replays my conversation with King Remme over and over again. How his eyes search mine so deeply, seemingly able to discern my secrets with a single glance. His insights into my motives leave me wondering how much he truly suspects.

Part of me is terrified that he knows who I am. That Halisar's staff has given me away as the thief who failed twice. But another part of me is curious. For once, it feels as if someone is seeing me for me, not for what they can get out of me.

I rise from my bed, slip on my cloak, and make my way to the royal gardens. As always, the cool night air and fragrant flowers ease my restless spirit. When I round a bend in the path, I catch sight of King Remme sitting alone on a stone bench. His familiar gold armor dim in the dark. He appears lost in thought, gazing up at the night sky.

I hesitate, unsure whether to make myself known. Before I can decide, King Remme turns his head and our eyes meet. He smiles slightly and gestures for me to join him. After a moment's pause, I accept his invitation and sit down beside him.

We sit in comfortable silence for some time, gazing up at the stars together. Though we do not speak, I swear I sense a connection forming between us—a meeting of kindred spirits who both seek something more. King Remme finally breaks the silence. "It soothes the soul to see the heavens, does it not?"

I nod. "Like a forgotten memory, reminding us of who we truly are."

King Remme turns to face me, our eyes meeting once again. I see warmth and something I can't quite put my finger on in his eyes.

He smiles. "Indeed."

We fall into a comfortable silence once more, gazing up at the stars. After a time, King Remme speaks again. "Tell me, Scarlet, what inspires your spirit?"

I consider my answer carefully. "The feeling of earth between my fingers as I tend my garden. The scent of roses after a spring rain."

King Remme nods. "Simple pleasures, yet profound."

"And you, Your Majesty? What brings you joy?"

He smiles softly. "The first blossoms of spring, signaling new life after a long winter. A well-crafted turn of phrase in a poem. A delicious piece of bread, fresh out of the oven."

I return his smile. "Wisdom and wonder, it seems, reside within us both."

King Remme chuckles. "It would appear so." He eyes me thoughtfully. "We are not so different, you and I."

"Perhaps not," I agree. "Two souls seeking connection among the lonely towers of rule and secrecy."

King Remme is silent for a moment, considering my words. Then he speaks, a note of wistful longing in his voice. "To be truly seen and known, without pretense."

I meet his gaze evenly. "A rare gift, that."

King Remme's eyes search mine before dropping to his cursed hands. "An impossible one, for me."

I hesitate, tempted to place my hand over his in comfort. But I quickly remind myself that King Remme is still a stranger and, well, a king—and I, little more than a contestant in his tournament.

Instead, I speak gently. "Only if you believe it to be."

Time passes as we sit in silence together. I am not sure if it is appropriate to leave or even if I want to. What do I do in a situation like this? If I'm not careful, I will be discovered.

The king points out a constellation of stars above us. "My mother would tell me that one was the Crown of the Wise King," he says wistfully. "She said if I studied the stars and learned their lessons, I would one day wear a crown worthy of their legend."

I follow his gaze to the constellation overhead. "Your mother must have loved you very much," I say softly.

King Remme sighs, a trace of sadness in his eyes. "She did," he says simply. He smiles faintly. "Yet her stories remain with me all these years later."

His raw vulnerability touches something within me. This guarded king has shared a secret piece of his soul, if only in a story.

I meet his gaze, somehow understanding this man needs nothing except the simple act of being heard. "Some memories never fade, no matter how long ago they were made," I say gently.

King Remme returns my smile, his eyes revealing new depths of feeling—gratitude, wonder. "And for that listening heart," he says softly, "I am grateful beyond measure."

I take a steadying breath. "My father loved the stars too," I begin quietly. "We often would lie in the garden and name the constellations together."

Warmth fills King Remme's eyes as he listens. Emboldened, I continue. "My mother died when I was young. My father followed several years later, taken by illness." My voice catches as old grief wells up within me.

King Remme's eyes widen slightly at my revelation, as if truly seeing me for the first time. I look away, ashamed at my tears.

"My kingdom is full of people," King Remme says softly. "Yet I find myself surrounded by strangers. Solitude is a heavy mantle to bear."

His honest words touch something deep within me. In him, I see reflected an echo of my own loneliness—two souls longing for connection in a world that does not truly see them.

I meet King Remme's gaze, tears still wet on my cheeks. "To have one who truly listens is a gift rarely given," I say, my voice thick with emotion. "And for that listening heart, I too am grateful beyond measure."

King Remme smiles, a beautiful and rare sight. "Some gifts are meant to be shared."

Our eyes meet again and this time, something unspoken passes between us—an acknowledgment of souls recognized. Though we do not touch, two kindred spirits have found each other at last.

***

The castle halls are still quiet as I make my way to breakfast, my footsteps echoing off the stone walls. Most of the court has not yet risen, taking full advantage of the lazy morning. My rumbling stomach urges me onward, thoughts of warm bread and sweet jam propelling my steps. The scent of freshly baked goods wafts through the air, and my mouth waters in anticipation.

As I turn a corner, Darius comes bounding up beside me. His presence is a welcome distraction from my thoughts. "Late start today?" he asks with a grin, his eyes twinkling with mischief.

I yawn, feeling the weight of the previous night's events. "A bit," I reply. My late night with King Remme has caught up to me, and the exhaustion is evident in my voice.

Darius nudges me playfully, his shoulder brushing against mine. "Plotting my demise?"

I chuckle, the sound mingling with the echoes in the hallway. "Saving that for the next trial."

We walk together, our laughter bouncing off the stone walls, creating a melody of camaraderie that temporarily eases the tension in my chest. Just as I start to relax, a figure up ahead catches my eye. King Remme strides into the hall, his presence commanding the space around him. He speaks in hushed tones with an advisor, their voices a soft murmur that blends into the background. My heart skips a beat, my breath catching in my throat as his eyes find mine from across the room. For a moment, the world seems to narrow to just the two of us.

Remme's lips curve into a small, almost imperceptible smile, and a rush of warmth spreads through me, rising to my cheeks. Butterflies flutter wildly in my stomach, their wings a chaotic dance of excitement and nervousness. I manage a hesitant smile in return, my mind racing with memories of our last encounter. The intensity of his gaze, the unexpected tenderness of his touch—these thoughts swirl in my head, making it hard to think clearly.

"Scarlet?" Darius's voice pulls me back to the present, grounding me. "You okay?"

I nod, though my eyes remain locked on the king. "Yes, just... lost in thought."

The advisor's animated gestures draw my attention. He waves his hands emphatically, stepping closer to Remme with each insistent word. But Remme, with a deliberate grace, shifts away, maintaining a clear distance between them. His face remains a composed mask, betraying nothing of his inner thoughts or emotions. This controlled avoidance strikes me as odd, and my curiosity sharpens.

Why is he so intent on keeping his distance? Remme's movements are always precise, intentional. This reaction feels almost... instinctual, something ingrained from past experiences.

I glance at Darius, who has also noticed the interaction. "Interesting," he muses, his brow furrowed in thought.

"Very," I murmur, my mind racing with possibilities. What could have prompted such behavior? Our kiss flashes through my mind, the memory vivid and electric. He's not always so standoffish. In fact, there have been moments when he's shown a surprising vulnerability, a glimpse of the man behind the crown.

As I watch, Remme's gaze shifts, his eyes locking with mine once more. There's something in his expression, a flicker of... concern? Suspicion? The butterflies in my stomach twist into knots, a mix of excitement and unease. What is he hiding? Why does it feel like he's looking right through me, seeing more than I want him to?

I notice a figure standing a few steps behind Remme—a female guard. Recognition dawns on me like a bolt of lightning. It's the same guard who conducted my first interview when I was trying to get into the trials. Her stern yet fair demeanor had left an impression on me.

She stands at attention, her eyes scanning the room with a sharpness that suggests she misses nothing. As the advisor steps closer to Remme with each emphatic gesture, she subtly positions herself between them, her movements almost imperceptible to anyone not looking closely. This subtle act of interposition stands out to me as odd. Why would she feel the need to create a barrier? Her presence here, so close to the king, intrigues me. What role does she play in all of this? Is she simply a guard, or does she hold more significance?

The advisor's frustration is palpable as he steps back, clearly unsettled by the guard's silent assertion of space. Remme remains unyielding, his posture a study in controlled distance. My heart pounds in my chest, each beat a reminder of the growing connection between us and the many questions that remain unanswered.

"Scarlet, we should keep moving," Darius says gently, his hand on my arm. "Breakfast won't wait forever."

I tear my gaze away from the king, nodding. "You're right," I say, though my mind remains fixed on Remme and his enigmatic behavior. As we continue down the hallway, I can't shake the feeling that the king's actions are more than just a matter of personal space. They speak of a deeper story.

Lost in my thoughts, I crash into a courtier coming from the opposite direction. We both topple to the ground in a flurry of limbs and papers. I scramble to help gather his scattered documents, mortified by my clumsiness.

"For goodness' sake!" the man grumbles, his voice laced with irritation. I look up to see that the courtier is none other than Lord Greystone, my forced fiancé. His face is a mask of annoyance, his sharp features twisted in a scowl.

"Watch where you're going!" he snaps, not yet realizing who I am. His tone is harsh, cutting through the air like a knife. My heart pounds, a mix of fear and anger bubbling up inside me.

"I-I'm sorry," I stammer, scrambling to gather the scattered papers. My hands tremble as I try to collect myself.

As he bends down to help, his eyes finally meet mine. Recognition dawns, and his scowl shifts into a smirk. "Ah, Scarlet. My dear fiancée. We must work on paying attention to every detail to avoid such accidents. It won't be acceptable when you're my wife," he says, his voice dripping with condescension. His proximity makes my skin crawl, a sickening mix of charm and dominance radiating from him.

Lord Greystone is tall and imposing, with a chiseled jawline and piercing blue eyes that seem to look right through me. His dark hair is slicked back meticulously, not a strand out of place, a testament to his vanity. He always dresses in the finest clothes, the fabric rich and adorned with subtle yet expensive details. It's as if he's trying to buy his way into respectability, but all I see is a man trying too hard to mask his insecurities. He exudes an air of over-confidence that borders on arrogance, believing everyone is enamored with him, and under his control. The faint scent of expensive cologne clings to him, almost as if he's trying to mask something unsavory beneath.

Darius steps forward, his expression serious as he intervenes. "My apologies, Lord Greystone. Scarlet has a lot on her mind this morning," he says, his voice steady and calm, offering me a lifeline in this uncomfortable situation.

I shoot Darius a small smile of thanks. "It's nothing," I assure Lord Greystone, forcing a smile. "I'm just tired from last night. And anxious about what the next trial holds."

Lord Greystone straightens, his eyes narrowing as he studies me. "The trials come with a lot of pressure," he says sympathetically, but the sympathy feels false. He gestures for us to follow and starts down the hallway. "But that pressure can be used to your advantage too! It'll drive you to do better and push yourself further than you ever thought possible." He claps me on the back in encouragement, but the gesture feels possessive, not supportive.

As we continue down the hallway, I glance and notice King Remme watching us intently. His face is a mask of neutrality, but I can see the tension in his posture. He has stopped walking and paused his conversation, seemingly ignoring the man speaking to him. What is he thinking? Why is he so focused on us? His eyes are unreadable, making it impossible for me to decipher his thoughts.

Lord Greystone continues to drone on about the importance of composure and attention to detail, his voice oozing with self-importance. "As my future wife, you must always be vigilant. You will be held to a higher standard," he says, his tone both commanding and patronizing.

My blood boils, and I force myself to remain calm. "I won't be marrying you," I snap, my voice shaking with barely contained anger. The words hang in the air between us, a challenge that I know he won't let go unanswered.

Lord Greystone stops, his smirk widening into a grin. "Oh, Scarlet," he says, amusement dancing in his eyes. "I do enjoy a good challenge."

I force a smile, my heart pounding in my chest. "I'll keep that in mind," I say, my voice strained.

Sensing the need for an escape, Darius quickly adds, "We should be heading to the dining hall. Competitors only, you know. Important to start the day right."

Lord Greystone's smirk widens as he leans in close, his breath hot against my ear. "You can try to avoid me all you want, Scarlet, but you can't escape this. Your stepmother and I have an understanding. I've always watched you, wanted you, and I always get what I want," he whispers, his voice dripping with possessive confidence.

A shiver runs down my spine, and I fight the urge to recoil. "Let's go, Darius," I say, my voice trembling slightly as I pull away from Lord Greystone's oppressive presence.

As we walk away, I feel Lord Greystone's gaze burning into my back. I glance back at King Remme again, who is still watching. Our eyes meet once more, and I feel a sense of reassurance. Despite the turmoil surrounding me, there is a glimmer of hope. The king's expression remains inscrutable, but his attention feels like a lifeline in the midst of the storm.

Darius guides me down the hallway, his hand a comforting presence on my arm. "Are you alright?" he asks softly, his concern evident.

I nod, though my mind is spinning. "I'll be fine. Thank you, Darius."

He gives me a reassuring smile. "Remember, you're not alone in this. We'll find a way through."

As we enter the dining hall, the tension begins to ease, but the weight of Lord Greystone's words lingers.

THE TRAP

SCARLET

The cobblestone streets echo softly beneath my boots as I walk home, each step a rhythmic lullaby that attempts to soothe the chaos in my mind. Life bustles around me in the marketplace, vendors calling out their wares, children laughing and playing, but I barely notice. Lingering heavily on my thoughts is the encounter with Lord Greystone, his menacing smirk etched into my memory. I replay the scene over and over, the way his eyes bore into mine, the subtle threat in his voice. My hands still tremble slightly, a physical manifestation of the unease that coils within me. I know I need to speak with Fairy Godmother; her wisdom and comfort are the balm I so desperately need right now.

As I near the edge of the marketplace, the familiar sights and sounds of home begin to seep into my consciousness. The manor comes into view, its serene facade a stark contrast to the turmoil I know lies within. My heart tightens at the sight, a mixture of dread and determination settling in my chest. This place, this property, is my inheritance, the legacy my father left for me. I love every stone, every flower in the garden he tended to so lovingly. Stepping onto the property, the muffled chaos of my family reaches my ears. Voices raised in argument, the clatter of something heavy falling to the floor—typical sounds of discord that seem to define my home life.

I pause for a moment, listening to the uproar. My stepmother's sharp voice cuts through the air, followed by my stepsisters' high-pitched complaints. A pang of frustration and helplessness stabs at me, tears threatening to well up in my eyes as I think about the injustice of it all. They treat this place like their personal kingdom, and me, just a pawn in their cruel game. Yet, I cannot abandon it; this manor is my sanctuary, my father's dream, and I must protect it until I can rightfully claim it as my own.

I make a conscious decision to avoid them, slipping through the side entrance that leads to the kitchen, my sanctuary. As I enter, the warmth and scents of freshly baked bread and brewing tea wrap around me like a comforting embrace. I close my eyes for a moment, allowing myself to breathe deeply and let the tension ease from my shoulders. This is the one place where I can find some semblance of peace, away from the judgmental glares and harsh words.

Fairy Godmother's presence fills the room, her soft humming a soothing melody that calms my frayed nerves. She is more of a mother to me than my own stepmother, her kindness and wisdom a guiding light in the darkness that often surrounds me. I know she will listen, understand, and offer the guidance I so desperately need.

The kitchen is warm and inviting. Fairy Godmother stands at the counter, her back to me, a soft hum escaping her lips as she works. My heart swells with a mix of relief and gratitude. I pause in the doorway, taking in the sight of her deft hands expertly preparing a meal. With a flick of her wrist, a knife begins chopping vegetables on its own, a small but impressive display of her magic.

"Fairy Godmother," I call softly, stepping fully into the room. She turns, her eyes lighting up with a mixture of surprise and delight at the sight of me.

"Scarlet, my dear," she says, wiping her hands on her apron before pulling me into a warm embrace. "I didn't expect you so soon."

"I needed to see you," I confess, my voice barely above a whisper. "There's so much to talk about."

She nods, understanding without needing further explanation. "Come, sit," she says, guiding me to a chair at the worn wooden table. I take a seat, feeling the weight of my worries beginning to lift. "The house is in good condition, I assure you. Your stepmother is none the wiser about my little enhancements."

I glance around, noticing the absence of the usual clutter and disarray. The floors are spotless, and the air feels lighter. "You've done wonders," I say, a note of awe in my voice.

She chuckles, her eyes twinkling with mischief. "A little magic goes a long way, my dear. Now, tell me about the trials. How have they gone so far?"

I hesitate, a knot of worry tightening in my chest. "Fairy Godmother, are they treating you well? My stepmother and stepsisters—they can be so cruel. I can't bear the thought of them mistreating you."

Her expression softens, and she places a reassuring hand on mine. "Don't worry about me, Scarlet. I can handle them in my own time and way." Her words are calm, but there's a steely resolve behind them.

I want to press further, to ask what she's done, but I can see she won't elaborate.

"Fairy Godmother," I begin, my voice trembling, "I don't know if I can do this. The trials... they've been so much harder than I expected. And then there's Rose..."

Fairy Godmother's brow furrows with concern, already knowing about Rose's presence. "What about Rose, dear?"

I sigh deeply, the weight of my emotions pressing heavily on my chest. "She's also competing for the crown. I thought it would just be me, but now... I feel like I can't compete with her. She's always been the perfect one, the one everyone admires. How can I possibly measure up?"

Fairy Godmother moves to sit beside me, her presence a calming anchor. She takes my hand in hers, giving it a reassuring squeeze. "Scarlet, you are more capable than you believe. You have a strength that Rose does not—a strength born from adversity and perseverance. The trials are not just tests of skill but of character. You have proven time and time again that you have what it takes."

"But what if I'm not enough?" I whisper, the vulnerability in my voice laid bare. "Rose has always been one of the best. She's so confident, so composed. And me? I can't compete in the same way she does. I can't afford to fail, but I'm struggling to feel like I haven't already done that."

"Do not underestimate yourself, child," Fairy Godmother says firmly. "The challenges you face are meant to reveal your true potential, not to compare you to others. Each step you take is a testament to your resilience and ingenuity."

I nod, though uncertainty still gnaws at me. "But why did you send Rose? I thought this was my chance to prove myself, to claim my father's legacy. And now it feels like she's here because you don't believe in me."

Fairy Godmother's expression softens with understanding and a hint of regret. "I sent Rose because you had stumbled twice in retrieving the Bodian Crown from the king. It wasn't that I doubted you, but the stakes are high, and I wanted to ensure our chances were as strong as possible. Rose is meant to be a backup, not a replacement."

"I've felt so alone," I admit, tears welling up in my eyes. "Like no one truly sees me for who I am. Everyone is so quick to judge, to dismiss me. Even now, I can hear them arguing, treating this house—my house—like it's theirs."

Fairy Godmother brushes a tear from my cheek, her touch gentle and comforting. "You are seen, Scarlet. I see you, and I believe in you. Your father's spirit lives on in you, and his dream for this manor will be realized through your strength and determination."

I take a shaky breath, feeling a glimmer of hope. "Thank you. I don't know what I'd do without you."

"You are never without me," she says, her voice a soothing balm. "Now, tell me more about the trials. What else have you faced?"

I recount the other challenges, the treacherous paths, the cunning competitors, and the fleeting moments of triumph. Fairy Godmother listens intently, her eyes never leaving mine, her presence providing the strength I need to continue.

"And then," I say, my voice trembling slightly, "there's the staff I found. The staff of Halisar, the god of thieves. It feels... powerful, but also dangerous. It could reveal things about me that I don't want anyone, especially the king, to know."

Fairy Godmother's expression becomes more serious, a note of concern in her eyes. "Power is often a double-edged sword," she says thoughtfully. "The staff holds great potential, but it also has the ability to reveal aspects of your character and past that you may wish to keep hidden. If the king becomes suspicious, it could complicate matters greatly. However, if you learn to use it properly, it could be a formidable asset."

Her words resonate deeply within me, instilling a newfound sense of determination. "I will try," I say, my resolve strengthening. "For my father, for this manor, and for myself."

Fairy Godmother smiles, a proud and loving expression. "That is all anyone can ask, my dear. Now, let's have some tea. You need to keep your strength up for the trials ahead."

As she moves to prepare the tea, I feel a sense of peace settle over me. With Fairy Godmother by my side, I know I am not alone.

A soft fluttering sound draws our attention to the kitchen window. A small bird, a messenger pigeon, perches on the sill, a tiny note tied to its leg. Fairy Godmother hurries over, her face growing serious as she unties the note.

"What's wrong?" I ask, a knot of worry forming in my stomach.

She hands me the note, her eyes filled with concern. "A mission is about to go very wrong. Lucius and Gen are about to get caught."

My blood runs cold as I read the hastily scrawled words. The weight of the situation presses down on me, my heart pounding in my chest. "We can't let that happen," I say, my voice trembling.

"The job was a trap," she says, her tone grave. "The king has been hunting us. This could expose everything."

I feel a surge of panic, the enormity of the responsibility overwhelming me. "What do we do?"

"I don't have time to find someone else. I need you to go and stop them," she says, her voice firm and unwavering. "But be careful, Scarlet. One wrong move and everything we've worked for could be lost."

I nod, determination hardening my resolve. "I'll do it," I say, my voice steady despite the fear coursing through me. "I'll save them."

Fairy Godmother squeezes my hand, her eyes filled with pride and worry. "Be safe, my child. And remember, you are stronger than you know."

***

The streets of the city are alive with the bustle of midday activity, but I move through them like a ghost. My heart races, the urgency of the situation pushing me forward. Fairy Godmother's warning still echoes in my ears: this mission is a trap. Gen and Lucius are in danger, and it's up to me to save them.

Dressed in black, with a mask concealing my identity, I blend into the shadows despite the bright sun overhead. The clothing clings to me, allowing for maximum agility and stealth. I've trained for moments like this, but knowing my friends' lives are on the line makes every step feel heavier.

As I approach the Merchant's Guild meeting house, the imposing structure looms over me, its stone walls radiating a cold, indifferent strength. I scan the perimeter, noting the increased guard presence. I didn't know that the king was looking for our guild specifically. The thought sends a shiver down my spine, but I push it aside. Focus, Scarlet. They need you.

I duck into an alley, taking a moment to assess my surroundings. The side entrance to the left seems less guarded. Timing is everything. I wait, heart pounding, until a cart rolls by, providing the cover I need. I slip through the gate and into the cool interior of the house, my footsteps silent on the stone floor.

Every sense on high alert, I move cautiously. Muffled voices reach my ears from a corridor to the right. I move towards them, my steps calculated and precise. The voices become clearer: Lucius's smooth, confident tone and Gen's more measured, focused one. Relief washes over me—they're alive.

I peek around the corner and see them in a small room, surrounded by books and scrolls. Gen is hunched over a table, working on disarming an anti-espionage enchantment, while Lucius examines a map. They look tense, but unharmed. I step forward, ready to join them, when a magical alarm blares through the house.

My blood runs cold. How did I miss that?

Guards burst into the room, weapons drawn. Gen and Lucius look up, shock and fear flashing across their faces.

"So much for never being caught before, huh?" Lucius quips, trying to lighten the mood. Gen shoots him a glare, frustration on her face evident.

I spring into action, throwing a smoke bomb to create a diversion. The room fills with thick, choking smoke, giving me the cover I need. I dart forward, taking down the nearest guard with a swift kick to the head. Another one lunges at me, but I sidestep and sweep his legs out from under him.

"What are you doing here?" Gen exclaims, relief evident in her voice.

"Surprise," I say, managing a small smile despite the chaos. "We need to move. Now."

Lucius nods, already recovering from the shock. "Lead the way."

We make our way through the house, the smoke giving us precious seconds to evade the guards. My heart races as we navigate the maze-like corridors. Every step brings us closer to freedom—or so I hope.

We burst through a door and find ourselves in a large hall. Relief washes over me, but it's short-lived. Standing in the center is the King's private bodyguard—she seems so much more intimidating here in this room, glaring down at us, than she did this morning in the hall. My heart sinks; if she recognizes me, it's all over. I'll be expelled from the trials, lose any chance at the crown, and worst of all, the King will discover my identity.

Her eyes lock onto mine, and a smirk plays at her lips. "Stop! Give up now and surrender," she says, her voice cold and menacing.

I tighten my grip on my weapons, my mind racing. She is a formidable opponent, and with the soldiers backing her, our chances of escape are slim. But I can't let fear paralyze me. My comrades are counting on me.

"Go," I whisper to them. "I'll hold them off."

"Are you crazy?" one hisses. "We stick together."

There's no time to argue. The bodyguard steps forward, drawing her sword with a practiced grace. Her eyes lock onto mine, cold and calculating. I meet her gaze, my resolve hardening. "Fine. But stay close," I whisper to my comrades.

She lunges first, her blade slicing through the air with deadly precision. I barely sidestep in time, feeling the whoosh of the sword as it narrowly misses my shoulder. I counter with a quick jab of my dagger, but she parries effortlessly, her expression unreadable.

She presses the attack, a flurry of strikes aimed at my head and torso. I duck, weave, and block with my daggers, our weapons clashing in a symphony of steel. Each strike sends vibrations up my arm, but I grit my teeth and push through the pain. Sweat trickles down my brow, stinging my eyes, but I don't dare blink.

Out of the corner of my eye, I see my comrades locked in combat with the soldiers. One of them disarms a guard with a swift twist of the wrist, while the other blocks a heavy blow, their faces set in grim determination. They fight with the skill and precision that only master thieves possess, but the sheer number of enemies threatens to overwhelm them.

The bodyguard feints left, then swings her sword in a deadly arc aimed at my neck. I drop to one knee, the blade whistling just above my head. Seizing the moment, I roll forward and come up behind her, slashing at her exposed side with my dagger. She spins, her sword deflecting mine at the last second, and we are once again locked in a deadly dance.

A soldier lunges at me from the side, and I kick him away, my focus never wavering from the bodyguard. Her eyes narrow, and she changes her stance, her movements becoming even more aggressive. She knows she has the advantage in numbers, and she's trying to wear me down.

My muscles burn with exertion, and my breath comes in ragged gasps. The bodyguard's relentless assault leaves me no room to think, only react. I block a downward strike with both daggers, our blades locked together, and I see the flicker of a smirk on her lips. She thinks she's won.

But then I hear a shout from one of my comrades. "Look, the window!"

Hope surges through me. I break away from the bodyguard, parrying a final strike that leaves her momentarily off-balance. "Cover me!" I yell, sprinting towards the large stained-glass window at the far end of the hall.

My comrades fight with renewed vigor, forming a defensive line to hold off the soldiers. The bodyguard recovers quickly and gives chase, her sword flashing as she cuts down anyone in her path. My heart pounds in my chest, each step bringing me closer to the window and our only chance of escape.

I reach the window and smash it with the hilt of my dagger. The stained glass shatters, raining colorful shards around me. "Go, now!" I shout, helping my comrades through the opening. The king's bodyguard is almost upon us, her eyes blazing with fury, but I can't afford to look back. We need to get out—now.

We scramble through the shattered window, shards crunching underfoot as we hit the ground running. The guard's furious shouts echo behind us, but we can't afford to look back. We dart through the narrow alleyways, our breaths coming in ragged gasps, the city's midday bustle a distant hum compared to the pounding of our hearts.

"Left!" I shout, leading them through a maze of side streets. The guards are relentless, their footsteps growing louder with each turn. We sprint around a corner, nearly colliding with a fruit vendor who curses at us as we pass. I throw a glance over my shoulder—three guards are still on our tail, and they're gaining ground.

Lucius skids to a halt beside a stack of crates. "I'll slow them down. Keep going!" He kicks the crates over, sending them crashing into the street, momentarily blocking the guards' path.

"Not bad," I pant, pulling him along as we continue our frantic escape. Gen, ever the strategist, takes the lead, guiding us through a labyrinth of alleys and backstreets. The sound of pursuit fades, but we don't dare slow down.

Finally, we reach an old, weathered door hidden in the shadow of a crumbling building. Gen raps on it in a specific pattern, and it creaks open to reveal a dimly lit passage. "In, quick!" she urges.

We slip inside, closing the door behind us. The passage is narrow and damp, the air thick with the scent of earth and mildew. Our footsteps echo softly as we make our way through the twisting tunnel, the adrenaline slowly ebbing away.

At last, we emerge into a hidden cellar beneath the guild tavern. The familiar sound of muffled laughter and clink-ing glasses seeps through the ceiling. Gen unlocks the door and the three of us find a table to sit at. Safe, for now.

Lucius collapses in a chair, a grin spreading across his face. "Well, that was fun."

Gen rolls her eyes. "You're insufferable."

I smile at their teasing, but the weight of my mission still hangs heavy on my shoulders.

"We did it. We got the information. Now we just need to get it to the right people." Gen says.

Lucius steps closer, his eyes twinkling with mischief. "And here I thought you just wanted to spend more time with me, Scarlet."

I chuckle, shaking my head. "Always the charmer, Lucius."

Gen groans. "Can you two please save the flirting for after we've saved our skins?"

Lucius flags over Polly, the barmaid, and she gives us a knowing look as she passes by. "Polly, three drinks, please. We've earned them."

As Polly nods and heads to the bar, I take a deep breath. "Listen, there's something you both need to know. The mission—it was a trap set by the king. Fairy Godmother almost found out too late and sent me to save you."

Their smiles fade, replaced by a sobering realization of how close we came to disaster. Gen looks down, her face pale. "That explains the extra guards."

Lucius tries to lighten the mood, offering a lopsided grin. "Well, we're not dead yet, right?"

We may not be dead, but this whole thing has sobered my wishful thinking. There is absolutely no way anything could ever happen between me and the king. If he ever discovered who I was it wouldn't be just my life on the line. It would be the entire guild. They are more of a family to me than my own.

Polly returns with our drinks, and Lucius raises his in a mock toast. "To not dying today."

I take a deep swig of the beer. We sit in silence for a moment. The chatter of the room the only noise.

Lucius breaks the silence and winks at me. "You know, Scarlet, one of these days, you might just fall for my charms."

I laugh, the tension easing slightly. "Keep dreaming, Lucius."

Gen nudges him playfully. "Seriously, give up. You never had a chance."

Missed Opportunities

Remme

The doors banging against the walls with an echoing thud as I storm into my private study. Sofia trails close behind, her usual composed expression replaced by one of barely contained frustration. I begin pacing, too agitated to sit still, my boots striking the polished floor in a staccato rhythm.

"How?" I demand, whirling to face Sofia. "How did they slip through your grasp again?"

Sofia's jaw clenches, the only outward sign of her irritation. "They had someone on the inside tip them off. Knew we were coming."

I slam my fist down on the heavy oak desk, making the neatly arranged papers jump. "Damnable thieves!" I snarl. "Like rats scurrying back to their filthy holes."

Sofia waits silently, knowing better than to speak when I am in such a temper. She has witnessed my rages often enough over the long years of our friendship. I continue seething, stomping over to the window overlooking the castle gardens.

"After all the preparations, all the resources spent trying to apprehend them, still they evade me at every turn!" I grit my teeth, glaring out at the cheerful blossoms swaying in the breeze, oblivious to my dark mood.

"Sire, we will find them," Sofia says evenly. "We were close this time. Their luck cannot hold forever."

"Can it not?" I snap, whirling to face her. "Tell me, in over three years of hunting these criminals, have we ever once managed to capture their leader? Or uncover the identity of even a single member?"

Sofia's silence speaks for her. In all our years of dedicating guards, spies, and endless hours trying to root out this persistent thorn in my side, they remain as elusive as mist. It galls me to admit defeat, especially to Sofia, who has aided me tirelessly in this vexing pursuit.

I turn back to the window, planting the golden gloves that protect everything from my hands on the smooth stone sill. The contact helps calm my racing thoughts, allowing me to gather the frayed edges of my temper.

"Forgive my outburst," I say in a low voice. "I should not take my frustrations out on you." I hear Sofia step up beside me.

"You have every right to be angry," she says. "I let them escape when they were within my grasp." Self-recrimination colors her usually composed tone.

I shake my head, turning to face her. "You carry no blame in this, my friend. The failure is mine alone."

Sofia looks ready to argue, but I hold up a hand. "I am king. The security of this realm and bringing dangerous criminals to justice ultimately falls to me. If I cannot manage even that..." I trail off bitterly, despising the helplessness writhing within me like a caged beast.

"There must be a traitor close to the throne, feeding them information," Sofia muses. I nod grimly, having already reached the same conclusion. It is the only explanation for how they always remain one step ahead, slipping through my fingers no matter the preparations made.

I sink into my chair with a weary sigh. "I do not even know who they truly are or how to contact them openly. When we've tried reaching out before, it was grasping at shadows, uncertain if we were even speaking to the right people."

Sofia nods solemnly. "They cover their tracks well. But their random acts of defiance seem aimed at provoking you, not personal vendetta."

"Which perplexes me more," I reply, kneading my temples where a headache throbs. "With no way to engage them in discourse or address any grievances, they remain a cipher. Are they mere nuisance or more dangerous threat? Their antics breed doubt in my capability to lead! Already whispers spread, speculation that I am unfit to govern."

Sofia stands beside me, steadfast as ever. "Pay no mind to fearmongers and rumor mills. No one devotes themselves more fully to the kingdom's prosperity."

I draw strength from her staunch loyalty. "If only that were enough," I say bitterly. "With each brazen theft, faith in my rule wavers. Even my own council questions my strength, and some guards' loyalties twist."

I rise abruptly to pace, shaking off dark thoughts. "But how to stop them when we cannot even discover their true names or origins? We must end their ceaseless provocations."

Sofia's eyes flash with determination. "We will uncover the source in time and bolster security."

I stop before the window, gazing sightlessly at the city below. "But how? I have tried attacking directly to no avail. We need a new approach."

Then inspiration strikes. "The trials! Is the arena almost finished?"

"They are. We employed a company that uses magic users to speed up their construction times."

"Perfect. Such spectacle could draw them out into the open, tempt intervention."

Sofia's eyes shine as possibilities unfold. "Perhaps allow the crowds some engagement, sire? Cheering for favored champions, giving tokens of esteem, maybe even tools and items that could help them in the trials?"

"I like it," I reply, intrigued by the implications. "Public gifts could expose ties back to the thieves themselves if they already have any members in the trials themselves."

"And any suspect patronage would be in full view of all," Sofia adds.

"Now we're getting somewhere. Meddling in the games could entice them into reckless action."

I resume pacing, energized by this breakthrough. "Have the marketplace criers and broadsheet peddlers feature the participants. Stoke zealous support from all corners. Arrange a set of interviews with the participants by several of the papers as well. We need those with money to be tempted as well."

"A fine strategy, my king," Sofia agrees. "Generate fervent emotional investment in the victors."

"Make the people feel connected to the outcomes," I continue.

Sofia meets my gaze unwaveringly. "We set the stage for temptation few could resist."

"This just may work."

Sofia bows her head deferentially. "It will work. I shall prepare the arrangements at once, Your Majesty."

As the door clicks softly shut behind her, I wish I could share in her conviction. But doubt gnaws at me. I force the negative thoughts away, straightening to my full height. I cannot afford to show weakness or indecision, not when so much is at stake.

Striding to my desk, I sift through the dispatches and reports. Buried amongst them is the one that started this renewed fervor - a smudged parchment I have read over a hundred times since I wrote it several weeks ago. It describes in detail the infiltration of my private chambers, the attempt on the Bodian crown. But most unsettling of all, it speaks of a woman who somehow resisted my deadly touch.

I trace a finger over the hastily scrawled words, a phantom ache rising in my chest. She slipped through my grasp as insubstantially as a dream. But the memory of her lingers, the only living being to touch me and live in over a decade.

In the solitude of my study, I allow myself a moment of painful longing. What might it be like to feel the warmth of another without fear of death? To touch and be touched beyond the borders of my gilded cage? I banish the treacherous thoughts almost as quickly as they form. Such foolish fanciful wishes will only bring misery.

Still, questions persist. Who is she who can withstand my curse? Some dark sorceress? A mistress of ancient arts? Or perhaps merely someone immune, a random quirk of fate? I know that at my coronation I was given a blessing of someone who could withstand and help me control my curse, but no details as to why. What makes them so special?

I pace to the window once more, staring unseeing at the cloud-strewn sky as my mind turns over possibilities. Something nags at me, some instinct that circumvents reason. The timing of this mysterious thief targeting my most treasured possession feels too coincidental.

My jaw tightens as pieces begin falling into place. The Bodian crown would fetch a fortune for any common criminal. But if their intention was mere profit, why risk twice attempting the same heavily guarded target? No, this speaks of a deeper motive.

I tap my fingers on the stone sill, thoughtful. When gossip of the attempted theft spread, it undermined faith in my rule further. As if this faceless woman mocks my inability to stop her.

Could the two be connected? This elusive guild rises as my authority wanes. The more brazen their antics, the more pressure mounts for me to rectify the situation. Have they positioned themselves as symbols of my supposed weakness?

The thought sends a spark of fury through me. How dare they! Manipulating perception and politics to cast doubt upon my crown. If this is some coordinated ploy, I swear they will regret toying with forces beyond their capability.

I glance down at the dispatch, possibilities turning over. The mysterious woman who can withstand my touch - if she is one of them, it would make sense. An attempt to unbalance me, make me seem feeble and distracted.

My hands tighten into fists, crumpling the parchment. Very well. If it is a game they want, I shall oblige. They seek to manipulate me with my own desire for connection? I will find this woman and learn her secrets, by force if necessary. And when I unravel whatever grand scheme they have devised, the retribution will be swift and merciless.

I smooth the parchment carefully, a predatory anticipation building within me. "Enjoy your brief rebellion while you can," I murmur to the silent room. "Soon enough your games shall come to an end."

The thieves guild has overplayed their hand this time. I shall turn their attempts to undermine me against them. Find the weaknesses in their armor and tear the whole rot-ten enterprise down once and for all. They believe themselves so clever, so untouchable. But even mist disperses before the light of the rising sun.

Soon there shall be nowhere left for them to hide. And when I am through, not even memories will remain of their sedition. Power and rule belong to the crown alone. These lingering shadows will threaten my kingdom no more.

Of one thing I am now increasingly suspicious of - the mysterious thief who breached my chambers could be connected to this thieves' guild. If she is one of them, I may be able to find her and through her, trace the lines back to unravel their entire web. She may prove the loose thread that threatens to destroy everything they have built.

And I now possess potential bait to draw her out again, tempt her into the light where she cannot evade me - the Bodian crown. She has revealed interest in stealing it, and I could use that to entrap her if she is indeed one of them. Soon we may see who ensnares who in this game of shadows.

I roll up the parchment carefully and place it in my desk drawer. Sofia is right, I must have faith. This contest is not over yet. If and when we clash again, perhaps the advantage will be mine. I touch two gloved fingers to my lips, recalling the mysterious thief's brief warmth. If she is one of them, we shall meet again, my elusive thief, under circumstances of my choosing. She may come to regret ever provoking my ire.

The shadows have lingered too long already. It is time for the light to pierce every crevice and extinguish them for good. My kingdom has no place for those who deal in deception and defiance. Order and obedience shall be restored.

Interviews
Scarlet

The solarium's warm, golden light filters through the large windows, casting intricate patterns on the tiled floor. Despite the tranquil atmosphere, tension hangs thick in the air. I trace the carved patterns on the table, seeking solace in the intricate details as Rose's self-assured smile burns into me from across the table. Darius sits beside me, his smile plastered on. It's clear his goal is to charm everyone here.

A petite journalist with kind eyes and her hair piled high on her head with a spare quill stuck in it takes a seat, her quill poised over her parchment. "How are you all feeling about the tournament so far?"

Before I can respond, Rose leans forward, exuding an almost smug confidence. "Challenging, but certainly not anything I can't handle." Her eyes glimmer with a hint of challenge as they meet mine. "Some of us thrive under pressure, don't we, Scarlet?"

The dig doesn't go unnoticed. I square my shoulders, refusing to be baited. "Indeed, some of us do," I reply evenly, holding her gaze. "Though others seem to simply enjoy hearing themselves speak."

Rose's smirk falters momentarily before she masks it with a sip of tea. Darius, seated beside me, grins mischievously. "You know, if this were a contest of who can make the most enemies, I think we'd all be champions by now," he says with an amused laugh.

I smile at his teasing remark, the tension easing slightly. Darius has a way of lightening even the most charged situations. My gaze falls on the tray of refreshments, the sight of the cranberry-orange scones offering a small comfort. I take one, savoring the burst of tart sweetness as it melts on my tongue.

The petite journalist leans forward, her gaze inquisitive. "Could you elaborate on the artifacts you uncovered in the catacombs? What significance might they hold?"

I glance nervously at Rose and Darius before answering. "The ancient wooden staff I found seems important, but I'm unsure of its true purpose yet," I admit haltingly.

Rose doesn't miss a beat, her confidence unwavering. "The golden scarab symbolizes power and transformation—quite fitting for an artifact from these trials, wouldn't you say?" She shoots me a pointed look, almost daring me to contradict her. A flash of annoyance runs through me, but I bite my tongue, refusing to rise to the bait.

Darius chimes in, holding up the intricately carved lute with a lopsided grin. "I think mine is just telling me I need to pick up a new hobby."

The journalist quirks an eyebrow. "Can you play the lute?"

Darius smirks, his eyes twinkling with amusement. "I mean, technically anyone can play a lute. The question is if they could play it well. Personally, no. Not at all."

A surprised laugh escapes my lips before I can stop it. Trust Darius to lighten the mood with his dry wit. Rose shoots him an exasperated look, but I can see the hint of a smile tugging at the corners of her mouth.

The journalist scribbles furiously in her notepad. "And what do you believe these artifacts represent in relation to the upcoming challenges?"

I exchange a glance with Rose and Darius, considering my words carefully. "From what King Remme explained, the artifacts will be used to sort us into teams for the next phase of the trials," I say, recalling the king's words before we entered the catacombs.

Rose nods in affirmation. "Forming effective teams will be crucial for success moving forward. The artifacts are likely symbolic of the strengths and roles we'll need to complement each other."

"An intriguing prospect," Darius muses, his fingers absently tracing the intricate carvings on the lute. "It will be interesting to see how the teams are divided and the dynamics that emerge." A wry smile tugs at his lips as he glances between Rose and me. "Though with personalities like ours, I imagine it could get...lively."

I chuckle at the understatement, my earlier nerves easing.

The journalist seems satisfied with our responses, her pen still dancing across the page. "There have been rumors of an arranged engagement for you, scarlet. One to a rather well off nobleman. Care to comment?"

A hush falls over the room.

My heart sinks, frustration burning hot within me. I meet the journalist's gaze, my voice steady and resolute. "I have agreed to no such engagement. The outdated notion that a parent can dictate someone's future spouse is not only antiquated but harmful. Besides, both of my parents are dead." The weight of my declaration hangs in the air, the room falling silent save for the frantic scratching of pens against notepads.

Rose regards me with a mixture of surprise and begrudging respect, no doubt taken aback by my candor.

"Well, Scarlet has never been one to shy away from defying expectations," she remarks.

FROM THE SIDELINES

REMME

From my concealed vantage point in the tunnels between the walls, I watch Scarlet as she boldly declares her refusal of any arranged marriage. She's certainly bold enough to be the thief I've been seeking, I muse. Her defiant stance and unwavering conviction intrigue me.

As Rose remarks on Scarlet's tendency to defy expectations, the challenge in her emerald eyes hints at the fierce rivalry between the two women. Perhaps one of them is trying to undermine the other's efforts. Darius' teasing holds a subtle respect when directed at Scarlet that gives me pause. He is meant to be my eyes and ears, but could his judgment be clouded?

When Scarlet speaks vulnerably of her desire to forge her own path and find a true sense of belonging, I find myself momentarily disarmed by her sincerity. For a fleeting instant, I see not a suspect, but a kindred spirit yearning for the same freedom I seek. Get ahold of yourself, I chastise inwardly. She could merely be an accomplished deceiver.

As the interview concludes, I remain skeptical of taking Scarlet's words and actions solely at face value. If she truly wishes to prove herself, she must do so through deeds, not rousing speeches. An intriguing notion starts to take shape - arranging a more...intimate opportunity to observe her unguarded and put her motivations to the test. She's certainly bold and headstrong enough to potentially be the thief. Perhaps a private one on one is in order, a chance to unravel the truth behind that carefully sculpted persona.

I can't deny the flutter of anticipation at the thought of an encounter where her every nuance would be laid bare, quickly tempered by an inward grimace. This is merely a strategic ploy to confirm her loyalty...or lack thereof. Nothing more. Yet a increasingly insistent voice whispers that after the tenderness I glimpsed between us in the palace gardens, a private meeting could reveal depths I have determinedly ignored until now. Would it really be so bad to find someone I could be close to?

No, I can't let myself get hopeful like that. I know exactly what happens if anyone or anything gets too close. My luck wouldn't be good enough for the one person that I wouldn't harm to be someone I actually cared for.

Pushing aside the distracting thoughts, I slip away with renewed determination to orchestrate a discreet rendezvous with this infuriatingly enigmatic Scarlet. Only by observing her in an unguarded, intimate moment can I hope to separate illusion from reality and discern if she is friend or foe. The stakes are too perilous to be swayed by a lovely face and honeyed tongue.

THE ARENA

SCARLET

After the interview, I make my way back to the competitors' quarters alongside Rose and Darius. The questions from the journalist still linger in my mind, especially the probing ones about my personal life and motivations for entering the tournament. As we walk, Rose shoots me a sidelong glance, her expression unreadable. Anger simmers beneath my skin at the reminder of my stepmother's meddling in my life once again.

"Well, that certainly wasn't what I expected," she remarks, a hint of disdain coloring her tone.

I grit my teeth, fury rising at the journalist's audacity to bring up that wretched arranged marriage in a public setting. When I signed up for this tournament, I never expected my personal struggles to become fodder for public entertainment and gossip.

"Did you know they were going to pry into our lives like that?" I ask Rose and Darius, unable to hide the irritation in my voice. "I thought this was supposed to be about our combat skills, not parading our secrets before the entire kingdom!"

Rose shrugs, though I detect a flicker of discomfort. "Clearly the king wants to put on a real spectacle. Get the people invested in more than just our fighting prowess."

Darius gives me a sympathetic look. "I can't imagine it's easy having such personal matters dragged into the light like that. But look at it this way - now you have a chance to control the narrative on your own terms."

Before I can respond, a palace attendant approaches us. "Competitors, please return to your quarters and change into your training attire. You are to meet outside the main hall in one hour," she instructs crisply before turning on her heel and striding away.

"You're not actually considering marrying that asshat Greystone, are you?" Rose asks with a derisive snort as we head back to our rooms.

I shoot her a withering look. "Of course not! My step-mother is the one forcing this engagement for her own gain. I won't be a pawn in her games."

Darius shakes his head. "If the king allows this invasion of our privacy to continue, the entire tournament will become more of a circus act than a test of martial skill."

"Exactly!" I exclaim. "We are here to compete, not have our lives put on display like animals in a menagerie!" The thought of Lord Greystone watching me with his lecherous gaze sickens me to my core.

Rose raises an eyebrow at me, a silent challenge passing between us. Darius simply shrugs good-naturedly.

An hour later, ornate carriages arrive to transport us. To where, I have no idea. No one will tell us anything. As someone who rarely does anything without knowing the route, alternate routes and back up plans this is only putting me even more on edge.

As our carriage jostles into motion, I gaze out the window, my fingers unconsciously tracing the hilts of my daggers tucked at my waist.

Rose seems to sense my discomfort, arching an eyebrow at me. "Relax, Scarlet. The people crave spectacle - play to their fancies and they'll be eating out of your hand," she remarks smoothly. As one of the Thieves' Guild's envoys often tasked with public-facing roles, she is far more at ease with the spotlight than I.

I frown, unconvinced. The crowds thronging the streets seem thicker than usual, scores of people all headed in the same direction as us. "And if I have no taste for being a sideshow act?"

Darius chuckles, unfazed by my irritation. "A true warrior doesn't shy away from spectacle. Embrace it, and you might even find you enjoy the roar of the crowd." He winks mischievously.

If only he knew, I'm no warrior. I'm a thief and we are trained to work around and bend if not break the rules.

As our carriage finally draws through the palace gates, the opulent vehicle slows to a halt. I steel myself before getting out, determined not to betray my awe. But as I catch my first glimpse of our grand new stage, I can't help but gape - a colossal stone arena looming ahead, its towering walls etched with intricate carvings depicting epic battles of ages past.

Awestruck, I take in the sheer, breathtaking scale of the structure, my breath catching in my throat. This is no mere training ground - this is a spectacle fit for legends. As we approach the gaping entrance, the guards part ranks to reveal King Remme himself, resplendent in his royal attire.

He surveys us with a measured gaze, his expression inscrutable. "Esteemed competitors," he begins, his voice carrying across the hushed crowd, "welcome to the true trials of skill and endurance. This arena will be your proving ground."

His eyes seem to linger on me for a moment before sweeping over the others. "From this day forth, your abilities will be on display not just for my scrutiny, but for all the kingdom to witness. The people will be permitted to fill these stands, to cheer for their champions and offer gifts to aid you in your quest."

A murmur of surprise ripples through the competitors at this pronouncement. The king raises a hand, commanding silence once more.

"Indeed, this tournament shall serve a greater purpose. The funds raised from these spectacles will be divided—the victor shall claim not just the Bodian Crown, but a share of the monetary rewards proportional to their performance. The remainder shall be distributed to aid those in need across my lands."

My mind races at the implications. Hearing the journalist mention it was one thing. Actually hearing it from the king is different entirely. Not only will our skills be tested before a crowd, but their favor—and wealth—could sway the outcome. Numbers run through my head. If I can play this right and win, I won't only get paid out for collecting the Bodian Crown but also the extra money that's now been added to the prize could last me years if I played my cards right.

I glance at Rose, wondering if she grasps the full significance of this development. Her face is enraptured with a mix of calculation and intrigue.

King Remme's gaze finds me once more, and I could swear I see a glimmer of...something in his eyes. A challenge? An invitation? "Use your time here wisely," he says, his voice low yet carrying an undercurrent of steel. "For the arena will reveal the true measure of your character, as surely as it exposes your abilities."

With that cryptic pronouncement, he sweeps away, leaving us to contemplate the trials ahead and the eyes of the kingdom upon us.

"You heard His Majesty," one of the king's guards barks out. "The stands are open to receive spectators. This is your first chance to show your worth and gain supporters." His steely gaze rakes over us, daring any to protest.

The immense scale of the arena leaves me awestruck as we enter through the towering archway. The smooth stone floor extends before us like a grand stage, surrounded by soaring tiers of curved seating ascending majestically towards the heavens.

My gaze is instantly drawn to the lavish private viewing boxes dotting the higher levels, already occupied by finely dressed nobility appraising us like prize livestock

Fitting considering among them is Lord Greystone lounging arrogantly in one of the lavish private boxes, no doubt poised to leer and mock from his lofty perch when he gets wind of my defiance. Just imagining the smug look being wiped off that pompous face when he finds out I denounce our engagement brings a vindicated smirk to my lips. Let him choke on his wounded pride when this so-called "future wife" rebuffs him before the entire kingdom. I'm no wilting noble's daughter to be brow-beaten into submission anymore.

Greystone isn't the only set of eyes boring into me from on high. Movement from the largest, most opulent box catches my eye as King Remme himself emerges, commanding presence flanked by his intimidating honor guard. As if sensing my scrutiny, the king's piercing stare finds and holds me amidst the sea of competitors. I meet it unflinchingly, refusing to be the one who looks away first in this silent clash of wills.

"Breathe, Scarlet," Rose murmurs in a low aside, reading the tension in my clenched jaw. "Let your skill speak for itself. Don't give that lecher the satisfaction of seeing you flustered." Her tone hardens. "We have a chance here to rewrite our stories on our own terms. Don't squander it on petty grievances."

As infuriating as Greystone's presence is, Rose is right. This grand arena is our stage now to rewrite the stories that have been imposed upon us for far too long. No more being bound by the expectations of others. This is where we seize control of the narrative through undeniable feats of skill.

Pushing aside my rage, I pivot to survey our training options. Various racks of practice weapons line one wall, from sturdy staves to glinting blades. Hanging sacks and straw dummies provide targets for sharpening strikes.

A sly smile curves my lips as an idea takes shape. Without a word, I catch Rose's eye and jerk my chin towards the sparring circles, a silent challenge glimmering between us...

Rose's face lights up with wicked glee as she grasps my intent. "I thought you'd never ask." Without further preamble, she peels off her outer layers until she's clad in just a fitted tunic and leggings, all harsh lines and coiled readiness.

I mirror her actions, shrugging off my cloak and jacket until I'm similarly unencumbered. My fingers caress the worn leather wrappings on my palms and knuckles - earned through years of fighting, from alleyway brawls to carefully orchestrated strikes. This is my element, my truth laid bare.

Around us, the other competitors are splitting off to warm up in various ways - some stretching, others taking tentative swings with practice swords. But it's the stands that draw my eye as they begin filling with a steady trickle of spectators. I spot a section roped off specifically for scribes and royal reporters, quills at the ready to document our every move.

Rose murmurs, following my gaze. "Time to give them a real show, don't you think?" Her eyes glint with feral anticipation.

I grin fiercely back at her. "I'm ready. Don't know what's taking you so long." With that, we launch into motion.

Rose darts in first with a flurry of jabs and feints, her whole body a whirling dervish of controlled violence. I sway back, absorbing and deflecting her through sheer muscle memory and instinct honed over countless back-alley melees. When she overextends her left side, I seize the opening - ducking low and aiming a sweeping kick at her legs.

She leaps back with a breathless laugh. "You're getting sloppy in your old age, Marheart!" Rose taunts through a fierce grin.

A hot thrill rushes through me, all other concerns falling away as the world narrows to Rose, myself, and the primal dance of strike and counterstrike. We flow together in an intricate cadence, exchanging blows and parries in an ever-accelerating tempo. The exhilaration of battle singing in my veins drowns out everything - the murmurs of the crowd, Lord Greystone's presence, the weight of the tournament itself.

At some point, my back slams against a column with enough force to rattle my teeth. Rose's forearm presses against my throat as she bears down, her face flushed and eyes alight with the thrill of the fight. An explosive series of hits and blocks has left us both sucking in ragged breaths.

"Getting...sloppy...yourself," I gasp out through a grin, barely feeling the strain in my muscles. This is glorious.

Rose's expression abruptly sharpens and she eases back a fraction, her demeanor shifting subtly. I recognize that particular microexpression - a warning that I'm pushing things too far, drawing unwanted scrutiny. "I hope that worked out your anger because you need to cool it," she whispers in my ear.

With an internal wince, I belatedly remember we are supposed to be maintaining an air of civility, not unleashing our full deadly skills. Fairy Godmother will be furious if we give too much away. We need to be careful to not do anything that could potentially connect us to the guild. I need to be more careful of the moves I use. Some are specific and could be recognized. I wasn't paying close enough attention to make sure I avoided those.

Dragging in a steadying breath, I force my body to ease its coiled intensity, letting the frenzied high of combat bleed away into a more restrained looseness. Rose mirrors my shift seamlessly, our exchange slowing into something more akin to a formal sparring session.

I twirl the dagger in my hand, the familiar weight and balance grounding me as I face Rose across the sparring circle. My eyes glance to the king's opulent viewing box, where King Remme sits observing with an intense, calculated gaze. A flutter of nerves dances in my stomach as our eyes briefly meet, that same electric connection from our moonlit garden rendezvous reverberating through me.

I shake my head slightly, pushing aside the unbidden thought. Surely the king's scrutiny extends to all the competitors, not just me specifically. Yet...a treacherous part of me can't help replaying that surprisingly intimate conversation we shared, how he seemed to truly see me in a way no one else ever has. Get a grip, Scarlet. He's studying us as combatants, nothing more.

Before I can dwell further on the peculiar yearning his piercing stare sparks within me, Rose explodes into motion with a ferocious attack. She launches herself forward in a blistering flurry, dagger flashing as she rains down a blinding series of slashes and jabs. Instinct propels me to deflect her onslaught, my own dagger a mere blur as I absorb and redirect Rose's furious strikes in a whirlwind of parries.

The clashing of our daggers rings through the arena, the low murmurs of the thronging crowd fading into a muted backdrop as I immerse myself fully in the cadence of combat with Rose. Sweat beads along my hairline as I deflect her blistering combination of jabs and slashes, every fiber of my being narrowed to this primal ebb and flow of traded strikes. This lethal grace is my essence stripped bare - not the delicate noble's daughter, or the maid that my stepmother has forced me to become, but a tempered force of controlled ferocity normally sheathed in the shadows.

A sudden swell of raucous laughter from one of the nearby spectator sections catches my peripheral attention. My focus wavers just a hairsbreadth, gaze flicking towards the disturbance against my will. In that fractional moment, my eyes are instinctively drawn back to the king's box where he sits observing, posture erect and expression inscrutable as his penetrating stare finds and pins me amidst the whirlwind of motion.

Heat rises unbidden to my cheeks as every nerve ending thrills to his undisguised interest, his eyes seeming to pierce straight through my controlled facade into some deeper, unseen truth.

"Stay in the moment, Marheart!" Rose's bark cuts through the din as her dagger clips my forearm in a stinging graze. I barely avoid a more devastating strike, realizing with a jolt how dangerously distracted I've allowed myself to become.

With an inward curse, I redouble my efforts, raining down a blistering hail of attacks that has Rose rapidly backpedaling and struggling to keep pace. I can't afford such lapses, not here on this grand stage where the slightest misstep could undo everything. The weight of the king's lingering stare caresses over me like a physical touch, simultaneously thrilling and disquieting in its implacable judgment of my every minute tell.

Is he so inexplicably drawn to me? Or scrutinizing my defenses for weakness, for flaws to exploit? That nagging uncertainty forces me to throttle back the full extent of my lethal skills, even as some reckless part of me craves to let my unvarnished truth blaze forth before his discerning eyes.

In a momentary lull where we break apart, both breathing hard, I risk another furtive glance towards Remme's secluded viewing box. A tremor runs through me as his penetrating stare finds and holds me. He watches me with solemn, unwavering focus...and perhaps the barest glimmer of challenge sparking in his eyes.

A strange sense of giddy daring blossoms within me then, this defiant part of me that thrills at the unspoken invitation to unmask and bear truth before his discerning scrutiny.

Letting out a breathless laugh that startles even myself, I surge back into our lethal exchange with renewed determination.

The tempo of our dagger sparring accelerates into a fever pitch, the entire world narrowing to the dizzying cyclone of metal clashing against metal. I relish each stinging blow, each jarring impact sending adrenaline-fueled euphoria blazing through my veins. This is who I am in truth - uncompromising lethality sheathed in grace, undaunted by kings or circumstance.

At last we break apart again, both sucking in ragged breaths as the roaring crowd once more reasserts itself in a deafening swell. Rose watches me through narrowed eyes, her chest heaving, silently questioning the newfound intensity blazing within me. I meet her gaze with a fierce grin, whole body thrumming with the lingering high of unleashed passion.

Only then do I dare to fully turn my focus back to the king's viewing box. And my breath catches in my throat at the naked acknowledgment blazing in Remme's eyes as they find and hold mine. Gone is the opaque mask, the impenetrable wall he normally wields - instead I'm pierced by an incendiary look of molten approval, challenge...a nd undisguised yearning that leaves me both shaken and strangely emboldened.

You Need to Win

Scarlet

The clash of weapons fades into a distant murmur as the crowds gradually disperse from the arena, the day's exhibitions drawing to a close. I linger behind, feigning interest in one of the vacant training rings as the competitors and spectators filter out around me.

My gaze continually strays to the now-empty king's viewing box, and a strange sense of loss tugs at me.

I'm the last to eventually exit the shadowed expanse of the arena. The walk back through the winding city streets allows my mind to wander, replaying every heated look, every charged moment shared with the king in an endless, dizzying loop.

My feet steer me not to the dorms, but to my family home. It's been too long since it was a place that I felt safe and like I belonged, but it is mine. I need to own up and take control of things before they get even more out of hand.

Raised voices and clattering objects greets me as I reluctantly step inside. Squaring my shoulders, I make my way towards the sitting room from which the disturbance seems to originate.

Stepmother stands in the center of the chaos, eyes blazing and lips pursed in her signature look of disapproval as she stares down my bickering stepsisters. At my entrance, her ire pivots towards me in a sweeping shift of demeanor, a serpent-like smile spread thinly across her face.

"What are you doing here," she simpers in saccharine tones that instantly set me on edge. "I thought you would be gone the entire tournament. Have you already been eliminated? You never were very good at much." Her gaze holds a knowing look tinged with veiled menace.

Refusing to be cowed, I lift my chin in silent defiance. "I have only stopped by for a moment. May I have a word alone?"

"Of course. In fact, I feel we should have a private discussion to realign expectations," she states, gesturing towards the study with an imperious wave. "Girls, see to having tea brought for us."

An uneasy silence falls over the room as my stepsisters eye me with undisguised dislike before scurrying to obey.

Forcing an insouciant expression, I trail behind Step-mother, bracing for the onslaught to come.

She wastes no time once the study door closes behind us. "I hope you realize how very fortunate you are that Lord Greystone has developed...certain intentions regard-ing you," she begins without preamble, mouth pursing contemplatively. "His status and connections could secure our family's future where your own failings have left us perilously vulnerable."

The words are like a slap to the face, driving the breath from my lungs in a harsh exhale. "My failings?" I echo, dumbfounded.

"Silence!" she hisses, palm cracking against my cheek with enough force to make my head ring. I taste copper on my tongue as my jaw clenches stubbornly against the wave of pain.

"You ungrateful wretch," Stepmother seethes, livid eyes boring into me. "Your foolish whims and defiance have cost us more than you could ever comprehend. Your fa-ther's legacy - this estate and all it represents - is nearly lost."

A leaden knot of dread forms in the pit of my stomach as her words seem to echo from somewhere far away. Surely she doesn't mean...?

"What did you do?" I spit out.

Her expression softens into one of feigned remorse. "The truth is, I made certain...investments in an attempt to shore up our dwindling assets. Very ill-timed investments as it turned out."

She pauses to let the weight of her admission sink in. My throat works convulsively as I struggle to process the implication. The estate...my inheritance...in jeopardy?

"For my lack of prudence, I accept full responsibility," Stepmother continues smoothly, an undercurrent of steel beneath her placating tones. "But that still leaves us in a rather precarious position. One that could be handily resolved were you to embrace the future Lord Greystone has so generously arranged for you."

My pulse thunders in my ears as the floor seems to tilt dangerously beneath my feet. After everything—the missions, the brutality, the deceptions—it all may be for naught?

A tremulous tide of rage surfaces then, shoving aside my disorientation as I level a look of pure venom at the woman before me. "You selfish, grasping viper," I spit through gritted teeth.

Stepmother's expression shutters closed, mouth flattening into a severe line as she straightens to her full domineering height. "Mind your tongue, girl," she hisses in clipped tones.

Her next words are slow, measured, and laced with serpentine certainty. "Accept Lord Greystone's proposal and a portion of your inheritance may yet be preserved for you. Defy me..." Her gaze grows flinty and merciless. "And all shall be forfeit - your wealth, your status, even this home stripped away to settle the debts."

"What will you do if you lose the house? You have nowhere to go," I ask.

"That won't happen. As long as I live this home will be mine and if you hope to ever inherit it you will be a good girl and do as I say."

As she sweeps from the room without another word, her ultimatum hangs in the air like a sword's keen edge pressed to my throat. Dimly, I register the muffled clink of china and footsteps signaling my stepsisters' imminent arrival with the tea service.

But I am numb, frozen in the throes of gut-wrenching dismay and fury. How could she have been so recklessly careless? So staggeringly selfish? And now she would sacrifice my future - my very identity - to the lecherous whims of Lord Greystone for her own survival? If he was such a catch she would be offering her own daughters, not me. No, she knows exactly what she's doing.

A soft rap on the door breaks through the heavy silence that has descended. I hastily swipe at the lingering tear tracks on my cheeks as Fairy Godmother slips into the room, a steaming cup of tea in her hands.

"Here, drink this, my dear," she soothes, handing me the fragrant brew before settling herself in the chair beside me. Her warm eyes take in my disheveled state, lips pursing in a concerned moue. "That dreadful woman has put you through the wringer once again, I see."

The gentle understanding in her tone is my undoing. I crumple forward with a hitching sob, cradling the teacup in a white-knuckled grip as hot tears spill down my cheeks anew. Fairy Godmother simply waits with infinite patience, letting me unleash the roiling tempest of heartache and fury that batters me from within.

"How did you even know I needed you here, Godmother?" I ask bluntly, swiping at the dampness on my cheeks.

Fairy Godmother lets out a dry chuckle, perching herself on the arm of my chair. "Please, Scarlet. I'm the one who trained you myself since you were a tiny thing. You really think I can't sense when my girl is in turmoil?"

I manage a watery laugh at that, comforted as always by her no-nonsense manner.

"So is there any way out of this fresh hell without having to marry Greystone?" I ask, unable to disguise the desperate longing in my voice. "Some angle you've got worked behind the scenes?"

She considers me shrewdly for a moment before shrugging. "You know I can't divulge everything I've got cooking, girl. Not until it's go time."

I huff out an exasperated sigh - of course she's playing a longer game here, as always. "Will your 'cooking' at least let me hang onto Father's legacy without being leashed to that lech?"

Fairy Godmother's expression turns deadly serious. "There's only one surefire way out, Scarlet," she states, locking eyes with me. "You need to win."

***

I need to win. That sounds so simple and somehow like a guarantee when I am in Fairy Godmother's presence, but as I walk back to the dorms that hopeful delusion dissipates and reality sets in. I'm still competing with many of the best of the best. Not to mention Rose who was also trained by Fairy Godmother. I can hold my own, but I also feel shackled by the parts of me I can't reveal in the trials so as to not give away too much of myself.

Lost in my meandering thoughts, the muted crunch of gravel pulls my focus outward with a start. A sleek black carriage rolls to a halt beside me on the deserted path, its elaborately wrought door unlatching to reveal a dimly lit interior. My heart leaps into my throat, any number of sinister scenarios flitting through my mind before an unmistakable voice drifts out on a satiny baritone.

"A bit late to be wandering the grounds unescorted, my lady," comes King Remme's rich tones, laced with a thread of dark amusement. "One might be tempted to enact a few...creative forms of recompense for such brazen defiance of propriety."

I almost laugh. My lady? No one has ever called me that. Also, is he flirting? The curtains part further, revealing the king himself lounging amidst the plush seat cushions. He cocks one dark brow in an imperious arch, wine-hued lips quirking in a devastating smirk.

"Need I remind you this kingdom strictly prohibits banditry and assaults on nobility?" I manage to retort through my breathless stupor. "Unless you are confessing a penchant for disregarding your own laws?"

A rich chuckle spills from his lips, the sound caressing me with indecent intimacy. "For a woman of your spirit and fire? I may be sorely tempted to make an exception," he purrs, crimson eyes glinting with wicked promise in the dim carriage light. "But tonight I come in peace - merely offering an escort to ensure your safe return before the castle's more...delicate inhabitants take to the halls."

My mouth curves before I can temper the response. "And just why should I trust the word of an admitted criminal?" I rejoin lightly, the thrill of our playful repartee dancing through my veins. "You could be luring me into some nefarious scheme under the guise of nobility."

"Perish the thought," King Remme gasps in feigned horror, pressing one hand dramatically to his chest. Then his expression sobers infinitesimally, that intense, brooding edge seeping back into his gaze. "Though I would sorely grieve any circumstance that robbed me of your intoxicating presence before I had a chance to...appreciate it more fully."

Heat blazes across my cheeks at the blatant implication, my breath catching in my throat. I can only gape at him, mind whirling at the dizzying path our flirtation has taken. After what feels an eternity suspended in that smoldering look, he quirks one brow in wordless invitation, lips curving in a slow, sensual smile.

Is it really sensual or am I just reading into this? Why exactly am I responding like this to him? We've only had one intimate moment before this. Most of our interactions he didn't even know it was me.

With a shaky inhale, I step into the carriage, conscious of King Remme's heated regard tracking my every movement. As the plush cushions dip under my weight, our eyes meet and hold in another soul-searing look - a world of unspoken promises and illicit, delicious temptation.

The carriage lurches forward with a subtle creak before Remme finally breaks the weighted silence. "So tell me, Lady Scarlet - what deep philosophical musing occupies your mind on this fine spring eve?" he rumbles in that rich timbre. "Family woes? Court intrigues? Or perhaps...more intimate considerations?"

His gaze drops briefly to my mouth before flicking back up, weighted with unmistakable hunger.Does he know? Why would he be looking at my lips if he didn't? He doesn't appear to be drunk. Is he putting on an act to merely probe?

"I...find my thoughts lately turn to the subjects of choice and consequence," I manage at last, inwardly cursing the tremor in my voice. "The ever-tightening bonds of expectation, and the escalating price we pay for resisting them."

His expression turns contemplative. "You speak of rebellion against convention - casting off the shackles we so obediently adorn," he muses, something like approval tingeing his tone. "No small risk for one of your standing, Lady Marheart."

For someone of my standing? He he really just say that?

I hold his weighted stare, a reckless frankness taking hold. "One I've already paid steep coin for on more than one occasion, I fear," I counter. "And yet the allure of breaking those restraints only grows more intoxicating with each passing day."

Why am I having fun with this? I shouldn't be. I need to stay far away so he doesn't discover who I am. But yet, my gaze lingers on King Remme's lips, memories of our searing kiss at the masquerade ball flooding back vividly.

When our mouths finally clashed in that electrifying fusion, the sovereign's firm yet achingly tender kisses coaxed exquisite ecstasy from my very core. This is all feeling very familiar and I don't hate it. For a moment I allow myself to imagine what could be between me and the king if things were different.

A sly, satisfied smirk curves my lips at the memory of how we taunted each other until we kissed. The moment would have been perfect if I hadn't messed up stealing the crown.

The king regards me with intensity. Awareness thrums between us, charged and potent, before he speaks again in a low rasp.

"Does the mere notion not set your soul ablaze, my lady? Of escaping the restraints and giving in to whatever you heart desires?" Remme rumbles, those molten eyes glittering with unspoken invitation and wicked promise. A promise I find myself wishing he could fulfill. I know that I shouldn't, but I do.

His low rasp strokes me in a way I am almost ashamed to admit to.

"More than you know, Your Grace," I breathe boldly, holding his heated gaze in playful defiance.

Remme's eyes bore into mine, his expression intense. "The idea thrills me," he says finally, his voice a low rumble. "To willingly give up control, submit to someone I choose out of my own free will. Someone whose wildness and fire stirs a part of me I've kept locked away."

He pauses, holding my gaze. "It would be freeing to let loose that side of myself with someone whose spirit resonates with my own. To open up and quench this thirst I've felt for real, raw connection for so long now."

The open vulnerability and magnetism of his words send a shiver down my spine. His eyes smolder like embers, daring me to make the next move. The air between us feels electric, weighted with possibility.

My heart thunders in my ears.. I can barely draw breath. That part of me that desperately wants to be seen and loved and cherished above all others is soaking this up.

Then, before I can find coherent response, the carriage rolls to a shuddering halt outside what I recognize as the dorms on the castle grounds. In an instant, that heated, tenuous connection between us severs like a bowstring snapped taut. I straighten automatically, wrestling back the impenetrable mask of propriety even as that untamed creature within me howls and claws in visceral protest.

I clear my throat, trying to appear unfazed despite the charged energy crackling between us. "Thank you for the ride, Your Majesty. But perhaps a chaperone would be wise in the future." My voice comes out a bit shaky.

One of Remme's dark eyebrows quirks up, his lips curving in that damnably attractive smirk. "The future, you say?" His voice drops lower, laced with temptation.

His bold words make desire flare hotly through me, leaving me momentarily paralyzed under the searing intensity of his gaze.

Seeing my flustered reaction, Remme moves closer, surrounding me in his earthy, masculine scent until I'm practically dizzy with want.

"Until next time, my lady," he murmurs, his voice a rough caress as he reaches to my side.

Why do I suddenly want him to touch me?

The door swings open before I can attempt coherent reply, and I find myself deposited in a daze, the carriage already drawing away at a brisk clip. Did he open it?

Reality crashes in in an unwelcome wave. I was just flirting with the king. He was flirting with me. Right? It's dangerous to get too close to him. On the other hand, I could use this to my benefit. Get close enough to possibly find another opportunity to steal the crown.

A last glance at the carriage before it turns a corner and disappears entirely from view twists my insides into a knot. Maybe the king could be another way out. Maybe letting myself open up to him wouldn't be so bad. If I played my cards right, he could be another way to escape my engagement. No one would refuse the king, right?

POINTS

SCARLET

The breakfast hall is a flurry of activity as I enter, the ornate double doors swinging open to reveal an array of aromas wafting from the long tables laden with food. My gaze is immediately drawn to the new large board dominating one wall, its surface covered in neatly written lines detailing donations and gifts received for each contestant.

I scan the names quickly until my eyes land on mine - Scarlet Marheart. A respectable sum. I quickly skim over the rest of the names and find Rose. Our totals are similar, but hers are from a spread over more donors. I'm sure many from admirers she's gained while on the job.

Looking over my own list of donors my fiance's name glares back at me, the amount listed next to it like a slap in the face. Heat rushes to my cheeks as anger surges through me. How dare he! I won't accept it. I want nothing to do with him and won't have his money taint my name.

I whirl around, scanning the crowd until I spot one of the event coordinators. "Excuse me!" I call out, waving to catch her attention. The woman turns, a polite smile on her face as she approaches.

"Lady Marheart, how may I assist you?"

"This donation..." I gesture at the board, struggling to keep my tone even. "From Lord Greystone. Is there any way I can refuse it or have it redistributed?"

Her brow furrows slightly. "I'm afraid not. Once a donation has been made, it is final and cannot be returned or transferred."

"But surely there must be some exception?" I protest, my voice rising slightly.

The woman shakes her head apologetically. "I'm sorry, but those are the rules. No exceptions."

I open my mouth to argue further, but a familiar voice cuts through the din.

"There you are, darling."

Lord Greystone strides toward me, that insufferable smirk playing on his lips. Grabbing my hand he drags me behind him to an empty hallways nearby. He holds up a folded newspaper and steps towards me. "You'll never guess what the headline says about us."

I straighten my shoulders, bracing myself as he draws near. Too near, his body crowding into my space in that way he knows I can't refuse. The familiar woodsy scent of his cologne surrounds me as he leans in, his breath warm against my ear.

"Problem, love?" he murmurs, low enough for only me to hear.

I turn my head, our faces inches apart as I fix him with a hard stare. "I won't marry you. I am owned by no one."

One dark brow arches. "I'm your fiancé. Of course you will marry me and do exactly as I say. Or have you forgotten?" His hand slides possessively around my waist, pulling me flush against him.

I try to squirm away, but he's immovable, trapping me against the hard planes of his body. "I will take care of my families own debts," I hiss. "You have enough of your own."

Anger flashes in his eyes, but he smothers it quickly, the corner of his mouth quirking up. "Such concern for me and my finances." His fingers tighten on my hip in subtle warning. "How touching. Afterall, soon they will be yours as well."

Before I can retort, he produces an embossed envelope from his jacket pocket and presses it into my hand. "We're expected at Lord Everton's fete this evening. As my fiancée, your attendance is mandatory." His tone brooks no argument. "I'll see you there, dressed and ready at seven sharp."

With that, he releases me and strides away, leaving me flushed and seething in his wake. My fingers curl tightly around the invitation, crumpling it as I fight the urge to stamp my foot like a petulant child.

The crumpled invitation feels like a lead weight in my hand as I stare at his retreating back. Every fiber of my being screams to throw it at the back of his arrogant head and reject him outright. But a harsh reality settles over me - I haven't won the tournament yet. As much as King Remme's attentions bolstered my confidence, his flirtatious glances don't guarantee me a way out of this wretched situation. For now, playing the dutiful, happy couple is my only viable option, and the thought makes my stomach churn.

Gritting my teeth, I tuck the invitation away, forcing a neutral expression as I make my way back to the crowded hall. Rose smirks at me from across the room, her gaze calculating as if she can sense the inner turmoil roiling beneath my calm facade. I'll not give her the satisfaction of seeing me crack.

Tonight, I'll don the costume of the perfect nobleman's fiancée, all smiles and graciousness on the surface. But beneath, the defiant embers continue to burn bright. This battle isn't over, not by a long shot. I am no fragile butterfly to be mounted and displayed, but a phoenix rising from the ashes of my circumstances.

One way or another, I'll find my freedom from my fiance's grasp. Even if I have to burn his gilded cage to the ground to do it.

***

The rhythmic clop of horses' hooves on cobblestone heralds the arrival of the ornate carriage, its gleaming black lacquer reflecting the warm glow of the lanterns lining the drive. I smooth my hands over the sumptuous emerald silk of my gown, taking a deep, steadying breath. Tonight's performance begins now.

As the carriage rolls to a stop, the footman swings down and hurries to open the door, offering a white-gloved hand to assist me. I place my fingers lightly on his and step out, the skirts of my dress pooling around my feet. Before me looms the imposing façade of Lord Everton's estate, its grand façade softened by the meticulously tended gardens and artfully placed lantern light.

My gaze is immediately drawn to the figure waiting at the entrance – Lord Greystone, already swaying slightly on his feet, a crystal tumbler in hand. His free arm sweeps out in a grand, if somewhat unsteady, gesture. "My darling Scarlet! You're positively radiant this evening."

I paste on a serene smile, dipping into a shallow curtsy. "You flatter me, my lord."

He snakes an arm around my waist, pulling me flush against him as he leans in, his breath hot and sour with spirits against my cheek. "Let's keep the niceties between us, pet. You know how I detest..." he wavers, catching himself, " detest the need for propriety in our...private dealings."

A shiver runs through me, his words sending a clear message – he expects my full compliance tonight, no matter how boorish or entitled his behavior. Refusal is not an option, not with the tournament and my family's future at stake.

"Of course, darling," I murmur, allowing him to steer me through the arched entranceway.

We're immediately submerged in a sea of finery – brocaded gowns that shimmer with every movement, gentlemen in expertly tailored suits, the air thick with the scents of polish, perfume, and barely-concealed ambition. Nobles and wealthy merchants alike cluster in throngs, speaking in bright, brittle tones that belie the calculating pursuit of status beneath every polished word.

"Lady Marheart!" An older matron in dove gray sweeps toward me, a sickly sweet smile plastered across her lined face. "What a pleasure to see you attending Lord Everton's little...soirée." She casts a pointed look at my fiance, who merely offers a mock salute with his glass.

I summon up my most gracious smile. "The pleasure is all mine, Lady Rutherford. You are too kind."

Her gaze drops in an unmistakable perusal of my gown. "My, that is a striking color on you. Not quite proper for a lady of refinement, but...bold. Quite fitting, given your penchant for theatrics in the tournament so far."

The backhanded compliment stings, but I keep my tone light and airy. "You're too generous. I simply aim to make the most of the opportunities I've been given."

Lady Rutherford releases a tinkling laugh. "Of course, dear girl. Do give us a good show, won't you? My Edgar has quite a stake riding on your continued success. We've read wonderful things about your performance in the first two trials. Made quite the impression. We look forward to seeing you personally in action." She leans in conspiratorially. "And if you should happen to require any...additional support, you need only ask."

Of course. They all have bets placed, viewing this entire spectacle through the lens of their own greed. Gritting my teeth in a polite rictus, I incline my head. "You are most generous, my lady. I shall endeavor not to disappoint."

As she sweeps away in a waft of cloyingly sweet perfume, I feel Lord Greystone's arm tighten around my waist, his fingers digging into the pliant silk. "Well handled, pet," he purrs against my ear. "But don't make too many missteps. We've appearances to maintain."

I open my mouth to retort, but a fresh wave of well-wishers descends, eager to ingratiate themselves and press me for details about the upcoming trials. Plastering on my most practiced smile, I wade into their midst, holding court and sprinkling just enough vague promises of entertainment to whet their bloodthirsty interest. All the while, I keep a watchful eye on the man who will torture me this evening, his glass never remaining empty for long as he drifts from group to group, shamelessly flirtatious smiles and wandering hands following in his wake.

Between the ingratiating and the subtle digs, the weight of maintaining my composure grows heavier by the moment. I catch glimpses of furtive movement from the servants drifting through the crowd, their mannerisms and positioning too calculated to be mere chance. Members of the guild, no doubt here on an assignment. This is a high risk event to try running an operation during. What could be worth that risk?

My thoughts are broken by a hush rippling through the crowd, every head turning in unison. My gaze follows and lands on the unmistakable figure of King Remme descending the grand staircase, his golden crown glinting in the candlelight.

The king moves amongst his subjects with regal poise, offering greetings and small smiles, though he keeps a careful distance, never quite making physical contact. His usual bodyguard close behind, whispering in the king's ear from time to time. I notice his hands remain firmly at his sides, the golden gauntlets of his armor precluding any chance of an accidental touch. When a server offers him a crystal flute of chilled wine, he demurs with a polite shake of his head.

Before I can ponder his peculiar behavior further, a booming voice cuts across the din. "Lady Marheart! A moment of your time, if you please?"

I turn to find Lord Percival Avery bearing down on me, his ample girth straining against the seams of his burgundy velvet doublet. His florid face shines with an excited gleam as he leans far too close for propriety.

"I simply must hear your thoughts on the upcoming trial. The people are positively buzzing over the possibilities!" He lets out a hearty guffaw, bits of spittle flying. "Gave quite the performance in that last bout, you did. Had half the noblewomen in tears at the drama of it all!"

Smothering an inward cringe, I paste on my most polished smile. "You are too kind, my lord. I can only hope to continue providing ample entertainment as the tournament progresses."

As I feed him artfully vague responses about the challenges ahead, my gaze drifts over the crowd once more, searching for that unmistakable golden figure. But the king seems to have vanished amongst the glittering throngs of attendees. An odd sense of disappointment settles in my chest that I can't quite place.

Giving myself an inward shake, I refocus on Lord Avery's rambling monologue. One distraction at a time - first I must maintain this facade long enough to cultivate what favor I can from the attendees. Keeping my courtly mask firmly in place, I politely extricate myself from his company with a few well-practiced pleasantries.

My gaze darts around the crowded ballroom, searching for an escape route. In the far corner, I spy a set of glass-paned doors leading out onto a balcony. Making my excuses, I slip away from the stifling press of bodies and weave my way towards that beckoning promise of fresh air.

Outside, the balcony is mercifully deserted, offering a welcome respite from the cloying atmosphere within. Ornate stone railings give way to a panoramic view of the estate's immaculately landscaped gardens below, the grounds bathed in a warm orange glow from the strategically placed lanterns. A light breeze stirs the gauzy fabric draped over trellises, creating a dreamlike quality to the whole scene.

"There you are." That rich, sonorous voice seems to envelop me like a warm embrace. Turning, I find King Remme approaching with his trademark easy grace, a playful glint in his eye. "I was beginning to worry you'd run off for the evening already."

I can't help but return his teasing smile, though heat prickles at my neck. "And deny myself your charming company? I think not."

He joins me at the railing, near enough that the subtle notes of his cologne - woodsy with a hint of citrus - washes over me. Up close, I can make out the finely etched detailing of his golden armor, candlelight gilding him in an almost ethereal glow.

"You seemed quite...cozy with that Lord Greystone earlier," he remarks, feigning nonchalance even as that piercing stare clouds with something darker. "Despite your public assertions of being unattached."

Is that jealousy I hear? Part of me thrills at stoking such delicious fire in the king. But pragmatism reminds me I must tread carefully - one ill-timed disclosure could see this fragile spark snuffed before it fully ignites.

Holding his weighted gaze, I offer an enigmatic smile. "My situation is...complicated, Your Majesty. That man represents an obligation I find increasingly difficult to accept, despite what circumstances may imply."

The king considers me a long moment, that uncanny perception of his no doubt parsing the deeper truth in my veiled admission. At last, he gives a resigned dip of his chin. "I see. Well then, Lady Scarlet, perhaps I can offer a welcome...diversion from your troubles this evening?" His voice lowers to an intimate murmur as that smoldering look returns.

Maintaining my carefully coy expression, I lean fractionally closer, holding his burning stare. "One can always make room for...diversions, Your Majesty, should the right opportunities arise."

I'm nearly knocked over as an arm plops across my shoulder. The smell of alcohol wafts over me.

"Your Majesty!" Lord Greystone's feigned joviality grates on my every nerve. "So good of you to grace us with your presence." His grip on me tightens to the point of pain.

King Remme eyes him with thinly veiled disdain. "Lord Greystone. I was merely admiring your...companion's poise, given the circumstances."

Lord Greystone's gaze sharpens, but his smile remains smugly fixed in place. "Yes, well, my Scarlet knows her duty. Don't you, pet?" His fingers dig into the tender flesh of my arm in pointed warning.

I swallow hard, holding King Remme's stare as I murmur my assent. "Of course."

The king holds my gaze a moment longer, his eyes glittering with some indecipherable emotion, before nodding once and moving on to greet the next cluster of guests.

He waits until the king's out of earshot before leaning in close, his whiskey-scented breath hot on my cheek. "Get a grip on that tongue of yours, darling, before you go making trouble for us both."

I open my mouth – to argue, to lash out, I'm not even sure – but a deafening crash slices through the music and laughter, drawing every eye. Near the back of the room, a motionless liveried footman lies crumpled amidst the shattered remnants of a priceless porcelain vase. But it's the skittering of jewels across the marble floor that causes the guests to erupt into shocked exclamations.

And there, fleeing through the debris amid a flurry of skirts and curses, is a familiar face from my dealings in the guild – Tabitha, one of our youngest and most skilled infiltrators, clearly having been caught in the act of some heist or another.

Around me, the crowd erupts into chaos, the unctuous nobility devolving into a frenzied mob of outrage and re-crimination. In the maelstrom, I catch Greystone's eye, his mounting rage simmering behind his own rapidly crack-ing façade of control.

My gaze darts back toward the escape route Tabitha took, the footman she struck down still lying motionless on the floor. Chaos swirls around me in a dizzying spiral of color and sound, but one thought alone rings clear in my mind – I have to help her, heedless of the cost.

I surge forward, buffeted by the crush of bodies, fighting through that churning sea of silk, jewels and fury toward the door. Just as I'm nearly through, a crushing grip seizes my arm, whirling me around to face my fiance's contorted mask of rage.

"And just where do you think you're going?" he snarls, spittle flecking his twisted mouth.

"I...!" I cry, struggling against his unbreakable hold. " Please, Lord Greystone, I need to check something! Make sure no one is hurt."

He lets out a bark of sardonic laughter, grip tightening until I know bruises will mottle my flesh come morning.

"You seem to have forgotten your place, pet. You're mine
, or have you conveniently forgotten that little fact again?
You do exactly as I say when I say."

Frantically, I cast about for any ally, any whisper of
sympathy from the assembled crowd, but there is only
blind panic and righteous fury leveled at the absent thief.
Tabitha is on her own, as is so often the way in our world.

He snatches my chin in his bruising grasp, forcing me
to meet his smoldering glare. "Consider this a lesson, my
sweet. You will get these silly, noble whims under control,
or so help me..." His thumb digs into the tender flesh beneath my jaw in subtle threat. "It's about time you learned
your lesson once and for all."

My breath catches in my throat, the ultimatum and his
implications both achingly clear. With a derisive sneer, he
releases me, sending me staggering back a step.

The damage is done, the die irrevocably cast. I am once
again bound, my wings clipped before I'd even tasted true
freedom. Bowing my head in defeat, I permit Lord Greystone to steer me away from the wreckage and the shouts of
the newly summoned palace guards, wisps of smoke from
the fallen lantern already staining the elegant scene with
twinges of ruin.

My defiance remains, that inner spark refusing to be extinguished despite Lord Greystone's best efforts, banked now, but glowing hot. For tonight, I retreat.

But this battle is far from over.

Touch Her Again and Die

Remme

The crash of shattering porcelain reverberates through the grand ballroom, drawing my attention as a hush falls over the assembled guests. Near the back, a young woman scrambles to her feet amidst the debris, jewels spilling from her skirts in a telltale spray. A thief from the guild, no doubt - bold enough to attempt such a brazen heist here, tonight.

As she flees, weaving through the throngs of outraged nobility, I catch the eye of my bodyguard Sophia. A silent look is all it takes; she gives a sharp nod and moves to pursue the would-be criminal, flanked by two of my palace guards. They'll see her captured and brought to the dungeons for interrogation.

I scan the crowd, searching for a familiar curtain of golden locks amidst the milling guests. But Scarlet seems to have already departed in the wake of the disturbance, whisking herself away before I could seek her out. Disappointment settles in my chest, an emotion as novel as it is unwelcome. I had hoped to...what? Continue our earlier banter? Unravel more of the mystery she keeps so craftily veiled?

With a frustrated huff, I turn on my heel, striding for the grand entrance. Let the nobility sort out their disarray; I've more pressing matters demanding my attention. But I've barely made it through the ornate double doors when a woman's scream slices through the clamor, raw and laced with panic.

My steps falter as every ingrained instinct urged me toward the sound. I change course, following the commotion out a side corridor and around a corner.

The sight that greets me has my blood boiling in righteous fury.

Scarlet huddles against the wall, back pressed to the intricately carved wainscoting as she fends off the looming threat of a man twice her size, Lord Greystone. His meaty fists are clenched at his sides as he leans over her, features twisted into an ugly mask of rage.

"You'll get those high-minded notions under control," he snarls, flecks of spittle flying from his twisted mouth, "or so help me, I'll beat the obstinance out of you once and for all!"

With a harsh shove, he sends Scarlet crashing back against the wall, her head connecting with the wood paneling in a sickening thump. She crumples towards the floor, only to be hauled back up by her hair, a low moan of pain escaping her lips.

It's that broken, helpless sound that detonates every last shred of restraint within me.

"Ler her go," I growl, the command dripping with lethal promise as I stalk forward. "Now."

The man freezes, his beady eyes going wide with shock and dawning horror as he finally registers my presence. Scarlet sags in his grip, dazed and shaking, as he whips around to face me fully.

"Y-Your Majesty!" he sputters, hastily releasing his brutal hold and attempting to straighten to a properly obsequious stance. "F-Forgive me, I meant no disrespect. I was merely...instructing my betrothed on the boundaries of her position."

He juts his chin towards Scarlet, still hunched against the wall in obvious pain. "You understand how these...sp irited birds require the occasional firm hand, yes? A man must keep his woman in line when her fancies grow too lofty."

Loathing courses through me at his sneering, utterly unrepentant words. This ingrate dares invoke my understanding over brutalizing the very woman who has captivated my interest with her poise and courage? My fingers itch to unleash my curse upon his despicable form and rob the world of his stain.

But even as that virulent impulse blazes hot, pragmatism smothers it. I cannot afford for Scarlet to discover the truth of my curse, not when she could well be the key to breaking it. Not when she remains the sole object of my obsession.

Reining in my anger with an effort that leaves me physically shaking, I level the man with a look of pure, unvarnished disgust.

"You mistake my indulgences, sir," I bite out from between clenched teeth. "While a firm hand is occasionally required to guide the steps of the unruly, what I just witnessed was the behavior of a base coward striking out at his defenseless subordinate. It won't be tolerated, certainly not in my presence."

My gaze slides to Scarlet, now hunched against the wall with her knees drawn up in front of her. Her eyes shine with unshed tears of defiance and humiliation as she stares resolutely ahead, refusing to meet my assessing look.

Guilt lances through me at having been the unintended audience to her mistreatment and loss of dignity. More than anything, I ache to reach out and offer her comfort, to let her know her suffering was not unseen nor unjustified.

But I cannot. A single graze of my skin against hers and she'd be forever lost to me, transmuted into an exquisite golden statue - beautiful yet unfeeling, immutable. As devastating as her plight is to witness, I cannot allow my selfish impulses to put her in jeopardy. Not until I find a way to finally break this godforsaken curse. Not until I find the thief.

Shoving down the maelstrom of emotions churning within, I round back on the blustering cretin who put her in such a state.

"Take your leave, sir," I growl, "before I summon the guards and have you forcibly removed in a manner befitting your appalling conduct."

For an endless, heated moment, his beady eyes lock with mine in a silent battle of wills. Every fiber of my being screams for action, to unleash the rage simmering low in my belly at his unforgivable offense.

At last, he gives a sullen little bow, insolence etched in every line of his coward's form. "As you command, Your Majesty." He sneers the title like a slur before slinking away down the corridor, leaving us mercifully alone.

Once he's vanished around the corner, I risk a glance back towards Scarlet. She hasn't moved from her crumpled position against the wall, her face a frozen mask of mortified fury. A blossom of mottled bruising already darkens the delicate skin of her cheekbone, stark against her pale complexion.

The urge to go to her side, to offer whatever paltry comfort I can despite my limitations, gnaws at me with relentless insistence. But I cannot - won't.

"That man had no right to lay his hands upon you in such a way," I murmur, keeping a careful distance as I study her shrouded form. "May I take you back to your dorms? If you need to see a royal physician I can also call one to your room as soon as we get back."

For a long moment, she remains resolutely still and silent, the strap of her gown slipping down one freckled shoulder in silent testament to the struggle she so recently endured. At last, a small sigh escapes her, and she straightens incrementally, still not meeting my concerned stare.

"I appreciate your... intervention, Your Majesty," she says, her voice hoarse yet measured despite her visible disquiet. "But I'm afraid my situation is not so easily extricated."

She fiddles with the rumpled fabric of her skirts, unwittingly drawing my gaze to the trellis of vivid blossoms twining her bare arms. Small scratches score the tender skin, no doubt from fending off her assailant's advances. My hands curl into helpless fists at my sides.

"That reprehensible excuse for a man..." I have to pause, forcing down the thunderous rage that clouds my vision at the mere thought of him. "He claims to be your betrothed. Is this what you want your life to be like?"

Her jaw works silently as she finally raises her haunted gaze to meet mine head-on. What I see burning in those turbulent blue-green depths lances straight through all my defenses - fear and resignation warring with naked longing. Longing for what, I cannot say.

"No," she says at last in a voice scarcely above a whisper. "It is not."

Those two words, spoken in such a soul-weary tone, reverberate through me like physical blows, each more devastating than the last. She does not want this promised union, that much is unmistakable. And whatever circumstance binds her to enduring such mistreatment clearly weighs heavily upon her spirit.

Instinctively, I take a half-step towards her, palms upturned in a silent entreaty for understanding. For trust. "If you would permit it, I can help you. You need not reside any longer under...his dominion."

Her mouth twists in a rueful, one-sided quirk of her lips. "You are gracious beyond measure to offer such haven, Your Majesty. But freedom is a luxury I cannot yet afford. My...situation remains unchanged, for the present."

The bitterness in her tone slices me to the core. To be bound to such hateful circumstances against one's will...

My jaw clenches hard enough to crack bone as I strive to project an aura of steady confidence, despite the maelstrom of useless rage swirling within. What is going on that she thinks this poor excuse of a human could fix whatever has her bound to this man that her king could not?

"Please let me take you back to your dorm, at the very least," I attempt a reassuring tone, hoping against hope that she'll take this final offered kindness. "It would set my mind at ease to ensure you arrive without any further...u npleasantries this night."

For an interminable stretch, she holds my gaze, weighing my words and the sincerity behind them. At last, giving the barest incline of her chin, she rises to her feet on legs that only tremble a little.

"Very well," she acquiesces in that same threadbare tone. "I would be...grateful for the escort, Your Majesty."

Suppressing my sigh of relief, I turn and begin retracing my path towards the entrance and the awaiting carriages beyond. From the corner of my eye, I track Scarlet's progress as she follows a respectful pace behind, back straight despite the ordeal she's clearly just endured.

My heart aches with useless outrage at the injustice of her circumstance. To be so strong and proud, yet still bound to the whims and cruelties of lesser men. Were I not so intimately acquainted with the crushing weight of forces beyond one's control, I might not recognize that subtle, telltale despondence lurking behind her eyes.

Sophia and the palace guards remain conspicuously absent from the entrance hall as we make our way through the vaulted space. No doubt they've already escorted the captured thief to the palace dungeons as I instructed.

At last, we step through the looming oak doors and out into the temperate spring night, the light illuminating Scarlet's striking presence in crisp detail. The dark blossom of bruising stands out in vivid relief against her fair complexion, the line of her jaw set in a defiant tilt.

A sleek, black town carriage awaits with its doors flung open in readiness, the driver eyeing our progress with polite disinterest. I turn back to Scarlet, gesturing for her to precede me up the carriage steps. For a fleeting instant, our gazes lock, a strange frisson seeming to shiver through the air between us.

"I feel I must reiterate my disgust over the treatment to which you were so unjustly subjected, Lady Scarlet," I murmur, holding her eyes with a weighted look. "No woman should suffer such degradation at the hands of her sworn protector. You have my deepest apologies that my presence brought you into the path of such indignity."

Her teeth sink into her full lower lip, worrying the tender flesh as she ponders my statement. At last, she seems to reach some internal decision, shoulders squaring beneath the thin straps of her gown.

"With respect, Your Majesty...you should reserve that censure for the true offender," she states, her tone hardening to adamant steel. "I am no shrinking blossom, easily cowed or abused. What you witnessed was but a temporary setback towards a cause I still endeavor to see realized."

That fierce, blazing look in her eyes sears straight into my soul, igniting answering embers of determination and...something far more primal that I dare not give name to. Here, bathed in moonlight and the faint glow of the carriage lamps, she appears well and truly formidable rather than fragile - a being of incandescent strength and conviction despite her evident trials.

Perhaps it's that undeniable force of presence that proves my undoing in that singular instant. Or maybe it's simply been far too long since I've glimpsed such vibrant, unapologetic intensity from one of my own subjects. But whatever the impetus, the words slip free before I can grab hold of my treacherous impulses.

"You are...captivating, my lady." The hushed utterance seems to reverberate through the stillness like shattering crystal. My jaw goes rigid, bracing for the inevitable censure over such an unforgivable breach of propriety. Particularly after having just been the audience to her mistreatment at the hands of another.

But Scarlet meets my gaze head-on, her expression revealing not outrage, but somber acceptance of the raw truth laid bare between us. "I somehow doubt Your Majesty is given to such...untoward flattery without underlying motive," she murmurs, watching me carefully through her lashes.

Her words slice through my conscience with unerring precision, every instinct screaming to cover my careless indiscretion with the usual dismissive prevarications. To preserve the pristine distance I've cultivated between myself and my subjects for fear of the horrors my accursed touch could inflict.

And yet, something in her guileless stare seems to strip away even those most ingrained defenses, leaving me raw and mercilessly, recklessly honest.

"You aren't wrong," I admit in a rough tone, the compunction to lay my soul bare feeling very much like wrenching open a barely-healed wound. "I have not been afforded the luxury of...indulgence without intent in longer than I care to admit."

Her lips part around an indrawn breath, whether in surprise or outrage I cannot say. Pressing my advantage while I still can, I close the remaining distance between us in two long strides, utterly heedless of the impropriety of such an overt advance.

I lean in close and speak in a low, intimate tone while looking into her eyes. "I'm not gonna lie to you and say sweet nothings, Scarlet. You've...captivated me in a way I didn't expect. I can't say if you meant to or not. But just know, I won't forget the fire I saw in you tonight anytime soon."

Her eyes widen fractionally at my emboldened admission. For a handful of suspended heartbeats, the night seems to still around us, the scented air crackling with some indescribable, perilous energy I have not felt in...longer than I dare recall.

At last, her tongue darts out to wet her lips in a gesture of unconscious invitation that sends a molten shock of yearning lancing through my entranced senses.

"Be careful with such words, Your Majesty," she cautions in a low, throaty tone rife with thinly veiled warning. "One would not wish for such indulgences to be...misinterpreted on false premises."

The inference hangs unvoiced between us, searing and unmistakable - a portent of entanglements yet unknown that could prove disastrous if mishandled.

Yet I cannot heed that voice of carefully cultivated restraint urging me back from this precipice. Some reckless part of me longs to career over the edge into those perilous depths, drawn by the promise of true connection after so many years of deprivation.

"I assure you my regard is not lightly bestowed," I murmur, spearing her with an intent look that leaves no room for misapprehension. "Nor shall its implications escape me, however unanticipated they may have been. But fate does love a bit of...inadvertent meddling to set events askew from time to time, does it not?"

A daring smirk curves my lips as I drink in the picture she makes, bruised yet unbowed despite her circumstance. Beneath the gauzy layers of her gown, the flickering lamplight of the carriage sculpts every lush curve and dip of her form, fanning embers of desire I'd thought long since banked.

Scarlet's gaze lands on my face. I can feel her calculating. But no words escape her lips. The carriage jostles as it runs over a loose cobblestone and she winces. It takes everything in me to not reach out and help her. Her pained eyes meet mine for a moment, and then turn away. I wish the gods were kind. I both wish and desperately hope that she is the thief who attempted to steal the crown. But if that were true, it could be both of our condemnation.

THE PRISONER

REMME

It's nearing midnight by the time I've settled arrangements for a discreet physician to attend Scarlet and ensure she's not too gravely injured. Despite her outward bravado earlier, that disturbing encounter left little doubt as to the severity of the mistreatment she endures. My insides twist with a potent mixture of residual fury and impotent concern.

She could have ended that engagement to the pathetic excuse for a man - should have, by all propriety. Yet her evasive responses imply she dare not, for reasons I cannot yet fathom. But I'm fast developing an interest in unraveling whatever unsavory obligations tether her to such a man. If nothing else, her own family should be helping her with this situation. An interest which, if I'm being painfully honest with myself, extends well beyond the bounds of mere curiosity or subjects' welfare.

I shake off my thoughts about Scarlet and head towards the dungeons. Daydreaming won't help me figure out if this thief is part of that secret guild. Plus, the next trial is only a couple nights away. Giving Scarlet a break to recover could help her in the challenges ahead.

The heavy iron doors groan as the guards push them open, leading me into the dank prison tunnels underneath the palace. Flickering torchlight casts creepy shadows along the damp stone walls, like bony fingers reaching out. An eerie feeling hangs in the air down here - you can sense all the tormented souls who suffered in these halls over the years

At the far end, angry shouts and the meaty impacts of fist on flesh echo from behind the thick oaken door leading to the interrogation chamber. I feel a muscle tick in my jaw as the unmistakable sounds of brutality filter through, setting my senses on edge. A dungeon guard meets me on the other side, fist raised for another blow as he looms over the slumped figure strapped to the rack.

"A moment, Karrack," I interject before he can deliver the impending strike.

My steely tone seems to penetrate the man's bestial haze; he blinks and, realizing my presence, hastily backs away from the unconscious prisoner with a curt nod.

"M'lord King," he rumbles out in brusque greeting. "My men and I have been...questioning the prisoner, as you instructed. Just havin' a bit o' trouble getting her to divulge her tongue, is all."

As he steps aside, I get my first clear look at his detainee - the would-be thief from Everton's ill-fated revel. Young, painfully so, her slight form looking dwarfed and fragile amidst the cruel confines of the rack. Tattered remnants of her silk gown cling to her battered skin, ribbons of crimson streaking her thighs and abdomen. One eye is already swollen grotesquely shut, her split lip caked with drying blood.

Revulsion curls in the pit of my belly at the excessive display of brutality. This is no hardened criminal or assassin...just a starry-eyed girl who likely wanted to earn a few coins for an idle heist. One poorly considered but hardly deserving of such wanton sadism.

"What of her accomplices? Any details she may have revealed before..." My gaze cuts to the blood-flecked whip and other unspeakable instruments laid out on the side table, "...before more forceful measures were required?"

Karrack's beefy shoulders rise and fall in an indelicate shrug. "Aye, she did let slip a name when we started getting...persuasive." A nasty leer twists his features. "Mind you, the little wench tried to bite off her tongue after spouting it, the foolish quim. Had to give her a few lashes to keep her from doing herself further harm."

Her rasped, hitching breaths seem to echo louder in the dank space as I regard the trembling girl. A sense of implacable dread creeps over me, my instincts screaming out a warning of things far more foreboding than simple thievery afoot.

"Well?" I snap, impatience transmuting to a slow ember of anger. "Out with this precious name you extracted, Karrack, and quickly!"

The guard captain sneers, crossing his thick arms over his chest as he issues me an insufferably smug look. "Aye, m'lord. 'Course you'll be wanting to know that."

He leans back and takes an ostentatious breath. "The wee thing hollered out somethin' in a language I didn't recognize. Sounded a bit like...'Smarshtrooz Garrakoole en...'"

The guard trails off with a baffled look as he completely mangles the string of fluid syllables into a butchered tongue-twister. He clears his throat and tries again, the sounds becoming even more fractured.

"No, wait - 'Scloshturian Garghoudian...'"

A mounting sense of disquiet prickles along my nape as the captain continues vainly trying to reproduce what was likely the name of the shadowy thief collective. A different unintelligible stream of indecipherable syllables trips from his thick tongue each time, compounding the dread pooling in the pit of my stomach.

It couldn't be. But it would make sense. Could it be that the reason the name of this guild has remained obscured all these years is that some form of enchantment guards its identity, twisting the tongues of those who dare utter it aloud into incomprehensible jumbles?

Even under the most brutal torture, it seems this girl cannot give up its true name. A fresh gout of rage surges through me at that realization, quickly metamorphosing into bitter resignation. Of course nefarious sorcery is at play - why would it not be?

"Enough." I growl out the command, holding up a peremptory hand. Karrack grinds his teeth together but obeys, falling blessedly silent.

As I turn away from the interrogation rack, my eye catches on an odd pattern of markings spread across the reddened expanse of the prisoner's back, peeking through the scandalously rent remains of her dress. Leaning closer, I let out an involuntary hiss of dismay.

A gnarled emblem mars the unblemished flesh there, the shape of a snake biting its own tail, creating a stylized letter 'g' that appears to slither and shift eerily beneath the flickering torchlight. But there's something off about the design - flecks of gold seem to shimmer within the ink, almost like they're calling out to my cursed touch. Blots of crimson seep from where its raised tendrils bisect the raw meat of her savaged skin, lending the brand an essence of sheer malignancy.

A chill runs down my spine as I realize this is no ordinary tattoo. There's magic worked into those inky coils, I can feel it trying to tug at the power within me. This girl has been bound by some kind of spell or ritual, marked as a vessel to contain secrets.

No wonder she couldn't just blurt out the guild's name - that sigil has enchanted her very essence to stay silent, no matter how much pain they inflict. Brutality won't make her talk when wicked magic is sealing her lips.

I step back from the tortured prisoner, fighting to keep my expression neutral despite the unease prickling over me. This is more than just a gaggle of street thieves - there are powerful, dark forces at play here that I've been naive to overlook.

"That will be enough for tonight, Captain," I grit out, each word dropping like lead ingot onto the filthy stone floor. "Have the prisoner unbound and placed into one of the isolation cells. Given the...unique protections she's been granted," my lip twists in distaste at having to refer-ence the obscene branding, "more conventional interroga-tion tactics will prove useless against her. For now, she can remain confined while we determine alternate methods of extracting information."

Karrack fixes me with a look of sullen disbelief, but I slice him with a chilling stare before he can voice any objections. Reluctantly, he signals for two burly guards to retrieve the girl's unconscious, blood-streaked form from the rack. My stomach turns as the crude manacles bite into her already raw wrists, but I force myself to remain impassive.

Turning on my heel, I sweep from the chamber and back down the dank hallway, pausing only long enough to toss a curt order over my shoulder.

"See that she receives basic care for her injuries and is fed before being transferred to the cell. I'll not have the girl expiring needlessly before we determine her relevance."

Unease prickles along my nape as the guards murmur acknowledgement in my wake. There is a far more malignant force at work here than simple thievery or material greed - a truth I have willfully turned a blind eye to for far too long.

Tonight's grim discoveries in the dungeon have shaken me out of my naive delusions. I can no longer afford to turn a blind eye to the dark forces controlling this twisted thieves' guild. Whether I want to face it or not, I have to confront their malicious influences head-on before they smother what little light remains in my kingdom.

Squaring my shoulders, I stride back towards the palace and my private study. In the solitude of those secure walls, I can finally dive into the reports and records detailing suspected guild crimes over the past years. Analyzing the patterns may reveal their true agenda and who could be orchestrating it all from the shadows. Only then can I gather the knowledge to dismantle this collective piece by piece

After all, to combat the dark, one must first forge themself a candle to light the way.

CHAOTIC TAROT
SCARLET

The morning light filters through the narrow window, casting a soft glow over the sparse furnishings of my shared dorm. I sit on the edge of my cot, running a brush through my tangled tangled hair as I mentally prepare for the day ahead. It's always an entire process detangling my hair after a formal event. The complicated updos do a number on my hair and Lord Greystone only made it worse.

A sharp intake of breath draws my attention to Rose. She's staring at me, eyes wide and lips pressed into a thin line. It takes me a moment to realize she's fixated on the mottled bruises peeking out from under my tunic sleeves.

"What happened?" she demands, crossing the room in two long strides to grasp my arm.

I flinch involuntarily at her touch on the tender flesh. "It's nothing."

Rose scoffs, pushing up the fabric to better survey the damage. Purplish splotches mottle my skin in an unsightly map of pain. "This doesn't look like nothing."

Shame burns my cheeks. The last thing I want is her pity or concern over something so trivial compared to the stakes we face. "I had a run-in at the event last night," I mutter, tugging my arm free. "But it wasn't a fight that did this."

The words hang heavy between us as Rose's expression darkens with realization. "Greystone," she spits out, venom coating the name.

I avert my gaze, unable to meet the simmering fury in her eyes.

"We're going to make him pay for this," Rose vows, fists clenched at her sides. "At the first opportunity, I'll—"

"No." I cut her off, shaking my head firmly. As much as justice calls to that primal part of me screaming for retribution, I can't allow her to jeopardize everything we've worked towards here. Not when there are larger stakes at play than just my own suffering. "That's not why we're here."

Rose opens her mouth to protest, but I forge ahead before she can argue. "Besides, we have bigger concerns right now." I suck in a steadying breath. "I received word that Tabitha was captured last night during that charity event debacle."

The anger drains from Rose's face, replaced by a stricken expression. "Tabitha? But she's just a kid..."

"She stopped being a kid the day she joined the guild," I remind her grimly. We were no older when we pulled our first jobs, though the memories still make my stomach churn. "But you're right - she's too young and inexperienced for something of this magnitude. If she's been taken into King Remme's dungeons..."

Rose shakes her head, mouth setting into a grim line. "Then she may already be as good as dead. Those dungeons are infamous. People go in and never come out."

A lump forms in my throat at the thought of what Tabitha might be enduring in those dank cells, scared and alone. The kid has spunk, but she's hardly equipped to handle the dungeon's rumored brutality. We can't leave her to such a grisly fate.

"Then we have to get her out. Quickly, before it's too late." My hands curl into white-knuckled fists, nails digging into my palms.

Rose nods, some of the fiery determination rekindling in her eyes. "You're right. It's too risky for her to be here. But breaking into those dungeons?" She lets out a low whistle. "It won't be easy."

"Since when is anything we do ever easy?" I shoot her a wry look, trying to inject some levity into the situation.

A ghost of a smile quirks the corner of her lips before the somber mask slides back into place. "Fair point. But where do we even start?"

I rise to my feet, crossing to the rickety table to retrieve my staff - the item I found in the last trial. My fingers trace the intricate carvings, and a flood of possibilities blooms in my mind. "Well, for starters, we put these artifacts of ours to good use. If they'll play a role in the next trial like I suspect..."

Rose's brow furrows as she catches my meaning. "Then we'd better learn how to wield them properly. Who knows - maybe there are advantages we've been overlooking."

A determined nod, and we gather our things to head for the training arena. If we're going to pull off this hare-brained scheme of infiltrating the kingdom's most secure location, we'll need every advantage we can find. How hard could it really be? We are already staying on palace grounds. No one is better set up to rescue Tabitha than us.

As we stride through the palace corridors, my mind whirls with strategy and contingencies. Getting into those dungeons will be the easy part compared to finding Tabitha amidst the labyrinth and making it out alive. But we have to try. I won't abandon one of our own.

***

I drag myself back to my room, sweat-soaked and completely spent from training. Working with this stupid staff is kicking my ass. I'm so used to the finesse of dagger work - swinging around a giant chunk of wood feels ungainly and awkward as hell.

I pause at my door, leaning against it as I try to catch my breath. My whole body aches and I can already feel nasty bruises forming under my clothes. How the hell am I supposed to get decent with this cumbersome thing before tomorrow's trial?

Gritting my teeth, I finally push inside, only to spot a neatly folded piece of parchment on my pillow, weighed down by a small velvet pouch. Intrigued, I snatch it up, the cool material sliding pleasantly against my palm.

An invitation? But from who? My curiosity deepens as I examine the elegant handwriting requesting my presence for some private rendezvous this evening. I open the pouch to find a map marking a secluded door somewhere in the palace. Well, well...looks like someone has something clandestine in mind.

My eyes scan the elegantly scrawled lines, curiosity piquing as the words sink in.

Lady Scarlet,

Your endeavors in the tournament have not gone unnoticed by those in lofty positions. If amenable, present yourself this evening at the discreet location marked on the enclosed map. An audience has been requested - one that necessitates the utmost discretion on your part.

Opportunities such as this are seldom extended. I trust you will prove worthy of the privilege.

R

A secret rendezvous? Now who could have sent this kind of scandalous invite? My eyes narrow as I reread the vague yet undeniably suggestive lines. The overly self-important tone practically screams "royalty" - seems someone High and Mighty has taken an interest in little ol' me.

A smirk tugs at my lips as I consider the possibilities. Could it really be the king himself summoning me?

My gaze drifts to the heavy pouch, fingertips toying with the drawstring. With a steadying breath, I tug it open. A folded map tumbles out, the thick vellum bearing an intricately rendered layout of the palace grounds, a single red X marking a nondescript door tucked away in a secluded alcove.

An invitation, a map, a summons shrouded in enigma ...I should be far warier of stumbling heedlessly into unknown territory. And yet that defiant spark that so often governs my actions prickles with temptation to unravel the mystery. What sort of illicit game is the king playing?

My sore muscles protest as I strip off my tunic, wadding the rank fabric into an unceremonious ball to discard later. Lukewarm water from the basin does little to revive me, but at least I no longer reek quite so foully.

Donning a lightweight linen shift that hangs loose and unrestrictive, I tug a pair of well-worn boots onto my feet. Simple, unobtrusive…just in case stealth proves necessary wherever this rendezvous may lead.

Clutching the folded map, I slip out into the hushed corridor, carefully pulling the door shut behind me. A few candles flicker in rusted sconces, casting wavering shadows that turn every nook into a potential hiding spot for prying eyes.

Keeping to the edges, I make my way through the winding passages, my path traced on the map in my mind. Right, then left at the portrait of the fat Count Woolridge, continue on until the alcove with the crumbling griffon statue…

My knuckles connect firmly with the weathered oak door, the sound echoing hollowly in the deserted hallway. For several tense beats, everything stays maddeningly silent. Then the rusty grind of a latch, and the door cracks open a sliver.

"Who goes there?" a deep voice rumbles from the other side, guarded but calmly authoritative.

I clear my throat, keeping my tone level. "I was called here for a private audience."

The single eye peering through the opening gives me a long, scrutinizing once over. Then it disappears, replaced by the door swinging inward to admit me. There in the entryway stands the unmistakable figure of King Remme himself.

"You may enter," he says, stepping aside to allow me passage. As I slip past, my gaze sweeps over the intimate study - plush rugs, shelves crammed with ancient tomes, a fire crackling invitingly in the hearth. Two chairs are drawn up before it, flanking a small table laden with a sumptuous spread of fruits, bread, cheese and ruby-red wine.

"Make yourself comfortable," King Remme gestures as he closes and latches the door behind us. The heavy thud of the lock engaging sends a shiver down my spine.

We're utterly alone, away from prying eyes and watchful ears.

He moves to the table, unhurriedly filling one of the crystal goblets. "I trust your evening has been an...invigo rating one so far?" His piercing gaze finds me again as he proffers the glass.

"You could say that, Your Grace," I murmur, accepting the goblet with a small dip of my chin and draining the drink immediately. While I know I should hold myself back tonight with the next trail being tomorrow, I'm also in desperate need of an escape. Even if only for a moment.

A ghost of a smile plays about the king's lips as he settles into one of the chairs, golden bracers glinting in the low light. With a wave of his hand, he invites me to join him. "Then let us pursue more...restful diversions for a time. I've found a well-cultivated mind craves intermittent reprieve from the relentless onslaught of the day's rigors."

He leans back, holding my stare with an intensity that sends that same delicious frisson shivering through me.

Heat prickles along my neck and cheeks. The wine's rich, earthy notes tantalize my senses as I take a delicate sip, allowing the flavors to linger on my tongue.

The king seems to study me as an expectant silence stretches between us. At last, I find my voice again. "You mentioned wanting to discuss the trials...?"

King Remme stands and casually trails his gloved fingers along the spines of the leather-bound books lining the shelves. He seems to be choosing his words carefully when he finally speaks.

"I'll be frank - I had an ulterior motive asking you here tonight." His expression darkens briefly. "I wanted to ensure you were recovered from the unpleasantness with Lord Greystone at the soiree. He would do well to remember his place."

My breath catches at hearing Greystone's name stated so bluntly. There's a protective edge to the king's tone that sends a subtle thrill through me.

"You honor me with your concern, Your Majesty," I say, holding his intense gaze over my drink. "But any troubles I have are nothing compared to ruling a kingdom."

King Remme considers me for a long moment, his eyes revealing a glimpse of empathy. "Even so, Greystone's behavior cannot be tolerated. No woman deserves such mistreatment from one who wishes to have their lives forever connected."

I sense genuine anger simmering beneath his controlled exterior.

"Greystone is only a temporary annoyance," I reply dismissively, though my skin still crawls recalling his unwanted proximity. "I assure you, I can handle him."

King Remme's intense stare seems to peer directly into my soul, seeing past the nonchalance I try to project. His jaw clenches and shoulders tense, as if holding himself back from acting on some sudden impulse. When he speaks again, his voice resonates with quiet authority.

"I promise you, Greystone will learn the cost of mistreating someone under my protection."

His bold words hang heavy between us. I feel both thrilled and unsettled. Is the king saying I'm under his protection? Does he mean as a participant in the trials? Why do I have a part of me that hopes it more?

The king crosses the room and retrieves a small wooden box from a shelf. I notice the gilded scrollwork matches the designs on his armor.

He places the box on the table and lifts the lid, revealing a colorful deck of cards illustrated with mystical symbols. "Perhaps a reading can offer guidance to face the challenges ahead?" he suggests, quirking a conspiratorial eyebrow at me.

I tilt my head, intrigued by this unexpected development. "You read tarot cards?"

"A private hobby of mine," Remme admits with a roguish grin, shuffling the stack of cards. "I find the artwork fascinating, even if I don't fully grasp the arcane meanings."

I laugh at his candid admission - trust the king to dabble purely for the aesthetic appeal. I take another sip of wine, eyeing him over the crystal rim with interest. "Well then, reveal my future, oh wise magician. What secrets lie ahead for this lowly subject?"

He places the shuffled deck on the table and begins deliberately turning over cards, studying each colorful illustration intently.

"Let's see what guidance the cards offer for the path ahead," he says, eyes glinting with mischief.

He flips over the first card to reveal a gruesome image of a stabbed figure. "Ah, the Ten of Swords. A painful betrayal by someone trusted," King Remme explains, tracing the bloody sword hilts with one finger. "A wound cut deep to your core."

I lean back in my chair, eyebrow raised skeptically. "Or maybe just a bad night at the theater."

His lips twitch, suppressing a grin before schooling his features again. He turns over the next card depicting a bountiful harvest.

"The Seven of Pentacles - patience and perseverance finally rewarded with prosperity." His gaze flicks meaningfully to my cleavage. "Fulfillment in all aspects of life's bounty."

"My eyes are up here your highness," I tease.

His throat bobs as he turns over another card—the Two of Cups.

"A profound spiritual and physical bond between two souls," he declares, arching a suggestive brow. "Blended together in...sacred carnal ecstasy."

I nearly spit out my wine at his provocative insinuation. The king grins unrepentantly before moving on to the next card—the imposing Devil.

"Dangerous temptations that must be resisted, lest they lead one astray," he intones with mock gravity.

I set down my goblet, unable to restrain my snort of laughter. "Is that so?"

The king's eyes dance with humor, though his expression remains serious. "The cards impart deep wisdom for those who look closely."

I lean in, emboldened by this flirtatious game. "Well don't leave out any sordid details, Your Majesty. My future clearly depends on it."

The king's intense gaze remains locked with mine as he turns over the next card - the Eight of Swords.

"Ah, a card that has more to it than meets the eye." he proclaims with dramatic flair. "It shows a figure blindfolded and bound, trapped by unseen restrictions."

His eyes bore pointedly into mine. "Perhaps it represents feeling shackled to toxic relationships or obligations that sever you from your true path in life."

The king traces his finger along the illustrated figure's bindings. "Base attachments that blind the spirit and must be severed, no matter the cost, or they will utterly consume you. Plus there's eight swords total so the ending may be brutal. Stab it. A lot. End it."

"Well then." I raise my goblet in a mock salute, thoroughly entertained by his heavy-handed "reading" at this point. "Here's to severing toxic bonds and finding my true spiritual union," I retort airily. "All great journeys begin with a single step - or stabbing, apparently."

The king seems to drink in my reaction, a speculative glint in his eye. But his mask remains firmly in place as he gathers the scattered cards once more. "It seems I still have much to learn in the realm of tarot divination," he remarks. "Perhaps you'd care to display your own mastery?"

"Me? I'm afraid I don't have the gifts for divination," I say lightly, shuffling the deck while I gather my thoughts. In truth, my only experience is the card tricks I used to swindle gullible marks in my youth.

But perhaps some artful deceit is called for to keep our game going. A sly smile tugs at my lips as an idea forms. Let's see if I can turn the tables on His Majesty.

I flip over the Ten of Swords, depicting a brutal backstabbing. "Betrayal by someone trusted," I proclaim in an exaggerated gasp. "Tell me, does this represent a devious advisor? A jilted lover out for revenge?"

The king's jaw tightens almost imperceptibly. A hit already - interesting.

I flip over the next card, revealing The Moon. "Ah, a card shrouded in shadows and mystery," I say, giving the king a meaningful look.

"It often represents things hidden beneath the surface, secrets and illusions that distort the truth."

I trace my finger along the card's crescent moon, watching Remme closely. "Perhaps deep down you conceal something that could shake your very rule if revealed?"

almost imperceptibly, though his expression remains guarded. I'm struck by an intuition that my theatrical reading has hit uncomfortably close to some truth he wishes hidden.

"But let's move on from such gloomy cards, shall we?" I continue breezily, turning over the next illustration. "So many more secrets left to unveil, Your Majesty..."

I embellish my act with wild predictions, all the while scrutinizing Remme for any reaction to my prodding about concealed truths. His disciplined mask reveals little, but I sense the Moon's imagery troubles him. What damning secret might the king be hiding? His reactions has me only more curious.

Undeterred, I press on to reveal the Two of Cups between two embracing figures. "How romantic - the start of a deep, passionate union. Tell me, does someone have the King's affections?" My eyes dance with wry humor.

"Some delicious court scandal to spice up these mystical ponderings?"

The slightest muscle ticks in King Remme's chiseled jaw, a subtle tell that I've struck a nerve somewhere. Resisting the urge to crow in delight, I consider my next probing move carefully.

When the Hierophant emerges with his haughty, patriarchal glare, I can't resist one last playful barb. "Oof, what an arrogant old fool who fancies himself above the world," I spew out dramatically. "Stubbornly blind to the vibrancy and progress unfolding all around his crusty, shriveled existence. I'd hate to be in his royal doghouse!"

An impish grin curves my lips as I take in King Remme's reaction - the slight flush, the muscle twitching in his chiseled jaw. Clearly my thinly veiled taunts about scandalous unions and carnal cravings have struck a nerve with the usually unflappable king. I lean back in my chair, feigning nonchalance as I study him over the rim of my goblet.

"Why Your Grace, one might get the impression you find certain...interpretations rather provocative," I murmur. "Though I can assure you, my interest lies solely in understanding the deeper mystical truths the cards reveal."

I flip over the next illustration - the Eight of Cups, depicting a solitary figure turning away from a series of full chalices. "The endless quest for something more meaningful than mere material comforts and shallow pleasures," I proclaim solemnly. "A courageous soul's journey to slake an unfulfilled inner yearning."

My gaze holds his as I add with pointed significance, "Even at great personal risk, one is compelled to abandon the safe, known path to pursue deeper, soul-nourishing purpose."

The king's throat works as he swallows hard, something flickering in those depths. Is that understanding dawning in his stare? I resist the urge to hold my breath as the weighted silence stretches between us.

At last, his lips twisting wryly. "You spin quite the captivating tale, my lady. Although, sometimes the meanings can be difficult to grasp."

Back to my lady are we?

The subtle challenge in his words sends a delicious shiver of anticipation down my spine. Slowly, deliberately, I turn over the final card - The Lovers, an entwined couple gazing into each other's eyes with unabashed adoration.

"Does it?" I murmur huskily, holding his heated stare as my fingers trail over the intimate illustration. "See, here we see the ultimate spiritual and physical union - souls destined to converge, no matter what conventions or obstacles fate puts in their path."

My breath catches as Remme leans closer, the magnetic pull between us becoming nearly irresistible. Yet some primal part of me yearns to prolong this delicious game of truth and daring just a little longer.

Forcing a blithe tone, I gather the deck again with slightly shaky hands. "But enough divination for one evening. Shall we move on to...lighter diversions?"

King Remme's eyes fairly smolder into mine as his lips curve into a slow, knowing smile. "By all means," he rumbles in that sinfully rich timbre. "I find myself quite diverted already."

The Third Trial

Scarlet

The roar of the crowd swells to deafening levels as we take our places in the arena, hitting me like a physical force. My heart is pounding as I gaze up at the lavish private viewing boxes dotted along the highest levels.

Of course the privileged nobles get the best seats, peering down their noses at us like prize livestock. I sneer as my eyes land on one box in particular - there's Lord Graybastard himself, smirking arrogantly and no doubt poised to brag at the first opportunity. Just wait until he gets a load of the stunt I'm about to pull.

Before I can map out my opening gambit, a wizened old announcer stalks out to the center of the arena floor, leaning heavily on an ornate staff. The craggy lines of his face hint at decades of shouting over rowdy throngs just like this one. He shushes the crowd with an imperious wave of his hand.

"Competitors!" he barks in a gravelly bellow that carries easily. "You shall all be divided into teams based on the divine artifacts you retrieved earlier. Represent your patrons well through skill and guile!"

As his voice echoes off the stonework, a group of fur-cloaked acolytes start ushering and directing us towards the different team pedestals arrayed around the arena's outer ring. I exchanged glances with my unlikely new "teammates" that have been grouped with me - representing the gods of trickery and illusion based on our retrieved items. This should be...interesting.

I survey my appointed teammates with a critical eye - a motley assortment to be sure, but one uniquely suited to this trial. First, there's Tarin - a coltish archer lad whose wide-eyed stare betrays just how far out of his pastoral depths he finds himself. His calloused hands grip his bow with such eager tension, I'm surprised the wood hasn't cracked yet. He carries a quiver of arrows imbued with misdirection runes. My lips quirk wryly at his earnest naivete, though something about his transparent sincerity also stirs a long-buried pang of wistful nostalgia in me.

Next comes Olena, swathed in silk finery that must've cost more than most common folk will see in a dozen lifetimes. Her icy noble disdain encompasses our shabby arena surroundings and Tarin's dogeared tunic with equal revulsion. Something about the way her pale eyes linger on me, though, hints at an incisive hunger kindling behind that insouciant mask. A thirst to transcend the gilded cage of her birth through whatever means required. She possesses an ornate handheld mirror capable of casting potent illusions.

Last in line is Marek, the obligatory grizzled veteran whose stone-faced scowl and closely-cropped hair accentuate the old scars etched across his craggy features. I recognize the look of a man intimately familiar with bloodshed and its grim practicalities. His body is a tightly-coiled spring of leashed violence, practically radiating skepticism towards whatever "deception" our illustrious hosts have in store for us rabble. Smart man. Marek's broadsword can conjure shrouds of disorienting fog.

As for me, I clutch the trickster's staff tightly in my grip, its wooden length etched with sigils of artifice and subterfuge. This twisted relic represents the very essence of my life's skills, practiced from necessity rather than mere sport. Deception has kept me alive on these unforgiving streets when nothing else could. My daggers and other gifts from Fairy Godmother are strapped to my body since I wouldn't trust my skills with this staff, well... any further than I could throw the damn thing.

As I join my new team members to prepare for the trail, I look to see where Rose and Darius ended up. Rose offers me the barest hint of a nod, emerald eyes glinting with that familiar steel I've grown accustomed to over our years working in the guild. Darius simply smiles that easy, carefree smile of his, as if this grand spectacle is all just another lively song to be played out. I can't help the small answering grin that tugs at my own lips in response.

Before I can ponder my teammates further, a flustered attendant appears bearing a tray of assorted "gifts" from anonymous admirers. With a simpering flourish, he stops before me and presents an ornately carved box, the raised Greystone family crest glaring accusingly from its lacquered lid. I snort derisively, recognizing Lord Graybastard's baubles from a league away.

He always did lack subtlety, that arrogant cad - this ostentatious display being the latest in his ongoing campaign to try and publicly lay claim to my...assets. The thought has me biting back an acidic bark of laughter. Not a chance in all the hells I ever belong to the likes of you, you lecherous, worm-ridden pustule. Not after everything.

I'm scanning the nobles' viewing area, trying to ignore Lord Greystone's smug grin as he ostentatiously brags about the ornate box he sent me, no doubt expecting me to swoon over his entitled "affections." The arrogant prick.

Before I can make a rude gesture his way, movement from the king's private box catches my eye.

There's King Remme himself, observing the proceedings with that signature stony glare. Our eyes meet for an instant. To my surprise, a subtle tightening around his eyes conveys displeasure - at me? No, that wouldn't make sense. At Greystone's blatant spectacle is more likely. A hint of shared annoyance bolsters my defiant spirit.

That pompous ass won't be the only one getting a public rebuke today. With a disdainful sneer in Greystone's direction, I snatch up the box and hurl it aside to shatter dramatically against a nearby column. The crowd's raucous cheers swell in approval at my show of contempt.

I don't spare them so much as a sidelong glance. My focus remains utterly pinned on the king, holding that iron stare until at last he inclines his head a single, infinitesimal degree. A subtle nod of acknowledgement? Approval? My breath catches in my throat as the raw realization lances through me - for one ephemeral heartbeat, in rejecting my detested husband-to-be's lecherous overture, I'd pleased the king himself.

The feeling is at once exhilarating and earth-shaking in its sheer disquieting audacity.

The announcer's gravelly voice echoes across the arena once more. "Brave competitors! As the third trial commences, those teams not representing the spheres of trickery and illusion are asked to adjourn to the designated waiting areas. You shall be summoned when your turn arrives."

A chorus of grumbles and hushed whispers ripples through the assembled crowd. I watch with narrowed eyes as Darius, Rose, and the others are ushered away, disappearing through arched doorways that lead off the main arena floor.

Tarin fidgets anxiously, constantly adjusting and readjusting the strap holding his quiver of enchanted arrows. "So...what now? They didn't exactly give us instructions beyond waiting here."

"Patience is a virtue, young Master Tarin," Olena chides primly, not even deigning to spare him a glance as she runs one delicate finger along the gilded etchings of her handheld mirror. "Clearly this first trial involves demonstrating our adeptness at perceiving deception. No doubt we shall be tested shortly."

Marek grunts in tacit agreement, one calloused hand resting on the pommel of his sheathed sword. "Doubt it'll be simple. They'll want to root out our true capabilities more...intimately."

I can't help but share his skepticism. There's a tension building in the air, an anticipatory hush rippling through the crowd despite their earlier raucous cheers. They can sense the true game is about to start.

Sure enough, distant chanting begins to swell, rising in liturgical cadences from beneath the arena itself. The ground before us parts in a widening spiral, ancient stone giving way to reveal a circular pit rimmed with candle-studded braziers. A wizened figure emerges, bent and twisted, swathed in mottled crimson robes that seem to slither and coil of their own unnatural volition.

Olena's sharp intake of breath matches my own spike of unease. There's an unmistakable aura of power radiating from this new presence, seething with a palpable weight that sets every hair on my body standing on end. Whatever is about to unfold, it will wield energies far more primal than the magic that Fairy Godmother uses.

The robed figure gestures languidly, movements flowing with impossible grace for such an ancient form. Tendrils of luminous vapor begin coalescing in intricate whorls, solidifying into spectral humanoid shapes that drift and sway in midair around the arena. Their mouths gape in perpetual, voiceless screams of rapturous agony as their limbs undulate hypnotically.

"Spirits of the ether realm," the crone rasps in a voice dry as scorched parchment. "Heed our summons and bear witness to these mortal vessels who dare aspire to deceive you!"

The ghostly forms seem to turn as one towards our team, their empty sockets burning with eldritch flames. I tighten my white-knuckled grip around Halistar's staff.

As the ghostly phantoms converge, Tarin looses arrow after arrow with his enchanted shafts, but the projectiles pass harmlessly through their vaporous forms.

"Your tricks are useless here, boy!" the crone cackles. "We command the ethereal ether itself!"

Marek charges in undaunted, his broadsword slashing through the apparitions and summoning forth gouts of blinding fog to shroud us in murky disorientation. Through the eddying gloom, I grab Olena's arm urgently.

I hiss intently. "We'll need to counter their summoning directly if we want to break them!"

Olena meets my stare with dawning realization before nodding crisply. Raising her gilded mirror, she begins weaving a counter-spell that scatters prismatic force beams through the fog. Wherever they impact manifests brief pockets of clarity, allowing me to glimpse the arena's true state beneath.

But the true heart of the deception is that twisted old crone, her crooked staff conducting the entire phantasmagoria like a malefic orchestra. If we don't disrupt her conjuring, this maelstrom will only escalate further. Gripping my staff tightly, I draw upon every ounce of arcane craft and mental focus Fairy Godmother's teachings have imbued in me. To be fair, it's not much and frankly, I've never shown an ounce of actual magical ability before but if the gods gave me a magical staff they sure as hell have better given me the ability to use it. God of thieves, you had better not let me down.

Emerald beams of magic shoot from the staff, piercing and dispelling the crone's summoned spirits one by one. Her hollow shrieks rise in impotent fury as more and more of her illusory veil frays apart under our concerted assault. But even as her constructs begin unraveling, her own power swells in desperation.

With a thunderous roar, she raises her gnarled staff towards the heavens. The ground underfoot bucks violently as a shockwave of eldritch force radiates outwards. The torchlight dims as if the very air were turning to poisonous smog. Marek and Olena cry out in shock, reeling and staggering from the debilitating onslaught.

Gritting my teeth, I reach for the deepest wellsprings of my own mysterious magic, the runes along the trickster's staff flaring with crackling power. But even as I do, a presence unlike anything I've encountered stirs within that ancient wood - a sentient, willful force of cunning and beguiling guile.

As the crone's noxious miasma swirls menacingly around us, I feel a strange, intangible force stir within Halisar's staff clutched in my hands. It's as if the relic itself carries a sentient essence, a primal spirit of cunning guile given form. Without conscious thought, I open myself fully to that inscrutable presence, allowing its unfurling power to intermingle with my own.

The effect is instantaneous and profound. What was once a choking, poisonous haze twists and distorts into a shimmering vortex of incandescent motes. The vapors transform into a kaleidoscope of sparkling dust that swirls and dances around us in dazzling, diaphanous patterns. I can sense the intoxicating thrill of pure deception coursing through my veins, the intangible essence of the God of Thieves himself lending me his mystic gifts.

Olena's eyes widen in breathless awe at this wondrous metamorphosis, the crone's jaw hanging agape in stunned denial as her vile summoning is usurped and subverted by a far more ancient power. I feel her focus waver under the onslaught of this divine trickery, her control slipping like grains of sand through cupped palms.

Seizing the opportunity, I move with a serpentine grace utterly disconnected from my own mortal form. Halisar's divine essence guides my actions now as I whirl the twisted staff in an impossibly fast overhand spiral. The runes blaze forth with scintillating emerald light, bending and focusing my will into a searing torrent of pure arcane force.

The blazing beam lances across the arena to slam into the wizened crone with the fury of an avalanche, her fragile form hurled backwards into the shadowed pit like a broken marionette severed from its strings. As she disappears into the darkness with a despairing wail, the last vestiges of her summoned phantasms dissipate into wisps of glimmering ether.

Silence hangs heavy in the arena as the dust settles. Tarin gapes in slack-jawed awe, while even the grizzled Marek and cynical Olena regard me with bemused respect bordering on trepidation. For my part, I simply stand motionless, reveling in the lingering tingle of that alien power before allowing Halisar's divine presence to recede fully back into the trickster staff's carved recesses.

My heart pounds with the intoxicating aftershocks of having channeled such a primal, mystic force. Yet even as exhilaration courses through me, a small kernel of unease takes root. If the God of Thieves himself has marked me as his champion, aided me so overtly in this trial...then how can I hope to keep that truth concealed from King Remme's gaze?

The triumphant cheers morph into screams of shock and horror as the arena floor itself violently shifts. A deafening rumble like the earth wrenching itself apart reverberates through the stones underfoot. My stomach drops as fissures split open, jagged obsidian shards erupting in a crystalline maelstrom.

I barely have time to register the threat before searing agony lances through my body. Razor-edged shards shred flesh and muscle alike as they burst forth in an unstoppable onslaught, punching through my torso and limbs. White-hot fire seems to consume my very nerves as the jagged obsidian violates and eviscerates without mercy.

A scream tears from my throat, hoarse and primal, barely recognizable as my own voice. Warm wetness blooms across my shredded tunic, the coppery tang of blood thick in the air. Distantly, I am aware of Olena shrieking in horror while Marek bellows helpless fury, but their voices seem to echo from a vast chasm.

With a final explosive burst, the crystal storm subsides as abruptly as it had begun. I crumple to the arena floor in a broken, bleeding heap, agony lancing through me with every feeble movement. The last thing I glimpse before oblivion claims me is the king's stunned face, mouth agape in his private viewing box, our eyes finally locking across that impassable divide.

Then darkness rises to enfold me in its cold embrace. My final thoughts scatter like ashes on the wind as unconsciousness drags me down into its bottomless depths...

Questions that Can't Be Left Unanswered

Remme

The world seems to blur around me as Scarlet's form crumples to the arena floor in a broken, bleeding heap. My heart clenches almost painfully in my chest at the sight, an icy fist of dread gripping my insides. Through the ringing in my ears, I'm dimly aware of the crowd's shrill cries of shock and horror, but my gaze remains transfixed, utterly unable to tear itself away.

Scarlet's teammates reactions surprise me at how extreme they are considering I hadn't seen them interact with her before this trial. To be honest, my own reaction also surprises me a bit. Olena shrieks wordlessly, hands clawing at her face in a paroxysm of dismay. Even the grizzled Marek appears shaken, bellowing furious oaths that are swallowed up by the swelling pandemonium. But their responses are mere background noise, meaningless din drowned out by the roar of my own pulse thundering through my skull.

All I can see is Scarlet's battered, motionless form amid that crystalline hellscape, rent flesh and torn garments painting a gruesome tapestry in shades of crimson. My gloved fists clench with such force that the metal bites into my palms, dread threatening to hollow me out from the inside.

Some rational corner of my mind knows this is likely just another deception, an elaborate illusion crafted for my benefit. I'd instructed the arena masters to test the competitors' skills to the utter limits - to separate the authentically gifted from the pretenders through any means necessary, no matter how traumatic. But another part of me cannot shake seeing Scarlet so horrifically broken before my eyes.

My jaw clenches hard enough to creak as I force my expression into stony impassivity once more. I cannot afford to let the court or citizens see even a flicker of the roiling tempest burning within me. One misplaced tell, one crack in the facade, and it could undo everything, leaving my obsessive yearnings laid bare for all to mock and condemn as weakness.

As the medical acolytes hurry to cart Scarlet's limp form off the field on a stretcher, I finally tear my stare away to sweep across the assembled viewing boxes. Predictably, it doesn't take long to pinpoint the source of the blusterous outrage echoing above the din.

Lord Greystone has surged out of his plush seat, flushed face contorted in a mask of rage as he pounds his meaty fists on the ornately carved balcony railing. A thin sheen of spittle froths at the corners of his mouth, strings of acidic vitriol no doubt pouring from his lips though the exact words are lost amid the general tumult. The blustering oaf seems damn near apoplectic at the sight of his prospective bride-to-be left in such a gruesome state, never mind that the entire debacle was almost certainly theatrical in nature.

I curl my lip in a sneer of disgust, unable to fully mask the contempt I feel for the man's greed and entitlement. As if he has any true claim or right to Scarlet, to dictate her heart or determine her worth based on his pitiful, lust-addled ambitions. The mere notion makes my stomach churn in revulsion.

My eyes drift inevitably back to the spot where Scarlet fell, now only marred by spatters of crimson amid the cracked stonework. Something in me clenches tighter at the sight, the urge to rush down and see for myself her state almost overwhelming my restraint. But no…I cannot compromise my position or give the game away to those circling vultures just waiting to seize any perceived weakness. I am the king, impartial and untouchable as the laws of nature themselves.

At least, that is the role I must play, otherwise all will be lost and I will not only put myself, but also Scarlet into danger.

Gritting my teeth, I force my attention back to the arena floor as the next team, including Rose, takes their position for the trial. My stomach clenches as I watch the old crone materialize in the center, the same haunting figure that tormented Scarlet's team with illusions and deceptions.

As the trial begins and the crone weaves her dark sorcery, Rose suddenly breaks formation. Taking one long last look around, she darts forward, mirroring the desperate move of the thief who infiltrated my castle. In a blur, she grabs the crone's foot and pulls as hard as she can, knocking the large woman to the ground in an eerily familiar takedown.

My breath catches in my throat as realization washes over me. That technique…that audacious, fluid strike - it's the same I witnessed the night the Bodian crown was nearly stolen. The same skill that allowed the thief to evade capture and slip away like a wraith into the night.

Is it mere coincidence? Or has Rose been the mastermind behind the kingdom's security breaches all along, methodically honing her skills for this grand performance? Is she part of the thieves guild I'm hunting as well? Is Scarlet connected to that as well? It can't be a mere coincidence that she just channeled the god of thieves magic. I felt it as did everyone else in here. Rarely does a god interfere with mortal events, but when they do, they never do it subtly.

The notion that my own personal fixation may have blinded me to her possible connection to the thieves guild is sobering. While part of me recoils at the idea of Scarlet allying herself with such nefarious elements, I cannot discount the damning weight of evidence piling up - her flagrant disdain for authority, her remarkable skills at infiltration and subterfuge, and now this disturbing display of channeling forces beyond mortal ability from a picky god. All the pieces align in an almost inescapable pattern of guilt.

And yet...the part of me that thrills at her indomitable spirit, the fiery defiance kindled behind those eyes, cannot reconcile itself with condemning her so readily. There is an honesty, a raw authenticity about Scarlet that transcends the shadowed realms of deception and larceny. A part of her soul shines with the brilliant, uncompromising light of a bonfire piercing through the veil of deepest night. To extinguish that would be a tragedy beyond reckoning, an act from which I may never recover.

With an almost physical effort of will, I force my thoughts away from such perilous meanderings. There will be time enough to unravel this riddle and stake my heart upon the truth - whatever form it may ultimately take. For now, I am the implacable arbiter of these trials, and I must play that role flawlessly if I have any hope of claiming the prize that so consumes my every waking moment.

The rest of the day's events pass by in a blur of strained focus, my gaze constantly tracking Rose for any further anomalies amid the flurry of illusions and deceptions un-folding in the arena. Though she acquits herself admirably, I cannot shake the lingering suspicion first sparked by that peculiar shadow-play, that seemingly sentient aura which clung to her for those few, fleeting moments.

When at last the final gong reverberates through the arena to signal the day's end, I waste no time in rising from my viewing box and hurrying from the stifling confines. Affecting an aura of regal dignity, I nonetheless keep my strides brisk and purposeful, gradually allowing the court-ly facade to slough away with each echoing footfall on the marble corridors.

Soon enough, I find myself standing before the door to the arena's auxiliary infirmary wing. A pair of armored guards snap to attention as I approach, leveling their pikes in crisp salutes. I wave them aside brusquely.

"Leave us," I growl in a tone that brokered no argument. "And ensure I am not disturbed unless the arena itself is burning down."

The men exchange a confused look but know better than to defy a direct order from their liege. With rigid bows, they retreat back up the corridor to take up positions flanking the intersection, their clanking footfalls fading into silence.

I let out a slow exhalation, feeling some of the weight sloughing from my shoulders the further I move from prying eyes and wagging tongues.

Pushing open the heavy oak door, I step into the dimly lit chamber to find Scarlet lying unconscious on a cot, her torso and limbs thickly wrapped in linen bandages. An elderly physician mutters beneath his breath while preparing a dressing tray of unguents, but he barely reacts to my entrance beyond a deferential nod of acknowledgment.

One way or another, Scarlet's role in all this will soon reach its end. Either she will prove innocent of any involvement with the thieves guild I've vowed to extinguish, finally laying my obsession to rest...or else that uncompromising spirit will flare brilliantly one last time before I am forced to snuff out its radiant pyre, forever damning a piece of my own humanity in the process.

As I approach the cot and gaze down upon Scarlet's peaceful features, I reach out to gently brush an errant lock of golden hair from her brow. My throat tightens imperceptibly as the fingertips of my golden gloves ghost across her pale skin, and I feel a phantom ache blossom somewhere deep within my soul. I so desperately wish to touch her directly, but a part of me knows that will never be.

"What secrets do you harbor?" I murmur, the barest of whispers as if giving voice to my yearning may somehow break this fragile spell. "And once they are out in the open, what cruelties will I be forced to bear in turn?"

Unconsciousness has smoothed the lines of defiance from Scarlet's features, leaving her looking almost vulnerably young in repose. It's all too easy to be lulled into seeing her as the innocent she may never have truly been, a beguiling fantasy to quell the tumult of my doubts. But I know better than to blindly entertain such indulgent delusions any longer.

One way or another, I tell myself as I finally turn away from that cot, the truth will be dragged into the unforgiving light soon enough. Should it prove my darkest fears true and Scarlet stands revealed as irredeemably en-twined with the black-hearted guilds...then so be it. I will burn away that tangled web of treachery and deception by whatever means remain, no matter how deeply it leaves me scorched and hollowed in the process.

It's the only path left to me now. The sole flicker of hope still smoldering in the ashes of my existence.

No matter how dearly it may cost me, I cannot - I won't - allow that light to be extinguished before its secrets are finally, painfully laid bare

The Gift

Scarlet

Everything hurts. I don't want to wake up. But nature calls and it has almost become more painful than the rest of my body. Slowly I crack my eyes open to find that I am wrapped from head to toe. I attempt to lift one arm and moan in pain. This isn't going to work.

"It's about time you woke up," a familiar voice says out of my view.

I turn my head towards the voice, surprised that that actually didn't hurt beyond the pounding headache, to find Rose leaning back in a chair, her feet propped up on a table in front of her.

"What the hells are you doing here?" I ask.

"Some parties were concerned about your well being. In fact, quite a few were," she responds with a sweep of her hand.

Somehow I had missed the pile of items beside her.

"Those are mine?"

"Yep! Some are a mix of people who saw you breaking your fiances gift and thought to reward it. Others, sent healing aids and potions. Not that you've needed them. You've been closely monitored by the royal physician."

My brain took a few moments to process what she was saying. "Wait, how do you know what's in the boxes?"

Rose smirks. "I was only checking for your safety. Make sure there were no traps or hate mail delivered. Orders from the highest."

I want to tease her or tell her off, but knowing Fairy Godmother, I know there's a good chance that she really did tell Rose to check things out for me.

"I hate to ask, but Rose, I need your help."

Brow raised she puts her feet on the ground. "What do you need?"

"Mother nature calls and as you can see, I can't exactly move around well enough to take care of it myself."

"Nope! I'm out. That's not part of my job description. Wait there and I will get you help."

The scraping of her chair makes my head throb as Rose gets up and leaves the room. Soon after, a man in robes enters. His silver hair pulled up high on his head, worried creases on his forehead.

"You needed me my lady?" he says.

"I need to relieve myself. Please."

"Of course! One moment please."

I watch and wait. Assuming he will grab a chamber pot or come over to help me move. Instead, in my frustration, I find him to be standing the same spot mumbling to himself. I can't hold this much longer. With a grunt I begin to prop myself up on my elbow and shift when pain hits me everywhere I just put pressure. With a cry I collapse back down.

"Are you going to help me?" I grown at the man.

He only holds up a single finger in my direction, still mumbling to himself.

A tingle in my stomach begins as a warmth moves from under my bust on down. To my surprise I no longer have any feeling to need to use the chamber pot after the feeling disappears.

"What did you do?"

The man approaches me and looks me over. "Magic my child. You are a lucky one. The king himself has put me over your healing and comfort. Now, how are you feeling?"

"Like I was stabbed all over."

He snorts. "A bit literal aren't we?"

"How long have I been out?"

"Half a day. I thought you would sleep longer. I can bring you a draught to help you sleep until you heal fully.

With the spells working on you currently it should be less than a day."

"You're serious? How could I possibly be healed that quickly?"

He only gives me a look as if asking if I was serious.

Remembering that he had just magicked my own pee out of myself I guess I shouldn't disbelieve his abilities so quickly. Momentarily the man leaves and returns with a goblet and a golden box. He places the box and cup on the table beside my cot.

"Let me help you up for a moment. Make sure to drink all of this. It will work within a few minutes."

I allow him to help me sit up enough to drink the concoction, fully ready to disappear into the silent bliss once again as more wounds I didn't know of screamed from the effort of moving. After helping me lay back down he takes the cup away and as he exits the room Rose reappears.

"Oooh a new pretty? That wasn't in the pile."

I turn my head to look at the box. Something about it seems familiar, but I can't put my finger on it.

"Can you give me that? I just want to look at it," I ask.

Rose pulls a chair beside the cot and sits down. Her eyes widen a bit as she lifts the small box and hands it to me. Immediately I drop it from the weight directly onto my stomach. Tears well at the edges of my eyes from the pain. What is this made of?!

I dig the nail of my thumb, one of the only parts of my body not currently wrapped up fully, into the box and to my surprise it dug in. This is actually gold?

I gently pry open the heavy golden box, curiosity overpowering the pain radiating through my battered body. Nestled inside, I'm surprised to find not jewelry or riches, but instead a carefully packed meal - slices of roasted pheasant, goat cheese,the same scones I ate way too many of at the interviews, and vibrant winter fruits. My stomach rumbles reflexively at the sight and scent of food, despite the lingering nausea from my injuries.

I notice a small folded note tucked beneath a cluster of grapes. Wincing, I extract it and undo the wax seal bearing the royal crest. The message inside is penned in elegant script:

My Dearest Lady,

I hope this small token finds you recovering well. Please partake of these refreshments that you may regain your strength. I could not help but notice your enthusiasm for the scones at the interviews. Consider this a sampling of Cook's finest creations, along with my fondest wishes for your swift return to health.

Until we meet again,

R.

A warmth blossoms in my chest as I read the king's words, touched by his thoughtfulness.

I lift a slice of pheasant to my lips, savoring the burst of savory juice. As hungry as I am, I force myself to eat slowly, making each mouthful last. The food truly is exquisite - perfectly seasoned and cooked to tender perfection.

By the time I've finished half the meal, my eyelids grow heavy, the healer's draught taking effect. I reluctantly seal the box again, stowing the remainder of the king's gracious gift for when I wake. As darkness creeps into the edges of my vision, my fingers brush the note once more. A smile touches my lips as I'm lulled into tranquil, dreamless sleep.

***

Scanning the small room, I notice the untouched golden box on the bedside table. A warmth kindles in my chest at the memory of King Remme's thoughtful gift, his elegant handwriting wishing me a swift recovery. It has been ages since someone cared for me so genuinely, without tangled motives or transactional intent. The intense look on his face just before I was skewered will forever be seared into my mind. But even intrusive thoughts of the king send a nervous prickle down my spine now. Too much has happened; the connection between us, however scintillating, could prove disastrous if mishandled. But if it isn't... no. I can't let myself think about that right now.

A scraping at the door shakes me from my reverie. Rose saunters in, raking a critical eye over my remaining bandages. "Well, you look less like death warmed over at least. How are you feeling?"

I grimace, trying to shift to a seated position. "Well enough to get out of here. I'm assuming that's why you're here?"

Rose smirks. "Am I that transparent?" She steps closer, voice lowering. "FG sent word. We need to move tonight."

My brow furrows. "Tonight? But Tabitha..."

"I know," Rose cuts in briskly. "But it can't wait. Godmother received intel that the king plans to transfer Tabitha somewhere even we can't reach. This is our one window to get her out. You and I are the least likely to be killed if we are caught sneaking around the castle grounds. We can always claim we got lost while exploring or something."

My heart sinks, even as I know Rose is right. Fairy Godmother's network of informants is unparalleled. Combine that with the magic she keeps hidden from most and if she says time is running out, that is the stark reality we face.

With a grimace, I force myself upright. "Then we better get moving. Help me dress at least semi-decently for travel."

Rose nods and fetches my rumpled training clothes and boots. She works swiftly but gently to unwrap the bandages and ease the simple garments over my injuries. I bite back small hisses at the pull and sting, trying not to reveal my lingering weakness. But I can't fully hide the occasional wince or intake of breath.

"Sorry," Rose mutters after one particular nip of pain flashes across my face. "I know it still hurts like hell."

The rare apology takes me aback. She and I have been childhood rivals, only growing more competitive over the years. Vulnerability does not come easily, for either of us.

I give a strained chuckle. "At least I'm mobile. I'll manage." I meet Rose's eyes briefly. "But thank you. For coming to get me."

Rose looks faintly surprised by my sincerity but simply nods and eases my cloak over my shoulders. "Think you can walk or should I pinch a set of crutches? I'm sure you will be especially helpful as a distraction. Toss you to the wolves when it all goes wrong."

I inhale slowly, bracing myself. "I'll walk." I tentatively place weight on my legs and bite back a groan. My thighs tremble with the effort, sending twinges through my abdomen. But I remain standing.

Rose hovers a hand near my elbow, ready to grab me if I stumble. When I continue standing steady, Rose nods approvingly. "Right. Let's get the hell out of here then."

We slip out the door and navigate the winding back passages of the castle. More than once, I have to muffle a pained gasp and lean against the wall as my injuries throb. But I refuse to slow our progress or risk capture by stopping to rest. I am a member of the Triple G's, damn it. I will not falter during a mission.

The last sliver of sun disappears below the horizon as we finally pass beyond the outer castle walls. The fresh night air helps revive me somewhat, though I still have to concentrate to put one foot in front of the other.

Rose leads the way through a maze of side alleys and hidden passages only the guild knows until we reach the concealed underground door of the GGG tavern. The familiar taproom with its scarred tables and crackling hearth envelops us in welcome warmth. Fairy Godmother sits waiting, worry creasing her brow.

"Thank the heavens you made it, child," she rasps, fussing over my wan appearance. "When I heard what happened in the trial..."

I wave off her concern. "I'll live. What's the plan for Tabitha?"

Fairy Godmother's eyes harden. "Right, to business then." She unrolls a parchment map, tapping a section past the dungeons. "My sources say they've held Tabitha here, in an isolated cell. But at midnight she's to be transferred by covered wagon to Lightspire Hold."

"Lightspire Hold?" Rose cuts in, aghast. "She'll never make it out of there alive!" The mountain fortress is almost impenetrable, its dungeons carved into the sheer cliffs themselves.

My stomach turns over. Tabitha is just a kid, too green for a mission of that caliber. If we fail her now...

Fairy Godmother jabs a gnarled finger at the parchment. "Which is why we must act before then. Word came at a price - the king has tripled the dungeon guards. She wouldn't be getting moved there and getting the extra attention if he had gotten anything out of her. We do not want her to become another missing person poster caused by the king." She eyes me pointedly.

I grimace. "So what do you propose?"

"I have made a map of an entry to the castle that is in the process of being repaired. A side entrance for servants." Fairy Godmother traces a hidden passage through the catacombs. "You can find that here. You two are going to go in through that and get Tabitha out."

It isn't our most daring plan, but time is short and Tabitha's life hangs in the balance. I straighten, resolve hardening. "Consider it done."

Rose nods grimly then cracks a wry half-smile. "I do so enjoy causing trouble."

We drink a fortifying draught of Fairy Godmother's brew, the heady concoction dulling my pain. Too soon, it is time.

I hug Fairy Godmother fiercely. "Be safe, my child," the old woman rasps. "You as well, Rose. Look after each other."

Rose clasps her shoulder briefly. "We'll bring our girl home."

I meet my rival's - no, partner's - determined gaze and give a single sharp nod. We will succeed, or die trying.

Fairy Godmother secures my cloak around me. "Remember, timing is paramount. You must reach Tabitha's cell by midnight or she won't be coming home."

With that sobering reminder, we slip into the damp tunnels winding beneath the city. Faint torch glow illuminates crumbling stonework that marked foundations long forgotten. I focus on navigating the treacherous route, each step echoing in the oppressive gloom.

How much time has passed? The uncertainty eats at me as we descend deeper into ancient catacombs. We have to reach Tabitha before the transfer wagon departs. Failure is not an option.

At long last, I pick out the iron-banded oaken door Fairy Godmother had indicated, tucked away in a shadowy dead end. Fresh tool marks surrounding the lock show its recent construction.

With bated breath, Rose pulls out her pics and works on the lock itself for a moment until a soft click can be heard. We ease open the door just wide enough to slip through. The temperature plummets as we creep into the heart of the dungeons. I bite back a shiver, moving as silently as possible despite the waves of pain rippling through me. The barest scuff of our boots on stone sounds deafening in the heavy stillness.

We cling to the shadows, evading the guards' torchlight on skulking patrols. Fairy Godmother's map guides us un-erringly deeper through the labyrinth until I we find the heavy iron door to Tabitha's isolated cell. I sag against the wall in relief and shoot Rose a grin - we've made it.

Rose listens intently at the door but shakes her head - no sounds come from within. I swallow past a lump in my throat. Is Tabitha even still alive? Please, I pray desperately. Let us not be too late.

With agonizing care, I ease my lockpicks into the ancient mechanism while Rose stands watch. The minutes crawl by, each scrape of the tools echoing like thunderclaps to my hyper-aware senses. Finally, the lock springs open with a muted click.

We slip inside, and my breath leaves me in a whoosh. Tabitha lies crumpled on the filthy straw, face swollen and limbs at unnatural angles. But the shallow rise and fall of her chest confirms she still clings to life. I dash to her side, heart in my throat.

"Tabitha," I whisper urgently, cradling the girl's battered face. I hardly dare jostle her broken body, but we are running out of time. I tap her cheek insistently until her eyes slit open with a whimper.

"Hush, it's alright, we're getting you out," I soothe. With Rose's help, we lift Tabitha as gently as possible. She bites back screams as her shattered bones shift, my vision spotting with white-hot pain from my own barely healed injuries.

But together, we manage to awkwardly maneuver Tabitha between us, bearing the brunt of her weight. Step by agonizing step, we stagger towards freedom and slim hope of escape. Boots thud in the distance - the changing of the guards. Panic lances through me. "Faster," I urge through gritted teeth.

Navigating the lightless maze with our precious cargo feels endless. But miraculously, we reach the cellar door that Fairy Godmother had marked undiscovered. Panting and trembling, we ease it open - straight into the path of an oncoming patrol.

"You there! Halt!" The guard's shout reverberates down the tunnel as they fumble for their weapons.

Without hesitation, I lower Tabitha gently against the wall and step forward, my daggers in my hands in a heartbeat. My injuries scream in protest as I drop into a crouch, but I push through the agony. The darkness is my ally here. I creep forward on silent feet honed from years of stealth training. As the first guard comes into range, I strike. My dagger hilt collides with his temple and he drops without a sound.

Before his companion can react, I whirl and slash at the back of his knees. He crumples with a garbled yell, but my second dagger pommel crashes into his skull, cutting it short. I pause, panting, as pain ripples through my torso. We have to move. Now!

Rose grabs my arm to steady me. "Nicely done. But can you keep going?" Her voice is taut with concern.

I clench my jaw and nod curtly. The alternative is capture or death. My body trembles with the effort to remain upright as we drag the unconscious guards into the shadows. But I refuse to fail our mission. "Let's go," I rasp.

Digging deep, we forge ahead into the bitter night, leaving my ephemeral sanctuary of recovery behind for good. I can scarcely draw breath around the fire in my abdomen, and warm blood seeps through my bandages. But Tabitha's life depends on us getting her to safety. I won't let her down.

Satisfaction surges hotly, but I sway, drained. Rose grabs my arm to steady me. "We need to move. Now!"

Rose notices my faltering pace, the sheen of sweat on my brow. "Scarlet?" Worry cracks her usual gruff tone.

I shake my head doggedly. "I'll make it." I have to. For Tabitha's sake, and for everyone relying on us finishing this. One foot in front of the other, just a bit farther...

Voices echo from the tunnels behind us, guttural and full of violence. Torch beams bounce off damp walls, casting our pursuers' monstrous shadows. My pulse roars in my ears. I can't fight with my daggers again and I need Rose to carry the majority of the force of Tabitha. My body is becoming too weak.

Just ahead, a tall and skinny dark shadow catches my eye. Halisar's carved staff leans innocuously against the tunnel wall as if waiting for me. I'm stunned. I hadn't seen the staff since the arena trials, assuming it was locked away in my room by someone. Why has it appeared to me now? How did it get here?

I hesitate only a moment before grabbing the staff. Its polished wood feels familiar under my palm. As much as I want to deny it, I know my body wasn't ready for a mission of this magnitude. The staff's support may make the difference between life and death at this point.

The ancient runes flare to life at my touch, crackling with divine power. Halisar's might flows through me, bolstering my flagging strength. But I clench my jaw, resisting the god's tempting offer to take control. The magic isn't mine...using it could expose everything. But if it allows us to survive this night, it will be worth the sacrifice. I tighten my grip on the staff as we plunge deeper into the darkness.

Rounding a corner, we skid to a halt. Two figures stand haloed in flickering torchlight, features obscured. I sag in dismay - a dead end. How did we follow her map wrong? Fairy Godmother never gets it wrong.

"Go!" I forcefully whisper to Rose. "I'm only going to slow you down at this point. Take her and the map and get out. I will meet up with you later."

Rose only pauses for a moment before she offers a silent nod, shifts Tabitha's weight on her back and turns around to find a way out.

I inch my way back so I can't be seen and lean on the wall and Halisar's staff for support. As I peek around the corner, the shadowed figure lifts one hand.

"Captain Karrack," Remme bites out, voice glacial. "Did I not instruct you earlier to cease your excessive methods with the prisoner?"

Karrack's voice cracks. "But sire...the girl refused to talk. I took action to get result."

King Remme's eyes flash with cold fury. "You disobeyed a direct command. And now you dare hinder those I charged with retrieving the prisoner by force?" He turns his frigid stare on each guard in turn. "You have disappointed me greatly and I can't have anyone thinking their power is above mine. I am king."

Suddenly, Karrack begins screaming, limbs contorting unnaturally as his skin ripples. Before our eyes, his entire body transforms into solid gold, face frozen in a gruesome rictus.

Terror unlike anything I've experienced crashes over me, obliterating thought. The remaining guards' frenzied screams seem to reach me from underwater. This can't be real, it isn't possible...

I have to get out of here. Now!

Stumbling blindly through the tunnels, I clutching Halisar's staff in white-knuckled hands. Sobs choke my throat but I scarcely notice the tears streaking my face. My mind is still trapped in that horrific moment, playing over and over - the king's pitiless eyes, the guard's twisted screams as his body warped into gold... how is that even possible?

I had foolishly begun to hope that the king could be my escape from the gilded cage of my family, the iron shackles of my impending marriage. Our moonlit talks and longing looks wove a fantasy of freedom and affection that pierced my guarded heart.

But now that fragile dream lies shattered. I know the truth - his gentle words hide a monster. He is not a man at all if he can do that to someone.

And I...I am destined to be condemned to a loveless union, my hopes turning to ash. The bitter taste of despair fills my mouth as the last flickering light of hope gutters out inside me.

He is lost to me.

At last I reach the secret entrance we had entered at and collapse, spent. My body shakes with bone-deep sobs but no more tears will come. A heavy numbness 0settles over me, exhaustion and heartbreak dragging me down like stones.

Soft footsteps approach and I flinch before a gentle hand grasps my shoulder - Rose.

"Scarlet! Look at me, dammit. We can't stop now. We have to get Tabitha out of here before we are all caught and sent there."

I blink hard, clinging to Rose's voice through the haze threatening to swallow me. "H-how..." I choke out hoarsely. "His body, he just..."

I just shake my head mutely, blinking through the images burning behind my eyes - the king's merciless gaze, the guard's agonized screams as his body warped to gold... But I cannot tell Rose of the impossibilities I witnessed.

Rose searches my face, then her expression hardens with resolve. "Nevermind, there's no time. We need to get you both back to the others now."

She pulls my arm across her sturdy shoulders, bearing most of my weight and Tabitha's as we hurry through the winding streets. My head spins and my injuries blaze, but I force my feet to keep moving. We have to get Tabitha to safety. I cannot let the guild down now.

Questions burn on Rose's tongue, I can feel it. But she only asks tersely, "Can you make it a bit further?"

Each breath feels like broken glass in my lungs, but I manage a jerky nod. Rose is right - the mission isn't over yet. I can't fall apart, not when lives depend on us finishing this.

With Rose's help, I stagger the rest of the way back to the guild tavern. But the image of that guard transforming into gold feels seared into my mind. Nothing will ever be the same again.

When we finally reach the tavern, Fairy Godmother lets out a ragged sob at the sight of bloodied, battered Tabitha cradled between us. She ushers us inside, shouting for the healers. I collapse into a chair as chaos erupts around me, the pain and chaos of the night finally crashing down like a tsunami.

Fairy Godmother kneels beside me, gripping my hand with surprising strength. "You did well, child. Tabitha will recover, thanks to you both."

I manage a weak nod. I have completed the mission. But the cost feels unquantifiable as Remme's cold eyes haunt me, his deadly power laid bare. What else have I glimpsed, unintentionally unveiling his most guarded truth? And where does that leave us now?

I sit numbly as chaos swirls around me in the guild tavern. My mind feels disconnected, like I'm watching it all unfold from underwater. The healers shout grimly to each other as they work to stabilize battered Tabitha. Other members dart about to gather bandages, tonics, anything that could help. Their faces blur together, full of fear and purpose.

A gentle hand grasps my shoulder and I startle, blinking up to find Fairy Godmother gazing down at me in concern.

"Come with me, child," she says quietly. "Let us talk in private."

I nod mutely and allow her to guide me between the crush of bodies to her study at the back of the tavern. The small, candlelit room feels like a sanctuary, sealing out the frantic energy beyond the door. My knees nearly buckle as the adrenaline abruptly drains away, leaving me hollow.

Fairy Godmother eases me into a cushioned chair and presses a cup of honeyed tea into my shaking hands. The warmth seeps into my chilled fingers as I clutch it like a lifeline. She settles across from me, watching me intently.

"Scarlet, look at me. What happened down there tonight?" Her voice is gentle but firm. "You look as if you stared too long into the abyss, and I need to understand why."

I open my mouth but the words lodge in my throat. Flickering images dance behind my eyes - the king's pitiless gaze, the guards' frantic screams, skin melting into lifeless gold... A choked noise escapes me and I squeeze my eyes shut, willing the visions away.

Fairy Godmother leans forward, gripping my hands tightly. "Breathe, child. Take your time. But I need you to tell me what you saw."

Haltingly, I force out the words between shuddering gasps. "The king...his touch transforms people to gold. I saw him...curse a guard right in front of me for disobeying orders. His whole body just...changed. Twisted metal where living flesh used to be."

I dare to meet Fairy Godmother's eyes then. "He's not human. His power, it's monstrous. And I..." My voice drops to a horrified whisper. "I let him get close to me." Shame mixes sickly with fear in my gut.

But Fairy Godmother simply squeezes my hands, expression thoughtful. "So the rumors hold truth after all. I had my suspicions, but no proof." She shakes her head. "You bear no blame here, Scarlet. How could you have known? But thanks to your courage, his true nature now stands exposed."

I let out a long breath, her calm rationality easing some of the panic constricting my chest. Of course - if anyone can make sense of this nightmare, it is my wise Godmother.

"What do we do now?" I ask hoarsely. "If the king finds out I discovered his secret..." Fear prickles my spine at the thought.

Fairy Godmother leans back, steepling her fingers. "For now, we keep this knowledge strictly contained. Tell no one beyond this room until I can investigate further." Her eyes bore into mine intently. "Can I trust you with that, Scarlet?"

I straighten my shoulders, lifting my chin. "Of course. Not a word leaves this room." The firm purpose helps steady me. Whatever else, I am still a member of this guild. I will not fail our code of secrecy.

She nods approvingly. "Good. In the meantime, we should discuss how you came to escape at all after witnessing such a thing." Her shrewd gaze drifts down to the staff still clutched in my white-knuckled grip.

I follow her eyes in surprise, having almost forgotten about the carved object anchoring me to reality. "I...this staff appeared to me in the tunnels. I think Halisar guided me to it."

Fairy Godmother hums thoughtfully. "May I?"

I hesitantly pass the staff to her weathered hands. She runs a palm over the ancient runes, brow furrowing. "Yes, I can feel his power resonating within. Is this the staff that was mentioned in the papers from the trial?"

I drop my gaze, shame burning my cheeks. "Yes, but I don't know how it got to the tunnels. I didn't bring it with me and I can't help but wonder..."

"Hush now, none of that." Fairy Godmother tilts my chin up gently. "You did well to make use of it, child. Halisar himself clearly meant for you to have it. You've been blessed by the god of thieves. None of the other guild members can claim that. Not even me." She lets out an almost conspiratory chuckle. "It's almost as if Halisar has sanctioned us himself."

I let out a shaky breath, managing a faint smile. She always knows exactly how to settle my anxious thoughts. We sit in comfortable silence for a few moments as I finish the cooling tea. My limbs feel leaden, but my mind is clearer.

Fairy Godmother watches me closely, her wise face lined with fresh worry. "I know tonight has been rough, Scarlet. The days ahead may be difficult as we navigate this revelation." Her eyes are sad but warm. "But never doubt that you have the strength within to overcome whatever comes. Our choices define us far more than any magic."

Emotion wells up in my throat at her steadfast faith and I cling to her words like a light in the dark.

Fairy Godmother grips my shoulders firmly. "Remember you do not walk this path alone, my child. We will unravel the way forward together."

I cover her weathered hand with mine, vision blurring with grateful tears. But for the first time since stumbling from those lightless tunnels, hope flickers tentatively inside me. The world may have shifted on its axis tonight, but I will find my footing again.

Dark and difficult days are coming. But with my guild - my family - at my side, I will survive this storm as I have every other. And we will emerge wiser, stronger, bound tighter than ever through adversity.

I rise slowly, legs still shaky but spine straight. There is work yet to be done tonight. But I will rest easier knowing Fairy Godmother's steady guidance is there to light the way forward through the shadows. We will navigate this together, one step at a time.

I pull my wise mentor into a fierce embrace. "Thank you," I whisper hoarsely. There is nothing more that needs to be said.

She returns the hug just as tightly, love and pride shining in her eyes. Then she pats my shoulder and turns me gently toward the door. "Go check on the others now. We will talk more tomorrow."

I nod, squaring my shoulders and stepping back out into the bustle of the guild tavern, my spirit bolstered. The truth remains a heavy burden, but I do not carry it alone. And together, we will find a way.

A Confession

Remme

Today is the day - I will finally confess my feelings to Scarlet. The time for discreet flirtations and stolen moments is over. I must know if what burns between us could truly ignite into something more.

Butterflies swarm my stomach at the thought. I, a cursed king, as nervous as a green squire! Yet the thought of laying my guarded heart bare makes me more anxious than facing an army ever could.

A soft chuckle draws my gaze to Sophia sitting by the hearth, mischief dancing in her eyes. "Who would believe it? The fearsome King Remme, conqueror of realms, felled by something as simple as young love."

I shoot her a wry glance, my pacing finally stilling. "It is far from simple, as you well know. You always see straight to the heart of things, don't you my friend?"

Her amusement fades, keen intellect weighing my words. "I see the loneliness etched beneath your strength, Remme. But this path is tangled with thorns. She is still only a participant in your tournament who is probably susceptible to your curse."

I shake my head firmly. "The trials will conclude soon and I will finally master my powers. I think I've figured out who it is, but am waiting for the last trial to verify. Once no more risk of harm remains, we can explore what lies between us." I meet Sophia's skeptical gaze. "I will not lose this chance at happiness. Not when I have already lost so much."

Sophia sighs, rising to stand near me. "Your curse makes any relationship dangerous. If you touch her..."

Pain lances through me at the thought. "I know," I say hoarsely. "But I am experienced in control. Simply having her near, eases the isolation like nothing else."

Sophia searches my face with those piercing eyes that see far more than most. I open my heart to her, unwilling to hide even the most vulnerable parts.

At last she nods slowly. "Your feelings run deep. Who am I to discourage you from pursuing a balm to long-borne wounds?" Her expression turns solemn. "But promise you will take care. Scarlet may become hurt in all this, and not just physically."

I clasp Sophia's hand, immensely grateful for her wisdom and honesty. "You are a true friend for speaking so plainly. I know there are many risks, but turning away from love does not guarantee safety. I must try, Sophia. She deserves that much."

Sophia's gaze softens. "As you say. I wish you every happiness, if it is meant to be." Her lips quirk wryly. "But you had better prepare an especially moving speech to win her heart."

I chuckle as nerves resurface. "I intend to. Speaking of which, I have final preparations to make." I glance out the window at the sinking sun. "Scarlet will arrive soon. Will you ensure we are not disturbed?"

Sophia inclines her head. "Of course. I will keep watch outside." Her expression grows serious once more. "And Remme...be cautious. Follow your heart, but keep your wits about you."

I smile softly, infinitely grateful for her protective presence. "Always, dear Sophia." With an encouraging squeeze of her shoulder, I sweep from the study, buzzing with anxious energy. The time has come. Tonight, I bare the fullness of my heart. May the fates be kind.

I descend through empty castle corridors to the lovers' garden kept locked and overgrown since my curse began. Tonight, I have transformed it into a haven worthy of Scarlet. Candles adorn the vine-wrapped gazebo in a warm glow. Plum blossoms and hyacinth perfume the air with sweetness. A spread of delicate fruits, cheeses and wine awaits atop embroidered linen.

Most importantly, the space is utterly private. No curious eyes or listening ears can intrude upon what will be the most vulnerable conversation of my life. Here, surrounded by beauty cultivated through neglect and time, I will finally voice the depth of longing in my soul.

At the stroke of moonrise, a hesitant footfall reaches me. I turn, breath catching as Scarlet's figure materializes on the garden path. She is resplendent in a flowing gown the deep crimson of pomegranate seeds, hair spilling loosely over her shoulders. The candlelight softens her features, wide eyes darting nervously to take in the intimate setting.

I step forward, pulse thundering. "Scarlet, thank you for coming. Please, make yourself comfortable." I gesture to the cushioned chairs and try not to reveal how desperately her answer hangs on the air between us.

She perches tentatively across from me, spine stiff as a caged bird poised to take flight. I ache to put her at ease, but first, I must speak my vulnerable truth. Clearing my throat, I begin the speech I prepared with such care:

"From the first moment we spoke, you stirred something in me I thought lost forever. At the time, I told myself it was mere curiosity at your audacity." I smile sadly.

"But my heart knew better. Our every encounter kindled a growing spark, even through trials and mistrust."

I meet her eyes then, willing her to see the earnestness of my words. "You are unlike any I have ever known, Scarlet. Bold, principled, compassionate...you challenge me in ways no one else dares."

Scarlet's eyes shimmer in the candlelight. "Your Majesty, I'm flattered, but..."

Gently, I reach across the table to clasp her hand with my glove. "Please, let me finish. There is more I must say."

She watches me warily and I notice her flinch slightly, but she remains silent. I forge on through the reckless thrumming of my pulse.

"I know you still see little more than a king. But you have awakened something good in me, Scarlet. I wish to become a man deserving of your affections, a man freed of his past."

I slide from my chair to kneel before her, hesitant hope rising within me. "What I ask is simply a chance. Continue competing in the trials, remain here at the palace where I may court you properly." My voice drops to a fervent whisper. "Let me prove myself worthy of your love, for you have long ago won mine."

For a moment Scarlet simply stares, eyes shimmering with emotion. When she finds her voice, it wavers with uncertainty. "Your majesty...you honor me deeply. Truly. But this...I can't."

Agony spears through me at her words. I cling tighter to her soft hand, desperate not to lose this lifeline. "Why? If you feel anything for me at all, please do not turn away without giving us a chance."

Scarlet's breath shudders out as she gently pulls her hand from mine. "Too many things are stacked against us. I need to focus on the trials. The cost of losing... you don't understand. I need to focus.." Her eyes radiate sadness and something more complex I cannot name. "I am promised to another. And you...your duties must come first, as a king."

I rock back on my heels, shaken to my core. How can she speak so dispassionately of destiny and duty at a moment like this?

"Duty be damned," I retort hoarsely. "I have been king for a decade. With you by my side, we can help bring the people peace. We can create a better world for them. I know that you care for the people as well." I search her face beseechingly. "Scarlet, if you feel anything at all for me still, do not let your fear of shadows rob us of light."

Scarlet stands abruptly, chin trembling with emotion. "My king...you move me more than you know. But some risks are too profound. I am sorry."

With that, she sweeps from the garden, leaving the fragrant air cold and lifeless in her wake. I lean back heavily in the chair, breathless with grief. It feels as though she took a piece of my soul when she walked away.

Could I have misjudged her feelings so terribly? My mind races through the times we've been together and what I've seen from her so far. The unreasonable anger and protectiveness that I already felt for her after seeing her apply for the trials. Our moment under the stars baring our souls to each other. Her teasing and the tension between us as I tested her in the carraige. The queen of cups she playfully dealt me in her 'reading', hinting at introspection and unexpected new love. Seeing her broken and almost lost after the last trial had decided it for me.

So how, after all that, could doubt now crush the budding flower of hope between us? What could hold her back, if her heart yearned for me as mine does for her?

The lingering image of sorrow in her eyes haunts me. She hides something beneath the surface, some unspoken fear or burden. I wish she had opened herself to me, so we might face it together. But the fates haven't decided it's time, it seems.

Perhaps the differences in our stations still weigh too heavily. I see only the fierce, radiant woman, but she remains conscious of the weight of being king. Or maybe her family obligations truly do bind her too tightly. What right do I have to ask her to turn away from duty, however much it pains us both? I would help her though. There is nothing that I wouldn't fix for her if she only asked.

But surely our connection deserves a chance to blossom before being severed so abruptly! There must be some way to bridge this vast divide separating us. I refuse to surrender so easily.

Heart aching but resolve hardened, I rise slowly and make my way back through the now oppressive gloom of the castle. The coming days may be bleak, but while breath remains in me, I will keep fighting for the woman who stirs my dormant soul. The fates have sown bitter trials before me, but with Scarlet's light still beckoning in the distance, I will endure.

Sophia's knowing eyes find mine as I pass her in the hall on my way back to my rooms. My frantic heart still yearns to chase after the golden-haired woman haunting my steps. But tonight, rest will not come easily under the stars now grown cold and remote.

Heartbreak

Scarlet

I paste a smile on my face as I step into the bustling town square, bracing myself for the performance ahead. The scents of roasted meat and fresh bread mingle with laughter and music in the air. The charity feast we competitors organized overflows with townsfolk eager to support our efforts.

I move through the crowd, exchanging greetings and well wishes. Despite my inner turmoil, I take time with each person, offering sincere thanks or listening patiently to their stories. Their beaming smiles lift my weary spirit.

Near the central fountain, a gaggle of children dance in circles singing a playful rhyme. My eyes crinkle as I watch their joyful abandon. It reminds me of carefree days in my own childhood - before fate began hemming me in on all sides.

A brave lad darts up and tugs my hand. "Play with us!" he pleads. I hesitate, knowing I should mingle with the noble patrons. But the child's delight melts my restraint. Laughing, I allow him to pull me into the circle.

I spin and twirl with the children until all are breathless and giddy. For these stolen moments, my ever-present worries fade away. Too soon, the children are called away to eat, waving reluctant goodbyes. My cheeks ache from grinning but my spirit feels lifted.

Continuing through the square, I pause often to speak with workers and craftsmen who assisted in preparing the feast. Though exhausted from their labors, they beam with pride in what they accomplished for the less fortunate. I thank each one by name, humbled by their tireless generosity.

At the banquet tables, I laugh as heaped plates are pushed eagerly into my hands by local families. I sample a bite of each dish, complimenting grandmothers on secret recipes and fathers on luscious roasts. Their gifts of food may appear simple, but I understand the care infused in each one. I accept them with heartfelt gratitude.

Between conversations, my gaze drifts inevitably toward the royal box where King Remme holds court. My chest tightens remembering his agonized confession in the moonlit garden. How badly I wish I could forget everything and have said yes. I look quickly away. Even from a distance, the weight of his presence still affects me like the sun's inescapable gravity.

Nearby, Lord Greystone's annoying voice carries over the crowd as he talks with nobles seeking his favor. They laugh loudly at his bad jokes, hoping to get on his good side. Greystone looks very pleased with himself. He doesn't even glance my way.

I frown, feeling uneasy. I know Greystone has a shady past gambling and chasing women. But now he's suddenly popular with the royal court, like his reputation doesn't matter. When did all these vipers start sucking up to him so hard? Something strange is going on here. But right now Greystone holds all the cards. The thought leaves a gross taste in my mouth.

Shaking off my misgivings, I put on a smile again as I continue through the festivities. Whatever plots and schemes churn behind the scenes, today is about bringing cheer to the people. I cling to that purpose, pushing down the helplessness gnawing beneath my breastbone. I can only live in this moment. Tomorrow's trials will come soon enough.

Just as my mind was distracted from my least favorite person here - Greystone's grating voice sounds behind me. "Scarlet, my treasure! There you are." Before I can react, he presses against my back and slides a jewel-encrusted bracelet onto my wrist. "A small token for my future bride."

I plaster on a smile and resist the urge to hurl the gaudy thing into the dirt. "You spoil me, my lord." My skin crawls as he nuzzles my neck possessively. I cannot stomach his touches, not when my naive heart still yearns for another.

"Nonsense, you deserve the world," Greystone murmurs as onlookers titter and stare. "Come, you must sample the fowl. It's delicious."

He steers me to the banquet table before I can object and piles my plate obscenely high. I force myself to nibble daintily under his watchful gaze, my stomach churning. All I want is to flee this false charade, but appearances rule my days now. I've turned down my only hope of escaping this fate. If I fail the last trial tomorrow and don't win the trials as a whole, marrying Lord Greystone is my only option. Greystone's investment in my stepmother's estate has us both in golden shackles. The thought nearly drowns me and I am already wading too deep in my emotions today dealing with the king.

"Wonderful as always," I lie demurely, continuing the slow torture of my plate. Greystone preens, but his satisfied smile slips when a harried maid spills wine down his doublet.

"Clumsy wench! This is Atrian silk!" he thunders. My pulse spikes in alarm at his fury. The surrounding conversations quiet.

The maid pales, stammering apologies and bowing low. I step between them before Greystone can raise a hand. "My lord, do not trouble yourself. The dressmakers can easily remove a small stain."

Greystone's eyes flash dangerously at my interference. With effort, he smooths his features to haughty indifference. "Of course, you are right. But the help should mind their place." His stare bores warningly into me before he turns on his heel. "Come, Scarlet. I grow tired of these meager festivities."

My nails bite into my palms in frustration as I allow him to escort me away. A cold knot of anger twists in my gut. He acts as though he already owns me.

Outside the square, Greystone shoves me against a shadowed wall. "Do not undermine me again, wife," he hisses. "You belong to me. It would be unwise to resist your duties." His smile turns cruel. "Unless you wish your dear stepmother to find herself...homeless?"

Rage and despair war within me. I long to drive my dagger through his black heart. But my family's fate hangs by a financial thread only Greystone can secure. I don't care so much if my stepmother is homeless, but by making that happen, I would lose my inheritance as well. So I bow my head in apparent submission.

"Forgive me," I grit out. "I spoke rashly."

Greystone grasps my chin almost gently. "I know change is difficult. But you will learn obedience in time." With a patronizing kiss to my forehead, he releases me. "Now stay and help clean this mess. I'm returning to my estate." He sweeps away smugly.

Only after he vanishes around a corner do I release a shuddering breath. A familiar ache of helplessness threatens to pull me under. But I force my spine straight and head back to the bustling square. I will finish this task with chin high, no matter how inescapable my cage seems now.

Once I rejoin the volunteers, the work of soothing ruffled feathers and clearing the feast proves a welcome distraction. By the time the sun sinks below the city walls, little evidence remains of the day's festivities. Weary to the bone, I slip into an alley shortcut towards the guild tavern, wanting only to drown my sorrows away for a night.

Raised voices and the crackle of magic make me freeze just before turning the corner. Risking a peek around the crumbling brick, my eyes widen. Half a dozen masked figures in thieves' garb surround none other than King Remme, weaving violent spells. His head guard lies crumpled against the far wall. My heart leaps into my throat.

The king fights like a cornered wolf, vicious and desperate, but the attackers slowly force him back. As one assailant binds his legs in shimmering wire, another strikes his chest with a bolt of energy. He crashes hard onto the grimy cobblestones with a pained shout.

Time seems to slow. I should run, get help...but these men could kill Remme before anyone arrived. They seem prepared, too prepared. Ice-cold calm settles over me. Sometimes you must deal with threats personally. Cursing under my breath, I tear several strips from my gown's silk hem and wrap them around my head and face - a thin disguise, but it will have to suffice.

Taking a deep breath, I slip one of Fairy Godmother's paralysis darts and a throwing knife into each palm. Then I step silently into the alley's mouth.

Two of the assailants have their backs to me. I let the darts fly, striking them both in the neck before they realize I'm there. They drop like stones. The others whirl, snarling curses. I fling my knives in rapid succession, catching two more in the chest and shoulder. They fall screaming.

The final masked pair charge recklessly, hurling twin fireballs. I somersault beneath the sizzling arcs of flame. As I roll to my feet, I draw my daggers and slash viciously at the nearest foe's hamstrings. He collapses with a howl.

The last one tries fleeing but I tackle him fiercely, pinning him against the alley wall and pressing both blades to his throat. "Who sent you?" I demand. But he only gurgles blood through the knife slashes on his neck. Snarling in frustration, I knock him unconscious with the dagger hilt.

Trembling with adrenaline, I scan the bodies to ensure all are neutralized. My disguise seems intact but my skirts are badly shredded from the fight revealing the Triple G's tattoo on my thigh. I freeze as my eyes land on Remme, stirring weakly as the binding spell around his legs fades. There's no time - I have to disappear before he sees me.

I sheathe my daggers and melt into the nearest shadows, pulse pounding. A few frantic turns later, I'm sprinting full tilt for the guild tavern, mind racing. How could King Remme have been ambushed and left undefended like that? What will I do if he saw anything to identify me. The dress is new and I can toss it and change in the guild tavern so he never sees it again. My stomach sinks. I can only pray he did not glimpse my face through the thin covering or tattoo in the chaos.

As soon as I arrive at the tavern I change hastily, throwing the dress and face covering into the hearth at the tavern and swapping my slashed gown for nondescript trousers and tunic.

I want desperately to check that the king is alright after the attack, but I dare not risk being seen. Clenching my jaw in frustration, I tread softly to the back office and knock. At Fairy Godmother's gravelly welcome, I slip inside.

Candlelight casts a warm glow over the familiar space. Fairy Godmother looks up from her ledger, gray brows rising in surprise.

"Child, you're back early. How was the feast?"

I hesitate, unsure how much to reveal. But something in me needs to unburden, if only partially. "It went well. But on my way home, I witnessed a group of masked thieves attacking the king in the alley near Darren's bakery." Technically true, if lacking context.

Fairy Godmother's eyes sharpen. "Masked thieves, you say?" She leans forward intently. "Were they displaying any sigils or colors to identify who?"

I shake my head. "They wore plain clothing. Definitely weren't anyone from our guild. But they used violent magic - spells meant to maim or kill." I suppress a shiver at the memory.

"Hmm." Fairy Godmother rubs her chin in thought, brow furrowing. "It's dangerous to have an unknown moving withing our territory. I will look into this."

I sag slightly in relief. If anyone can uncover the truth behind the attack, it is her.

She studies me closely. "You seem very shaken. Is the king alright?"

"He was stirring when I left."

"Did he see you?"

I shook my head no, "I don't think so."

She crosses her arms and looks me up and down. "Scarlet, I know you've grown fond of the king. Is there more to this you aren't telling me?"

I meet her probing gaze. "I've said all I can for now. Please trust that I'll explain everything when the time is right."

She holds my eyes for a long moment before nodding slowly. "Very well. Get some rest, child."

I embrace her, gratitude welling up. She always knows when not to push. With a murmur of thanks, I retreat out of the room before she can read anything more in my face. I hate deceiving her, but have no choice for the moment. I can only pray my omissions do not create deeper problems down the road.

All I can do is pray my impulsive actions have not destroyed any last chance of escaping my hopeless fate. Please, Halisar, if you've truly decided to bless me, please let King Remme remain ignorant of my role in all of this. If he unmasks me now, after coming so agonizingly close to freedom, I do not know how my weary heart could bear it.

THE FINAL TRIAL

SCARLET

The waiting chamber echoes with nervous energy as we competitors huddle together, straining to hear the muffled crowds through the arena walls. I wring my damp hands, trying to ignore the anxious flutter in my stomach.

Rose gives me a bracing smile from across the room.

The chamber doors grind open and we all flinch. Another competitor's name is called. She rises unsteadily, face bloodless but resolute. We watch her go with shared dread.

"Reckon it's a pit of vipers out there?" someone jokes weakly. A few manage thin laughter. Anything to distract us from toxic thoughts.

"Maybe they finally perfected that skeleton army," pipes up a scrawny youth. More strained chuckles.

My lips twist wryly. "It's a baking contest, clearly. Dragon egg souffles." The tense group latches onto the absurdity, tossing out equally ridiculous guesses to release nervous energy.

But all too soon, the doors open again. "Scarlet Mer-heart." My name rings out and the room stills. I stand slowly, my legs wooden.

The walk through the torch-lit stone corridor stretches endlessly, my blood rushing loud in my ears. But I keep my spine straight and head high. Let the final challenge come. I may have barely been able to sleep last night from my mind never shutting up about everything between me, the king and Lord Greystone, but I am ready.

The attendant gestures me wordlessly through the heavy iron door and I stride into the unfamiliar circular chamber beyond, shadows dancing across robed chanting figures...

My heart hammers as I'm led not toward the arena gates, but down a torch-lit stone corridor. None of the previous trials began this way. Apprehension and confusion churn in my gut. Where are they taking me?

The passage ends at an imposing iron door engraved with arcane symbols. My escorts gesture wordlessly for me to enter. Squaring my shoulders, I step through into a circular room ringed by robed figures chanting in an ancient tongue.

Their strange melody reverberates through me as I'm directed to stand in the room's center, marked by a wide circle filled with similar runes. Power builds on the air, raising the hairs on my nape.

The lead mage approaches, pressing a smooth black stone into my palm. "Hold tight. And remember - perception is fleeting, only courage endures." Before I can question the cryptic words, the chanters raise their voices. Blinding light floods my senses.

I'm falling...falling through a vortex of screaming color and noise. It seems to last an eternity, until my knees abruptly strike earth. My vision swims back into focus under a blistering sun. The robed mages are gone. In their place...nothing but scorched desert sands in all directions.

Disoriented, I gain my feet and scan the undulating dunes. The arena is nowhere in sight. How is this possible? Some powerful spell must have transported me elsewhere instantly. But why?

Hot wind buffets my face as I turn slowly, searching for anything besides repetitive miles of baked sand. In the distance, something catches the light - an enormous glass wall. My eyes follow it and to my surprise, I find myself entirely surrounded by this glass wall that extends to create a bubble over my head high in the sky.

My mind races to make sense of it all. This must be the final trial - some conjured world meant to test our limits. Focus, Scarlet. What did the mage say? Perception is fleeting…only courage endures. He failed to mention that with the sun glaring into the glass I will bake in here if I take too long. Suddenly my cooking joke seems funny to me in a whole new way. Or perhaps I've already had my mind lost to the heat. Either way, I need to do this fast. Whatever it is I need to do.

As I look at the sand near my feet I notice it's slowly moving. All in one direction. With no other unique identifiers I decide following that would be my best bet.

The sun beats down unrelentingly as I trudge up yet another massive dune. Sweat dampens my back and brow, sand grinding between my teeth. My throat is parched, every swallow painful. But I conserve my limited water rations carefully.

The glass looms no closer despite the endless miles crossed. The repetitive slopes taunt me with false nearness. All I can do is grit my teeth and put one aching foot in front of the other.

Some time later, movement on a nearby ridge catches my eye. Three bulky silhouettes crest the dune, lumbersome bodies swinging. I freeze, squinting against the harsh sunlight.

My hand goes to my dagger. Some desert creatures perhaps? I count only three. If they attack, I may be able to dispatch them swiftly and conserve strength. I sink into a crouch, slow breaths steadying my nerves.

As the figures trudge down the sandy slope toward me, deep furrows trail behind their footfalls. Closer now, I make out thick limbs, oversized torsos, misshapen heads. No natural beast moves like that.

My mouth goes dry for reasons unrelated to thirst. These lumbering giants are each easily twice my height. Their hulking bodies seem to roil and reform constantly amid plumes of sand. Realization hits my tired brain - these are elemental creatures, their frames composed of animated desert sands. Sand gollems!

Fear sinks icy claws into my chest. No ordinary weapon can fell such conjured behemoths. I must flee!

I surge upright and sprint desperately for a rocky out-cropping nearby, my stiff legs screaming protest. Risking a glance back, my heart stutters. The gollems are already halfway down the dune, ground shuddering under their purposeful strides.

I pour every ounce of strength into my flagging limbs. But my head start shrinks rapidly on the shifting sands. Angling toward the outcropping, I scramble frantically upward on burning thighs, lungs heaving scalding air.

A massive hand sails past my ankle, seeking purchase. With a final grunt I crest the ridge and half-slide, half-fall down the opposite side, crashing in a breathless heap. Gulping air, I claw behind a tall boulder and huddle trembling. My gambit worked, for now.

Heavy footsteps circle the base below. I clench my eyes shut, trying to slow my ragged gasps. Maybe they'll miss me and continue on...

The boulder blocking me shudders violently under a thunderous blow, sand raining down. I bite back a scream as one enormous gollem after another batters the rock, seeking to dislodge it.

Wedging myself further into a crevice, I fumble desperately for options. I dropped all my gear in my reckless flight. Without tools or magic, I'm utterly defenseless.

The stone shielding me cracks down the middle under the ceaseless assault. We're running out of time! I look about wildly and spot a chunk of the boulder broken loose nearby. An idea sparks.

I wedge my hands beneath the basketball-sized fragment and heave with all my might. It barely budges. Clenching my jaw, I gather my legs under me and push with everything left in my burning muscles. The chunk rises, wobbling.

With a guttural cry I half-lift, half-kick the massive stone at the weakest gollem battering the boulder beside me. The heavy missile catches it squarely, forcing it back a step.

Sand spills from its torso like blood but quickly re-forms. Not enough!

Fury overtakes fear. I will not cower helplessly as death looms! Grabbing more broken debris, I hurl every stone and shard within reach at the trio of gollems. They stagger under the barrage but keep coming.

My teeth split against each other from the force of my screams as I continue flinging every loose bit of the environment I can wield. Bloody scrapes cover my hands and arms from wrestling with rubble nearly too heavy to grasp. Still I rage on. If these are to be my final breaths, I will fight 'til the last!

Finally, a lucky stone propelled by adrenaline and desperation strikes the wounded gollem's head clean off. The enormous body hesitates, sand swirling uncertainly. Then the whole form collapses into a harmless pile, blown away swiftly on the desert winds.

The sight reignites hope's guttering flame inside me. They can be defeated! Shouting hoarsely, I redouble my efforts against the remaining two. Step by agonizing step, I force them back under my desperate barrage.

At long last, the second gollem's chest shatters into clumps. Before it can regenerate, I tackle it bodily and we crash down the slope in a tangle of limbs. Its body dissolves completely beneath me as we roll to a jarring stop on level ground.

I lurch up, head swimming with exhaustion. Only one adversary remains now. It pauses warily at the ridge top, observing its decimated allies. Then, with an eerie moan, it turns and retreats the way it came.

My legs give out and I collapse onto hands and knees. Half-crazed laughter bubbles up between ragged gasps. I defeated them. Somehow, impossibly, I held my ground and survived!

As I search for and retrieve my daggers from where I dropped them, I process how long I've been in here. None of the others before me had been gone as long as I feel I have been. Was I sent somewhere different? Is there some magic at play affecting the lapse of time in here?

I have to keep going. I've lost all sense of time at this point.

After what feels like hours later of following the moving sand as it slowly sped up, hurtling to who knows where, I stand at the top of a sand dune. Strange tubular plants cling to the rocks around the swirling vortex of speeding sand in the center, trembling oddly.

The sand is moving too fast. If I get too close it will pull me in. I don't understand. What am I suppose to do?

I pause as movement catches my eye in the sand, running towards me from behind. The lone surviving sand gollem. It roars, sand whipping up around it as it stomps at a speed that shouldn't be possible, seeking to reach me. I'm trapped between it and the deadly vortex.

Heart pounding, I scramble along the interior perimeter, the tubular plants providing handholds even if they are burning my skin to touch them. I can hear the golem roar as it closes in.

I desperately cling to the slippery plants as the vortex's pull strengthens, dragging me towards its waiting maw. Their tendrils dig agonizingly into my skin but I don't dare let go.

A thundering crash shatters my hopes - the gollem breaches the top of the sand dune above me. It storms towards me, even as the sands yank my legs over the rim. This is it, I can't resist both forces!

But the mage's riddle repeats in my mind - perception is fleeting, only courage endures. This is a trial. It seeks to test me. I must surrender control and make the bold leap into the unknown.

Gasping a prayer to Halisar, I release my hold on the plants. The vortex instantly swallows me down in a roar of sand. The world disappears as I'm swept rapidly down, down through flaming darkness...

THE HOURGLASS
SCARLET

Abruptly, the sands spit me out, dropping me into a dim cavern. I crash to my hands and knees on the stone floor, coughing and shaking sand from my hair. It's done - I made it through. Relief and elation well up in me as I regain my feet, squinting into the gloom. Above me is the towering flow of sand pouring from high above. Without magic, that fall alone would have killed me. I wonder... a quick glance around and I can see more glass in the far off distance surrounding me still, but the shape is almost upside down from where I just was.

It can't be. A laugh escapes me. I must be going crazy. Did they throw me into a giant hourglass? A hint at time running out for the last trial?

A blinding flash suddenly illuminates the cave, and I am no longer alone. Surrounding me stand a dozen figures wearing each competitor's likeness. More magic? Confused, I turn slowly, taking in the circle of doppelgangers.

Their faces show no emotion, but they mirror my movements exactly.

Perception is fleeting... My own double's dagger lifts in warning. These must be shadow selves summoned to challenge me, mimicking me perfectly. I cannot beat them by matching skill for skill. I must be unexpected.

I charge first, faking left then rolling right and springing up inside the guard of one double. My dagger slides smoothly into his heart and he dissolves into black vapor. The real fight begins.

I abandon all defense, aggressing relentlessly with blinding strikes from all angles. The doubles react a blink too slow, and two more fall to well-placed blades. My confidence builds - I can win this!

But slowly the tide turns as my initial fury spends itself. The remaining doubles adapt to my onslaught, the perfect match for my every attack. My lungs burn, injuries blazing as I frantically parry and dodge their encircling blades. I cannot keep this pace forever.

In desperation, I flip atop one double's sword, slash and kick off his chest, to vault over the circle. I hit the cavern floor and sprint into the dark before my shadows can pursue. I need a new tactic, quickly.

The sound of rushing water reaches my ears. A river! Following the sound, I find a swift underground channel cutting through the chamber's far side. If I can cross it, perhaps the doubles will struggle with the terrain...

Sheathing my weapons, I dive into the biting cold waters. My sodden clothes try to drag me down but I kick furiously, angling against the push. Halfway across, a shadow appears above - the doubles found me.

One dives in after me, swimming powerfully to intercept my path. With a grunt of effort, I crash into and overturn the double beneath the surface, then continue towards the opposite shore. My feet finally hit silt and stone.

I stagger from the river onto the bank, collapsing to my hands and knees and vomiting water. A splash tells me the remaining doubles have entered the river after me. It will slow them, but not for long. I push back to my feet and run on trembling legs down a passage leading away into more unknown darkness. There has to be an escape somewhere ahead. Otherwise this trial is unwinnable.

The footfalls behind me gain ground in the winding tunnels. Up ahead, a rope bridge spans a gaping chasm, barely visible in the gloom. It will have to do. I sprint out onto the swaying bridge, my added weight making the ropes creak alarmingly.

Halfway across, the planks under me give out and I crash through into open air beneath. Instinctively, my fingers catch and clench around one of the rough ropes as I swing out over the inky void below. I cling desperately, breath frozen. Don't look down.

Far above, footsteps carefully make their way onto the weakened bridge as the doubles follow me out over the gorge. The ropes jerk and twist in their hands. They will cut my anchor any second!

Swallowing back fear, I begin hauling myself up the rope, muscles screaming protest. I cannot defeat them, but perhaps I can still evade them. The lead double's blade flashes down toward my white-knuckled hand.

Letting go, I allow myself to plummet into the abyss. The wind roars in my ears for seconds or hours - I lose all sense of time. Is this what dying feels like?

Just as I abandon all hope, the fall abruptly ends. My body slams into an icy pool, the shocking cold driving the breath from my lungs. I sink into shadow before clawing back desperately for the surface.

I break into blessed air again, coughing violently. Jagged stone walls loom all around, barely visible in the gloom. But above, a soft light glows, pulsing gently.

I flip onto my back, floating as strength flees my thrashing limbs. Craning my neck, I realize the radiance emanates from the highest point of the hourglass above. It seems to beat in time with my slowing heart as I drift, mesmerized by its hypnotic rhythm.

With a final bright pulse, the last golden grains fall and settle into the giant cavern. The glow fades. Understanding washes over me – the sands of my trial have finally run out. Time is up.

I roll over, slowly pulling my leaden body through the dark waters toward a sandy shore just ahead. Relief floods me as I crawl onto blessedly solid ground and collapse, every muscle trembling with exhaustion.

Perception is fleeting, but courage endures. When you have nothing left but breath in your body, that is enough. I have passed the final trial. But was it enough to win?

MY THIEF
REMME

I take my seat overlooking the arena's center after stretching my legs, where an ancient hourglass structure stands. This mystical relic projects the competitors' experiences overhead through complex illusion magic, compressing hours into minutes. The crowds will witness highlights of the trial as though watching through a window to another realm.

Aiding the magic, the sands' slow vortex represents flowing time itself. The projections have always proven insightful, though never has so much hinged on what truths they may reveal. I pray the magic exposes the final clues I seek.

Rose steps forth boldly to enter the trial after Scarlet. While Scarlet prevailed through clever caution, I know Rose will unleash her unrelenting fierceness. She does not comprehend surrender.

Rose vanishes into the churning sands. Immediately scenes flare overhead - our magical window into the conjured world. The crowds gasp and cheer as Rose battles lumbering sand beasts under the blistering illusory sun. Her dual blades carve through them relentlessly until they nick the soul stones holding them together, and they disintegrate.

In the strange caverns against her doubles, she fights viciously, refusing to yield ground. The spectators are mesmerized by her aggressive onslaught as she carves through two opponents. But her boldness isn't without costs - trapped in the raging river, rocks bash Rose mercilessly. Still she drags her battered body from the water through will alone, to the crowds' approval.

By the time she attempts crossing the ruined bridge, Rose is clearly exhausted, injuries slowing her usual agility. Yet still she flings herself recklessly over the crumbling edge, heedless of the danger. The onlookers applaud her unrelenting determination.

When the dark waters finally spit Rose out, she crawls onto land on bloodied nails, swaying with fatigue.

The scenes fade as Rose is half-carried back into the arena, peering about wildly through tangled hair. Her clothing is utterly shredded from the merciless trial. As her sleeve falls away, I gasp - a familiar tattoo is revealed on her bared shoulder. A brightly colored mermaid swimming down Rose's shoulder, her tail curving around on itself to create a familiar shape. Much like the snake did creating a g on the young woman that escaped my dungeon.

Shock roots me in place. Rose bears the mark of the thieves guild I've been pursuing. I press my temples against a pounding headache. After last night's attack, I swore one of my rescuers bore the same sigil on their thigh. But I took a hard blow to the head.

All will be revealed after she is crowned the winner of the trials. Once she has been given the crown I will know for sure if she is who I think she is.

I Give Up

Scarlet

My heart hammers an erratic beat as the competitors are led back into the muted daylight of the arena. The crowds still roar from the last nail-biting trial through the mystical giant hourglass. Its sands yet swirl lazily, projecting swirling fractals overhead now that the scenes have ceased.

I glance over at Rose, leaning heavily on a healer as she limps along. Her clothing is utterly shredded, one sleeve torn completely off to reveal the thick bandages swathing her shoulder. Our eyes meet and understanding passes between us - the tattoo beneath is now exposed.

Rose gives an almost imperceptible shake of her head, guessing my thoughts. We cannot speak safely here. But I read the resolve in her steady gaze - no flinching or fleeing now. We will see this through, no matter the cost. I draw strength from her courage, squaring my shoulders. Let the fates fall where they may.

Too soon we are arrayed before the royal box, the crowds silencing in anticipation. My stomach feels sick as I clutch Rose's hand like a lifeline. In moments, hopefully I will be crowned champion and this will be all over. I will be able to complete my mission, turn in the crown and maybe find a way to escape from the arranged marriage. My recent donations have been sizable. Perhaps it will be enough to pay off my stepmothers debts.

A fanfare blares and King Remme rises slowly, his face unreadable. But his eyes linger on me a heartbeat longer than the rest. Hope and dread war within me. How do I miss him so much when there was never truly something going on between us? But he presents only calm resolve as he addresses the expectant arena.

"People of Ovehan, you have borne witness to extraordinary courage these long weeks. Any who complete the trials are proven worthy of honor and respect." Nods and murmurs of agreement ripple through the stands.

King Remme continues, "But three among them exemplified the virtues of compassion, justice and sacrifice beyond all others." My nails bite into my palms, apprehension rising. "Bronze medalist, representing perseverance - Darius Fellcipher!"

Polite applause rises as a shocked Darius ascends the wooden winner's platform erected hastily in the arena's center. He appears humbled by the recognition after barely surviving each round through clever tricks. I clap sincerely along with the rest. However devious his methods, he persevered when many faltered. And his skills did save my life once. He has earned this honor.

Too soon the noise dies away and Remme raises a hand for the next pronouncement. "Silver medalist, representing courage and integrity - Lady Scarlet Merheart."

Ice water trickles down my spine. Silver? Weeks of sleepless nights and grueling trials ending in...second place? The arena seems to tilt around me. This cannot be real. I blink back traitorous tears, fighting to keep my composure before the expectant crowds. But inside, grief threatens to pull me under entirely.

Somehow my wooden limbs carry me up the winner's platform steps. I avoid looking at the king, unable to bear what I may see lingering in his eyes. Pity? Or worse yet, disappointment? Focusing on keeping my chin high is taking every shred of willpower I possess.

If I am not champion, then I have failed completely. Nothing can save my family estate now other than being sold off. No escaping Lord Greystone's vile clutches. A bleak future awaits me at home, shackled "duty" to a cruel man. This tournament was my only chance...and I just lost everything.

I jerk back to the present as raucous cheers erupt, jolting me from my spiral of despair. Rose has been named champion and now ascends the platform, beaming triumphantly. Though she sways with exhaustion, her good eye glows with fierce joy. This victory is hers alone - she earned it through blood and sacrifice. I summon up a smile through the anguish, embracing her gently so as not to aggravate her injuries.

"You did it," I whisper hoarsely.

Rose squeezes me fiercely with her good arm. "We did it," she insists. I can only nod, not trusting my voice. At least one of us succeeded today. I will celebrate with her later. But right now, grief scrapes at the ragged edges of my soul. I only wish to escape the probing eyes and find somewhere quiet to nurse my wounds.

Rose seems to sense my need, releasing me with an understanding look. As the king places the victor's wreath of golden laurels on her head, I slip quietly down the platform steps ignoring the cheering masses. Their joyful triumphs are salt in the raw wound of my loss.

I wind silently through emptying passageways under the arena, not paying heed to direction. I want only solitude, to unleash the black wave building within me before it drags me under in public view. This may be weakness, but I no longer care. The trials demanded every ounce of courage and strength I possessed. With the finish line lost, what reserves are left?

At last I stumble out into the street outside, empty still with the stands full. Soon the masses will swarm out. Gasping raggedly, I stagger to a bench nearby and deposit my worn and tired body into the seat.

I surrendered everything - my good name, my inheritance, my happiness - for the slim chance at victory here. And still I failed. Now I am utterly alone against the cold future looming before me. No options or hope remain.

Anguish and fear crash through me until I am spent. Somewhere in my fit, I scraped my knuckles the bench. But the physical pain barely registers through the yawning hollowness within. I am hollow, emptied of light and will. What purpose is left to me now?

The heavy tread of footfalls eventually intrudes into my fog. I tense, hastily wiping the tear tracks from my face. But I remain seated with my back to the entrance - I cannot muster the strength to don any mask before strangers just yet.

A hesitation, then soft footfalls approach my sheltered corner. Whoever it is, they tread lightly as one wishing not to startle or impose. I hear the whisper of cloth as they settle on the flagstones a respectful distance away. For long moments we both simply breathe, two islands alone in the street.

At the scrape of footsteps, I tense. But the tread is too light for a guard. A dark silhouette limps closer, backlit by the distant setting sun.

"Fairy Godmother?" I rasp in surprise.

She settles beside me with a sigh. "I thought I might find you here, child."

I look away, fresh tears threatening. "I apologize for slipping away. I just...needed space."

She lays a wrinkled hand on my shoulder. "No apologies needed, my dear. I cannot imagine the pain this brings you."

I clench my fist. "I sacrificed everything for victory. But it wasn't enough!"

Fairy Godmother rubs my back gently as I fight to compose myself. She doesn't fill the silence with false assurances or platitudes. Simply listening, sharing the sorrow. It steadies me like an anchor in a storm.

Finally I sit up straighter, the immediate anguish spent. Fairy Godmother squeezes my hand.

"What comes next feels an impossible weight," she says. "But remember, the future is not fixed. It can be reshaped."

I look at her questioningly. She takes a deep breath as though bracing herself.

"There are secrets I must share, pieces that may bring clarity. But you may see me differently after." Worry creases her brow.

I clasp her weathered hand. "Nothing could change how much you mean to me. Please."

She searches my face, then nods slowly. "I didn't fully know, but I had suspected, that I may have been unintentionally involved in the king's curse."

I sit up straighter. She's rarely spoken of her history.

"I was there the night it was cast," she admits quietly. "A dear friend got me access to the secret gathering of mages after the coronation. We were told the new king was in mortal peril, cursed with something that would destroy everything. My friend thought my healing gifts could help."

I listen intently as Fairy Godmother continues her tale. "When I arrived to the secret gathering, the king lay close to death, wracked with agony by the curse's dark magic. We were told only that it would kill him and any he touched. To stay far away. I found it odd that he was dressed entirely in gold as was the bed the king lay on, but I figured that was just part of the coronation. Showing his wealth and power... typical egotistical royalty stuff."

Her eyes take on a faraway look. "I have some skill with blessings, so I wove a counter-spell to negate the curse's lethality. I also granted him the gift to not need food or drink, to sustain him."

She focuses on me again. "Without knowing the curse's effects, I made one final addition - a catalyst that I hoped would allow him to eventually gain control of the magic inflicted on him."

I absorb this silently. Fairy Godmother had been there at the start, trying to help.

She continues, "I never learned what powers were invoked, or saw what artifact they used to bind as his catalyst. But after seeing his reaction to you trying to steal the crown...I began to suspect it was the implement chosen."

I sit up straighter in dawning realization.

Fairy Godmother pats my hand. "I wanted you to know the full truth."

I squeeze her weathered hand. "Thank you for confiding in me. Your actions saved his life - do not carry guilt for that kindness."

She smiles sadly at my determination.

I sit quietly for a time after Fairy Godmother finishes her tale, turning over this new information in my mind. One question nags at me that I cannot let go unspoken, even if only in my own head.

If the curse was going to kill him and anything he touched, how was I able to make contact without harm?

When I grabbed his leg and he fell as I escaped or when we kissed…

This didn't make sense.

I Was Wrong

Remme

After weeks of trials, today I finally bestow it upon the champion.

Rose waits in my private chambers, believing this merely an audience to receive her rewards. She has no inkling of the trap about to spring. I feel certain now - her build, her skills, even the flash of recognition in her eyes when viewing the crown before. She must be the thief who triggered my curse.

I school my features to impassivity and enter my chambers. Rose rises from her seat by the hearth, wincing slightly from her injuries but grinning.

"Your Majesty, I'm honored you wished to see me."

I force an easy smile. "The honor is mine, Champion. You have more than earned every reward." I lift the crown from the desk, no longer in the box I gifted Scarlet when I thought she was the thief. The idea finally removing these golden gloves has me wanting to rush, but I know better. "But first, I have a gift to celebrate your historic victory."

Her eyes widen at the sight of the jeweled crown. I watch closely as I lift the ancient artifact reverently. Is that fear in her gaze? Or perhaps greed?

Before she can react, I step forward swiftly and place the crown atop her golden curls. As I draw back my hand, I let my fingers deliberately brush her neck.

She gasps and stiffens, face freezing in a rictus of horror. Cracks spiderweb rapidly across her skin as gold overtakes her flesh. I leap backwards in shock as she lets out an agonized scream, hands clawing at her gilded face.

Moments later only a golden statue remains, captured eternally in her final throes of terror and pain. I sink to my knees, gut wrenching with anguish. No! This cannot be real!

I was so certain she was the thief. Her skills, her tattoo.. .it made perfect sense. But instead I just brutally murdered the true champion. What have I done?

None of this adds up. If she is not the thief, then who? None of the other competitors showed her cunning or subtlety. Could it be...Scarlet?

She hid her skills so cleverly in the trials. Only revealing her capabilities when absolutely necessary. The thief must have done the same to escape the castle undetected.

And her presence always stirred something in me, even then. An unconscious recognition? Is it possible I overlooked the one closest to me this whole time?

If so, the curse has claimed an innocent life through my blindness. I cradle my head in shaking hands. When will this madness end? I thought solving the puzzle would bring peace. Instead, it only multiplies pain and questions.

But one truth shines clear as day - I have failed catastrophically in my judgments. No more half-measures or groping in shadows. If Scarlet is the thief, I must handle this with wisdom and compassion. Too many lives hang in the balance.

Steeling myself, I drape cloth reverently over Rose's golden body. She deserved far better than falling prey to forces beyond her control. I vow to free her from this as soon as possible. For her, and all who suffer for my curse.

The path forward waits, but I cannot walk it alone. If I am to salvage meaning from this tragedy, I will need Scarlet's light to illuminate the way. But the next steps must be taken with utmost care. Too much depends on what comes to light in the darkness ahead.

A GRAND WEDDING

SCARLET

My hands tremble uncontrollably as I smooth out imaginary wrinkles in the voluminous white skirts. Today I walk the aisle to be bound forever to a cruel man I despise. Even the soaring cathedral arches and elaborate floral displays do little to settle my roiling nerves.

This dress feels like a ridiculous costume, the layers of silk and lace suffocating me. I wish I could tear the whole farce away. Nearby, my awful stepsisters preen and gossip loudly in their gaudy bridesmaid dresses, ignoring me completely. I have never felt more alone, an island adrift in a churning sea of expectations.

Too soon the musicians strike up a lively processional. With shared smirks, my odious stepsisters sashay haughtily down the aisle, chins lifted as if on parade. Now only I remain, rooted in place by cold dread.

Drawing a shaky breath, I force my leaden feet to carry me forward. The interminable walk stretches before me like a death march. All eyes turn my way, hundreds of faces blurring together as the crowds "ooh" and murmur over my dress's ridiculous ruffles and sequins. My corset squeezes so tightly I can scarcely breathe. I keep my gaze locked straight ahead, every step towards that altar taking monumental effort.

At the front, Lord Greystone waits with a satisfied smirk that makes my skin crawl. How I wish I could rake my nails down that smug face. The officiant gestures for me to take what feels like the final steps over the gallows trapdoor. On wooden legs weighed down by despair, I climb to stand frozen beside the vile man who will soon claim me.

This cannot be happening. Someone, anyone, please halt this madness!

Greystone's grin widens like a wolf baring its teeth. His clammy hand on my lower back makes me want to retch. Clenching my jaw so hard it aches, I stare fixedly ahead. Steady yourself, Scarlet. Just get through this nightmare. Do not shame your family by fainting or fleeing like prey.

The officiant drones on in a nasal voice, the cloying incense threatening to smother me. Or perhaps that is the restrictive dress, tight as a noose around my throat. When the officiant finally bids us recite our vows, bile burns my throat. I force the hateful words out past stiff lips. Each one feels like a nail in the coffin sealing my fate. Beside me, Greystone beams, reveling openly in his triumph.

Panic beats against my ribs like a trapped bird. This isn't happening! I must escape! But there is nowhere left to run. No more options or gambits remain. Checkmate.

"If any object to this union, speak now or forever hold your peace," the officiant declares. My heart leaps. Surely someone will intervene! The silent moments crawl by, no one stirring. Despair crashes over me. There is no escape.

"I object."

The strong voice rings clearly through the cathedral. Shocked gasped ripple through the crowds. I snap my gaze up to see King Remme striding fiercely down the aisle, eyes blazing.

"On what grounds?" Greystone demands through gritted teeth.

Remme mounts the altar steps until he stands mere feet from us. His palace guards file into the cathedral. "That you are an honorless coward who does not deserve her." His words slam into me. Could he truly still care so deeply?

With a growl, Greystone draws his sword. In a blur, Remme twists his arm viciously behind his back. "Think carefully, cretin. You are gravely outmatched."

Chaos erupts throughout the cathedral. Armored men pour in through every entrance, weapons bristling. My heart drops to my feet. Greystone's private guard.

With a savage kick, Greystone breaks Remme's hold. "You should not have come, your majesty. Now your curse will be your undoing." He rips off one leather glove, tossing it at Remme's feet in challenge. "My men wear enchanted items. Your touch cannot harm them. But theirs will end you."

The guards surround us, grinning cruelly. Remme holds my gaze. "Then we will face darkness together and emerge shining," he vows. My eyes sting at his faith. I do not deserve it, yet cannot resist its kindling flame.

With matching roars, Remme and I throw ourselves at the enemy forces swarming the cathedral. I drive my elbow viciously into the first attacker's throat before flipping another over my shoulder, not holding anything back. Their enchantments may shield them from Remme's power, but not my daggers and fury.

The once-cheering crowds flee screaming before the vicious onslaught, but I stand firm at Remme's side. We battle in flawless tandem against the endless waves, our skills complementing each other seamlessly. Though exhaustion burns in my muscles, I refuse to yield any ground.

A pained shout draws my gaze - Darius materializes from the shadows behind Remme, sinking a cruelly barbed dagger into his side. The king crashes heavily to the floor, crimson flowing freely from the grievous wound. Rage and anguish white out my vision.

"Traitorous snake!" I scream, my voice ragged and raw.

Darius' eyes glint with malice and triumph. "Surprised? You should choose your friends more wisely."

Before he can strike a death blow, I tackle him with savage force. We crash to the ground and I pin him down, blade to his throat.

"Why?" I demand through gritted teeth.

Darius laughs coldly, a sick gurgling sound. "I've served Greystone from the start. Always been a member of his family's court. Told him of the curse." His lips twist in a bloody smile. "You'll never win."

With a feral cry, I drive my dagger down in a blind fury, stabbing over and over. Hot blood sprays across my skin as Darius finally goes limp beneath me, eyes staring vacantly into nothingness.

I stagger back in shock, bile rising in my throat. He had been my friend once, or so I believed. This betrayal cuts deeply, but I force down the pain. I cannot afford sentiment now.

Chest heaving, I look down at his mutilated corpse. "May your treacherous soul find no peace." I turn my back, steadying my heart. Mourning will have to wait - the battle still rages. I leap back into the fray, blades flashing. There will be time later to make sense of it all.

I whirl back to defend the king, heart in my throat, but we are badly outnumbered now. His body guard fighting desperately to protect him. Despair threatens to crush me. Unexpectedly, shouted war cries ring out as the Triple G members smash fearlessly into the attackers' flank, evening the odds.

White I was distracted the king had attempted to make a move on Lord Greystone, but it doesn't appear to have gone well. Eyes blazing with cold purpose, I carve my way toward the altar where Greystone fights. He will pay dearly for threatening those I care for and masterminding this bloodshed. Today his vile machinations end forever.

I find Greystone fighting a weakly struggling Remme. Seeing me approach, murder etched on my face, Greystone's expression twists with hatred. With callous force, he hurls Remme's limp body down the altar's stone steps.

I throw myself desperately in Remme's path, barely catching him before he crashes onto the unforgiving floor. Gently I lower him down, unable to look away from the ugly wound still bleeding heavily. Please, Halisar, do not take him from me now! Not when we have come so far together.

Greystone descends the steps toward us, magic crackling ominously around his hands. "I knew you were trouble from the start, witch," he spits viciously. "After I finally end your miserable life, his Majesty will serve my ambitions nicely."

His hand flashes out, vile magic bursting towards me like a bolt of venom. I twist Remme behind a protective marble pillar just in time, the spells shattering stone right where we stood. In Greystone's moment of distraction, I slip a knife from my belt and hurl it in one smooth motion straight through his shoulder.

Greystone clutches the wound in dumb shock. A body slams into me as a member from my guild takes down one of Greystone's men, pulling my eyes off of Greystone for a moment. When I looked back, he is gone. Cursing under my breath for letting him escape, I'm half tempted to chase after him, but I can't pull myself away from the king.

I turn Remme as gently as possible, though he remains limp and terrifyingly pale. At the sight of his freely bleeding wound, something inside me finally snaps.

"No!" I scream in primal anguish, clutching Remme's body tightly. Around us the battle still rages, my companions barely holding back the endless attackers. We are gravely outnumbered. At this rate, we will all be slaughtered.

Desperation and fury roar through me. I cannot lose him like this! With a ragged cry, I call out to the only one with the power to save us. "Halisar, give me strength!"

In response, an ancient wooden staff materializes in my hands - the God of Thieve's own weapon, overflowing with divine magic. I grip it tightly, allowing Halisar's essence to flow into me, granting his supernatural skills and strength.

Raw power surges through my veins like lightning, sharpening my senses. I gently lay Remme down and rise to my feet, eyes blazing. With a thought, I summon eight of the discarded daggers to float in the air around me, poised like fang-filled vipers ready to strike.

The remaining soldiers advance warily. With a guttural scream, I unleash my rage and pain through Halisar's staff. Blinding divine light explodes outward, disintegrating the attackers instantly. Their ashes drift to the ground, all threat removed in a breath.

At the altar, Greystone watches in wide-eyed terror, unable to flee. With icy calm, I command the circling daggers to shoot forward, pinning his limbs to the marble. He howls in pain and fear. But my onslaught is not through.

I stride forward until I stand directly before the whimpering man. Making eye contact, I pour all of my grief and fury into one final strike. The daggers yank free and converge as one, driving straight through Greystone's blackened heart in a deadly metal bloom. His screams echo, then fade to silence.

The staff tumbles from my shaking fingers as I fall to my knees, fully spent. The divine presence recedes gently from my mind. Halisar's aid was given freely, not forced.

Fairy Godmother's arms encircle me comfortingly. "It's over, child. You are safe now."

I cling to her, exhausted and hollowed out. But despite it all, we endured. And with Fairy Godmother's guidance, perhaps in time these wounds will heal as well.

She begins rocking me gently like a child as my wracked cries echo emptily through the bloodstained cathedral.

Healers hurriedly enter the cathedral, I can feel their hands on me but I push them all away. Mumbling something about the king. I don't matter. Only he does. I can't help him now. I need him to live. I have too many unsaid things that are bursting from within that I need to share. He can't be gone. I won't let him.

I Can't Hurt Her

Remme

Everything is dark and muffled, like I am underwater. Distant shouting echoes around me, but I can't make out the words. A heavy weight presses down on my chest, making it difficult to breathe.

Where am I? The last thing I remember is the battle raging in the cathedral, and the searing pain as Darius' pierced my side. After that, only darkness.

Sensation begins returning slowly. I become aware of softness beneath me and a dull throbbing in my abdomen. With great effort, I pry my heavy eyelids open. Blurred shapes and colors swim before me, gradually coming into focus. I am in my royal bedchamber, weak sunlight filtering through the arched windows. The familiar opulent gold furnishings and silk draperies surround me.

Turning my head is a monumental effort. I see a figure slumped in a chair beside the bed, face hidden by cascading golden strands of hair. Scarlet. She is here. I try to call out to her, but only manage a faint rasp. Still, it is enough. Her head jerks up, eyes wide.

"King Remme!" Scarlet cries, leaning forward to grasp my hand. "Thank Halisar, you're awake!"

I reflexively flinch away from her touch. A look of confusion and hurt flashes across her face. My chest constricts at that, but I have to be cautious. The curse is still upon me. I cannot risk harming Scarlet too.

"I'm so sorry. I shouldn't have," she mumbles as she pulls herself away.

I sigh, my voice still rough and weak. "No, please. It's old habits. I just don't want to hurt you."

Understanding dawns in her eyes. They soften with sympathy, but she respectfully moves her chair back a bit. "Of course. I'm just so very relieved you're recovering. We were all terrified we might lose you."

My lips quirk up slightly. "Come now, you know me better than that. I don't fall so easily." I slowly push myself more upright against the pillows with a wince. My side still aches fiercely, but the bleeding appears to have stopped. One of the perks to having to always be healed with magic and no physical touch is that all of my healing happens quickly.

Scarlet gives a small smile at my bravado, though her eyes are still shadowed with lingering fear and grief. She has endured so much hardship. I wish desperately to comfort her, but do not dare get closer. Her eyes flick down and I realize that I'm naked and only covered slightly by a golden blanket covering only the most important parts at this point. I adjust it so more of me is covered but find myself enjoying the way her eyes are soaking me in.

An idea comes to me then. "Scarlet, please open the top drawer of my desk. There is something inside I need you to bring me."

She looks puzzled but does as I request without argument. I watch her closely as she slides open the drawer and freezes. Even from across the room, I see her breath hitch and eyes widen. Gently, reverently, she lifts out the bejeweled golden crown and carries it over.

"Why...why does Rose not have this?" Scarlet asks softly. I can see the struggle on her face to contain further questions.

"Because I made a mistake." I take a slow breath before continuing gently. "I must know something, Scarlet, and I beg you to answer me honestly. Was it you who broke into the palace to steal this crown? Twice?"

Shock flits across her delicate features. She stares down at the glittering crown cradled in her hands, conflicting emotions warring on her face. I hold my breath, praying I have not made a grave mistake in my suspicions.

"I promise, you will not be punished. I just need to know."

Finally Scarlet lifts her gaze to meet mine directly. "Yes," she admits in a near-whisper. "That was me." Then, before I can react, she reaches out and lays her hand softly upon mine.

I freeze, stunned. Her warm, living flesh does not harden to gold at my touch. She is immune to the curse. Which can only mean...

"It really is you," I breathe. "How did I get so lucky that the one who can help me control the curse is also the one I want at my side?"

Scarlet's eyes shimmer with relieved tears even as she nods. Overcome with emotion, I clasp both her hands in mine tightly. For the first time in over a decade, I feel the skin of another. And not just anyone - the woman fate herself intended for me.

I pull her onto the bed beside me and reverently caress Scarlet's face, still barely daring to believe this is real. She leans instinctively into my touch, eyes drifting closed. My thumb gently traces the silken skin of her cheekbone. I have forgotten such tender intimacy could exist between two people. It overwhelms me.

"I thought I might lose you before we ever had the chance to share this," I admit raggedly. "When I saw you walking down that cathedral aisle..."

Scarlet's eyes fly open, filled with sorrow and regret. "I never wanted any part of that," she says fiercely. "Greystone and my stepmother forced me into it. I despised every moment in that monster's presence."

I smile sadly and draw her closer until our foreheads touch. "I know. Forgive me, I did not mean to imply otherwise. You showed such courage facing him."

She lets out a shaky breath, tension slowly leaving her body. We stay that way in silence for a time, simply reveling in each other's presence and the knowledge that we are both safe. I gently stroke her hair, still hardly able to believe she is real and unharmed. She silently traces the golden tattoos that cover my body. Her fingers brushing over my skin giving me thoughts that I shouldn't have but are only natural considering I haven't felt anything this tender in so long.

At length, Scarlet pulls back to meet my gaze. "I need to be honest with you about something else as well. I know."

"About what?"

She waves her hand around the room. "About your curse. With us being together now, is it over?"

I shake my head wearily. "No, I fear it remains. I was never going to have it disappear. I was sixteen and foolish. In my arrogance, I thought curses were only tales told to frighten children. I thought I could outsmart them by asking for a way to increase my riches in the kingdom without taking from my people. To give them a better life." I give a hollow laugh. "How wrong I was."

I look down at my hands, which have brought nothing but suffering.

"But that doesn't fit what Fairy Godmother said," Scarlet mutters to herself. A look of concern and confusion on her face.

"Who?"

Her eyes widen when she realizes that I heard her.

"She's a sort of mentor to me. Someone who was there when they looked for a solution to your curse. It was her who cast the spell for you to gain control over it. Wait! She never said it would be broken. The curse will be controlled, not eliminated. Could you do me a favor?"

I look at Scarlet curiously. "Of course, anything for you."

She scans the room, eyes landing on one of the golden blankets folded at the foot of the bed. "Try turning that back from gold to fabric," she suggests.

My eyes widen in surprise. In all these years under the curse's influence, it had never occurred to me to attempt to reverse its effects. I had assumed items transformed to gold were lost to me forever.

I focus intently on the glittering blanket, my foot stretched out to touch it so I don't have to let go of Scarlet, calling up every ounce of willpower and picturing it as soft woven wool once more. I gasp as the metal ripples, then begins slowly reforming into pliant cloth. Within moments the blanket is fully restored, looking as if it was never touched by my curse.

I shift just enough to reach out a trembling hand to grasp it, almost afraid this is a dream that will shatter at my touch. But the blanket remains blessedly warm and pliant. I clutch it close, overwhelmed by the simple pleasure of feeling something soft once more. My eyes burn with emotion.

After a moment I become aware of Scarlet watching me with a tender smile. There is no judgement in her gaze, only warmth and understanding. Embarrassed to have been so undone by something so mundane, I try to subtly brush the moisture from my eyes.

Scarlet's hand covers mine, stilling it. "It's alright," she says gently. "You have endured so much loneliness with grace. Do not hide your joy now that we can share this burden together."

Her compassion dissolves the last of my restraint. I pull her close, clinging to this sweet miracle in my arms - both the blanket and Scarlet herself. She holds me as the tears fall unchecked, murmuring soothing words. We stay entwined together as my shaking subsides.

Finally I take a deep, steadying breath and draw back to meet Scarlet's eyes. "Thank you," I say hoarsely. "For this gift, and for having faith there was still some humanity left in me after all this time locked away."

Her answering smile outshines the sun. "Of course. We will get through this, one step at a time." She nods encouragingly. "Now, can you try turning it back? We should see if you can control the transformations."

I nod, filled with new conviction. Focusing once more, I watch the blanket morph back to lifeless gold. Another deep breath, and it softens anew at my command. I let out an incredulous laugh.

Scarlet grins and squeezes my hands excitedly. "Control. You truly get to have what you wished for now." In her joy, she throws her arms around my neck. I cling to her, blanket wrapped snugly around us both, cocooned in fragile new beginnings.

The Thieves Guild

Remme

The grand ballroom buzzes with excitement as nobles and dignitaries from across the kingdom stream through the ornate doors. Liveried servants scurry about, offering crystal flutes of chilled wine and delicate canapés as the orchestra strikes up a lively waltz. Almost as extravagant as the masquerade where we had had our first kiss. What a cute story that we will never tell our children. The cleaned up version will be much simpler.

I survey the festive scene from my position on the dais, resplendent in tailored crimson silk robes adorned with intricate gold embroidery. My hands flex unconsciously at my sides, the feeling of the rich fabrics still novel after so many years trapped in a suit of living gold. A faint tremor runs through me at the memory of that long purgatory - but I quickly shake it off. Those dark days are finally behind me.

"Are you alright my king?" Sophia asks, her eyes on my fidgeting fingers.

"I'm fine. Thank you. Just adjusting."

"Of course. I understand." A warmth reaches her eyes that I haven't seen in a long time. "I'm glad you get to be yourself once again. I look forward to seeing you become the kind of king you always dreamed of."

"Thank you Sophia. Me too."

Thanks to Scarlet's loving patience over the last few weeks, I have unlocked control over the curse that once rendered my very touch lethal. No longer will I be forced to wear concealing gloves and armor, unable to experience the simple joy of human contact. I can finally begin reclaiming my humanity piece by piece.

As if summoned by my thoughts, Scarlet appears at my side. My breath catches at the ethereal vision she makes in a flowing sapphire gown that brings out the striking blue-green of her eyes. The sweeping neckline accentuates the elegant column of her throat, while gossamer chiffon sleeves float around her wrists like whispers of smoke. I ache to reach out, to trail reverent fingertips along the silken expanse of that exposed skin. Ever since I gained control of my curse it's as if I crave the constant touch of things. My soon to be queen being my favorite.

As always, Scarlet seems to read my mind. A sly smile curves her lips as she offers me her hand, the barest hint of a challenge glinting in her gaze. "Shall we go mingle, Your Majesty?" The honeyed lilt of her voice caresses over me like a physical touch.

Unable to resist, I capture her proffered hand in my own, savoring the simple thrill of feeling her warmth against my palms. "I believe we shall, my lady." The endearment slips free before I can rein it in, that dangerous flare of want I keep so carefully banked threatening to consume us both.

But Scarlet only arches one shaped brow playfully. "We mustn't shock the court too severely on the first night, my lord. They are here to celebrate our engagement. Not that kind of show. " she purrs in a tone meant only for my ears. The heated undercurrent blazes between us, awakening baser instincts long suppressed within my iron restraint.

Chuckling despite myself, I reluctantly release her hand and gesture for her to precede me in descending from the dais. My eyes shamelessly track the gentle sway of her hips beneath the diaphanous skirts with every unhurried step. Gods let tonight get over quickly...

Once on the ballroom floor, we meander through the glittering crowd, exchanging smiles and pleasantries with the curious nobles craning to get a closer look at their returned king. I can sense the weight of their appraising stares, no doubt taking in the vibrant wardrobe and changing familiarity I can now offer my people.

But one group in particular proves bold enough to probe that very mystery. Lady Aramina Greystone, a handsome matron known for speaking as uncouthly as she adorns her ample frame, steps squarely into our path with a proprietous sniff. She's lucky I have no desire to punish entire families for one person's actions, considering she's the mother of the man my love just killed. Although, considering the woman in front of me, the whole batch may be bad.

"Well, well," she drawls in that grating accent, raking her cynical stare overtly along the shimmering fabric swathing me from collar to cuff. "Look who's finally emerged from their gilded shell." The barb hits its mark, judging by the titters from her equally discourteous companions.

I feel Scarlet bristle beside me, but I squeeze her hand in a subtle caution before pasting on my most inscrutable smile. "Indeed, Lady Greystone. One might say I merely wished my subjects to become...reacquainted with a proper sense of aesthetics after so long."

Aramina snorts indelicately while her friends titter again behind raised fans. "Is that what we're calling it these days?" She leans forward conspiratorially. "One does wonder at the inspiration behind such an...awakening. Or should I say, who might be responsible?"

Her beady eyes slide meaningfully towards Scarlet, undoubtedly noticing the lingering glances and unconscious proximity we share. I tense despite myself, my protective instincts flaring hot and bright where Scarlet is concerned. But she only lifts her chin with serene poise, caressing my knuckles with her thumb in a wordless show of solidarity.

"You give me far too much credit, my lady," she demurs with saccharine sweetness. "His Majesty has simply...embraced the notion of balance and control in all aspects of life. A lesson from which we might all benefit, I daresay." Her smile remains firmly in place even as her eyes glint with subtle challenge.

Aramina blinks, clearly taken aback by the polite rejoinder. After a long moment of tense silence, she emits another derisive snort and gestures for her little group to move along before I can formulate a courtly response. As they retreat into the crowd, I find myself shaking my head in disbelief.

"You, my dear, have the soul of a diplomat," I murmur admiringly, toying with the soft ribbons lacing the back of Scarlet's gown. "Though I confess I nearly lost composure when she began speculating about...us." I trace the word delicately, watching in delight as her fair complexion pinks ever so slightly.

Scarlet's lashes sweep demurely downward, but the coy curve of her lips reveals her own sense of gratified triumph. "One grows accustomed to sidestepping impertinent assumptions in certain circles. Would it really be so bad though? It is our engagement party after all. Everyone knows what that means long term."

I chuckle at the mild understatement, though a part of me longs recklessly to defend her honor by exposing every last rumor and innuendo for the worthless drivel they are. But practicality stills my treacherous impulses - for now. Too much has occurred to potentially jeopardize the fragile path forward I now walk with Scarlet by my side.

"Shall we avail ourselves of some wine before I become too intemperate?" I suggest instead, subtly guiding her through the crush of people towards one of the refreshment tables.

We make our way through the crowded ballroom towards the long banquet table laden with decadent refreshments. As we near, I spot a familiar face chatting animatedly with one of the servants.

"Rose!" Scarlet exclaims, quickening her pace.

"Scarlet!" she cries, embracing Scarlet tightly. They chatter happily, exchanging pleasantries and compliments on their attire.

I hang back a few paces, watching the reunion unfold. She had been among the first of my victims that I reversed the curse on. Like the others, she seems to have no memory of those days encased in metal. A small mercy for which I am unspeakably grateful.

"And our king, you look simply dashing this evening," Rose declares, turning to grin impishly at me. "Who would have thought you cleaned up so nicely after all those years clanking around in armor."

I chuckle, inclining my head. "You look radiant as always, Lady Rose."

"How dare you! It's quite the insult to throw at a woman of my standing to call her a lady," she scoffs, swatting my arm playfully. "We're all friends here. Now tell me, how did you convince him to finally emerge from his fortress of solitude?" She fixes me with a probing yet kindly look.

Scarlet slides me a sly glance, mirth dancing in her eyes. "Oh, I simply helped him embrace the merits of...balance," she murmurs, echoing her earlier words.

Rose arches a brow. "Is that what we're calling it?" she asks dryly, tone uncannily reminiscent of Lady Greystone's. But where the matron's words held scorn, Rose's reflect a happier and well intentioned tone.

Before I can formulate a reply, a bright, genteel voice catches my attention. "Well now, I hope my girls haven't been accosting the courtiers without a chaperone."

We turn in unison to find an elderly woman sweeping towards us in a swirl of emerald brocade.

Scarlet's face lights up. "Godmother! You made it." She embraces the woman warmly.

"Of course, my dear. I wouldn't miss this for the world." The woman's keen eyes meet mine over Scarlet's shoulder.

Sensing my confusion, Scarlet turns back to me. "Your Majesty, allow me to introduce Fairy Godmother, a dear friend and mentor to both myself and Rose."

"A pleasure to meet you, Madame Godmother," I respond politely, inclining my head. Inwardly, I am startled to finally put a face to the name I have heard whispered in select circles. She seems the epitome of gentility, yet I know her to secretly be one of the kingdom's most cunning outlaws. What game is she playing by arriving here tonight, I wonder.

"The pleasure is mine, Your Majesty," Godmother returns cordially. "I'm delighted to see Scarlet looking so happy on the eve of her engagement." She winks conspiratorially. "I always knew you two would suit marvelously."

Scarlet's lips quirk in a tiny, knowing smile. "I'm sure you did. You always seem to be able to see more than you should."

"Should is a strong choice of words," the elderly woman nods briskly. "But first, Scarlet my dear, won't you permit an old crone her moment? I am actually here on business and desire a word with both of you."

Rose and Scarlet pass a look that I can't quite place, but something tells me Fairy Godmother is not someone to displease.

"Of course."

"Excellent. Perhaps you could show me to somewhere more private where we can discuss this matter?" Fairy Godmother requests cordially.

I nod, offering my arm to Scarlet. "Of course. If you'll both follow me."

I lead them from the grand ballroom towards my private study, the sounds of revelry fading behind us. My mind races, wondering what exactly the infamous outlaw plans to propose. I have my suspicions, of course, but best to let her lay her terms plainly first.

Once secluded in my study, I gesture for them to take a seat as I move behind my desk. "Please, make yourselves comfortable. Now, you mentioned urgent business?"

Fairy Godmother folds her hands primly, leveling me with an assessing look. "Yes, well, I believe it's past time you and I had a frank discussion, Your Majesty. As I'm certain you've deduced, I lead a particular...collective that has operated in your kingdom's shadows for some time."

I incline my head, keeping my expression neutral. "Go on."

"Recently, after a rival faction perpetrated an attack on your person, I realized our uneasy truce could not stand any longer. For everyone's safety, it's time we legitimized our presence."

I nod slowly, memories of the incident she references flickering through my mind. I'm curious as to how she knew about it though. "What precisely do you propose?"

"A royal decree sanctioning our activities, in exchange for taxes and loyalty to the crown. We can provide services and access to information no legal force could and would consider negotiating the types of jobs we can take on."

I consider her words. Having the underground network on my side could be beneficial. "I believe an arrangement could be reached, with careful negotiations. I will have my advisors draw up an initial draft come morning."

Fairy Godmother smiles. "Excellent. With our powers combined, your rule will usher in a new golden era."

"Golden era? Really Fairy Godmother?" Scarlet groans.

The woman only shares a wide grin that reaches her eyes. She's clearly pleased with herself for that.

We shake hands solemnly. I feel Scarlet's tension abate with relief. clearly this accord carries significance for her as well. I make a mental note to inquire after their full history later.

Fairy Godmother rises, smoothing her skirts. "Well, I believe I've taken enough of your time for one evening. We can finalize details later."

I stand as well, clasping her hand warmly. "Of course. I look forward to a prosperous alliance."

With a gracious smile, she takes her leave, exiting the study in a swirl of emerald brocade.

I turn back to Scarlet, who moves to follow. But I step swiftly to the door, blocking her path with one arm braced above her head. She gazes up at me, lips parted in surprise.

"Leaving so soon, my lady?" I murmur, leaning close. "The night has only just begun."

Scarlet's eyes darken. "The guests will wonder where we've gone," she protests weakly.

"Let them wonder," I breathe, tracing one fingertip along her collarbone. Her breath hitches. Taking advantage, I capture her lips in a searing kiss, backing her against the door.

She responds fervently, hands tangling in my hair. I trail kisses down her jaw, nipping at her neck. My fingers skim her leg, lifting the skirt up to bare one creamy thigh.

I pause, spotting an intriguing mark. A crescent moon with a woman sitting on the end. If you knew what you were looking for it would look like a capital G. I trace it, sensing subtle magic. So she's a member too. I was correct.

"Well now...it seems you have your own secrets, my dear," I murmur.

Scarlet tenses. I tilt her chin up gently. "It's alright. I suspected as much already." I kiss her reassuringly. "But later, I would like hear the full tale."

She relaxes with a sigh, kissing me lingeringly. There is clearly more to her past than I realized. But I only find myself even more intrigued.

TOGETHER

SCARLET

Heat floods my veins as Remme traces the mark on my thigh, his fingers leaving trails of fire across my skin. He knows my secret - my affiliation with the underground guild.

I tense, holding my breath. But his tender kiss reassures me. He's not angry, merely intrigued by this new revelation. And still desires me fiercely, if the smoldering look in his eyes is any indication.

"Later," I acquiesce breathily, twining my arms around his neck to pull him into a fervent kiss. Explanations can wait - right now I need to feel him against me.

His hands resume their sensual exploration, pulling up my skirts and pulling down my undergarments to caress the smooth skin of my hips and backside. I gasp against his mouth, molding my body to his. Two can play at this game.

I undo the clasps of his shirt, slipping my hands inside to splay across the hard muscular planes of his chest. He groans appreciatively. I rake my nails lightly down his torso, eliciting a pleasured shudder from him.

"Minx," he growls, nipping my earlobe in retaliation. I whimper, arching into him. His knee nudges between my legs and I grind shamelessly against his thigh, chasing that sweet friction.

Remme brackets me against the door with his body, hands roaming everywhere, stoking my desire to an inferno. I fumble with the laces of his breeches, needing to feel him.

"Scarlet..." he rasps in warning, even as his hips rock involuntarily against mine.

"Please, Remme," I gasp, reckless with desire. Propriety is the furthest thing from my mind. I need him, now. The tension and all of the touching has had me feel as if I was on fire for weeks.

With a groan of surrender, his mouth claims mine again in a bruising kiss. Just a little longer, I tell myself deliriously. The guests can wait.

I gasp as Remme's thigh presses deliciously against me, the friction sending sparks of pleasure through my core. My hands grip his shoulders for support as I grind harder, chasing release. A particularly skillful swivel of his leg has me crying out, so close to the edge.

Sensing how near I am, Remme's hands close possessively over my breast through the thin fabric of my dress. His fingers tease my stiffening nipple as his mouth finds the sensitive spot under my ear.

"Come for me, my Lady," he growls. His gravelly voice combined with the ceaseless motion against my aching center is too much. With a sharp cry, I shatter apart in his arms, ecstasy coursing through me.

I cling to him weakly as I come back to my senses. The evidence of my pleasure dampens his breeches but he seems unconcerned, only smirking in male satisfaction.

"Now, I believe you wanted something of mine," he murmurs, guiding my questing hand back to the laces of his pants. I nod eagerly, needing more. As I take him in hand, desire coils hotly within me again.

His talented fingers slip between my legs.

I can't seem to get close enough to him.

"Yes, Scarlet," he groans, his voice a deep rumble in his chest that vibrates through me like thunder during a storm. "Touch me."

Emboldened by his encouragement, I slide my hand down the length of him, feeling him pulse against my palm. He bucks against my touch, and I know he's as desperate as I am.

"Lift your skirts higher," he commands between ragged breaths. I do as he says without hesitation, hiking up the voluminous fabric until it pools around my hips.

"Wider," he growls, and I comply, spreading my legs wider against the door. He positions himself at my entrance and with one powerful thrust, he's inside me.

"Gods, Scarlet!" he gasps, burying his face in the crook of my neck as he begins to move within me. "You feel so good." His words are punctuated by shuddering breaths as he slows down to savor the sensation of our joined bodies.

I can't even form coherent thoughts anymore; all I'm aware of is the pleasure coiling low in my abdomen with each thrust of his hips. His grip on my hips tightens as if he's holding on for dear life.

With each thrust, I can feel him going deeper, touching parts of me that I didn't know existed. It feels so good, so very right, as if this is where we were always meant to be. His hips move in a primal rhythm, our bodies slapping together with a rhythmic intensity that echoes off the walls of the darkened library.

His lips leave my neck and find their way to my earlobe, nibbling and sucking on it gently. He pants, his voice raw with desire, "I need... I need to see your beautiful face."

Rising up on tiptoes, I meet his heated gaze, our eyes locked together as we move as one. The passion flaring in his eyes is mirrored in mine and we both know we're on the edge of something monumental.

"Tell me you want this," he growls out between thrusts, his grip on my hips tightening even more.

"Yes," I breathe out, unable to form any other coherent words. "I want this."

"Tell me you want me."

"Always."

Emboldened by my confession, he picks up the pace once more. It's animalistic and wild and absolutely exhilarating. And the way he watches me, as if I'm the most precious thing he's ever laid eyes on... it's intoxicating.

"Scarlet," he growls, his voice a low rumbling growl that vibrates through me like thunder in a storm. "I'm close."

I can feel the tension coiling in my own body, the pleasure building unbearably with each of his hard thrusts. I dig my nails into his back, legs shaking with the effort it takes to remain standing. "Yes, Remme. Gods, yes!" I pant out.

His breathing becomes ragged in my ear as I felt the pulsing of his length inside me. A warmth spreads through my core, and I cry out as my climax washes over me in waves, carrying me away on its crest.

Remme's final thrusts are deep and hard, before he stiffens against me, groaning out his own release. We remain joined for several minutes, catching our breaths and trying to regain some semblance of composure.

As our breathing finally returned to normal, I could feel the evidence of our passion seeping between my legs. Remme, still buried inside me, nuzzled my neck with his chin and said, "We should... clean up before anyone... uh... smells the evidence of our... indiscretion."

I couldn't help but giggle at his awkwardness. "Yes, you're right. Just... give me a moment."

He chuckled and reluctantly pulled out of me. He reached for a nearby handkerchief and gently wiped us both clean. The cool fabric against my heated skin was a welcome relief.

"Thank you," I whispered, tugging down dress, trying to make myself presentable again.

"My pleasure, milady," he purred, winking at his own double entendre before completely stripping off his pair of britches entirely.

I whipped around to hide my blushing cheeks but not before he saw the beginnings of a smile tugging at my lips. "You're insufferable, Remme Corliss."

"And yet, here you are," he said, pulling on a new pair that he apparently found somewhere in here. I make a mental note to ask about that later. "Shall we return to the party as if nothing happened?"

"Nothing happened," I agreed, adjusting the folds of my gown and willing my hair to cooperate. "Coming?"

"Always," he replied with a devilish grin.

JUST REWARDS
SCARLET

The carriage bounces along the road, taking me back to the place I once called home. Beside me, Remme radiates a comforting strength, our hands entwined. I'm grateful for his presence today.

Returning to my stepfamily fills me with more dread than joy. The wounds from them run deep, and seeing Stepmother marry the decrepit Duke Geralsh provides only cold comfort. After she tried to marry me off to that decrepit old man, he seems truly fitting for her.

I stare stonily out the window as we roll up the drive towards the sprawling manor that will soon be mine. What I've fought for for so long. It looks the same, yet feels foreign now. I'm not the same and I don't need it in the same way I once did.

Remme helps me down, keeping one supportive hand at my back. I stand tall, head high, as we proceed to the gardens. Inside I am a turmoil of emotions, but I won't give Stepmother the satisfaction of seeing it.

My horrid stepsisters Prunella and Starla preen nearby, shooting me envious glares which I pointedly ignore. They are beneath my notice on this day. All my attention is focused on the kindly woman waving at us from beneath a flowered trellis - Fairy Godmother.

"Godmother!" I embrace her warmly, blinking back tears. She was more family to me than my real ones ever were. "I've missed you."

"And I you, child." Her sharp eyes examine me fondly. "Chin up, today's a celebration. You look lovely."

I manage a brittle smile. "What do I have to celebrate? Stepmother being rid of me?"

Godmother pats my hand consolingly. "I know it's difficult, my dear. But it gets better."

She leans in conspiratorially. "Besides, I believe I've managed to give your step family a little taste of their own foul medicine."

I raise my eyebrows in surprise. Godmother chuckles. "Oh yes, I simply couldn't resist getting a bit creative behind the scenes. A few shifted finances here, some forged correspondence there." She winks.

"With a touch of magic, I ensured the good Duke received many desperate invitations in your stepmother's hand. She thought she was losing her wits when she couldn't recall sending them!"

Despite myself, I have to laugh. Trust Godmother to find a way to subtly punish Stepmother through her own schemes and run them all out of my house once and for all.

Godmother smiles indulgently. "I decided your stepmother deserved to learn how it feels to be manipulated and trapped. This marriage will be just reward for how she treated you, my dear. Besides, the Duke has always driven me mad and he is much too old to be after a young bride anymore. The man walks with a cane for goodness sake."

I squeeze her hand, gratitude swelling in my heart. Godmother has looked out for me as the mother I lost. And with this revelation, I feel the shadows over this day lighten just a little bit.

"Now chin up," she encourages gently. "Today marks the first step towards a bright new future for us all."

I sigh, unconvinced but appreciative of her optimism. Taking our seats, I pointedly avoid looking at Stepmother. I have no desire to see her here playing the radiant bride. She does not deserve such joy after poisoning my childhood.

The ceremony passes in a blur. I try to take strength from Remme's steady presence beside me, focusing on the feel of his hand holding mine.

At the reception, music plays gaily but I have no urge to dance. Remme seems to sense my mood and leads me away into the gardens seeking solace. We come to a secluded grove surrounding a small fountain that I remember from my childhood.

Bittersweet nostalgia washes over me. "Father used to bring me here," I confide softly. Remme squeezes my hand in wordless support. I know if he were here, Father would tell me to have courage and stand tall.

His voice breaks gently into my thoughts. "He would be so very proud of you, Scarlet."

I offer a trembling smile through the sheen of tears. "Thank you. I wish he could have seen this day." Remme's faith has given me strength I did not know I possessed.

We hold each other close beneath the dappled sun. In this moment with Remme, the future no longer seems so bleak or uncertain.

Drawing back, I meet his tender gaze. "What happens now?"

His answering grin warms me like sunlight after winter's chill. "Anything we wish."

Cranberry Orange Scones

4 cups plus 1/4 cup all-purpose flour
1/4 cup sugar, plus additional for sprinkling
2 tablespoons baking powder
2 teaspoons kosher salt
1 tablespoon grated orange zest
3/4 pound cold unsalted butter, diced
4 extra-large eggs, lightly beaten
1 cup cold heavy cream
1 cup dried cranberries
1 egg beaten with 2 tablespoons water or milk, for egg wash
1/2 cup confectioners' sugar, plus 2 tablespoons
4 teaspoons freshly squeezed orange juice

Awaken your oven to 400°F, the temperature of a gentle dragon's breath.

In a large mixing bowl, combine 4 cups of flour, 1/4 cup sugar, baking powder, a pinch of salt, and the zest of an orange. Add cold butter, cut into small pieces like tiny gemstones.

Mix in 2 whisked eggs and heavy cream, stirring gently as if blending a potion. Fold in dried cranberries (rubies of the forest) coated with a sprinkle of flour.

On a flour-dusted surface, knead the dough into a smooth orb. With a rolling pin, flatten the dough to 3/4-inch thickness. Using a 3-inch round cutter, shape the dough into circles of power.

Place these mystic rounds on a parchment-lined baking sheet. Brush the tops with beaten egg (the golden seal) and sprinkle with sugar (fairy dust).

Bake in your kitchen's fiery heart for 20-25 minutes, until the tops are browned like autumn leaves. Allow the scones to cool for 15 minutes, then drizzle with a glaze made from confectioners' sugar and orange juice.

CHAPTER 50

Thank you for reading Cursed by Gold! I always love adding a little behind the scenes for the books I write and this one has been on my radar for quite a while. In fact, I may have tried to convince a few author friends to write this in the past because I wanted to read it so badly. I only knew that I wanted a Cinderella retelling if Prince Charming was King Midas and that I wanted the hook to be "Everything he touched turned to gold... but her" but when this book first started that was all I had.

Oh the ride these characters took me on was quite the adventure. I knew the ending of this book pretty early on and the struggle of how to build that relationship without Remme finding out who she was for the entire book was so hard. Especially allowing them some intimate moments where she couldn't even let her touch her when she was a contestant was a challenge to figure out how to overcome.

One of my favorite elements of the book is actually the chaotic tarot reading that Remme does for her. I was trying to figure out a date that they could do which would let them try and challenge each other when I stumbled on a tik tok account. A man who does chaotic fake tarot reading. They are hilarious and so off the wall. I knew it would be perfect and in fact may be getting included in the PR and purchased experience boxes from readers.